SEVEN OF SWORDS

Also by Carole Nelson Douglas
published by Tor Books

SWORD & CIRCLET
Keepers of Edenvant
Heir of Rengarth

Probe
Counterprobe

CAROLE NELSON DOUGLAS

SEVEN OF SWORDS

SWORD & CIRCLET 3

A TOM DOHERTY ASSOCIATES BOOK
NEW YORK

This is a work of fiction. All the characters and events portrayed in this book are fictitious, and any resemblance to real people or events is purely coincidental.

SEVEN OF SWORDS

A TOR BOOK
Published by Tom Doherty Associates, Inc.
49 West 24 Street
New York, NY 10010

Library of Congress Cataloging-in-Publication Data

Douglas, Carole Nelson.
  Seven of swords / Carole Nelson Douglas.
  (Sword & circlet ; 3)
  "A TOR book"—Verso t.p.
  ISBN 0-312-93142-5
  I. Title. II. Series.
PS3554.08237S4 1989   88-39650
813′.54—dc 19   CIP

First edition: February 1989
0 9 8 7 6 5 4 3 2 1

For the late Kathryn Boardman,
a book critic of professionalism
in the face of friendly fire

PROLOGUE

Creation Day

THE BOY WHO HAD NO BIRTHDAY KNELT ON THE SHINY
black floor. Faint reflections of pale hands and face flickered at his movements.

He peered into the floor, trying to see past his own
image. The substance was slick but not quite glassy—
opaque as a faceted smokestone yet thicker than a frozen
wave from the Well of Endless Water.

Moments before, the floor had been a lake of dark, oily
liquid. Now the boy's trembling palm smoothed its new
magical solidity, as he would calm a favorite mount before
riding it.

Living threads of color braided through the common
creases of his palm—headline, heartline, lifeline—and
branded phantom impressions in the obsidian floor.

Once reflected, the shadow lines writhed like snakes and
burrowed deep into the bottomless black.

If the floor was midnight-dark, the ceiling was a moonless midnight—dark enough to remain unseen. Around the
boy, thunderheads high as houses tumbled over each other
at the beck and call of some unfelt force. The airy hulks

1

rubbed the boy housecat-hard, then buffeted away.

He ignored the attendant clouds, scowling at their peripheral presence. His hands smoothed the murky floor. In a moment, his reflection had parted in two. Then only a channel of limitless dark winked solemnly beneath him.

Winked! He drew back before being drawn inward again. Dark did not wink, he realized. Only light did. . . .

His face almost kissed the floor that adamantly refused to reflect it whole. A sound like sand tattooing stone rained through the vast, cloud-thick space.

The boy glanced over his shoulder, annoyed again.

"Go away!" he admonished something. "You were not to follow. He will be angry enough that I have trod on the Dark Mirror. I cannot uphold your weight as well."

The sound advanced unabated, making the boy grit his teeth and fist his glittering palms. His sundered reflection clapped together like hands, forming a whole image beneath him again. His expression was stern, intent.

"Go away! Go back." He was kneeling upright, urging retreat on the herd of black clouds, rebuffing the oncoming patter of the rain.

Nothing heeded him.

A thunderously black cloudlet continued to nudge his knee. The rain's icy patter dulled into the brittle thud of hail.

The boy shivered and rubbed his hands over his forearms. Sparks from the friction of his thread-jeweled palms speared the dark.

These flying embers of light struck companion fire from the advancing darkness—at least they appeared to. Three eye-bright ovals of henna color, a murderous marriage of brown and red . . . old blood and new . . . pierced the distance.

Something came, dark and shambling. It was impenetrable, only an outline, yet denser than the darkest thunderhead and as solid as the glassy floor.

Something of the coiled muscular cat shaped it—although, in a way, it blotted out all other shapes. Yet it was not quite cat. Or—perhaps—rather more than cat.

Nor was it quite dog, though its blunt muzzle skated along the floor as if following a scent across the odorless surface. Whatever breed of beast it was, the effect was large, shadowy, lithe, muscular, and quite, quite lethal.

With a bound it leaped the remaining gap between them and settled beside the boy it dwarfed. Something in its preening on arrival was distinctly birdlike.

"He will be angry thrice times seven!" the boy complained. The initial discipline in his voice had thinned to resignation. "At least be silent, then. I'm occupied."

The thing hunched into a lurking cliff of shadow beside the boy, three ruddy caverns of eyefire curving a smile into its unreadable face.

The boy's worry-whitened fingers swept the floor, brushing aside his own rejoined image as if he were used to parting the curtain on his own facelessness.

Again he leaned down until his shoulder-length hair brushed the obsidian floor. Light tendrils seeped up the dark strands, twisting into the colors of summer lightning.

"There was a glow far below," the boy murmured without expecting an answer. He spoke like one used to addressing clouds and shadows, and—if receiving no answer—acted certain of at least engaging a receptive ear.

Under the pressure of his light-etched palms, the darkly translucent floor softened to charcoal color. A channel of light drove deep and widened. Eddies swirled through the glassy gray, then a bubble rose between jet cliffsides and spent itself in a ring.

The ring itself expanded, defining a tunnel of water-washed light that brightened by the instant. A tinge of green, then blue, dappled its surface.

Far below, as if seen through an endless birth canal, a tiny silver needle dangled in the counterplay of currents. By turns it wafted up toward the boy . . . and impaled itself deeper in the well's farthest silver.

"To me!" The boy's flared fingers lifted above the circle of liquid light, as a puppetmaster's might play the strings of his five-pronged control wand.

Far below, a cat's whisker of silver threaded the dappled distance, drifting feather-light. Up and up, spinning and turning, dangling from the very heart of distance itself, the object drew nearer.

Veiled aquatic light rippled the thing's image—now it seemed a filament of albino hair . . . then a toothpick of skin-pale wood . . . a silver thorn . . . a scarlet pin . . . a quill . . . a needle again.

At last it neared, swelling to fill the circle of light between the boy's separated hands.

He leaned closer, his hair catching fire on the floor and burning a halo around his heedless face. His features were even and pleasant, yet unbalanced—a trace of childish complacency softened the hollow maturity of encroaching manhood. He was boy yet, for some reason that had naught to do with birthdays.

He would be the second to tell anyone that he had never celebrated any birthday—and was not sorry for it.

Not that he had anyone to tell anything to. He was always alone, except for one too Other to be considered— and for things like the shadow beast that were not quite there.

Besides, who would stay long enough to listen to him tell anything? He had one last characteristic that made his pleasant features moot, and he had seen it in mirrors dark and not so dark many times.

He had no eyes.

Oh, he saw . . . through features that seemed—at first glance—to be ordinary eyes. But in him, as in no one else of humankind, iris and pupil drank from the same dark bottomless well. Where sight should have its seat—and expression—was only absence . . . glittering empty, endless absence.

He saw quite well. He had studied his own empty-eyed reflection until he was sick of it and had turned elsewhere.

What he saw now was something that he had studied for many years, too—almost half the entire seventeen sandglasses of his life.

Beside him, around him, the great clouded being hovered. Its breath, hot as summer air before a stormfall, steamed the thin surface of the well of light.

The boy exhaled impatiently and passed his palms over the wavering surface. There—just beyond his reach—bobbed the rusted hilt of a sword.

The boy's fingers flexed. The thick rune-inscribed hilt looked too massive for his lean, youthful hands to encompass. Though his magic had been potent enough to draw the sword from the well of another world, his untried physical strength might fail to retrieve it. He grasped that notion even as the sword eluded the quick clutch of his fingers, the knob of his throat bobbing in swallowed frustration.

The shadow hovering beside him spat out a fanged grin below the three vigil lights of its eyes. A dark foreleg pawed the flat circle of radiance, claws like scimitars snagging the water's skin.

Something translucent stretched as the shadow paw lifted—a tent of silver erected above the water's mouth.

"You'll break it!" The boy slapped the huge, misshapen paw with one bright palm.

Shadow shriveled back, growling, untouched.

"The sword must break the barrier itself," the boy explained, ". . . of itself . . . by itself. I can only call it, not command it."

He shut his opaque eyes, though darkness seemed to dwell there without his needing to close them.

"Come to me," he whispered. "Come to my rune-scribed palm. I have bought you at great price, with great pain—Come. . . ."

Inanimate things usually heeded him. All that he knew were inanimate things that could be animated. For a moment, the sword's great rusted hilt nosed the thin skin between light and dark, water and air, there and here.

Eyes shut, the boy heaved a sigh of relief and triumph. Then his eyes flew open, the dark at their centers expanding.

He huddled over the pool of light. A brighter light—a flashing angular form sheathed in silver scales—surged upward from the bright pinprick impossibly far below.

Breathless, disbelieving, the boy hovered.

The light stalk drove upward, thorns and leaves bristling from its sinuous form. Hair or waterweed twined it, shining with the glamour of the secret depths. Like liquid lightning the vision struck, straight for the sword. It impaled itself on the long rusted blade, wrapping weedy locks and spiny limbs around the metal length.

The boy gasped out his hope. Surely nothing human could embrace so cutting an edge and survive—! He watched for veils of red to swirl into the bright water.

Something did come, a seeping pattern of dark ribbons binding figure to sword and sword to figure. Ribbons spawned schools of more ribbons that laced together into a latticework.

The boy could no longer tell weapon from claimer, steel from waterweed. The hilt lifted on the roiled waters, almost piercing the barrier. He reached for it. Even as his light-lined palm brightened its rusted surface, a face formed on the water's pale skin.

Not much of a face—just eyes, silver eyes as staring as any fish's. Not so much a visage as a piece of one—just the quicksilver eyes and the yawning dark hole of a mouth stretching wider and wider, blocking the light from below, stretching to meet the well rim with a dark scream that tore the barrier as nothing tangible ever could.

The wail made even the shadow behind the boy pale. It dampened the fire in his hands. The creature of light spread darkness. It spiraled back into the eternity of dark glass, riding an arrow of steel. The vanishing sword etched a silver trail until it could no longer be seen, and all was as before—solid, glassy darkness.

Only the scream still echoed—among every inanimate thing and bobbing thunderhead, heard by the lurking shadowbeast. And finally by one other.

He came in the thunder he commanded and called a name that did not want to be spoken.

"Eeryon."

And the floor became the sinking waters of a dark pool, and attempt became failure.

Eeryon's palms winked out as they flailed in the shadowed waters closing like ebony lips over his dark head and lightless eyes.

CHAPTER
1

"WELL," SHE SAID, ADDRESSING NO ONE, "AT LEAST I have some talent as a thief."

She sighed and regarded the empty land, ignoring the chatter of a nearby brook. The meadow shook its long green hair back and forth as if to dry it by the light of the three suns rolling slowly up the sky.

A slash of snow-frosted mountains glittered at the fringe of the rumpled land. Over her shoulder, where she glanced with guilty regularity, the spires of a sprawling city shone alabaster in the bright daylight.

The girl wiped her embroidered sleeve over her damp brow, simultaneously pushing back a corona of wiry brown hair. Next to her, a dappled bearing-beast pawed the turf.

"I know. I seldom ask you to carry more than myself."

She stretched to unbind a burlap-wrapped object fixed to the saddle. A tall girl, she still had to struggle to free the binding. The object swung toward the ground, shedding its homely burlap skin. Sunlight glanced off a length of naked steel.

8

She caught the falling sword hilt, grunting.

"Great, unbending clumsy thing! You'd be better used carving a banquet boar. Stand up, will you, until I say differently—!"

She braced the weapon upright, its six-foot length from point to hilt head topping her own by inches. It spun in her grasp as she balanced it uneasily on its point. The heavy hilt swayed from side to side, pulling her with it.

"Be still!" She pressed her hands down on the crossbar until the point bit the tough sod. "For a reputedly magical thing, you are most unwieldy."

She sighed again and regarded the rear for pursuers. A constant ripple of windblown grass and running water made both foreground and background shimmer. This earth was as dappled as her bearing-beast. Few trees punctuated the meadows. She had paused under the shade of the only one in view.

Tall and broad, the tree dripped green leaves, each centered with an iridescent blue eye. The girl's mother had compared them to a "weepwillow" tree in her birthworld. And then her father would smile at her mother and they would say no more of things that apparently mattered only to them.

The sword mattered to her father, the girl knew that— never mind that it had hung ceremonially on the walls for as long as she could see, and could remember what she saw. Her mother had insisted the sword was life itself to her father. She should not have taken it.

A sound made her start, sweaty palms sliding off the crossbar. She waited, but it did not recur. Perhaps it was only the . . . creak . . . of a tree branch. She wasn't used to such noises in a mostly treeless world. The tree was squeaking in the wind, showing off for a rare visitor, that was all, she told herself, wiping a palm on her braid-welted trousers.

Half-released, the sword's inevitable weight sank against her youthfully slight shoulder. She braced it with her own weight.

"What shall I do with you now that I have you? In the tales, such things have a tendency to speak and call one 'master.' You do not seem the talkative sort. Where, then, does your magic lie? What can you do for me?"

The sword was silent, its weight more eloquent than its reputed powers.

"Oh! I should not have taken you." She wanted to sit down, but dared not. Once she sank under the sword's weight it would overcome her. A daring exploit would become a laughable escapade.

Her arms shook, the muscles finally protesting their overwork of the past few hours. She had thought that by taking the sword, having it to herself, studying it, she could learn its magic. It did not seem to have any magic—except by reputation and that exaggerated.

She leaned the hilt against the bearing-beast's dappled shoulder, but it minced away on silvery hooves. Above, glossy leaves rustled, shifting colors as they moved—azure eyes blinking green and then blue again.

She'd never been near enough a tree to observe its vagaries. The magic the wind wove through its branches dazzled her more than the vaunted powers of the leaden sword.

As she watched, rings of translucent coils arched from the foliage, glittering like silver samite.

Stunned, she stood gaping at the display, as if the tree had suddenly turned into some Solanandor Tierze merchant slinging tricolor silks into the marketplace sunlight. . . .

"Javelle—the sword!"

She turned, long hair whipping her cheek. Something was cresting the hill behind her. A familiar yet unwanted face—twisted into an unfamiliar expression—hung over a bearing-beast's neck. The rest of the beast rose into view as if levitated as it galloped up the rise. The arrival was swift and surprising, thanks to silence. She couldn't hear its hooves pounding the turf until the entire creature was visible.

Despite the warning, the girl froze, surprise-stricken on two fronts. Around her the gauzy coils curled into a circle, assuming a serpentine shape.

Her alarmed bearing-beast tried to sidle away, but its shaggy side bumped the encompassing coils. The beast whinnied its distaste, then crowded closer to the circle's center, to the girl still upholding the long silver sword.

"Leaveweavers!" the advancing rider warned as he neared. "Strike them."

She looked to her feet, where the diaphanous lengths writhed knee-high. She no longer took them for webspin or ground mist or some phenomenon of the shimmering land, but an enemy, however unknown. She clasped the hilt's tapered crossbar and backed away, allowing the sword to angle almost horizontally to the ground.

Her fingers twined the rune-inscribed hilt, tightening until the cryptic symbols impressed her palms. No one knew the runes' meaning—no one living, at least that was what her parents claimed. Her shoulders tautened to lift the sword. Had all the weight been hilt-borne, she could have done it.

Instead, the weight ran like mercury down the entire six feet of hilt and sword. Attempting to control it with untried muscles was like trying to hold a wild bearing-beast on a line of meadow-floss.

The only magic she'd found in the sword was the way its inordinate length became a leash that bound her. She scraped the tip over the ground, watching grasses crushed rather than cut. The point prodded the leaveweaver bellies, but they only whirled away.

Beyond them, the oncoming bearing-beast pulled up

sharply as its rider pounded to the ground. He drew no sword, but reached out as though to wrestle the serpents' translucently twining bulks.

Inside her circle, the girl sank down beside the fallen sword and watched from within the ring of airy bodies. She didn't know what to expect, only the inevitable outcome.

The boy—he was younger than she, smaller than she—pressed his hands along the quivering surface of leaveweaver belly. An instant alteration made their spinning pause. Their glittering crystal coloration dulled, hardened. They became as pale as old bone and, like old bone, faded to ashes.

Leaveweaver substance sifted to the grasses, catching on the wafting blades, leaving a dust-mote haze in their wake. The boy looked up from odd-colored eyes—one amber-gold, the other quicksilver-gray. He panted, then squatted, studying the girl across the gulf between them as if leaveweavers still separated them.

"Why?" he asked.

She was the elder. "Why did you follow me?"

He grinned. "A notion that you were doing something you weren't supposed to. I always get an itch in my palm . . . when you're up to something."

"Itch! You only want to cause trouble."

"How can I when you're always there before me?" His head shifted sheepishly. "Javelle . . . I was worried Mother would find out about you riding off again. You know how she frets when you wander alone."

"I 'ride off' because I wish to be alone."

He glanced to the ashy ring of grass. "You would have been—with them."

During a pause she tore out a sheaf of grass and braided it.

"Thank you," she said without looking up. "I'd heard of grassweavers, but not leaveweavers. How did you know?"

He shrugged, his expression blending fifteen-year-old

wisdom with childish pride. "It just came to me. There's a lot more in Rengarth than anybody knows about—or will know about until somebody comes into the wildlands to explore it."

"I did," she reminded him.

"And nearly got eaten!"

The relish he took in the words made her laugh at last. "Oh, Thane, you are such a . . . an infant sometimes."

"Look at what being older got you. Mother may be worried, but Father will be—"

"Furious?"

"No." Thane broke off his own grass stem and chewed it thoughtfully. "Father's never furious . . . just disappointed, which is worse. I think he might even be stern about that sword, though, even if you're the one who took it. You know his life hangs upon it."

"I know his magic is tied to it! That's all I wanted—to . . . study it. I can't take magic for granted."

"Who can?" Thane dusted his palms together and rose, failing to observe the way his sister almost answered, then visibly held her tongue instead. "Well, what did you learn from the sword?"

"That it is too heavy to carry great distances. No wonder even Father hung it on the wall."

"Father doesn't need swords much anymore." Thane came close, then suddenly knelt beside his sister. "I've never seen it close up. Huge, isn't it?"

Javelle smiled, pleased that Thane would be as unable to handle it as she. "It's Father's. Maybe no one else will ever be big enough to carry it, will grow large enough to carry it."

"Who wants to? . . . I thought you said that."

"I didn't expect to use it as a weapon."

"What else good is it?"

She eyed him from under veiled lashes. "Magic," she whispered.

"Magic," he scoffed. "Oh, I suppose . . . once . . . it hoarded some small magic. But even Father no longer relies on it, or notices it, other than to guard it. It's one more of the things he and Mother never talk about . . . well, before we were here . . . things that were more then than they are now."

Thane rocked back on his heels and grew as stern as only a younger brother can when he's feeling smug. "But I believe Mother when she says the sword is vital to Father's survival. And, Javelle, it was safe on the wall in Solanandor Tierze! *We* were safe. How will we return it without anyone noticing?"

She smiled at the implicit aid Thane's question promised. "Nobody notices the old sword anymore. Nobody looks up at the wall. Nobody notices me much; that's how I took it."

"Well, I can't blame them for not noticing you," Thane said in a tone of brotherly baiting. Javelle didn't answer, but something in her face made him break off the taunt. "I'm sorry I got the magic and you didn't," he said gruffly. "I don't even know why you miss it."

"Because I never had it! That's the sort of thing a person misses most of all. I don't . . . fit."

"Fit? Where?"

"Here. With you all."

"Father'd take that sword broadside to your own broadside if he heard you say that."

"No, he wouldn't. Father's not like that. It makes it even worse."

"You are a gloomy girl!" The boy jumped up and paced to his grazing bearing-beast. "Come on, we'll get the sword back and I . . . I won't even tell."

"Thanks," she responded sarcastically, stung by the adult impatience tinging his voice. "I can't find any magic in it, anyway. It doesn't even talk."

"Should hope not. Listen, I remember Mother saying

once that Felabba sprang from the hilt in Edanvant! Wouldn't that be exciting, if we found old Felabba again after all these years?"

"Speak for yourself, brother. Father wouldn't thank you for that."

"Still—" The boy collapsed to the ground on the liquid limbs of youth. His hands traced the hilt runes. "I could try. Felabba—here, kitty, here, kitty . . . kitty—"

"Thane, stop that! You could actually start something. The worst that could have befallen me was getting eaten by leaveweavers. You might actually . . . raise something."

"Afraid? Here, kitty, kitty—"

"Thane!" Half-angry, half-panicked, Javelle tussled him for the sword, shoving his magical hands from the hilt as if pushing them from the fire. "You'll unloose something you can't contain, you'll—"

They froze together. Beneath their dueling hands the hilt shone with a soft white light. Their palms, reddened by the glow, drew back, although no heat forced them.

"It *is* magic, and it answers your innate magic," Javelle said dully, "but not anything in me. At least we know it still keeps its powers."

"This is wonderful." Rapt, Thane watched the light fade as his hands retreated. He pushed his palms forward. The light intensified at their approach.

Javelle sat back to watch her brother toy with the phenomenon. "Are you thinking of anything specific to make it glow?"

"Nothing. I'm just touching it."

"Oh."

He glanced over his shoulder, his face alight in the hilt-glow. "Javelle, you do have your birth-serpent."

Reminded of what she took for granted, her hand touched her waist. A slim silver belt of albino Iridesium was aglimmer with pale rainbow highlights. She sighed, her waist expanding. At the movement, the belt flashed, vanished, then reappeared to scale her arm and twine the upper portion. A delicate serpent's head froze into a new place near her shoulder.

"This mobile bauble . . ." Javelle dismissed it bitterly. "'Tis a nuisance, a thing of its own whim and not mine. *It* doesn't speak, either."

"Why must magical things always speak? You do enough of that for all of us."

"I can cure that."

He made a face and jumped up. "Help me with the sword, and we'll get back before anyone notices."

In silence they lifted the heavy sword, swaddled it in burlap, and tied it again to Javelle's saddle.

"Thundermist would be happy to leave it here," she noted. Her mount rolled a pale eye as the sword weighted its withers again.

"Mother wouldn't. You know how she frets over Father."

"Father can take care of himself."

"Daughter can't."

"If you hadn't come, she would have had to! Maybe I have no magic because you're always there first with yours."

He shrugged. "Maybe you have no magic because you're lucky. And I'm not."

"Thane, do you sometimes wish you . . . didn't?"

He stared across the shifting land. "I always wish—wish that I didn't have what I do and did have what I don't. Mother would say that's the Torloc in me. Come on, I'll race you home."

It was worse than their youthful imaginations could have conjured: they had been missed. The sword had been missed.

"Why?" their mother demanded, worry and ire striking mutual sparks from her eyes' normal silver serenity.

Irissa paced to release the tension that had coiled around her since midafternoon, when both disappearances had been discovered. Kendric sat on the edge of a table, looking troubled but unshaken, the sword lying aslant beside him.

They all met in the family common room—an innovation Irissa and Kendric had brought to Rengarth to safeguard their privacy. No one witnessed the children's belated shame, the parents' fear and anger, but themselves.

"You." Irissa swirled to a stop, her dark hair flying beneath the containing band of an Iridesium circlet at her temples. She faced Javelle, a paler, slighter version of herself whose amber-warm eyes held a sullen sorrow.

"You are the elder," Irissa told her daughter. "And apparently the instigator. You should have known better. At your age I was—"

"An ignorant barefoot seeress in Rindell," Kendric reminded her, his tone managing to be both fond and cautionary.

Irissa whirled on him, unleashing her tight-reined fear.

"She was—they were—out alone in the wilds of Rengarth, that even natives do not traverse lightly. And they had taken your sword—!"

"*My* sword. I am the aggrieved party; I should mete out rebuke to the degree I feel it necessary."

Irissa considered, then slapped her hands to her sides and went to stand beside Kendric. "Mete," she invited.

The children silently regarded their parents. Irissa and Kendric were awesome by any standards—child or adult. To the people of Rengarth, they had been Ruler and Reginatrix for the past eighteen years. More, they were legendary strangers, wanderers of many worlds, the first outlanders to find and enter Rengarth in generations.

To any who confronted the pair, they made a combination formidable in any world. Irissa, six feet tall, was a Torloc seeress at the long-lived peak of her kind's magical powers, like her kind still young-girl youthful and bound to be for many, many years. Yet she possessed a certainty only great inner and outer power conveys.

Kendric's uncommon height alone marked him in any world's crowd—seven feet from chestnut-thatched head to sillac-hide-booted feet. His birthright had claimed him the High Seat of Rengarth as heir of a fallen Ruler and Reginatrix. His pregnant mother had spirited him to another place through a magical gate—the world of Rule where he grew up as a warrior Wrathman and had encountered Irissa by a forest pond in Rindell.

Together they had survived many challenges to body, mind, heart, and soul. None had proved as deeply rewarding, puzzling, and frustrating as parenthood.

Kendric cleared his throat. "Tell me about the leaveweavers."

Javelle and Thane exchanged a glance, then Thane answered.

"Like grassweavers—or at least the grassweavers you and Mother encountered on the way to Frostforge years ago, before we were born."

"We know when it was," Irissa put in dryly, absently braiding and unbraiding her foremost locks, never a good sign.

"I named them leaveweavers on the spot," Thane said. "They looked like the grassweavers you described, only smaller."

"Smaller!" Javelle was disbelieving. "They were huge."

"They just looked that way because they had you circled."

"Circled?" Now Irissa was incredulous. "Javelle, you were surrounded by these creatures with no means to repel them?"

"With no *magic!*" Javelle answered, tears suddenly thickening her voice. "I had the sword."

"What happened?" Kendric interjected.

Javelle spun to face him, but was silent until Thane

broke in. "I caught up with her just then. I . . ." He looked to Irissa, explained himself to Irissa. "I . . . touched the leaveweavers to powder."

She nodded understanding. Torloc magic was an outpouring of hands and eyes, a kind of witchery with will. No Torloc male had borne such magic until Thane's Rengarthian birth. Irissa smiled to remember Kendric's expression when the wombwitch had presented their secondborn.

His joy at fathering a son shone dimly through a greater wonder at finding the infant eyes off-colored—one a strange, luminous gold; the other the pure silver of a Torloc seeress.

Irissa had immediately known Thane for a radical permutation on the Torloc family tree. Her Torloc kin—beyond reach in Edanvant—still did not suspect what a revolution in the ancient struggle for power between Torloc men and women was aborning and abrewing in Rengarth.

Perhaps they never would. She and Kendric, and their offspring, could no more leave Rengarth than they had been supposed to be capable of finding it.

Irissa smiled at her son, knowing he explored his powers in a world that accepted magic, knowing that he was not kept ignorant and manipulated, as she was at his age.

Kendric was watching Javelle.

"It's late," he said abruptly. "We are hungry and tired, all of us. I suggest we discuss this tomorrow. The important fact is that we are all safe and sound." His fingers played across the sword hilt in passing, as if including it in their family circle.

Irissa hesitated, then nodded, looking worry-worn despite her endless youth. Kendric's hand stroked her hair as it cloaked her shoulder. She softened suddenly, then moved to the children, a hand on each to guide them from the room and end debate.

Javelle turned.

"I'll follow in a moment," Kendric said. "I want to examine the sword. Javelle—"

She slipped her mother's light custody and came over as obediently as a puppy, anxiety riding high in her eyes.

Mother and son were fading from the room, speaking intensely. Thane would want to consult Irissa about his recent exercise of magic. It came instinctively to him, but not always the understanding of it.

Kendric didn't always understand magic, but there were other, less spectacular things he did understand.

"Javelle—"

"I'm sorry," she blurted. "Nobody paid any attention to the sword anymore. I didn't think anyone would miss it."

"We missed *you*. A ludborg noticed the sword was gone."

"Oh."

Kendric sighed and examined the chamber. The royal apartments, as Rengarthians insisted on calling them, had been redesigned to reflect the world in which he and Irissa had grown up. Their luxuries were plain rather than fancy—devoid of magic or Torlockian embellishments . . . and even of Rengarthian innovations.

Good stone made walls all around. There were solid stone tables and wooden chairs, a ring of Irissa's tapestries that chronicled earlier adventures—an empty fireplace quite useless in this land of endless summer except in the bordering mountains.

Even the sword looked quite ordinary in this setting, though it was twice-forged and in its second incarnation, being a mind-made copy of the original sword Kendric had borne—and abandoned—in Rule.

Now his fingertips traced the Rengarthian runes that inscribed the hilt. His touch—or perhaps his thought—polished the metal to a glow that grew torch-bright.

Javelle sucked in her breath.

Kendric glanced at her and lifted his hand. The light faded and all was ordinary again.

"Thane can do that now, too," Javelle said softly.

He nodded. "I wish I had seen the leaveweavers before they vanished. I like to catalogue the creatures of this place; no one here has thought to do that. Consequently legend and reality entwine each other. I like my reality well defined."

"They were strange, but not so frightening—"

"How much danger were you in?"

She shrugged. "I'm here."

"You had the sword. Why?"

"Because . . ."

He waited. She was seventeen now, a young woman in many respects, yet still a child. He would have to drag it out of her and, with Javelle, silence was always her worst enemy.

"Because—" Her eyes met his. He was struck by their purely human magic and perversely proud of it, although they came from no strain he recognized in himself or Irissa.

Javelle's delicate fingers played over the metal below the hilt. She would never touch the hilt in anyone's presence now that it had failed to respond to her. But she looked at it as she spoke, slowly.

"The sword showed you the road to your magic. I thought if anything would—"

"Did it?"

Her head shook, tendrils flying and glinting gold in the sword's dying hilt-light.

Kendric began to sound a bit angry at last. "If someone —something—had showed me the road to 'my magic' when I was your age, or even a great deal older, I would have turned my back on it and marched the other way."

"Why?"

"I didn't want magic. You call it mine, but I have always been its—and unwillingly so."

"Still—you have it."

"And?"

"And Mother has it. I know what I should have been born—a seeress! All the ludborgs predicted great things at my birth. . . ."

"And at Thane's. Ludborgs are prone to that sort of thing. They would have waxed eloquent at the birth of a marsh-midge, had Irissa and I had one."

Javelle smiled despite herself, out of the corner of her mouth.

"And—?" Kendric prompted.

She sighed. He always knew when there was another "and."

"Thane has it. He doesn't even have to try."

"Perhaps you try too hard." Kendric lifted the sword into the light and turned the hilt until the runes were almost readable. "So you took the sword and Thane followed. You remind me of myself."

"You!"

"I prefer action to inaction. Do you realize how much of Thane is what he is because he bears his own curse?"

Incredulous, she stared at him.

"He had to follow you. He is not even an heir of Rengarth, since he is not firstborn."

"But rulership of Rengarth is not important to you, to us! We spring from elsewhere, even though you were conceived here. If we could find a way to leave, we'd probably go home to—"

"To where?"

"Edanvant."

Kendric laughed and pulled her against the solid comfort of his shoulder. "Javelle, Javelle, such a glutton for punishment! You want to surround yourself with empowered Torlocs when you pine for power yourself? Believe me, you would not like it. No, not Edanvant."

"Rule, then."

"Ruined Rule. Yes, there are many there without magical

powers, as there are many here in Rengarth. But they ply other powers in Rule. You would not like them, either."

"How do you know!" she burst out, pulling away in conviction rather than anger.

He didn't answer directly, instead lifting the sword and balancing it on the floor. Even while he was sitting, the hilt only came chin-high on him. He manipulated the heavy steel as lightly as if it were a reed.

"You got it down yourself?" he said.

"Yes."

"How?"

"I climb well."

"And—"

"Getting something heavy down is always easier than putting it up again. I let its own weight bring it—and me—down."

"Then you got it—unseen—to the stables and atop Thundermist?"

"It isn't far from the High Seat chamber to the back kitchen passage. I chose the time between meals. And I wrapped it in burlap."

He nodded gravely. "Yet . . . in the leaveweaver circle, you were helpless."

"I never said—"

"That's how I knew. Irissa was right: your actions mired you deeper than you could withdraw. Don't blame your mother for becoming angry at your escapade; it masks her fear. You could have perished had Thane not followed you."

"He always follows me!"

"You're the elder. But, tell me, for all your plans, you learned nothing of the sword or of yourself that could have saved you?"

She shook her head in mute discomfort. "Only that . . . I don't even know how to court magic. And . . . only that you must be very much stronger than I to carry such a thing."

"Yet you got it."

"But I wearied of it. I don't know what I wanted, what I thought! I only wanted to *do* something."

"So you did." Kendric smiled and tilted the hilt toward her. "Take it."

"I can't!"

"Show me."

"I don't want you to see."

"Take it," he repeated, his voice and eyes adamant. He was not father anymore, but teacher.

She braced herself for the sword's wearing weight. Upholding it for one more time, one more minute, seemed unbearable.

"I've tired from battling it. I was *glad* when Thane came to bring me back and helped me with it. It's yours, not mine. I should never have taken it."

"When you believed in it, you could lift it. Now it is as heavy as your despair. *You* make it unsupportable. Raise it."

"I can't!"

He stood and walked away from the table, leaving her clinging to the upright sword. It seemed both weapon and young woman would sway and fall together. Javelle's silk-soft face looked gaunt, tired, in the torchlight. A father would have had mercy on her.

Kendric folded his arms. "Lift the sword—not high, just enough to lift it to an enemy, to defend yourself."

She regarded him aghast.

She had always seen him as her father. Of course he had seemed large to her childish eyes. Later, she had come to realize he seemed large to everyone else, that he *was* large beyond the ordinary measure of men.

Still, he had never been too large to crouch by her tottering first footsteps, to catch her when she fell. Nor had he been too great to pace alongside her first bearing-beast—a squat, odd-hided, snuffling sort of scaled creature Scyvilla the ludborg had produced from a Bubblemere exclusively for her, so he said.

Everyone had always heeded her father—except sometimes her mother. Even Thane at his most balkish had obeyed that deep, seldom-ruffled voice as it floated over their childhood heads until they grew tall enough to hear it on its own level.

Now her father asked Javelle to do something she feared she could not, something she always knew she was unworthy of. She was heir of Rengarth by birthright: by precedence, not merit. By customary right of gender and magic, she had no claim to anything.

Her father frowned. The torchlight struck random silver from his eyebrows and the borders of his dark hair that she had never noticed before. Javelle remained frozen, the act of holding the sword upright a test in itself after her long day of dragging it after her.

Kendric's frown deepened. She couldn't remember him looking so stern, like one forced to do something he loathed.

"If you won't lift it to satisfy me—lift it to save yourself." He could have thundered, but his voice had sunk, echoing vibrantly in the simple stone-walled room.

She shook her head, tried to shrug her shoulders.

Then her father's burnished brown eyes were no longer looking at her but staring within—within and Without.

The stones lurched under her feet. What bound them gave as they ground apart. A tentative hand reached through the gap, coarse hairs cresting its black skin.

Before her eyes the tissue of the floor gave way, rent like filmy gauzelin. Small red-glimmering eyes peered up at her; a length of hairy body rose from the crack in the floor.

Javelle saw yellow teeth, a profusion of hairy limbs, all clawed. She saw the glitter of a gold-studded leather vest on the beastly body. Beyond it she saw the stolid, conjuring figure of her father. The worst was knowing how Kendric hated to evoke anything with his magic, least of all a monster from his daughter's darkest dreams.

"It's not fair," she cried. "You claim you don't want magic, yet use it to make me confront my absence of it. Father—"

He was a wall of suddenly overly rational adulthood, impervious to her pleas. Between them his horrific evocation squirmed and thrust its scabrous nether regions through the widening chasm in the floor.

Javelle tightened her muscles until they cramped. The sword point lifted from the floor, then plunged to supporting stone again.

I can't, she told herself. *Not alone. Not without magic. Please . . . if anything of magic dwells within me or without me, upon me or about me, let it show itself. Let* me *show myself—*

Her arms strained to raise the blade, tautening until rills of fire ran down them. Her muscles swelled against the silver snake around her upper arm until she felt the metal would snap.

Perhaps in reaction to her struggle, the insensate but mobile thing unwound itself. Javelle felt blood throb back into her upper arm. The snake slithered down her arm to the wrist, wrapping it in a tight cuff of silver scales. The head arranged itself on the back of her hand, the tiny silver tongue that always protruded pointing delicately to Javelle's middle finger.

Pretty, she thought bitterly of this new dispersement by the snake ornament. Fear became anger at the fate that gave her no more than a bauble as armor against a dangerous world. Then—strength flowed into her arm and solidified, like blood made metal, like flesh made iron.

Her hands tightened on the hilt as she had always

imagined them doing, her arms and shoulders went rigid, she lifted . . . lifted . . . lifted.

The sword raised before her—a glorious shining length of edged steel, a thing that conferred a sweep of command several feet around herself.

Amazed, Javelle swung the sword like a gentle scythe from side to side. It was only incidental that the gesture truncated the hairy creature crawling from the shattered floor. Steel cleaved hair and skin and bones . . . and then a briny disintegrating smoke.

Beneath the passage of the sword's pendulum of moving shadow, the floor healed itself of the illusion of fracture. Everything was gone except her father, herself, the sword.

She stared again into her father's eyes, for the first time in her life not sure what she would see there.

Kendric recognized her new skepticism and said silent farewell to something he had hoped never to lose but knew he must someday. Then he smiled.

His hand waved modestly at the floor. "A mere illusion. Not my kind of magic, if any is, but I would not send blood and bone against you, daughter, to teach you respect for your own blood and bone. Someday you may have to rend something in your own or another's defense. You must know your own capacity."

Shaking, she let the sword lower to the floor. "It is enough?"

He nodded. "For now."

"But it wasn't me. Somehow this birth-trinket—"

"Ah, that." Kendric's amber-brown eyes lighted to gold as he stepped near to appraise it. His thumb touched the frozen serpent head, but it didn't move. "A puzzling thing, borne with you by your mother—only without herself, not within. It was born with you, too—leaving the Overstone egg that shielded it at the moment you left the shelter of your mother's body. But you know the story.

"In your eagerness for magic, don't claim such for it, Javelle." His hand massaged her shoulder, where the sword-pang had settled. "It was reputed to bear great power, but had somehow endured beyond the exercise of it. It is your external birthmark. It has always played hopstone over your person at some internal whim.

"This day your own efforts raised the invisible magic of your will. That is the lesson I wanted you to learn. You, not a sword or a perambulating metal serpent; you, Javelle, are your own best shield and your own best magic. Your will."

"Take it away," she said quietly in answer.

He did, lifting the sword from her numb hands and laying it again on the table.

Everything in Javelle ached, the least of which was not her heart. Her wrist throbbed as if the serpent—for the first time in the seventeen years that they had been entwined—had twisted around her far too hard, as had her father's expectation.

He was right, though, she thought, there are lessons I must learn.

Something told her that Kendric might not know the name of every one. It shocked her, this notion that he might unknowingly be wanting, despite the best intentions. If she could not remain as she had been, then neither could he.

She looked up at him, her awe and love intertwined and rebraiding into something else. He was large and the sword was heavy. But she was something else, and only the world would tell her what.

He was smiling at her, looking a little chagrined—what if she told Mother what ugly creatures he had pulled out of stones to frighten his only daughter with? She wouldn't tell, of course. She was no Thane to go spreading news into every idle ear, especially when it might not reflect well on the bearer.

"Believe in yourself, Javelle," her father urged, emphasizing every word with a desperate clarity foreign to him. "Not magic," he coaxed as he was wont when she was younger and set on a thing bad for her. "That is the best birth inheritance I can give you—not magic, though I'd give you mine if I could. Never magic, for it is never enough."

CHAPTER
2

SCYVILLA THE RENGARTHIAN WAS WAITING DINNER IN the hexagonal meal chamber when Kendric and Javelle joined the others.

Odd, Kendric thought, how he continued to regard Scyvilla as "the Rengarthian" when Kendric himself lived in Rengarth now, and ruled it. Still, neither he nor Irissa had come to think of Rengarth as home over eighteen relatively peaceful years.

And the children . . . Kendric eyed his son, a lad of normal height for his fifteen years, with none of the elongation of bone his father had shown at that age. Kendric succumbed to parental prerogative and admitted to himself that he knew next to nothing about how either of his children felt.

"I hope you weren't too hard on Javelle," Thane impishly greeted his father. "She means well."

"Speak for your*self*," Javelle retorted, "and let me represent mine."

Their squabbling caused a ripple across Irissa's seamless brow, but she refused to add parental reproval to the always inflammable relationship between the two.

It was hard to imagine a faceless dark hole like the interior of Scyvilla's hood conveying relief, but somehow it did as the squat figure skimmed over to Javelle.

"Safe?" he intoned anxiously.

"And sorry," Thane put in.

This time Irissa murmured "Thane" in rebuke.

"And the sword?" Scyvilla prodded.

Kendric nodded slowly. "Returned safely, as well."

"It would be catastrophic if the sword fell into the wrong hands." The crystal caster nervously tugged the cincture that celebrated rather than delineated his swelling middle.

"How?" Thane asked quickly.

"Never mind," Irissa said. "You two think too much about the sword already—and see to what mischance it has led you! Scyvilla has prepared a welcome-home feast with all your favorite dishes."

"Rulian red-pepper bread?" Thane demanded, proceeding to list his awesome array of favorites. "And sweet saffron savory, and minced ebonberry tart and suckling swanfish?"

"Ah—" Scyvilla began in denial.

"Who'd want suckling swanfish besides you?" Javelle pooh-poohed. "I'm sure it's tawny longcakes and ginger scones with rainbow melon."

Scyvilla's hood twitched from one young person to the other. "Not *all* your favorites, I fear. But . . . rainbow melon, surely, to begin."

Thane's face fell. Chilled fruit, no matter how extravagantly colored, struck him as cold comfort and no way to begin a proper meal.

Kendric, who privately agreed, drew up the mother-of-pearl inlaid chair that was his—not because it was richly made but because it was the strongest chair to be found in the palace at Solanandor Tierze.

"As for the rest—" Scyvilla began with trepidation.

"Surprise us," Kendric instructed. "I'm sure our delinquent lambs will appreciate anything you've made."

Two dark heads nodded in tandem—one curly, one smooth as an Iridesium helmet.

Irissa sighed softly as her family settled down to dinner. Though the years never touched her outer semblance, her inner self craved peace to the exact degree her growing children sowed dissension between each other.

Kendric constantly assured her that such raillery was normal, but they both had been solitary born, lacking one parent, and were unused to the vigorous banter of brother and sister.

Kendric's eyes met hers across the shank of table between them. Irritation shattered like an invisible gauze of glass as the day's worry dissipated. They smiled tolerantly at each other as Thane began kicking Javelle under the table, simultaneously denying her accusations to that effect.

"He's so . . . backward . . . for fifteen," Javelle complained in a tone of adult exasperation. "I fear he'll never grow up."

"Why," Thane returned, "if you're any advertisement for it?"

"Quiet down and at least eat in peace." Kendric sounded optimistic.

"You've done quite enough for the day." Irissa, firm.

Scyvilla settled matters by bobbling through the preparation chamber door, a parade of casting crystals poised in midair behind him.

"Ah," Javelle murmured, impressed by the rainbow highlights that quivered in the globes' glassy curvatures.

What was within each globe impressed her mother even more—a toothsome dish wafted invisibly toward each of them.

The rainbow melon lay within its many-colored rind, its juicy meat ranging from pink to lavender to orange and emerald and blue in inch-thick strips.

Each glassy bubble descended in front of a diner, then the casting crystal burst. The brittle "pop" made them draw back in startled unison before this novel serving system, their eyes squinched shut.

A ludborg's laughter was a bizarre sound—half wheeze and three-quarters giggle—and Scyvilla indulged in it.

The expected shower of shattered glass was not forthcoming. Only dust motes bright as sugar crystals sparkled in the air—a token of the globes' spectacular passing.

Scyvilla clapped his oliphant-eared sleeves together, keeping his hands concealed despite his delight. "Eat hearty," he suggested.

Kendric's curved dining knife was already peeling particolored strips of melon from rind.

"Do mine, too, please!" Javelle prettily passed her plate over.

His mealtime carving tricks had entertained the children since infancy—in a minute Javelle's plate was heaped with rainbow curlicues of melon.

Thane struggled to duplicate the feat on his own melon —to no avail—while Irissa watched with secret amusement. Thane's knife slipped one time too many for his impatience. He laid it down and regarded his plate with an intensity that made Irissa's mouth open in protest.

Before she could speak, Thane's melon sliced itself into a heap of curls, which then erected themselves into the likeness of a color-dappled miniature steed.

"I suppose you're so hungry you could eat a bearing-beast," Javelle taunted sourly.

Thane just shrugged and began consuming his melon-curl steed.

Kendric rapped his knife handle on the table, unaware of

the gesture, as no one else was. He could hardly accuse Thane of childishly playing with his food when he had been entertaining Javelle with as simple a trick.

Still, to be outsorcelled by one's own offspring at one's own dinnertable . . . Kendric mused gloomily. The boy relied too much on his magic when there were carving skills to learn. Why hadn't *he* run off with the sword?

"Ahem," Scyvilla grated amiably.

Kendric looked up to find another quartet of globes sailing past his shoulder. These were empty. When he opened his mouth to comment, one crystal settled between his fork and knife hands, directly over the empty plate.

With an upward waft, the plate was spirited away. Kendric twisted his head to follow it, only to find another hovering crystal at his shoulder.

Javelle giggled.

Kendric might have become angry then at Scyvilla's sleight of serving, no matter how much it distracted the children, except that the item arrayed on the next suspended plate looked suspiciously savory.

"Swanfire Lake hind?" Kendric asked, naming a rare example of Rengarthian wildlife.

"See for yourself," Scyvilla smirked.

Kendric leaned closer, but the torchlight reflected from the globe's shiny, curved sides blinded him. The item remained a tantalizing but undistinguishable brown mass, and he couldn't use his nose to determine the meat.

"A lavish display, Scyvilla, but more frustrating than seductive," he admitted. "It could be moonweasel tripe, for all I know."

Across the table, Irissa lifted a puzzled eyebrow. "You can't see it?" Her silver eyes turned to the globe politely suspended at her ear. "Obviously, it's Swanfire Lake hind, your favorite main course, could we come by it more than once a decade. 'Tis plain to see—"

"It's not plain to me—" Kendric began.

Just then the crystal floated around him, drawing toward the center of the table.

"Ah! I see it clearly now. The flame reflection fooled me. And a well-carved hind it is, too. Bring it nearer, Rengarthian. I thought your wish was to feed, not tease us."

"Of course," Scyvilla murmured. The globe obediently returned to Kendric and deposited its burden on the tabletop. Glass vanished with the customary "pop" as Kendric inhaled a visible veil of steam rising from hot, basted meat.

"Wonderful, Scyvilla," he approved. "I anticipate that you have forgotten none of our weaknesses in the rest of the meal."

Scyvilla bowed silently as Kendric began attacking his serving.

But Irissa held back from her portion, her dinnertable attention for once on her spouse instead of their rambunctious offspring. Her restraint was not only due to her inbred distaste for the meat of the hooved creatures that Kendric was as happy riding as rending.

Scyvilla, she feared, had inadvertently revealed a greater wonder than his crystal servants. She ate slowly, her mind elsewhere, worrisome speculation dulling her quicksilver eyes.

Scyvilla's choicest treat arrived after dinner—and after the young people had been sent to bed, an event already long overdue because of their escapade.

A last, single globe came floating between Irissa and Kendric at the table's center, filled midway with a green half-moon of liquid.

"Borgia!" Irissa raved. "We haven't seen borgia since Edanvant! How did you accomplish this, Rengarthian wonderworker?"

Irissa seldom complimented others on their magic—she took her own so for granted. Scyvilla's hood squirmed modestly in the candlelight.

"A . . . trade secret."

"Trade?" Kendric said sharply. "We are all condemned to remain in Rengarth. How can you trade with anywhere else?"

The hood drooped. "You forget. I was the only one of my kind to escape Rengarth, for a time, until your relived birth travail in the Crux Crystal weened me back—and I was ready to come! But what I have seen in the worlds beyond Rengarth's locked gate and tight lips remains somehow so vivid that I can at times . . . re-create it."

"And you will have none?" Irissa asked courteously, although she knew the answer of long custom. She had never seen a ludborg, which is what she and Kendric called Scyvilla's kind for reasons they had almost forgotten, eat.

"None, Torloc lady. 'Tis my pleasure to serve this night."

"Serve? In what, perchance?" Kendric inquired bluntly. "Must we lick the crystal—or break it and lap up the residue amid broken glass?"

"Ah, the former Wrathman of Rule is thirsty, I believe." Scyvilla sounded pleased that his offering had whetted Kendric's appetite. "Patience, please."

The large crystal floated down toward the tabletop, touching, and then spinning until the emerald liquid within swelled to fill the entire globe.

Irissa impulsively lifted her hands to still it. Kendric winced at the imminent loss of good glass and better liquor. The crystal, a silver and emerald blur now, had distorted its shape somehow. . . .

The spinning slowed. Kendric blinked. The crystal was reshaping itself, as if being reblown before his eyes. It divided in two and elongated. Then it sprouted wings of glass.

"Enough!" Kendric ordered.

The alteration had stopped. Two deep-throated crystal goblets stood at the table's center, formed of glass thin as a fingernail. A pair of delicately delineated swan's wings folded at the cups' bases.

"Much work for two minutes' quaffing," Kendric grumbled by habit, finding, as usual, that magic made more of itself the lesser the achievement. Nevertheless he snatched the fragile stem before he should lose the vessel's contents.

Behind him, the departing Scyvilla hooted hoarsely.

"It is a *bottomless* glass, wise Ruler. Treat it wisely."

"Endless borgia?" Irissa was impressed at last. She lifted the glowing green glass and held it before her as if inspecting a jewel. "I presume it is safe-brewed, that Scyvilla knew better than to import lethal borgia."

"What's lethal is the possibility." Kendric drained his dainty glass in one long draught and sighed, his shoulders relaxing. Empty for a brief instant, the glass glowed emerald-bright again. "Can it not return a half-portion? I hate to leave a glass half-empty."

Irissa sipped her draught with neat, catlike savoring. "Scyvilla was kind to prepare this meal—not only to relieve our minds of our day's worry. He knows what it is to be homesick."

"For where? Edanvant? You think you have a tangle with one unmagicked daughter and a magicked son—imagine what would happen if they shared their world with a who-knows-what—? He paused, flummoxed. "What would your mother Jalonia's child be to them but an . . . aunt of the same age?"

"If Jalonia bore a girl," Irissa mused, "as Scyvilla's casting crystal predicted and we assume."

"Do you . . . become curious after all this time?"

Irissa shrugged, the borgia warming her mind as well as her body. "I have always been curious, knowing I have a sister—or brother—I have never seen. You left no relatives behind in Rule when we left, and less behind when we were exiled from our former worlds here in Rengarth."

"I left custom behind . . . the way of people and things in a world I was used to." Kendric spun the glass until the borgia washed its delicate brim like a small, angry storm-green sea. "Familiarity is some comfort."

"But we have been well treated in Rengarth—acclaimed as its rightful rulers. There has been peace, even if the Liderions remain strangely aloof. You have found tasks to occupy you, as have I. Our children have grown, safe—save from each other and themselves," she added ruefully.

"Too safe," he returned. "And they grow too fast. Soon they will be of an age to bed-bond or marry. And there are none like them in Rengarth."

"Girl, boy—there are scores of those in Rengarth!"

"None like them," Kendric repeated.

"But . . . Javelle has no magic. She is like everyone."

"Perhaps." Kendric didn't sound convinced. "But what of your son, seeress, who is like no one who has ever lived—not Torloc, not wizard, not even overambitious Delevant?

"He is a born Torloc seer, the first of his kind, of his gender, to blend the Torloc women's inbred magic with the men's hard-won external powers. There may be those who if they knew of him . . . even Rengarth would not be safe enough. Perhaps they already do," Kendric warned.

Irissa set down her gaudy glass. Her face was parchment-white against her midnight hair, against the black slash of the Iridesium circlet that banded her forehead.

"You mean my father, Orvath, who has always feared—or desired—my inborn powers? He would not have the means to enter Rengarth or affect us here from Edanvant . . . not even with all the men's talismanic magic combined."

Kendric nodded thoughtfully. "Yes. But I wasn't thinking of Orvath."

Irissa stared uncomprehendingly into his eyes, then paled even more than seemed possible.

Kendric grunted, bending over to pull of his boots. They tumbled down the dais steps as they fell from his hands, wear-softened leather shanks slumping like drunken soldiers.

"You really should have some new boots cobbled," Irissa suggested from the other edge of their down-deep bed.

"Yes," Kendric agreed.

He always agreed when Irissa mentioned his need for new boots. Yet he never did anything about replacing the sillac hide, although time had scuffed the vibrant orange to a weak-ale shade. The boots were the last physical remnant of Rule he owned.

He glanced to the sword on its windowside table. It was mind-made—evoked by his acquired magic in a moment of need—not the true thing of Rule he had left to bleed gemstones and sink into Rindell Pond. As such, he could never regard it with nostalgia. Besides, it never changed, unlike his boots, which bore the crease of every passing day until the surfaces seamed, like the faces of old friends.

Irissa, despite her comment, had retrieved the boots and set them side by side, as upright as possible, against the clothes chest.

She paused at a dressing table surmounted by a mirrored crystal of smoked glass—a birthing present of Scyvilla's that permitted Irissa to consult her own image in three-dimensional form—and lifted her Iridesium circlet from her head.

"I even dream of you with that thing on," Kendric remarked suddenly. "I've never grown accustomed to seeing you remove it. It's like watching a cat displace its face."

Irissa turned, her hair permanently waved at the temples by the circlet's daily presence even in its nightly absence.

"How do you think I broke Sofistron's ring of mirrors, if not by removing the circlet and using it as a magical lock pick? But I know your meaning. Seeing you without your sword most of these years . . ." Irissa smiled at the weapon as it lay unsheathed in a sheen of moonlight. "We have grown staid, Wrathman, in the 'lost, limpid Rengarth' we have found. No wonder our children wear on us."

"Staid? Just . . . older."

Kendric spoke matter-of-factly, without thinking. He did not see Irissa flinch at his words, being too busy pulling the embroidered tunic over his head without scratching his face on the chain-of-gold threads worked into the design. Luxury was ever an impediment to a man of his simple upbringing and simpler tastes.

Irissa sat suddenly at her dressing table, regarding herself in the mirror, watching a smaller Kendric in the mirror's marvelously lifelike background.

"It's past midnight. Aren't you tired?" he asked. "Worry wears on one like water on rock, though I never knew it until I had offspring." He stretched long arms, yawning.

In the mirror, Irissa saw silver reflect off Kendric's dark brown head and the coiled hairs of his chest. She heard his joints crack, though he did not.

He did not seem to see or hear as sharply as she any longer—or perhaps she simply paid him more attention now that her children had grown independent enough to slip her eternal maternal watchfulness.

"Perhaps you have too little to worry about," Irissa said lightly. "Do you ever miss our earlier adventures, our quests through gates and worlds?"

"Miss lean rations and leathery meat and even tougher bedding? Miss magical hocus-pocus and Torloc pride and garrulous cats? No, if I miss anything, it is—"

"Yes?"

He paused so long before answering, Irissa began to worry all over again.

"My bearing-beast, Willowisp . . . my bond brothers of Rule. Sometimes my father, Halvag the Smith."

"You've never spoken of these things."

"They are the past. But you asked."

She nodded, hiding from her reflection in the glass. "I never miss anything. I am completely content. I don't truly miss my mother, Jalonia, for I never knew her. I don't miss my father, Orvath, for he confuses me. Finorian . . . frightened me."

"At least you have the living to not miss," he said.

"I am an ingrate, I suppose. Perhaps we should . . . visit . . . Edanvant. I might miss my grandfather, Medoc, a bit. And Dame Agneda."

"How . . . visit?" Kendric almost bellowed with pent-up frustration. "We cannot leave this cursed paradise of Scyvilla! We rule all we survey—other than being wary of an imperial poisoning by an ambitious clan with heirs it desires to install."

"Then you do miss the freedom of the early days!" Irissa pounced.

Kendric's big fists unfolded into a dismissive gesture. "Why miss what one cannot reclaim? We are trapped here, Irissa, as our children are. Perhaps it is safer than other lands; certainly it is safe from intrusion. No one has cracked a gate to Rengarth since we did it nineteen years ago."

"It seems like yesterday," Irissa mused.

"Look at your children. They make a glass, not of hours, but of years."

"I know. They . . . seem almost adult, but are still babes in everything other than body."

"They have been reared in a land that offers little to test them. And Javelle is a young woman."

"Javelle!" Irissa laid down an Iridesium comb so quickly

that a trail of coldstone sparkle momentarily slashed the air. "What shall we do with that girl?"

"More to the point, what will *Javelle* do with Javelle? She'll be fine, Irissa. You've always worried about her overmuch."

"Why should I not? She has no magic!" The anguish in Irissa's voice, the way the words seemed torn from her, made Kendric stiffen as if encountering an old enemy.

He was silent for a bit, as was she. The luminous walls and pillars with their living ornaments of water-bound fish rippled tranquilly around them. He finally spoke.

"So?"

"Not even a rudimentary talent, not so much as a trick with a talisman is in her! Even the Torloc men proved it possible to defy their birthright and acquire someone else's magic. Javelle is . . . magic-mute."

"So?"

"How will she protect herself? Were it not for me . . . us—"

"Javelle will protect herself as other women do. Most of them do not bear magic."

"She is not an 'other woman.' She is Torloc."

"Half-Torloc."

Irissa's silver eyes blinked into his mortal brown ones as she became aware of the blind alley into which her assumptions led. If Javelle had been robbed of magic, then perhaps a non-Torloc father was the thief.

Irissa shook her head, denying the charge that neither of them would voice. "I worry for her so," she continued softly.

"What about your son?" Kendric asked, a sharpness in his tone she had not heard before.

"Thane? Thane is . . . splendid. He is so gifted, so adept with his magic. I never expected a male Torloc child to be so blessed—it's almost frightening."

"He is lazy, Irissa."

She half-started up, appalled by the charge.

"I love him, too, but he relies on his magic instead of himself. He is indirect, self-absorbed; he expects everything to be conjured up in one of Scyvilla's crystals for him."

"Lazy! He saved Javelle!"

"When it would have been better for her to have saved herself."

"She wouldn't have needed saving if she hadn't run off with your sword—why would she do such a dangerous thing?"

Kendric regarded her, a reply in his transparently honest eyes that never reached his lips. His voice was softer when he spoke again, but firm still.

"At least Thane felt some obligation to follow Javelle— although most of it was probably to report her mischief later. Yes, I'm glad his magic was there to help her, but don't you see? Javelle has always had Thane's magic there to mock her lack of powers. She has always been older but has never been better."

"Wouldn't I give her half mine if I could? I should have, by birthright—"

Kendric moved to the dressing table, to stand behind Irissa. "I was born of Phoenicia, a powerful Rengarthian Reginatrix, yet I showed no more bent for magic in my youth than a toad. My Rengarth-forged sword evoked a bit; my alliance with a Torloc seeress conjured even more. Perhaps Javelle has not met her sword or her Torloc yet."

Irissa threw her hands up into the air, laughing wearily.

"We are too worn and too distraught to discuss such matters now. I never knew you felt so strongly about their different . . . natures."

"Why not? They do. Am I immune just because I am not Torloc?"

Irissa's seeress's eyes gentled. "I never said that, never thought that."

He sighed, and, being a large man, could have extinguished several banks of candles with it. "No, you merely succumbed to the human trait of worry." His hand moved to her shoulder, to the green-gold fastening of her tunic. "I know a cure for that. Are you coming to bed?"

Irissa slipped wordlessly into his embrace, her long, peerlessly dark hair sliding against him like satin ribbons. "A moment," she whispered.

She sank down at the dressing table. Kendric returned to the bed, and the illuminated aquariums dimmed as they always did when the couple retired.

Irissa pulled off a heavy bracelet of green gold, and a ring with an exotic stone. Her marriage ring, gate-welded to her middle finger, sparkled through its quintet of inner colors as her hands moved. One rested on the clasp at her shoulder, but first Irissa leaned close to the mirrored globe, so close that Kendric could not see past her hair-cloaked shoulder if he should try.

Scyvilla's globular looking-glass had other tricks than three-dimensionality. Irissa could call images into it and page through them like a book. Anything she had seen, she could see again.

So she had evoked her parents' likenesses from far-off Edanvant in her more pensive moments, though she would never admit the . . . weakness . . . to anyone, not even Kendric. So she had summoned the faces of old friends and old enemies on more than one occasion.

Now, for the first time, she called up the visage of an old lover. Her first lover, her only lover, Kendric as he had been in the Shrinking Forest of Rindell on the very day she had met him more than twenty years before . . .

The mirror rippled obligingly, painting a panoply of leafy trees such as she had not seen since Edanvant. Her silver eyes dwelled reminiscently on the weepwillow trees trailing in the dark water, on the darker form of a man clad in Iridesium mail and a blood-rusted tunic.

The Kendric of that day assembled in all the impressive impact of his seven feet of well-armed height, as Irissa had first seen him.

He pulled off his helm and Iridesium hood so she could see his face. Irissa stared, feeling the blood drain from her own face in the present as she confronted the visage from the past.

She had no notion—not then, not even now—of how much Kendric would change, *had* changed. Irissa leaned closer, as if to see more clearly.

How could she have not known, not noticed? Kendric had aged since she had met him. His hair—it had shrunk back on his brow like the Shrinking Forest itself, stalk by stalk, slow but inevitable. What now were silver strands embroidered to match his tunic's gilt richness had been solid, bark-brown hair to the root of each and every one then.

And the lines of his face that always faded before her fond eyes into a familiarity that would remain ever fresh— they were all additions and subtractions upon a visage that had been as smooth as his Iridesium helm before the first blow was ever struck upon it.

Irissa's palm spun the mirror away. The smoky globe teetered on its brass spit and turned back an empty face—empty even of Irissa's own reflection.

That suited her. She wanted no one to see her shock, least of all Kendric. Tears slid from her silver eyes, anyway. She quickly cupped her hand beneath her chin. The hot liquid that sped down her cheeks hardened like ice in an arctic wind before it reached her wrists.

Tears made into coldstone clinked dryly in her palms. No more than these few fell; they were too betraying. Irissa swept the sparkling stones into a pocket of her tunic, which she unclasped and shed like some outworn skin as she rose.

Donning an expression that she hoped hid her newest and gravest worry, Irissa joined Kendric in the dimness of their bed.

CHAPTER

3

HE FELL FOR A LONG, LONG TIME—THE BOY WHO HAD NO birthday. He fell so long he seemed to be flying.

He should have been swimming.

Water oiled past him, black and engulfing. Unseen things swathed his limbs and then released them with a pressure like clammy hands.

He began to discern lighter shades of darkness, all the more disturbing because there should be no variation in the bottomless midnight of the Dark Mirror.

Great greasy forms slid by, boneless tentacles of oily flesh. Eyes gleamed like stars, faintly red, blue, and green despite their abiding yellow-white glimmer.

He saw huge obsidian walls as thick as shadow—and even larger shadows passing on those walls. He looked above to find black water eddying like lace tatted over the water's skin. He breathed the turgid liquid and it breathed him back until he seemed to be part of it all—the darkness and the depths and the ever-present shadow.

Helpless, his limbs turned to jelly and his mind stirred around and around in some impenetrable stew. He drifted in the Dark Mirror's endlessly expanding universe. There was no point in protesting his fate until the one he had offended made his fate clear—and even then there was no protesting. There never had been.

So, consumed by a curiosity born of living in a strictly limited world, the boy began speculating about the beings that drifted so insensately against himself.

Were they as trapped as he—all gnats caught in some sticky dark web of not-quite-water? Were they air-breathers immersed in an alien element that for once forbore to smother them? Or were they water-sprites—creatures from the over-ocean's deepest underbelly—welcoming him to the eternal fathoms of their unlit worlds?

His calm, he knew, would not appease the one who waited above. Calm never did. Still, calm was the sin he had made into a personal virtue, out of some instinct too dim to name. Sometimes he thought another self hid within his outer semblance, a transparent, peeling kind of self that clung so close he could barely sense it.

Sometimes he thought he was not real at all, but a conjuring of the man above.

A phantom fish trolled by—an undulating length of fluted fins and serpentine muscle. Its rippling side butted the boy sideways. He saw that more than starry fish-eyes lit the depths. Far below, sand sparkled like ground jet beads and obsidian coral coiled into the frame of a mirror.

The mirror made up the whole bottom—one vast, smooth, shining plane of perfect darkness. Intrigued, he stroked for the emptily reflective mouth that yawned wider the nearer he flailed.

Then he saw the mouth shrink. He spotted two darker wells above it. Sharks cruised out of the cavern eyes—sleek and silver, seeming almost emissaries of some mammoth being's hidden expression.

A giant face resolved from the bottom sand and coral—a

woman's visage writ large in the element of hectic water, floating within it, on it, beneath it. Ghostly ropes of the weed called seaspit pooled around its black-featured face.

Then it came swooping up for him—all face and all mournful expression. All-consuming. Possessing in the simple cold-blooded way of a fish only an open mouth and then darkness, inner darkness.

Terrified at last, he tried to cry out. At least, his lungs and muscles and mouth moved in that manner. As in a nightmare, no sound came forth here, only the silent, rhythmic delving of the deep in its complacent and eternal turmoil.

No, he shrieked soundlessly as the great swallowing mouth expanded beneath him, around him. No!

He was being rapidly withdrawn from the depths, grasped in the jaws of some beneficent leviathan driving a tunnel to the surface. Below him the phosphorescent face of water and seaspit pursued, its gigantic features screwed into mask of anger and loss, bottomless loss. . . .

Screaming, he broke the water's oily surface. True air filled his lungs, not the bubble of fraudulent air that had belled him below.

The boy gasped, flailing to stay afloat, then realized he thrashed in an ankle-deep puddle. The water ran rings around him; expanding ripples shrieked to match the cry within his mind. The silver reflection of a face—eyes and mouth and nose—evaporated into reflected candle flames on a jet-dark surface. He looked up, gasping.

A man stood there at the mere's edge, water lapping at the hem of his long robe like some spirit-broken dog. The boy heard his own canine panting slow to regular breathing.

"Why?" the man asked. He was more than a man, though the boy didn't know how he knew it, having never seen anyone less than this man.

"The sword," the boy croaked, feeling toadlike squatting

there in the shallow water and getting uncomfortably damp at last. "I thought it was important. I almost called it up from the Well of the Worlds."

"It is important." The man withdrew gloved hands from the wide-hemmed sleeves he habitually folded them into. "It will be even more important when I say so. Get up, my son, and trod on Dark Mirrors no more. And bring your . . . pet . . . with you."

The man turned into the darkness and vanished.

The boy didn't move until he shared the darkness with nothing human. Then he stirred and looked around. A detached thunderhead with three lightning-bright eyes cowered near the mirror's congealing edge.

The liquid had the consistency of tar now. The boy pulled himself free limb by limb and backed away from the black spot on the floor.

The cloud-creature rubbed his legs like a cat, then puffed itself higher than a man. The boy patted a curve of cloud, even though his hand passed through it as through fog.

"There'll be much to say," he told his familiar. It seemed a substantial thing to bear no name, but the boy never knew what to name it. In some ways, he found the cloud-creature more real than himself. At least, it did not suffer from his terrible affliction.

Sighing, all triumph washed away by the drowning in the Dark Mirror turned black water, the boy slogged through the formless waste, looking for the shapeless door to what he called home.

CHAPTER

4

LUDBORGS BY THE DOZEN FLOCKED OUTSIDE THE PALACE of Solanandor Tierze. In their dun-colored robes amid the colorfully dressed populace—and given their nearly circular dimensions—they resembled nothing so much as walking mudballs.

Still, a ludborg was the center of attention wherever he went, and a flock of ludborgs expanded the center of attention into a circumference.

Cityfolk circled them, as they always did when these bizarre beings moved in a mass from their countryside caves into the public byways. In a land noted for strange forms of nature, ludborgs remained strangely *un*natural forms.

Javelle watched them gather from the shadow of the palace swangate. After a moment, she flung herself through the heart-shaped doorway made by facing swans, their long necks arched, into the sunlight beyond.

The palace boasted many entrances and exits, each more exotic than the last. But swangate, constructed by some long-ago Swan Clan Ruler, had always been Javelle's favorite point of departure. Each feather on the giant swans' graceful bodies had been carved from rare blackwood and buffed until it glowed with an almost natural sheen. Wood was a luxury in a land where trees were singular.

Not only Javelle had grown fond of swangate. As she left its shelter, a new shadow clung to the puffed swan's breast at the archway's side, then darted after Javelle. She sensed the shadow before she saw it. Whirling, her crinkled locks flew into narrowed eyes.

"Thane! You always follow me!"

He bowed. "You always precede me, that's all."

"Liar," she casually countercharged. Her attention had already been distracted by a flurry among the ludborgs. "Go home," she ordered.

He shrugged, having anticipated both the order and his subsequent disobedience. Once Javelle had joined the crowd clustering around the ludborgs, Thane slowly circled the gathering, trying to peer through thick bodies and akimbo elbows.

Javelle, a half-head taller, stood on tiptoe and ignored him with great success.

An "ahhh" from the crowd made Thane challenge the heedless wall of backs with small success. He continued to circle the knotted bodies, unworried about losing sight of Javelle.

Their own dark heads stood out among the lighter Rengarthian ones like a wren-brown ludborg in a peacock pen. Most Rengarthians were pale, with hair so flaxen it sometimes shone slightly green in sunlight. At most a Rengarthian might boast a cinnamon-dust shade of hair— or the rare red head of the Brenhall Clan.

Thane finally returned to Javelle from the circle's opposite side to ask her outright. "What is it?"

Utterly absorbed, she no longer begrudged his presence.

"Something from the Spectral City—a veil of spirit-spray, I think."

"Let me see!" His request went unheeded, despite his rank. Custom made Rengarthian heirs highly dispensable. And Javelle preceded him there as well.

Thane braced himself on his sister's hips and leaped so high his boot bottoms smarted when he came down again.

"Let go!" Javelle complained.

"I can't see."

"Then use your magic."

She shrugged him off, terribly adult for a moment in her superior height and irritation. Thane considered the situation. Thoughtless invitations were the kind he most liked to accept, especially when his sister issued them.

He squatted on the ground, observing a forest of variously clad calves. Feet scented by everything from bearing-beast dung to new-mown grass and crushed ebonberries milled in a manner expressive of their owners' health and gender.

Ground level, at least, offered a break in the solid circle of bodies—Thane could even glimpse the ludborgs' robes pooling on the dusty cobstones and something sinuous shimmering among them.

Another universal "ah" of delight above spurred his ambitions. He began looking at his nose until his oppositely colored silver and gold eyes crossed—a feat that had made his sister shriek with disgust since he was nine.

There was more to the trick than Javelle ever knew—or at least, had seen lately. His intent stare produced a visible beam of light as frail as mist from each eye. At first blade-straight, the emanations bent and kissed with an almost-metallic hiss, then twined. A slim gilt and silver rope began snaking along the ground among the forest of rooted legs.

It wove between the stately, swollen ankles of market-bound dames, around the thin, knobby joints of children and old men. It hobbled maiden and man, granddam, and even the odd infant set to the ground and temporarily overlooked.

In and out the glittering serpent of Thane's sight wove, sly yet slack, moving more by some interior stretching than an outward motion.

At last the questing tongue of thread came wagging back to him. Thane glanced up. Everyone was still absorbed, oblivious of each other and the lacing at their feet.

Thane grinned and leaped upright—and back. The rope his sight had woven jerked back with him. Amid shrieks and curses and much dust, people lurched into one another and then toppled. Javelle went down with a satisfying plop, already looking around for him with a sisterly instinct for brotherly mischief.

Thane sank back on his heels, the threads of his vision misting and reeling back into his eyes. Laughing, he easily saw over the fallen heads to the circle's naked center where rotund ludborgs buzzed in confusion.

"Ah," Thane said, seeing at last what everyone else had all along—a sheet of shimmering light dappled with rainbow colors on which figures moved and objects took fantastical shape.

Even as he watched, the veil stirred and collapsed, leaving a swarm of dust motes blinking out in the commonplace daylight.

"Satisfied, young sir?" a voice rasped behind him.

Thane swallowed a chortle in mid-glee and twisted his head over his shoulder. Scyvilla stood there, rocking like a disconsolate nursemaid.

Javelle scrabbled over. *"You* did it!"

"I saw what everyone else did," Thane answered Scyvilla.

"You had an opportunity to see *more,"* Scyvilla reproved. "Instead you ended all sight."

"It was marvelous, Scyvilla, what was it?"

"A piece of the Spectral City. Wherever the city pauses, it leaves a web upon the grasses with its going. Like dew, such remnants fade in sunlight. This fragment refused to fade; hence we conveyed it here to consult our Reginatrix, who alone among us forges some link to the phantoms that inhabit the Spectral City. But overexposure ended it. A pity. I believe it held something that you would one day give a great deal to know."

Thane remained quiet as the hood bowed deeply to point its eternal inner shadow directly at him.

"I wanted to see it, that's all," he finally said.

"So did your mother. That is why we . . . er, ludborgs, as they call us now, brought it hither."

Thane shrugged and tried to look indifferent.

"Did Thane's stupid magic banish it?" Javelle asked hopefully.

"Just his curiosity, I think," Scyvilla answered. "We may yet convey some tatters of this tissue to your lady mother. I will see to what remains."

Scyvilla glided away on unseen, and apparently unshod, feet.

"Midge-mind!" Javelle hissed at Thane. "I have never known anyone so set on ruining everything."

"You're just jealous because you couldn't make a flea jump from one end of Thundermist to the other."

"I can't do any harm, either," she reminded him.

"Certainly not," he sneered, "with a sword."

His comment had the desired effect. Javelle deserted seniority and dignity to chase him wrathfully through the tangled streets of Solanandor Tierze until they both should so tire of it that they would forget their quarrel.

Irissa stalked the limits of her greeting chamber wrapped in icy dread. She was alone. Rengarth, more than most lands, recognized that its Ruler's spouse had a role in public affairs. Every Reginatrix had her own official chambers in which she could conduct whatever business she wished.

Irissa's greeting chamber had been more of a retreat from rule than an outpost of it. Her tapestry screen commanded a corner, glowing softly blue. Intrigued by the ludborgs' ever-present blue-worms, Irissa had received a supply she was interweaving with more common threads to create an experimental blend that would shed light as well as magic.

She kept a pelt-draped couch there, strewn with Rengarthian reading matter from the city archives. The tabletops carried several flat glass bowls in which floated some of the rare singing flowers gathered from the empty grasslands.

The flowers—broad-petaled, fist-sized blooms of oddly dull colors—were dormant now. They cast only a thin, silvery hum into the air that Irissa found more soothing than their normally boisterous vocalizations.

"Seeress." Scyvilla was bowing in the doorway, a posture that was noticeable only in that his body now resembled a half-moon instead of a full one. Still, his tone had been suitably serious.

Irissa came quickly to the central table—a stone-supported wheel of polished weepwillowwood she had imported from Rule by means she never discussed.

"Lay it here."

Scyvilla complied, unfolding a thin iridescent rag in the table's center.

"This is all?"

"There was considerably more—I was compelled to enlist a full dozen of my kind to help convey the whole here."

"Then what happened?"

"Your son."

"Oh. Dare I ask?"

"In his eagerness to see it, he raised a ruckus around it. Dust, direct sunlight, wind—singly or together, they were too much for a thing of such elusive delicacy. I saved what few . . . shards I could."

Irissa's long fingers smoothed the wrinkled tissue, which was skin-thin. "He is—"

"Ignorant," Scyvilla obliged. "And a festy, high-spirited lad who should learn some responsibility."

"Easier said than done," she replied. "Have you offspring, Scyvilla?"

The hood was silent. "We do not . . . quite . . . do things that way. No doubt from observing others."

"Observe this fragment," Irissa suggested. "I would have been grateful for the whole, but if this is all we have—"

"Hmmm." Scyvilla's hood hovered over the remnant. The table's tight woodgrain pattern could be seen through the diaphanous stuff. Some other, opposite pattern moved in the gossamer threads, but faintly.

And then the fabric melted . . . or rewove itself. A subtle rearrangement of threads evoked a face in the cloth—a face shaped in whorls much like the grain of watered silk. It was a face seen in water, through water—moving water.

"Neva?" Irissa wondered.

"The fabric is pale, so it reminds you of that white-miened woman," Scyvilla cautioned her. "But it could be anyone. How long since you have seen Neva?"

"Not since . . . Javelle's birth, when the Spectral City overlaid its image on Solanandor Tierze so Neva and Aven could be with me, though both were only specters then."

Irissa frowned, then sighed, putting a hand to the Iridesium that braceleted her brow as if it bound her.

"I know not the price they paid to perform that wonder. I was . . . too weary and too wonder-worn myself at the time. But I have never seen them since, nor any trace of the Spectral City."

"Yet it comes . . . and goes. We ludborgs have seen it a

time or two—though never near and never very clear. It fades, Reginatrix."

"Forever?"

"Do not all things?"

Irissa wrapped her hands about her arms and paced, her midnight hair rippling with cobalt highlights in the glow given by the distant blue-worms.

"The Spectral City has always been part of Rengarth," she declared as if also asking.

"As far as we know."

"If it fades now, then my . . . our arrival has caused it." She paused at the fragment, at the glimmer of a face watching from within the delicate weave. "I must go there. I must find it again."

"To save them?" Scyvilla wondered.

The look Irissa gave him conveyed all her resolve and one thing else—her shame.

"To save myself again, as before."

"Some outer force threatens?"

Irissa smiled wearily. "No, inner."

"What then?"

"Life," she said, "and death."

"A journey—alone?"

Kendric had sought Irissa in her greeting chamber. He had not sought the news she gave him.

She sat at her tapestry stand, tranquilly embroidering a moonweasel into the design, which represented a bestiary of places they had visited.

He studied the cool blue of her profile as the blue-worms painted it.

"And you call *me* stubborn."

"You haven't even argued yet."

"Why should I?" He slapped his hands to his sides. "Yet I must point out that you propose to commit the offense for which you berated Javelle."

She eyed him over the point of the slender silver needle gleaming in the unnatural light.

"How? I will take nothing that is not mine, and certainly not your sword. I am not leaving without first leaving word of my departure. And I go armed with more than a sword—my mature magic. What have I to fear in Rengarth?"

"Geronfrey," Kendric reminded her brutally.

"We have heard or seen nothing of him since he slipped into a gate to the world Without with his . . . spawn."

"Nineteen years ago," Kendric snorted. "An eyebat to a life-prolonging sorcerer like Geronfrey. He called Rengarth his for more years than a Torloc lives. I doubt we've seen the last of him."

"Nevertheless, I must go."

"Why? You still cannot present a reason strong enough. And why can't I go with you?"

"Geronfrey," she retorted. "If he lurks, someone must stay and guard the children, the kingdom."

"The kingdom! I rule everything but my own family."

Irissa's head tilted. "Would you want to?"

He thought, then laughed. "No, you are more interesting unruly. But, Irissa, tell me at least the need for this sudden quest of yours. Does some danger threaten that you wish to spare us?"

Her face tightened.

"If you believe you spare us, you are wrong. You can never spare us our caring, our worry."

She almost answered, and what that answer would have been neither he nor she could have said. Instead, she pointed to the table, to the wafer of fabric lying there, dissolving there into the whorls of woodgrain supporting it.

"It's an . . . imprint of the Spectral City, Kendric. Of the Spectral City's soul, I think. The image fades even as we eye it. Can you not still read a plea for aid, even when it is inscribed on a cloud?"

"Who pleads? The face is familiar, but . . . unreadable."

Irissa watched Kendric hover over the fragile wisp, his strong hands braced heel-down on the table edge, his shoulders hunched. Her own face fractured—as if torn into emotions too various to fit into a single frame.

She stared at him staring at the fragment, then saw the blue light strike a silver glint off the hairs upon his knuckles.

Irissa's needle plunged into the tapestry and stayed there, like a sword driven home, a question asked and answered in the same breath.

"Whose face?" he asked again, racking his remembrance.

She rose and went to stand beside him. "A citizen of the Spectral City who is . . . was . . . very close to us."

"Neva?"

She nodded.

"Or . . . Aven?"

She nodded again.

"Both?"

Again.

"And more than they?"

"I believe so, but I cannot say. Unless I go."

He nodded then, putting a hand to her shoulder. "You never stopped me from meeting my fate, even when you thought the means crude and bloodsome. I find magic too refined and soul-curdling, but it is your medium, seeress. Make of it what you must."

They stood for a while like that, then Kendric turned and left the room.

Irissa bowed her head and put her hand to the tabletop, gently, upon the disintegrating shimmer. Her fingertips hushed the voiceless oval of the open, wailing mouth.

Around her, the floating flowers keened like a faraway wind.

She had traced, finally, the features, between the time that Scyvilla had left her and Kendric came to her. She knew the face now, and knew the name.

It was herself. Or a phantom of herself, or of that phantom. Had Kendric not been surprised by her decision, and sorely troubled, he would have noticed, Irissa thought, both glad—and sad—that he had not.

Her thumb reached to the betraying band of iridescence across the fading brow and erased it with a stroke.

CHAPTER
5

FROM ANY TOWER IN SOLANANDOR TIERZE, ONE COULD see Rengarth stretching willy-nilly in every direction and looking, in any direction, the same.

Yet the land exuded a wild abandon that made it more than magical. Wreaths of grass and singing flowers carpeted hill and vale. Hills cradled ponds and lakes and streams in thousands of amiable dimples. The land went on forever, and kept its secrets well.

After nearly twenty years to reclaim it, Kendric, who had been conceived but not born here, still found Rengarth alien. He brooded while watching Irissa guide Javelle's mount into the hock-high grasses that grew a spear's throw past the city gates.

Those who mowed the grass from the city fringes were ancestrally appointed guardians of a sort, more revered than gatekeepers. Some instinct told them to barber just so far and no more. And from that invisible point on, the grasses sprang up unfettered, hissing like snakes in the wind, hiding bog and burrow and the real, naked face of Rengarth.

Now Irissa rode alone into that deceptively open wilderness, on an errand she was uncharacteristically close-mouthed about.

"Mother need fear nothing in Rengarth," Thane offered in that odd blend of boast and empathy so common to lads his age.

Javelle, on Kendric's other side, simply bit her lip. Kendric glanced to her white fists on the rampart stones and smiled. She might not have shared her mother's magical powers, but Javelle had full measure of Irissa's passionate self-control. He suspected that what rode Javelle was not worry for her mother's safety, but a fierce wish to be in her place.

Kendric ruffled Thane's smooth hair and shook Javelle's knotted shoulder. It was comforting to have partners in puzzlement when confronted with another's eternal mystery.

"Your mother is a seeress," he reminded their children. "There are times when that . . . calling . . . overrides all else. It has never slain her yet."

His words comforted himself as much as any other. Once, long ago, he had presumed to spare Irissa knowledge of a hidden hazard he saw better than she. Now, he feared, the scale had counterbalanced, the boot was on the other foot. And it pinched.

At the brow of the hill dusted with the dawn's golden pollen, the rider paused. A silhouette against the rising suns, Irissa seemed to look back. Those on the tower top strained to see her daily familiarity in that tiny image about to plummet into unbridled Rengarth—all three—and failed.

Irissa, far below and far away, discerned little more of her watching family—just a distant peak bracketed by a foothill on either side standing dark against Solanandor Tierze's pale stones. The familiar juxtaposition made her smile.

She drew her shortsword and waved the bare blade in the

glare of Rengarth's three rising suns. Whether the watching figures saw anything was impossible to tell, but Irissa felt more optimistic for her exuberant gesture.

"Come, Thundermist," she urged Javelle's dainty mount, and it plunged down the hill into a sea of grass.

Before her Rengarth stretched, a blue-green carpet kept rolled too long and therefore lying lumpily over the earth. Several glistening trails overlaid the emerald grasses—pathwindings of the normally nocturnal grassweavers.

Irissa had no desire to encounter these huge translucent worms and reined the bearing-beast west, away from the dew-drenched grasslands. Where the Spectral City might lie now that it had proven shy was something only instinct would determine.

She rode most of the day, relishing the solitary pleasure of her own company and feeling a bit ashamed of that luxury. The only shadow on the earth was that cast by herself and her bearing-beast—a two-headed, many-footed monster that shrank or elongated as the suns swung high and then low again in the sky.

A selection of foodstuffs plumped out the bags that hung almost ornamentally from Thundermist's saddle. For drink there was an empty canteen fashioned from tough-scaled skin. Rengarth bubbled with water, as if situated over some constant wellspring. Irissa had only to dismount and fill her canteen at a nearby stream, pond, or lake. The water would be fresh and pure; nothing spoiled in Rengarth unless someone made it spoil. Poison was the greatest violation of Rengarth's nature, hence its people's favored weapon.

Irissa pondered this as she rode, remembering that a poison-taint from Rengarth had laid her low in Edanvant for a time. Hungry, she nibbled a tawny longcake left over from Scyvilla's celebration dinner. Dry, she scanned the rippled horizon for a glint of water.

"There!" she confided to Thundermist's obligingly

pricked ear. "You'd fancy a drop, too, I think." She brushed her trousered calves against the sun-warmed belly and the bearing-beast cantered forward.

The promised water turned out to be one of those solitary springs that sprinkled the land for no discernible reason. Irissa happily hurled herself off Thundermist's swelling sides—she was unused to going beast-back, and her leg muscles were protesting already.

The animal instantly dipped its muzzle to the water, unperturbed by the constant ripples that raced from the spring's ice-white center. No twin image of Thundermist's long, large-lipped head floated on the water's surface. Water was unreflective in Rengarth—not even the blue of the sky found reproduction there.

Water was more a window than a mirror in Rengarth. Clear as a coldstone, bright and chill and clean and cutting, water seemed to sharpen rather than blur the sight.

Irissa gazed down into the limpid land beneath the spring—a jagged ledge of crystal-white rock tunneling down indefinitely, until even light narrowed and white became gray, and gray . . . black.

Water flowed over her hands, over the canteen's submerged neck, not even distorting their images. Initially chill to the touch, it warmed—or she cooled. Liquid began to feel as unheralded as air and less bothersome than wind.

Irissa paused there, dawdled there. Still water had always fascinated her—not for its sly reflections, but for its quiet depths.

Then Thundermist's nose snorted back, spraying droplets.

Irissa leaned forward to glimpse what had startled the bearing-beast—a sudden star of light deep in the blackness that was the pupil of the spring's silver eye.

"What?" Irissa wondered, reaching a hand toward the spring's center. Behind her, Thundermist's anxious hooves milled the grass.

Of course the glimmer was fathoms deep, beyond reach. Irissa stretched for it anyway, intrigued into total impulsiveness.

The water seemed colder and a shadow had fallen over the suns.

Then it came to her, what it was . . . the fugitive glitter bobbing suddenly within reach of her hand. Her eyes widened as they recognized the hilt of a sword—not any sword, but Kendric's.

She leaned over, into the water, determined to capture the sword. The spring's clarity made misjudging its position impossible—the lost sword was here, right under the farthest stretch of her hand. . . .

Jewels glittered over the blade plunging into the water's dark heart, that expanding pupil of depth and dark and distance that should have stayed a mere pinprick. Gems scabbarded the sword's hidden length, reminding Irissa of another sword, another body of water, another day, and another land.

The hilt stabbed up through the water, smashing the smooth surface into drops sharp as shards of broken glass. Cold, they sprinkled Irissa's eyelashes and skin, cutting like early winter rain.

Instinct made her want to rear back; something else made her lean closer and grasp the chill hilt in her hand. Heavy; she had forgotten how heavy the weapon was. Here, in water, it weighed down again, drawing her with it. She felt her hand plunging into a substance colder than an ice-basilisk's breath.

Then the sword was spiraling through distance and time, drawing Irissa's mind behind it. She plunged to the center of the empty eyes lying in wait at the bottom blackness. A wail echoed in her ears, refracted over and over by the icewater clarity.

Some disembodied force took her in its vacant arms.

Another's purpose swathed her sense of self, her limbs, her mind, her magic. Twined as if in waterweed, Irissa's momentary weakness became another's strength.

That other was possessed of a single-minded intent Irissa had never encountered before. She felt the sword snatched from an iris of lighter darkness at the spring's deepest center, felt herself pulled up and back as if she were a blade being withdrawn from an invisible wound.

Cold and dark spun past her. She had not yet loosed the sword and it came with her. Only half her arm—and all her mind—had ever been in the water. Together body and mind broke the water's surface suction; together they burst into sunlight again, a fading wail echoing in both physical and mental ears.

Irissa flourished the prize still clutched in her hand, as if to assure distant watchers of her safety. She looked up, holding it against the sun to see it. A dark cloud shaped like a bearing-beast was sliding past the third sun. In the tri-light, a dagger-long glass shard glinted sharply. The cold, leaving her fingers, allowed Irissa to feel the shard's sharp edges. Blood trickled with water down her wrist.

In the spring, the ripples died away, as if something were diving again, very deep, and should not resurface again.

The shard was a piece of casting crystal.

Irissa, her cut hand swathed in a bandage of broad-leaved sagegrass, studied it that night over the small fire she had started with Kendric's flint and steel.

He had insisted she take the pieces and it seemed right to defer in a minor way, since she was set upon her own will in the major one.

Now she began to appreciate Kendric's reluctance to use magic for small wounds and smaller inconveniences. Rengarthian meadows were lonely, and not every beast on or under or over them had been catalogued. No moon softened the dark night sky. Even Thundermist overcame his kind's inbred fear of fire to hang his head closer to the sole orange spark in the darkness.

Irissa appreciated the company.

"I told you so," she imagined Kendric telling her, although he had not told her anything. "You think Rengarth so safe and yourself so dangerous that you go riding off on your own with no more notion than a blind-burrow of where you head or what you will find there."

It would have been more comforting had she truly had such words to resurrect. Serving as her own critic was a chill exercise and Thundermist was not a responsive listener. Irissa snuffled dismally—her arm's immersion in the spring had given her a chill the fire of dried grasses couldn't warm.

It was time to harvest more grasses for the fire. She rose and weighed the canteen's contents. After the springside incident, she had ridden on to skim her drinking water from a shallow stream. Soon after, night overtook her with a sudden sunfall unmitigated by a moonrise.

Sighing, she swished cautiously through the surrounding grass, reaching deep to their roots to pull out older, drier blades with her left hand. Despite the grass's evergreen appearance, dead leaves tangled beneath the surface. Irissa returned with full hands to refurbish the fire. She enjoyed the bright exhalation of flame with which it greeted her offering.

Thundermist neighed and minced back, incidentally breaking off more dead grass for the next refreshing the fire needed. Irissa sighed again, this time it was more of a grunt, and settled before the fire again, her eyes returning to the shard—surely a castoff of some long-ago ludborg's foretelling session. . . .

The shard was gone!

Or rather . . . it was . . . altered. Irissa hovered over what remained of the wedge-shaped blade—a lopsided, swollen blob of opaque white glass.

"It's melting. . . ." she began, but even as she spoke, the glass stretched like skin, in every direction, so that gradually a globe came into circular being on the crushed grass.

Flames danced in its reflective curves until two-tongued serpents appeared to be cavorting in the vicinity. This globe was smaller than those customarily conjured by Scyvilla and his kind. Perhaps, Irissa guessed, it was an instrument of another day.

Not quite transparent, the cloudy surface swirled, melding rainbow colors until it mocked a soap bubble. Then, like a bubble, it lofted into the air. It lifted slowly. Irissa rose from her heels to her knees. The upborne crystal passed her waist, then her shoulders. Directly opposite her eyes, it paused, spinning.

Startled, heeding an interior baritone voice of caution, Irissa veiled her eyes from any magic. Yet the bauble was so light and lovely, so . . . enchanting.

It drifted over the fire as if heat-drawn, the glass skin tautening, thinning, until it became translucent. Irissa's face and eyes followed it, studying the image she discerned within it—only a cloud, lumpish and unremarkable.

Then an emerald winked into being. Irissa blinked and pulled back. Another emerald, cut into a pointed oblong, paired the second.

Irissa felt her world reel. All Rengarth seemed to have leaped sideways, leaving Irissa plunging through unsupported space. Her right hand clasped her sword hilt, a slice of pain reminding her a moment too late of her injury.

The crystal floated higher. Irissa rose to her feet with it, keeping herself eye to eye with the emeralds. Still it ascended, until there was no action possible but the rash one. Just as the crystal threatened to waft into the roof of night's tenebrous mouth, Irissa's hands reached out of their own volition, both well and wounded, and snatched it back.

Light as air the brittle glass rested between her palms. She felt the breath-held responsibility a ludborg must feel for his casting crystal. At her feet, the fire stretched feeble fingers of light through the globe, illuminating a network of crimson and blue threads.

A living thing? The eye-bright emeralds seemed to read her thoughts. At least, one winked lazily shut. Irissa almost dropped the crystal. Speculation found an answer too unbelievable, too bizarre, too . . . likely . . . to be true.

The crystal's uncanny lightness affected Irissa's head. It went to her feet, too. She felt that if she didn't do something quickly, she would waft skyward with the globe, forever to be pointed out to her own children and their children's children as the "woman with the moon." Remember Hariantha of the Inlands, she warned herself; sheathe magic at your own risk.

Decided, Irissa bent her memory to the last occasion she had shattered a crystal—eighteen years before when Kendric had been subsumed into the Crux Crystal. As she had delivered him from his brittle womb, so she would release . . . what she would release.

In her hands, the crystal warmed—half-heated by the fire, half-fired by its native resistance to her invasive magic. Then the glass chilled until her fingertips whitened and seemed ready to break off like ice daggers.

Despite the ardures, Irissa clung with her hands and eyes to the crystal, penetrating it with a glance that ran hot against the cold and icy against the heat. Slowly, a spiderweb of fissures cracked the surface until only the pressure of her five fingertips held the ball whole.

Blood oozed out of fine black capillaries—whether hers or another's or simply illusion she couldn't say. The pressure became unbearable; her entire being squeezed the globe into the shape of itself.

It finally burst with a sizzle, glass bits sleeting past her into a glittering whirlwind above the fire. Irissa felt fire in her hands, and something heavy. She dropped it when it became too hot and gravid to hold—almost into the fire.

A white kitten landed on four splayed feet, its crossed green eyes blinking in the bright ground-level light of the dying fire.

Irissa crouched on all fours to regard it, disregarding her throbbing hands, the thin tracery of claw marks on her palms.

"Felabba?" she whispered, hoping no one could hear, no one could see her being so ridiculous. Of course no one could! And of course it was not—it *couldn't* be—Felabba.

The kitten's face tilted on its scrawny neck. Under the enormous ears, the eyes were a mature, deep green. A small mouth yawned open to reveal tiny teeth and a pink pad of tongue. The kitten regarded Irissa seriously and spoke.

"Merow," it said, quite clearly. "Merow."

CHAPTER
6

SUNRISE CAME ABRUPTLY TO RENGARTH. ONE MOMENT night in all its opaque darkness draped the land; the next moment blades of fresh-forged light obliquely sliced the grasses.

Irissa stirred stiffly, surprised—and worried—that she'd slept on the open ground. She had spent most of the night repulsing the kitten, which wanted to wreathe her neck in search of a warm nest of breath and hair.

Irissa had repeatedly thrust the small hot body to her cold feet, which could use a draping of fur. But the creature—with the blind, stubborn instincts of the young of any kind—persisted in clawing its way up her clothes to her head again, where it purred loud enough to wake a grassweaver. Now it slept, limp as death, in a crease of her tunic.

Sitting so as not to disturb the animal, Irissa looked around for signs of the giant nocturnal spinners called grassweavers. Not even their gossamer trails showed on the lilting grasses. She rummaged her food pouch and found a handful of dried meat—for the kitten, not herself. The scent wakened it, and it proved mature enough to gobble down the stringy meat, licking absurdly short whiskers afterward.

Thundermist had a whole world to graze and needed no feeding—the smallish bearing-beast stood at the end of his rein-weight, ready to bear again. Irissa lifted blanket and saddle to his back and drew leather girth straps through the Iridesium rings that secured them.

The kitten was another matter. It sat at her feet, regarding her with sober eyes, slightly crossed.

"What shall I do with you—whatever you be?"

It rubbed against her booted leg, almost toppling in its eagerness to ingratiate. Surely this . . . adorable . . . little creature was not Felabba, Irissa thought firmly.

Full daylight saw Irissa mounted and riding again. She had knotted her sash around her neck. In the cradle of that sling the kitten rode, curled into a sweetly sleeping ball. Irissa petted its downy head from time to time, attracted by such unprecedented feline docility even as she was annoyed by its helpless presence on a mission of some importance. She began to understand Kendric's long-ago impatience with the tag-along Felabba.

Despite Irissa's hopes, no magical instinct was guiding her to the Spectral City. Not only was the city wont to appear and disappear without rhyme, reason, or prior warning, but it seldom occupied the same location. Already Irissa saw the white jagged line of the Frostrim Mountains grinning on the horizon and she had seen no sign of the city.

If she rode much farther, she would likely see the towers of the forbidden northern city of Liderion, whose mysterious inhabitants dealt with the rest of Rengarth only through cryptic delegations.

Kendric had often threatened to mount a company, ride to Liderion, and demand entrance, but he had never done it. Even the ludborgs believed that Liderion was best left alone. Irissa was no more eager to confront alone the last of Rengarth's mysteries.

She reined Thundermist, who immediately lowered his head to gather grass sheaves. A quiet pond nearby thrummed with a flotilla of singing flowers. Falgonflies with yard-long wingspans glided over the lazy water. The kitten yawned and flared tiny claws on all four feet as it stretched.

"An idyllic day for a pleasure ride," Irissa announced to both mute animals. "But hardly what I sought. Where is that come-and-go city, hmm, kitty? Farsee and speak or forever eat grassweaver eggs."

She tickled the kitten's chin. If it really was Felabba in infantile form, such indignities would certainly flush out its true nature.

The only responses she got were typical: the kitten's pink tongue lashed its pristine bib of white fur and Thundermist stamped a shining hoof. Irissa rolled her eyes. She was used to danger finding her, not to riding to meet the unknown and encountering only a crystal-borne kitten.

Irritated by her quest's futility so far, she nudged Thundermist into pounding the rippling turf in wide, spiraling circles. The kitten, bath interrupted, jolted safely in its sling.

Grasses fell beneath Thundermist's hooves until Irissa could look back and presume grassweavers had been at work. As the bearing-beast made its looping rounds, Irissa let her mind coil into the past. She recalled her first passage through the ghostly city on the Hunter's back. Her memory repeated every sensation—clattering up the spiraling steps, along the misty ramparts, through the crooked, foggy streets.

Thundermist's route began to invoke that old reality to the same degree it echoed ever new in Irissa's memory. Dust from the pulverized grass coughed into the air behind the beast—cloudbanks of dust, drifting up, spinning in the sunlight, engendering phantom shapes in a mobile whirlwind.

Neva, Irrissa remembered, her mind conjuring the white woman of Rengarth—half-specter, half-dream . . . who had returned to her Rengarthian birthland from Edanvant through a Spectral City well, drawing her brother, Ilvanis, with her.

Irissa recalled Neva's reawakened Rengarthian other self—blithe, red-haired Aven and her scrappy brother, Sin. Aven and Sin were specters now, too, despite their youth and color, rejoined with their paler counterparts when the revived fire-salamander had lifted momentarily above the Frostrim and caught all Rengarthian things that had outlived their time in its fiery claws.

Irissa's thoughts screwed deeper and deeper into the past, into Rengarth's roots, grinding her memories into the very earth as Thundermist galloped in tighter and tighter circles against the tauter pull of the reins.

She lost sense of time, then place. Thundermist finally protested her instructions, rearing until his silver mane riffled like dry grass across Irissa's face. She saw only the glittering dust around her and smelled the sun-heated odor of bearing-beast and crushed grass. Against her breast, the kitten mewed helplessly.

Then . . . a sheet of dust glimmered into a tapestry woven with the pale outlines of arch, lintel, stair, street, and roof. Moths fluttered against the dust-mote curtain—people-sized moths clothed in ghostly raiment.

At last the Spectral City lay before Irissa, revealed by the dust as the dew betrays a near-invisible cobweb. Still, it was flat—unreal, hanging on the air rather than occupying a space within it.

Irissa urged Thundermist into the diaphanous image, but the bearing-beast balked, planting stiff legs. His hooves backstepped until Irissa felt likely to slide over the cantle and down his glossy hindquarters.

In the confusion, the kitten slipped its sling. It plummeted to Thundermist's withers, where it clung with every tiny claw and howled piteously at the motion and dust and its precarious perch.

Spurred by the panicked kitten, Thundermist kicked his heels to the sky and bolted straight into the settling dust.

Irissa felt a soft prickle, like warm snow. The sunlight grew cooler, if no less bright. The dusty veil retreated before her as if pushed back by Thundermist's intrusion. As the party penetrated the image, it in turn wrapped around them, gaining depth and distance.

Breathless, Irissa reined the mount and tore the kitten from his blood-pricked withers. Thundermist's head jerked as a phantom figure passed but a hand's width from his rolling eyes. More forms emerged from doors and byways, brushing by Irissa and her bearing-beast as if they did not exist.

She dismounted, anyway, carrying the kitten, leading Thundermist, and in no way prepared for a hostile encounter. Her sword jolted at her hip, its emerald hilt-stone shining slightly luminescent through the dust-laden murk of the Spectral City. Irissa did not remember it thus. . . .

An odd twilight air infected the city, as if it absorbed the rays of some ancient, everlasting sunfall. Its citizens, oblivious as usual to mortal visitors, seemed shrunken. Fainter. Irissa was tempted to reach out for . . . or even *through* . . . a passerby—had both hands not been busy beast-tending.

"Such a handful," she admonished the kitten. "At least your predecessor—your ancestor?—could walk, talk, and eat under her own power. Why bother coming uncalled if you are not to be of use?"

Taunts would not bestir a possible Felabba in the white kitten. It yawned again, in Irissa's face, then peered alertly about, threatening to sink its claws into her hand and bound away. She tightened her grip on the tiny barrel chest.

Who knew how a lost mortal animal might tip the Spectral City's delicate balance of reality and dream if left behind?

Thundermist whinnied hopefully, working his lips to show benign square teeth.

"A well, bright beast—I think you're right. Let's see if Rengarthian water still runs real in the Spectral City."

She led the bearing-beast to the circle of mortared stone in the middle of a ghostly square. Elusive citizens flowed past them, detectable only as outlines to her eyes, their passage felt as transient zephyrs across her skin.

Water bubbled over the well lip, creating a thin, constant veil of liquid that drained into a moat at the foundation. Thundermist drank greedily, his smacking the only sound in the Spectral City. The water seemed to revive and calm him. Irissa trailed a hand through the clear liquid—it felt dry and cool.

The kitten strained its tiny neck and sniffed until its whiskers twitched. Then its claws flailed in unison, its slippery little body writhed—and it was falling into the well, a screech like a wailwraith's echoing off the smooth stones.

"Felabba! Oh, no. . . ." Irissa leaned after it, heedless of specters.

Bead-sized borgia-green eyes squinted up at her as the kitten frantically trod water. Only its wing-sized ears, eyes, and pink nose kept above the waterline's silver surface. Irissa grabbed for a fist of fur, but her rescue motions only submerged the creature in a tiny tidal wave.

It resurfaced, legs churning, wet hair rayed like thorns on its head and ears. Irissa reached for it again; this time it sank before she could capture it. Horrified, she watched the small white form twist and sink, then claw wildly upward again.

Irissa pounced just as the kitten broke water again, sinking her fingers into wet fur and lifting it. The effort caused quite a splashing—water droplets dry as dust motes cindered her eyes and made her shut them. The kitten, waterlogged, seemed to have grown much heavier. Irissa pulled with all her strength until she clutched a sopping, sputtering burden to her chest again. She stepped back from the well lip and blinked water motes from her eyelashes.

"Unhand me," a light voice berated her. Something squirmed in her arms, something powerful enough to push clawed back legs against her breastbone and spring off.

Gasping, Irissa pushed the damp hair strands from her face and saw a white animal perched on the well lip. It was a white cat . . . but not quite cat yet—a rangy, adolescent creature whom submersion had not beautified.

"Felabba?" she asked suspiciously.

The animal was occupied in methodically tonguing its cowlicked coat and ignored her.

"I'm sorry you fell in—"

"Jumped," the cat replied in dulcet tones.

"Your bath seems to have . . . aged you."

"I am ageless," the cat answered between dedicated licks.

"But you speak now."

"That can be remedied." The cat gracefully leaped atop Thundermist's withers and promptly kept quiet.

Kendric, Irissa knew, would regard such silence with approval. She herself felt strangely cheated. But . . . her hands were empty and her quest was hers again. Irissa looked around the square. Fewer specters came and went. Perhaps her presence had tainted the area. The city did not welcome her as freely as when she had ridden the magical Hunter or visited it in the company of Neva and Ilvanis.

Irissa stood hesitating, somehow feeling as sopped and disarranged as the kit—the young cat . . . with about as much to say about it.

A gentle pull on her sleeve made her jerk around. Dust motes spun into a pair of silver whirlwinds—then Neva and Ilvanis were etched in coldstone glitter against the spectral street.

"Tell us," Ilvanis said eagerly, his voice but a wind-whisper, "about your marvelous cat."

"It's not my cat. But I think it was—or will be—a creature called Felabba that Kendric and I knew in Rule and saw again in Edanvant. Somehow falling into the well hastened its growth—"

"Remarkable!" Neva drifted in a silver-white swirl toward Thundermist. "Ilvanis and I were first drawn here by a well-window from Edanvant to Rengarth, but we have never seen a living thing enter a well without exiting it elsewhere. Your cat must be very magical."

Drier, the creature in question sank into its haunches and began purring with a self-satisfaction Irissa found wearing already.

"It was born—unasked—of a crystal shard drawn from a dark pond," Irissa said shortly. "What it will make of itself is not for me to say. I came here to find you, not discuss feline pedigrees or powers."

Another pull behind her—more sensed than felt—made her turn again. A duststorm of pale rose-colored particles was resolving into two figures—Ilvanis's and Neva's once-living counterparts, Aven and Sin.

"You look well, seeress," Aven greeted her. "Neva and I were sorry we missed the birthing of your second child."

"It was better you came for the first—I didn't know what I was doing then."

"Nor Kendric, I hear," Sin put in with a phantom grin.

Irissa felt sudden melancholy. It was hard to see those who had once been vibrant flesh and blood reduced to shadows of their former selves. It reminded her with a pang of her own mission.

"I seek a . . . gate from Rengarth and could think of nowhere else to try."

"A gate? There is no gate." Ilvanis sounded certain.

"There must be, how else would the sorcerer Geronfrey have drawn Kendric to Rengarth unwilling? And I crossed also through a window of Geronfrey's Dark Tower in Edanvant—"

Neva's spectral head was shaking sadly. "Kendric came not through a true gate, but one opened by Geronfrey's dark magic. Now that he is gone from Rengarth these many years, there is no means—"

"Do not make me regret that we rid the land of him!"

"Why desire this gate?" Sin wondered. "You are well and happy in Rengarth. Your family is safe, except for the danger of clan-poisoning. Other lands offer worse dangers for less reward."

Irissa studied Sin carefully. "How do you know that I am happy?"

"We . . . spectral citizens . . . sense these things. Happy enough, anyway."

"True. We would not stir from Rengarth even if we could now, I think. Save that . . . Kendric fails."

"At what?" Neva was indignant. "Kendric is not one to fail, and if he did, he would find some way to turn it to advantage."

"Not *at* anything, Neva. *In* himself, in ways too secret to see. He . . . ages, as I do not."

"Ah." Ilvanis nodded sagely. "He is not Torloc."

"But I am! And I have come to the Spectral City to discover if there is any . . . force . . . that can make Kendric Torloc in longevity at least, and where I can find it."

"Hmm."

They paced around the well, all four specters, though nothing so solid as feet touched ground and nothing so solid as ground underlay them all. Around they went in solemn procession, vaporous robes flapping soundlessly, the wellwater rippling at their passage.

"Apparently their brains have become as spectral as

themselves," the adolescent cat remarked from Thundermist's withers, "if it takes this much ceremony to think."

"If you are not Felabba, I shall have Scyvilla cook and serve you. Now, hush!" Irissa ordered angrily.

Like four phantom flames the figures flickered around the spectral well, one merging into another until—for a moment—it seemed that only two, integrated forms paced there. A phantom who was not quite Neva or Aven . . . and not quite Sin or Ilvanis . . . and not quite wolf or owl. . . .

"A comely combination," the cat commented again, squinting at the animal Irissa and Kendric had known as the Rynx.

Irissa ignored it as the semblance of the Rynx melted into the swirling vapors. Then motion stopped and the four settled into their separate selves again. In a line beside the well, they spoke in turn.

"You remember, seeress, that the wells of the Spectral City each hold a guardian face," Neva began.

"Yes! These are people not quite as spectral as yourselves."

"They are the faces of those who have died," Sin put in direly.

"But—" Irissa hesitated to tell her friends that they, too, were quite dead.

Neva smiled, her native warmth shining through her insubstantial form as flame surmounts glass. "We are specters because Geronfrey transformed us into animal or other semblances. All of us here have been so spelled and hence hang in a quasi-life in this semi-city."

"The dead in the wells," Aven explained with a toss of albino locks, "are those who have been *killed,* whose spirits are not merely homeless while some beast bears their soul, but who have died in some deeper, realer way."

"They linger for a while," Ilvanis said, "and then depart. Others always take their places. To us, *they* are the phantoms, as you and your beasts are also. But they see both sides of death, and one of those is life."

"And where there is at least a view of life, there is an answer to its quandaries," Neva finished. Her misty golden eyes darted to each of her companions in turn. "I think that Irissa must consult the Old Woman of the Well."

"I will consult a Gilothian fireworm!" Irissa burst out. "Only let it be soon."

In a body the specters had surrounded her. Irissa felt herself being wafted along in a cloud. A vaporous hand tugged Thundermist's reins. The beast plodded obediently along. Lengths and widths and breadths of Spectral City streets drifted by.

Encased by her escort's misty forms, Irissa felt almost that the city moved and she stood still, so smoothly did cobble and brick roll by in silent progression.

Then another square was before them—this one round —and another well wall. The four specters evaporated several paces back, and Irissa could see their vague forms more clearly. All were gesturing her to the well.

"She has not been here long," Neva warned, her clear voice rising like a bell, "and will stay even less long. We have felt a miasma of great power dissipating. Perhaps she can tell you of what you seek."

Irissa moved through the fading architecture, over the ghostly stones. "How did the faces in the wells die?" she wondered.

"They were *killed,* I thought you knew," Ilvanis said. His voice grew fainter with each step Irissa took, but she dared not look back.

"Killed?" she asked.

"Some Geronfrey transformed and banished. Others he killed by whatever means came readily—mostly magic."

"What?" Irissa could hardly hear the last words and risked a backward glance.

There was no one there. Of course, there never really had

been, but . . . She looked to the street and gasped. The cobbles were winking out, here and there, like stars. Green blades of grass grew through their gaps. The Spectral City was decamping, already!

She rushed to the well lip, unconcerned with how ghastly this victim of Geronfrey's might look. Already the constant sheet of running water that poured from its mouth was thinning into separate falls.

The well's surface water rippled—Irissa sought in vain for a face among the blurred rings of motion. Something white bounded to the well rim. Irissa took it for a departing phantom, but its solid side pushed against her arm.

"I know somewhat of wells," the cat said, crouching with its forepaws curled into the nonexistent edge, its green eyes scanning the water.

"Don't fall in again!" Irissa warned it. "I might not be able to save you."

"I have never 'fallen' into a well in my lives," the cat returned a bit indignantly. "Be silent and learn. And look for the Eye of Edanvant."

"The Eye—?" Irissa, dumbfounded, unintentionally complied with the cat's call for silence.

"Use your eyes!" it returned, as intent upon the water as if a fish cruised just below the surface.

Irissa envisioned the Eye of Edanvant—a great malachite iris inlaid in the center of the Damen Circle. She had seen that ancient eye swallowed by its own pupil. She had seen the Damen Circle abandoned by the women who used to gather there to share the Torloc powers. She had seen the Eye perverted by Torloc men greedy for an untoward share of the women's magic.

She had never thought to evoke a thing from her own and her kind's past again.

Yet it came to her magical call, rising in a green glow to the surface. Then it faded and a face floated in its stead—a wizened, whitened face not one whit spectral. A face Irissa had last seen written on a cloud above Citydell in Edanvant.

"Finorian! First Felabba, and now you? Does this mean I have aid upon my quest?"

"It means you dream backward, child, always a bad sign. You look back because you have glimpsed a future whose face you cannot regard. It must be a dire farseeing for you to come to the dead for soothing."

"Are you . . . dead?"

The Eldress's moon-white eyes rolled in merriment, or what passed for it with Finorian. "If I am not, I make a fine semblance of the dead. So once again I come to you over water, though I prefer the borgia of my earlier incantation. Much finer effect, to come floating into a green goblet and turn the Wrathman white with surprise. Where is he, your partner in quests?"

"Home. Here in Rengarth."

"Rengarth. Ah . . . so I have found myself where none can go voluntarily. Or leave. Is that what troubles you?" the Eldress asked with sudden insight.

"Yes. A gate. I must have a gate from here to—"

"Where?"

"Anywhere, for a start. But ultimately—to Rule."

Finorian's sightless eyes narrowed. "You do go back, child, when you seek your birthworld. Rule is . . . ruined. Magic has left it bereft of any light and mystery. What seek you there?"

"Some . . . clue."

"And you must go in person?"

"Yes, for only I will know what I seek when I see it."

"Which is—?"

"Hurry, Finorian, there is not much time—!" Even as she spoke Irissa watched the Eldress's face distort, its features pulling apart as if caught by the well's rippling rhythm.

"For you or for me?" Finorian's harsh voice demanded.

"For both of us, and the Spectral City, as well."

"You must tell me your quest."

"Kendric. . . ."

"Ah! I knew it. You push yourself to the extremes of your magic for only one cause. I told you he was yours, my girl, for better and more often for worse. What mischief has he fallen into now?"

Irissa was ready to wring her hands or Finorian's neck, were it physical. "There's so little time—now, for us—and forever, for Kendric. He ages, Finorian, hair by hair and joint by joint."

"Always the way of mortal man." The expanding mouth expanded farther as a mocking cackle drifted to Irissa's ears. "Did I not tell you? Good riddance, I say. But what of your child?"

"Children."

"Ah. A seeress—or two?"

"None. Our daughter, Javelle, is . . . unempowered."

"And the other?"

"A . . . boy." Irissa said no more.

Finorian kept silent a moment. "Bitter, bitter the answer to all my expectations. So now you are a loyal wife and mother, seeking to assuage mortal anxieties. What will you do when your half-born *children* age before you, seeress?"

"Find another answer."

"And if you go on alone, as I did, generation after generation?"

"I go on." Irissa straightened, feeling wind sifting through the vanishing Spectral City, feeling her precious time blowing away in stinging grains of sand. "Speak to me, Finorian, of gates and Rengarth and a remedy for Kendric's mortality. He is Ruler of Rengarth now, born of magic stock. Still, despite all that, he . . . ages."

"Even I aged—ultimately," Finorian snapped, "as you

will, too, should you be as unfortunate to live as long. What is that specter at your hip, that bit of white fog I cannot focus upon?"

Irissa smiled. "A cat. I found it in a well."

Finorian was silent for a good long time, so long her face fractured into isolated features upon the water—two askew eyes, some serpentine strands of white hair, a mouth in mid-sentence being driven into different directions.

Irissa despaired. Who would have thought the Old Woman of the Well would be one so innately hostile to Kendric? Although, at the end, even Finorian had softened toward him.

The phantom mouth was moving on the pale green water, quickly.

"You have come to the right well, seeress. Know this: there is no gate from or to Rengarth, save these wells. Be quiet! There is little time, as you said. Only one who is a specter—or part-specter—can pass. That is how the pale pair from Edanvant came to Rengarth through a well— they were mostly mere spirit already. I see nothing of the phantom about you.

"But. There is indeed a way to grant Kendric a life span as elongated as his body. And it is not magical at all. He left his sword, one of the Six Swords of Rule, in Rindell Pond when he left Rule with you. Only that sword will—melded with the mind-made sword he conjured in the Inlands— prolong his life. You must fetch it to him."

"How? If I cannot leave Rengarth? If there is no gate?"

Finorian's face was a glint of surface reflections. Beneath Irissa's weight, the well wall was eroding with every passing moment. She felt thin sunlight on her back and saw the city around her fading to morning mist.

Only the motion-dappled wellwater still kept its spectral shape. She leaned closer to read Finorian's disintegrating lips. The words came to her ears like a distant whisper.

"It will take more than a seeress's Far Focus to find a way

from Rengarth, more than a Wrathman's mighty arm and wayward will. More even than a white cat this time. I wish I could know the outcome . . . it promises to be interesting. You have always given me that.

"The sword," Finorian's revenant hissed. "The seventh sword, Irissa, will answer your need. And you are right, it lies in Rule, where even magic has died."

Irrissa leaned toward the dark water that was turning violently green, as everything around her was. She felt she was leaning into a bottomless glass of borgia in search of her own reflection.

A sharp reminder on her arm etched a warning into her flesh.

"Careful," a sardonic voice cautioned behind her. "You'll fall in and get more than wet in what's left of that well."

Irissa jerked back, finding herself standing in a Rengarthian meadow staring intently at a patch of green grass the wind whipped this way and that, as if trying to read fortunes in their patterns.

She absently put her hand to her arm. The palm came away with a pattern of red, random dots. The cat, weighing heavy on her shoulder, insinuated its gawky head next to hers again. Whiskers tickled deep in her ear, as did a low voice.

"Another journey—save that it can't be made. Your conversation has begun to ring a bell. I recall a rather overbearing fellow, all bluster and no finesse. I hope he is not to be involved in this inconvenient journey that is impossible."

"You *are* Felabba," Irissa accused softly, finding it as hard to believe her own words as she had found Finorian's unpalatable.

"Felabba, Melabba, does it matter? I have many lives and many names and more memories. Sometimes they do not all coincide."

"Then I shall call you Brittlebones, not Bitterbones as Kendric did," Irissa threatened, lifting the cat to Thundermist's withers for the ride back to Solanandor Tierze.

"Hardly appropriate." The cat arched its back into an agile half-hoop. "Kendric, hmm? I can hardly contain my desire to see this person that so rubs Finorian the wrong way."

The cat curled into a decidedly larger lump than before at the fore of Irissa's saddle, forcing her back against the cantle. Irissa gathered the reins, studying the vacant grasslands for a moment. Perhaps the Spectral City would someday vanish utterly. Even exiled spirits, like mortal men, must have a limited longevity. And Finorian, where had her essence gone? It was a marvel to evoke the Eldress again, even for a moment.

Irissa sighed deeply, a sign as much of resolve as of anxiety. She urged Thundermist into a canter that had the cat hanging on for all of its dubious lives.

"Despite doomsayers," Irissa announced, "I find myself optimistic. Finorian has told me what I craved—the sword that was Six is now Seven and is the answer to my quest. And where there are barriers, there are ways around them. And Kendric is *not* overbearing, but otherwise he has not changed a bit, Felabba. And it is *I* who can hardly wait for him to look upon you again—whatever age or incarnation you claim.

"It shall be," Irissa promised, "in Finorian's exquisite understatement, interesting."

CHAPTER
7

"THIS," KENDRIC DEMANDED INCREDULOUSLY, "IS THE sorry object of your quest?"

A silence prevailed, during which Kendric glowered at the object atop the table. The object atop the table glowered back. It was, of course, the cat.

"This," he continued after a strained moment, "is the prize to be pried from your mysterious journey, the purpose you would not speak of? And why not—it is indeed unspeakable."

Irissa burst into laughter then, as Kendric's highest dudgeon met its match in the lithe white cat's icy superiority. Secretly, she was much relieved. Her return with the cat obscured the true object of her mission. That she was not yet willing to confide.

Kendric, she knew, was as secretly enjoying his reacquaintance with an old adversary. He had planted huge fists on his hips as he stalked around the table, inspecting the creature from whisker to tail.

The cat's emerald-green eyes never left Kendric. Its head followed his movements with a liquid, lazy grace.

"It seems to have improved in the washing," Kendric noted at last. "The coat is brighter, the whiskers longer, the teeth . . . whiter. Still, not a prepossessing animal, by any stretch of the—"

The cat stretched an idle paw and batted Kendric's elbow as he passed. Kendric responded by pouncing on the narrow torso and lifting the cat high above his head.

"Strike me, will you? Such impertinence could leave you high and dry."

"Kendric, it's just a kitten," Irissa soothed.

"This one was never 'just a kitten,' if this is indeed a version of Felabba."

"It speaks."

"Not to me," Kendric answered in a tone that demanded demonstration.

The cat drooped over his hand limp-limbed, taking advantage of its tree-high perch to stare idly at the chamber's stained-glass ceiling. Since a flock of Rengarth's ample birdlife was suspended between the glass and a glittering net, the view was doubly interesting to the cat.

Kendric lowered his arms. "Flex your claws, will you? It is as untractable as ever, save it is blessedly silent."

"What would one say to a wall?" the cat asked tartly as its paws touched table again.

Kendric smiled grimly. "And contrary as ever. I knew if I praised its silence I should be honored with its voice."

"You are both unfailingly predictable," Irissa said fondly. "Now . . . Kitty. If you won't claim Felabba's identity or her name—"

"Not Kitty," the beast begged, turning in a circle as it settled down to bathe its hindquarters between interrogations. "Proper names are vital, didn't this . . . legendary . . . Felabba teach you this?"

"It is not the same cat," Irissa said, turning to Kendric as if she'd finally made up her mind. "As you say, it's much younger than the Felabba we knew."

"It speaks," he contradicted Irissa with her own earlier argument.

"It speaks. Yet it was born of a crystal shard pulled from some other world's water, and an immersion in a Spectral City well matured it. Still, it is young and has shown no great gift for magic. Perhaps it will entertain the children."

"They are getting old for such simple entertainment."

The cat paused, its tongue drooping roselike from its mouth. "My kind is never simple and rarely an entertainment," it suggested tartly.

"Felabba it is," Kendric named it. "In memoriam." He turned to Irissa. "I am glad to see you back, even with this in hand. How did you know such a creature lurked out there? Did it call you?"

"Something did," Irissa evaded. "Kendric, the Spectral City is . . . dying."

"All magical things are prone to . . . eventual evaporation."

"As are all mortal ones?"

"No, not so fast as mortal ones. But still, the city may have haunted these grasslands for centuries. You can't expect everything to wear as well as you do."

"No." Irissa thought a moment. "But I can try to make them."

"As well command a cat." He glanced to Felabba to find the disconcerting eyes focused on Irissa.

Kendric's unease swelled inside him like a secret. Part of his discomfort came from confronting an old familiar in new alien form. No matter what he called the cat, it simply had not the age and thorny wisdom of its namesake.

Most of his disquiet came from contemplating Irissa. She was becoming as inexplicable as their offspring—moody, secretive. He doubted he could survive three Torloc tempests that chose to brew at once.

He turned to the bottomless goblet of borgia, Scyvilla's for-once-apt gift, and drained it. The cat watched disapprovingly, as if miffed by his rough and ready consumption of such silken borgia. Kendric shrugged. He had never been a sipper at life, and didn't intend to start now.

"What do you think?" Irissa asked the children at sunfall when she presented the cat during the before-dinner family hour.

Silent for a change, Javelle looked to Thane. They burst out laughing together.

"Thane had hoped to find Felabba and produce her himself," Javelle tattled.

"He still can," Kendric put in. "This is a pale imitation of the real Felabba."

"How so?" Thane curiously circled the cat, which once again occupied a tabletop.

The animal yawned as Kendric enumerated the original Felabba's many gifts and good graces.

"This is too . . . young and sleek a cat. The real Felabba was somewhat crooked of spine as well as intention. Its coat was matted here and there from the lazy application of its tongue. Yet that tongue thought nothing of applying its sandy side to criticizing myself and your mother at every turn."

Felabba the Second yawned and began biting, with icy hauteur, the hair between its toes.

"Is it female, like the original?" Javelle wanted to know.

"I have not . . . looked," Kendric admitted. "Perhaps you two would care to investigate."

They started forward eagerly, Thane at the fore. The cat's gaze never left them. Its black pupils slitted to the width of one of Irissa's eyelashes, although no light had increased in the twilight room.

"Thane can do it," Javelle said, pausing.

He reached boldly for the animal's lean middle, then froze as if spellbound. "It can speak. Let it tell us."

There was a silence in which one could hear a cat's tongue rasp over its fur.

"Tell us," Kendric advised the cat. "There's no telling when Thane might get the urge to see for himself again."

Felabba regarded Thane intently. "He is a rude boy." Javelle crowed.

"Like his father," the cat added demurely.

Thane and Javelle held their breaths. No one talked to their father in that fashion, especially children and underlings. To their astonishment, Kendric laughed.

"This creature must share some passing acquaintance with its undistinguished forebear. It has learned the art of insult somewhere. I confess a certain . . . nostalgia for the noxious beast. I have heard nothing but courtly courtesies for so long. Here, young Bitterbones, have some borgia."

Kendric tilted his goblet, which had filled lip-high again the moment he drained it. Drops of borgia lay quivering like cabochon emeralds on the polished wood.

"Your hospitality, like your wit, is late arriving, Wrathman," the cat noted, hunching its face over the green liquor, "and it could use a bowl. Still . . . this is better than I have had in some time."

"How long?" Irissa sounded suspicious.

The cat quirked a whisker. "Long enough for me to keep the answer to myself. And as for my gender, I tend a riddle to test your offspring's wits. I am neither male nor female; make of me—and that fact—what you will."

"That's not a riddle!" Javelle objected. "That's a statement."

"Now you begin to grasp what Felabba was like," Kendric said.

All four people hovered over the table to watch the cat daintily lap the drops of borgia. A royal family's life in Rengarth was well ordered. Disruption of routine, even in a furred form, was welcome.

Despite its easy acceptance into the family and Javelle's pleas to the contrary, the cat was not allowed into the dining chamber. Instead it was borne off on the shoulder of a ludborg for a tour of the kitchens that were its proper environs.

"Let it beg for its supper and learn the humility that was so becoming to its predecessor," Kendric said sardonically, as the family trailed in to dinner.

"Why have we never seen a cat here before, Father?" Javelle asked.

"I don't know. They're common enough in other worlds. Common as coldstones."

"Cats don't beg," Irissa put in suddenly in answer to Kendric's next to the last statement. "They hunt. I wonder what this one is hunting in Rengarth."

"Us?" Kendric asked lightly in reply.

Irissa shivered a little, and his eyebrow lifted. "It's chill after sunfall, sometimes," she said, "despite the summer warmth."

"Perhaps our bones feel the chill more now," Kendric suggested without considering that Irissa's bones were in their infancy as Torloc life spans go. Sometimes he seemed to forget entirely that she was Torloc.

"Hmm," she murmured, then turned to the boy on her left. "Thane, I want you to sit with me this evening as I ply my tapestry. We should discuss the degrees of far-seeing."

"Oh, Mother, must I? I know farseeing backward and forward."

"Then you shall learn it from side to side. Yes, you must."

Kendric lifted his head from his plate of breaded swanfish at Irissa's sudden sharp tone. There was an urgency to her of late he could not explain. Sometimes he thought that being trapped in the same land for all these years had worn on her as much as it had on him.

Thane had recognized the maternal imperative as well,

though his face still looked ready to advocate his own wishes. In the brewing eye of a family storm, Javelle dropped her knife with a clatter that ended the discussion.

Kendric glanced to his daughter's face. It was set with a control he found alien in one so young. Perhaps Irissa should also speak privately to Javelle more often. . . .

Then the meal was done and the torches were lighting the chamber on their own initiative, as they always did after dinner. Irissa and Thane were pushing back their chairs in tandem. Kendric had a meeting with citizens concerned about an epidemic of poisoning among their livestock.

Once more a family dinner ended with more questions than answers—and every one of them unspoken. Kendric frowned as he patted Javelle's shoulder in leaving. She remained sitting at the table, looking as if her small frame harbored a world's worth of worry.

He would have to address the hidden family malaise soon, Kendric decided as he wound his way down the palace stairs to the council chamber. Very soon.

Thane roved around the chamber as Irissa settled herself on a stool by the tapestry stand. Other tapestries of her design—huge rectangles of oddly gossamer fabric—covered the gray stones.

Candle flames beat like moths' wings. The tapestry threads gleamed iridescent in the light. Wind rarely rested in Rengarth; even within the strongest stone walls some infiltrating breeze managed to shake whatever it moved among.

"You think embroidery work beneath a person of my powers," Irissa noted from her modest corner of the room.

Thane whirled, startled to have his thoughts read. "You are not a burgher's wife in need of occupation."

"I am a Ruler's wife, which is even worse, even more designed for idleness. But my work at this stand is hardly idle. Have you ever really looked at my weavings, Thane?"

"Of course. I've seen them since childhood."

Irissa smiled a little at that "since." She sheathed her needle in the canvas and turned to her son. "Look again," she suggested in such an understated tone that he obliged without question. She watched him comply with mixed feelings.

He was her tapestry, too, this child. This son. Braided before birth from the separate strands of her own and Kendric's selfhood, born to swell upon the loom of life until he stretched to meet the limits of his potential. Yet Thane was both the woven and the weaver of his fate. And his potential was unproven. He was the first birth-born Torloc wizard, a creature of unimaginable magic.

It was into this unproven, childish son of hers that Irissa now poured her deepest, most desperate hopes.

Thane's native impatience ebbed enough to let him survey the glittering tapestries. "They are histories, aren't they?"

"Recent histories. Of our travels from Rule to the Inlands of Ten to Edanvant and finally Rengarth. Of how we met, Kendric and I, and of what we met with on our journeys."

Thane waved a hand at the tapestries, that lifted and sank in the interior wind as if buoyed by seawater. The lulling motion lent the illusion of life to the figures worked into the fabric.

"I've heard all this," he said.

"Then listen again," Irissa said with an iron in her voice that no child of hers had heard yet.

Thane spun to face her, intrigued and ashamed at the same time. Irissa's long dark hair was stirring in the faint indoor breeze. Thane could see the dancing candlelight strike a rainbow reflection from the black strands. It seemed a length of living Iridesium, vibrant with Irissa's will and power.

Her silver eyes shone like stars in the dark, moonless Rengarthian sky. Thane had, at times in his development, found his mother both beautiful and powerful, though never at the same time. Now he saw the terrible beauty of her inborn power, and wondered how he could ever have underestimated her simply because she was his mother.

"The Torloc quest is sewn onto those walls in threads of blood and tears," she said. "But what is recent history to me and mine is twisted from a master thread of magic longer and older than even some of the worlds we walked, I think."

"You've never spoken like this before."

"I never had the need."

"I'll listen," Thane said with a humility new to him.

Irissa smiled, then felt a tear at her heart, as if the weight of its own being had ripped one of her tapestries along a hidden faultline. He was so *young!* She was about to ask so much of him. She began.

"You know of the gates we Torlocs followed from world to world in search of Edanvant. You know how they found that long-lost ancestral place, and how your father and I found the surviving Torlocs there—divided, bitter."

"But you reconciled them. You two built the bridge between city and forest, men and women. Why did you leave? I know you—we—can't leave Rengarth, that it is a forbidden world save to its own. But why did you leave Edanvant for here—and how?"

"That part we never told you and Javelle."

"Why?"

"We . . . didn't want to frighten you."

"I'm not afraid of anything!"

There it was, twelve-year-old bravado resurfacing in a fifteen-year-old face. So young, Irissa thought, yet . . . her only hope.

"We had an enemy," she told him, "a powerful sorcerer

who craved my powers and secretly knew of and feared Kendric's birthright to Rengarth. Geronfrey has dogged us through many worlds and always sought to . . . end us."

That Thane feared. He was still young enough that the unwelcome notion of losing his caretakers, his parents, struck with the impact of an arrow to the heart.

"Even here?"

"Even here. Especially here."

Thane dropped his head to hide his stricken eyes. "That is why you worry so when Javelle and I explore the land. I thought—"

"You thought your parents were simply . . . irrational. Foolish. Mean."

Thane's head dropped even lower.

"If my powers and Kendric's blood were so precious to Geronfrey that he must have them at any cost, think how your particular portion of both would . . . madden him."

"You . . . bested him?"

"We saw him leave—horribly, through a window to Without."

"Without permits nothing to survive itself, you said so!"

"So I thought. With Geronfrey, one can never be sure."

Thane took a turn around the room, staring at the tapestries. "So even in this safest of places, you never felt safe."

"Rengarth is not so safe. You forget their poisonous politics. Our . . . reign . . . has been brief. There is much time yet for other clans to usurp the role of Usurper from Geronfrey now that he is apparently banished—and overthrow us. And we never asked for this rulership!"

"No wonder Father worries. So." Thane turned eagerly. "You want something of me. What is it? You want me to find and destroy this Geronfrey, to free you all from his shadow?"

Irissa almost laughed, save that it would have shriveled

Thane's burgeoning confidence. If only it were so simple!

"No," she said calmly. "We have lived with Geronfrey—with the threat of Geronfrey—for longer than you have lived, and we can do so comfortably for many lifetimes. It is not Geronfrey I would have you duel, but a vaguer, more insidious enemy. Mortality."

Thane's face wore a puzzlement she had seen many times on Kendric's. He walked toward her, sensing an importance in her lowered tone that made power-mad sorcerers moot.

Irissa took Thane's hand in a way he did not resent, not as if he were a child, but an equal whose alliance she sought.

"Your father—" The words came hard. "Your father is aging, Thane, like the mortal man he has always claimed to be."

He jerked his hand away, denying her words. "Father? He is the biggest, the strongest man in Rengarth. He has magic to rival your own, you have said, although they are a patchwork of powers from many sources—his mother, Phoenicia; yourself; the sword. There's nothing wrong with Father!"

Irissa remained calm. "Nothing wrong with him were he wed to a mortal woman and sire to mortal children. Torlocs are long-lived, Thane, you know that. You share that heritage. Kendric does not."

"But—"

"Have you not seen the silver in his hair? The new runes time has etched upon his face? He was not always so. And he is becoming more so every year. Somehow, despite the magic he has accrued, he has not been granted the longevity to accompany it."

Thane paced, the first time Irissa had ever seen him do so. Beneath his knitted brows, his odd eyes glittered like spinning coins of gold and silver. She could not say which denomination was more valuable to her—the seeress's silver that conferred untold powers upon her son, or the golden glint that echoed his father's eyes.

Thane stopped. "He will die."

"Yes. As will I. In good time. But he will die beforetime, Thane, while you and I still have centuries before us. It is not . . . fair . . . and I will not have it."

"But . . . what can you do?"

"I have done it." Irissa rose. She towered over her son. "My quest to the Spectral City was an attempt to seek two things: a means of preserving Kendric's life for a time equal to mine—and a gate, for any answer must lie outside of Rengarth."

"And you found?"

"A cat who is not what it was." Irissa laughed ruefully. "It is good to see Kendric sharpening his wit on a worthy opponent, though. He was fonder of Felabba than he would let anyone know."

"But the answer!"

"I have it. It is the sword. Not the one here. That was mind-made, remember?"

Thane turned numbly to face a tapestry behind him—a red-woven vignette of crimson dust and flying robes, Kendric amid it all fashioning a sword from his memory and magic.

"In the Inlands against Ivrium's Heirlings," Thane described the scene. Suddenly the tales his parents told by candlelight as bedtime diversions assumed a reality he could neither believe nor deny. "Mother, if this sword isn't enough, what is?"

"The original. The only one of the Six Swords that Kendric carried in Rule when we met, that bridged us on my departure from Rule, that he dropped to"—Irissa paused, her voice taut—"to follow me through a Torloc gate. That is the sword we must have, that we must retrieve, to keep Kendric among us."

"How?"

"Go to Rule and get it."

Thane blinked. "But, Mother—then you must have found a gate at the Spectral City!"

"I found there is no gate, as there never was. Not in Rengarth. Oh, specters can come and go, but I am still merely flesh and blood and cannot pass."

"I'm sorry."

Irissa stared at her son, surprised at the adult tone of comfort in his words. He embraced her as he had not in several years.

"I'm sorry," he repeated. "What shall we do? And what can . . . I . . . do?"

"Find a gate!" Irissa held Thane fiercely, feeling his shock. "You are even better endowed than I to accomplish this. I know you can do it!"

"How? Mother, how?"

"I don't know. That's always the sting in the tail of magic. It seldom says how. But . . . I . . . know . . . you can do it. You are sublimely gifted, Thane. You have not even begun to unravel the knots of your magic. You are my sole hope. Your father's only hope. Follow your instincts. Think of your father, and trust your feelings."

"Father thinks I'm a freak," he burst out.

Irissa was struck dumb with shock.

"We're not alike," Thane went on sheepishly. "He seems afraid of my magical powers, the way they come to me."

Irissa straightened. "Kendric is afraid of nothing for his own sake. He may fear the price your unheard-of powers will demand of you, but that is understandable. He wishes you less trouble in life than he found—any parent does."

"He . . . might find immortality bitter coming from my hand, from my . . . freakish blend of powers."

"Thane." Irissa almost shook her son. "You *are* his immortality."

Thane shifted uneasily under the press of her hands on his shoulders. "I always wanted to be like him, when I was young—"

"You are! Yes, in ways neither of you sees yet."

"Then I realized I could never be like him, that I had things—greater magic—that he would never have."

"So do I."

"You don't understand—"

"Yes, I do, better than either of you thinks. This will resolve itself with time. Kendric was always uneasy with magic, even his own. You can't expect him to face your lavish supply of it without cold feet. It doesn't mean he doesn't love you, Thane. It doesn't mean he isn't proud of you."

"But . . . if his . . . survival is up to me—" Thane looked up at Irissa with a boy's anguished eyes, for all they gleamed magically silver and gold. "Perhaps my talents are not enough, perhaps *I* will fail him."

"Not if you don't fail yourself. Kendric more than anyone would understand that to try is to accomplish, even in the face of failure. No, neither he nor I would hold you to achieving your quest. Kendric wouldn't even let you attempt it in the first place. That's why he must know nothing of this, nothing."

"He is . . . hard to keep things from," Thane said doubtfully. "I always feel so . . . small."

"I know. That is what you get for your mother wedding an utterly honest man. But we are Torloc, Thane, and there is much iron in our Iridesium. Kendric would say we are a race that avoids looking naked truth in the eye. Perhaps our truth is simply hard to see. Will you try?"

"I'll try to find a gate, though I don't know how. I'll try to fool Father, though I'll hate myself. If I . . . get through, I'll get to Rule and bring back the sword though all Without stand between me and Rengarth."

"Hush." Irissa pulled Thane's smooth-haired head to

her shoulder. "Don't tempt Those Without by mentioning their fell domain. Without is not so easy to get into—or get out of—as you think. There'll be hazards enough in common worlds between gates."

Thane submitted to her mothering as he had not in some years. Irissa cherished this moment when she saw her son standing at the crossroads of child and adulthood. If he found a gate, he would not return the boy she had known, and that was a loss beyond counting, no matter how dear the gift that came borne on the blade of the seventh sword.

"What of Javelle?" Thane asked suddenly.

"Javelle?"

He looked into her silver eyes, so deeply she could feel him probe to the very quick of her mind. In asking him to use his magic for Kendric, she had permitted him to apply it against herself. "Javelle has no magical powers. What of *her* mortality?"

The question cast rings within rings, rippling the vast spaces of Irissa's inner self. She fought back coldstone tears.

"First," she said, "the sword and Kendric. Then there'll be time enough to worry about Javelle."

CHAPTER
8

THUNDER RUMBLED IN THE DISTANCE, AS IT ALWAYS DID.

The place in which he lived was vast, and dark—so dark that clouds roiled in its upper spaces and lightning snapped under the unseen eaves.

It contained many rooms, though the rooms themselves were so huge they felt unconfined. It was never easy to tell when he moved from one chamber to another. And it didn't matter, for every room mirrored every other room —dark and vast and empty.

Eeryon could hardly tell the passage of time, either, though it sometimes felt as if huge, lazy eons had rolled cloud-silent through these great rooms. At other times, he perceived days and months and years as no more than a clump of dustballs in the corners he couldn't see.

The only thing he had to pass the time—besides the company of his pet, a disembodied demon Eeryon had trapped in a passing thunderhead—was his lessons.

Today, he was learning how to eat.

"Why?" he had demanded. His existence had been whole from the first. Shattered memories revealed nothing earlier but more space and more dark and more commands from the Dark Man who commanded this space and time. His magic-master encouraged questioning, although he never brooked having his answers disregarded.

"Why?" Eeryon had asked. "I don't need to eat." It was true. Nothing here ate, except each other and that for reasons other than sustenance.

"You may need to be seen eating, in places you will be."

"Where?"

The magic-master encouraged curiosity but not challenge.

"In worlds where you will go."

"When?"

"When I say."

Eeryon sighed to recall that conversation, brief as lightning bolts. The two-pronged instrument the master had given him—calling it a fork—lay in his slack hand, the tines prodding a lump of some white mushy stuff.

"Eat," the master had thundered, "and ask questions later when you have proven your abilities."

This "eating" was perhaps the most distasteful task the master had required thus far. Eeryon shoved a sodden lump toward his mouth, his tepid senses recoiling from the mere approach of something with the smell, texture, and look of food.

He had never eaten, not even—as the master was fond of boasting loudly to the unseen spirits that called from time to time—"mother's milk."

Eeryon wondered what milk was. And a mother.

But there were many things the master did not see fit to tell him. He stabbed another lump of food into his mouth, then stiffened. The morsel never arrived, though he still felt the thrusting motion of his arm.

Eeryon held his breath, although that made no difference. Another of the Dark Moments had come. They never announced themselves. There would be a tingle in his limbs followed by a wave of weakness. His sight would dim, then paradoxically sharpen. Finally, he would feel himself fade from his own mind. His senses—never intense—withdrew as his consciousness was cloaked in a deeper dark than the night all around him.

He could not even feel his heart beat, though he knew that the master would be angered to know of this . . . defection of Eeryon's. The magic-master's words came back. "You must be reliable, Eeryon, or you will be of no use to me."

That which was of no use to the master . . . was not.

The Dark Moments had come more frequently of late, although Eeryon could not say for how long. There was no "long" in this place, no before and after, only a constant continuing.

He remembered first glimpsing himself in the Dark Mirror as it lay like a wet and sticky rug at the base of the deepest chamber. The black, gleaming surface had reflected him—all of him—except his eyes. Fascinated, Eeryon had stared right through those eyes into twinkling empty darkness and had understood his awful difference. Even the cloud-demon had eyes, albeit three of them.

During Dark Moments, Eeryon suspected, all the rest of him shrank into a tight impervious ball and escaped through his empty eyes.

Where he escaped, he didn't know. Although the master had educated him to a roster of many names—Rengarth, Rule, the Paramount Athanor, Rindell Pond, the Oracle of Valna, Mauvedona—none of them touched him any more concretely than a wandering cloud butting its way through the place's maze of massive rooms.

Eeryon felt a thickening of his face, felt his mouth gagged with cloud. The Dark Moment passed, and he was obediently swallowing the horrible food he must appear to like. Only one thing he took into himself truly sustained him, and that was knowledge.

"Very good."

The magic-master was there, towering, his gloved hands folded into his sleeves.

Eeryon glanced down at his empty plate. It looked whole again, relieved of its pasty burden. Why couldn't he remain uncontaminated, too? But the magic-master always had a reason. Now he shared a minute portion of it.

"You may be required to exercise your eating talents sooner than you suspect. The worlds Within await you. You will find them close and confusing, but you are . . . to the press of power born. You will adapt well." It was an order.

"What of the sword?" the boy asked in the face of this unprecedented confidence.

"The sword . . . moves in the water, attracting more eyes than mine—and yours. Premature as your fishing expedition was, I may have to send you sooner than I thought."

"To—?"

"To the worlds forbidden us, as ours is forbidden them. You are my heir, Eeryon, but first you must prepare the way for my return, so there is something for you to inherit."

"Heir?" The word was new to him.

"Never mind. Just serve me as you have— unquestioningly. You know your purpose."

"To acquire the sword."

"You know your goal."

"To bring it back to you."

"You know your means."

"Magic," the boy said promptly. "All the magic that I may command."

"Against any foe."

"Against any foe—mortal or magical."

"In any world."

"In any world—Within or Without."

The mage nodded, his golden beard and eyebrows glinting in the dimness. He pulled an arm free of his robe, his iridescent leather glove moving to Eeryon's head. Such a gesture was so unheard-of that the boy feared the glove would pass right through his brain.

But his senses remained solid, and the weight of a bony hand followed the curve of his skull.

"You are my son, my heir," the magic-master intoned with a deep undercurrent of emotion. "You are my key that will free me from the . . . terrible empty wastes of Without, where only my powers keep my small domain here free of consumption. You will return me to the worlds Within that are mine by right of magic. My survival rides on your untried powers."

"I almost called the sword to my hand from the Dark Mirror!"

"The sword may be called, but will not answer. You must capture it in the common, mortal way, by questing for and claiming it. You must bear it back, fighting all obstacles. A sword can take life, and that sword—in the wrong possession—will take my long life from me. To win immortality, one must risk mortality. You must engage upon a trial of bone and blood as well as magic."

"What do I know of such things?"

"Little," the magic-master admitted. "But you will learn, quickly. Your talent is inborn." He turned in that motion that preceded his abrupt departure, then paused. "I give you a parting gift, my son."

Eeryon's face looked up, expectant. He had received no gift but lessons and loneliness.

"My name," said the mage, smiling fire-white through the golden bush of his beard. "Geronfrey."

The name was only the second Eeryon had heard applied to anything he had seen, besides his own, and he had not really seen himself.

In that moment, the magic-master's quest became his, as he became the magic-master's, as he became son to father and mage to mage.

CHAPTER
9

"THANE? ARE YOU BECOMING A RECLUSE?"

Javelle idled on the threshold to her mother's greeting room, fresh from a ride on Thundermist. Her clothes were wind-creased, her coiled hair even more ruffled, and her cheeks were burnished apple-red.

With the shutters half-drawn, the chamber was dim, lit by the random glitter of the tapestry threads. Thane sat cross-legged atop the table in the room's center. He was gazing intently at the walls.

"Thane?" Javelle clumped into the room in her riding boots, forcing her presence into his view.

"I'm thinking." He sounded as if that should quiet her.

"Thinking." Her tone managed to make the pursuit seem unprecedented. "Well, that is a departure."

He ignored her, keeping his chin cradled on his fists, which were braced in turn on his akimbo knees.

"Mother will have your skin for scratching her weepwillow tabletop," Javelle tried next.

"I haven't scratched it."

"You will." Javelle's fingertips stroked the glossy surface. Wood was rare in Rengarth; this table was polished to a glaze just shy of mirror-bright. She kept silent, regarding her brother's profile. He withstood her scrutiny, or worse, ignored it as easily as he did Javelle herself.

"I haven't seen you for three days," she said.

"Lucky you."

"Yes, but . . ." She boosted herself atop the table beside him. "Oh, this wood is chill . . . ! Thane, is something the matter?"

Javelle would never admit it, but her brother's absence had revealed how much she depended upon his presence for company, motivation, and invigorating doses of aggravation.

"I'm just studying these tapestries of Mother's, that's all. I never really looked at them before."

"These?" Javelle eyed the somber walls with their rectangles of storied patterns. Worms of reflective thread writhed across the woven surfaces as the air shifted the hangings. "Perhaps you need light—" She moved to jump down and go unshutter the window.

"No!"

"Thane, why not?"

"I can . . . see them better in the semi-dark, that's all. If I half-close my eyes, the . . . things . . . in them move, live again."

"That's the wind, silly. They always waver like that. Thane, you never cared about the tapestries before. You never even noticed them. What *is* the matter with you?"

"A nosy sister."

"Merely curious. It hardly concerns me if you wish to stay indoors and moon over some moldy hangings."

"If Mother made them, they will never molder."

"Anyway, the scenes they show, the things that happened in them, are all in the past. Father once said to think of them as a map to yesterday."

"Father said—?"

"Yes, you never listen to him. But I . . . did, anyway, years ago, when you were only an infant and too young to remember."

"I walked at six months and spoke at nine. I remember almost everything but my birth," he protested. "What would you know that I wouldn't?"

"Something, precocious one. Perhaps there were simply things you didn't pay attention to."

"Such as—"

Javelle's hand swept toward the tapestry before them.

"This. You were always too busy playing with magic and consulting with Mother. Father had less spectacular ways of entertaining me. He told me stories."

"Of the weavings?"

"Of what's in the weavings. Why do you finally want to know now?"

Thane gritted his teeth. Javelle would take her pound of penance one way or another. "Yes. I finally want to know now. I have an idea. . . ."

"An idea? For weaving your own tapestry? I thought that was women's work."

"Magic was supposed to be women's work, too, among Torlocs, yet we defy that tradition."

"You didn't have to say 'we' just to include me in what I've always been excluded from."

"I'm sorry, Javelle . . . no, I mean it. I look at things a bit differently now. I . . . need your knowledge of the hangings. I shouldn't have reminded you of what you can't bear to remember."

"No, you shouldn't have." Javelle shrugged, finding his concession tepid. The exhilaration of her recent solitary ride was dissipating into the old despair she always felt when confronting Thane's magical superiority. "Anyway, if you want to know about the tapestries and don't want to ask Mother, ask Father." She stood to leave.

"I can't!" His panic was genuine.

"You can't?" Suspicion had tinged Javelle's voice.

"I mean . . . Father and I have never had much in common."

"You are both male. Perhaps he'd welcome a chance to tell his son about his old exploits. He wasn't always a dull Ruler in Rengarth."

"Still—" Thane thought rapidly. "I'd rather hear it from you, Javelle. I wouldn't want Father to know how ignorant I've been."

Appealing to his sister's superiority was a brilliant stroke. Javelle softened and preened at the same time.

"I should think not," she agreed, jumping back on the table. "Which one do you want to hear about first?"

"That one." He pointed to a mysterious interior scene—a room of many windows each overlooking a different, alien vista.

"But that's one of the least interesting ones." Javelle indicated another hanging, where Kendric, sword raised, fought a whirlwind of crimson dust and robed warriors. "What about this—when father mind-made the sword and bested Ivrium's Inlands spawn? Father and Mother aren't even sewn into that other tapestry."

"No." Thane leaned more intently forward. "It's the only one they're absent from."

"And do you know why?"

"Tell me."

Javelle leaped down and strolled to the wall, standing so as not to obscure the design. She began her lecture.

"They are absent because this hanging depicts Geronfrey's many-windowed tower room just *after* Father and Mother had found the proper window back to Edanvant. There were eight gates—some to places of unimaginable horror . . . and some to the dead past. But Father magically sensed the right one and led them both safely through it."

"Mother must have had a notion, too."

"Perhaps." Javelle moved past the other hangings, her eyes tallying scenes of other days, other worlds.

"Do you notice anything about Father in the tapestries?" Thane asked suddenly.

"Notice?"

Javelle paused to stare at a larger-than-life-size Kendric bridling an Empress Falgon in a cave while Irissa waited beside a shoulder-high egg. An iridescent armament of embroidered feathers sheathed the falgon's massive body. Crimson threads glinted in Kendric's dark hair while azure accented Irissa's night-black locks.

"I notice only that I sometimes forget that they were more in other worlds than we see them as here," Javelle commented.

"More," Thane prompted, some unspoken worry nagging at his voice. "More what?"

"More . . . mighty, magical, more adventurous, more—" Something lingered at the back of Javelle's mind, a word that refused to step forward. "More . . . glamorous. Is that what you meant, that we only see our parents woven in plain threads now?"

He shook his head. "I don't know what I meant, or I wouldn't have asked. But I mean to study these hangings as closely as Scyvilla reads his casting crystals. There is more in them than meets the eye."

"I know them by heart," Javelle said. "Or at least I did when I was young. If you must mope, I suppose it's better that you do something constructive with your time."

She moved to the door, hoping that Thane would unkink his legs, leap off the table, and follow, saying, "I'm ready for a ride myself. Where were you and where are you going?"

This time he didn't. This time he didn't even say good-bye.

Javelle hesitated on the threshold, turning back to see her

brother circled by dimly glimmering tapestries in which figures moved as if shaken by a gentle, unseen hand.

She wished she could shake Thane, jolt him out of this new and disturbing reverie. He was ruining the balance of their contrasting characters, leaving her no ground of her own. *She* was the thoughtful one who cherished past and present. *He* was the impulsive one hurtling ever forward to the future. Now he had usurped her emotional bent as well as her magic.

She took a last summation of the depictions of her father. Nothing was "different" about them—whatever did Thane mean? Father didn't change, Javelle told herself, his children did, and that was natural. Children grew and parents grew older, save that Irissa and Kendric were magical exceptions to the rule.

Javelle shrugged and left Thane to brood among the fragile thread-worlds wafting against the walls.

But she found the palace strangely deserted, her mood too vaguely despondent to share with others. She had never realized how much Thane's antics had counterbalanced her more somber nature. Without him, she was like a ball deprived of its bounce. She finally wandered into the kitchen and began rummaging food chests in search of something she couldn't name and that most likely was not edible.

"'Tis but an hour or two 'til dinner," Arzino, the cook, sang out from behind his chopping block. The heads of coriander roots flew like woodchips.

"I'm hungry now."

"You won't be then if you eat now."

The kitchen staff still resented Scyvilla's usurpation of their role the few nights before. Rengarthians of ordinary talents—that is, unmagicked people—were proprietary about serving their rulers, a sentiment Javelle normally sympathized with.

"I'm starving!" she repeated, pulling a string of tongue-sweets from a hamper. The multicolored droplets glistened like beads. Javelle unwound a couple feet of them—observed Arzino's disapproving eye and unreeled another two feet of candy.

"A most merciless huntress," said a voice at her feet.

She looked down to see the white cat coiled imperially into a discarded flour sack as if reclining on swansdown-stuffed ermine. It had laced its plumy tail through its entangled legs so that all four feet and its face—nose and toe pads rosy with sleep—rested on a cushion of fur.

"You don't look as if you could hunt a midge," Javelle taunted.

"Looks deceive," the cat replied, yawning until its whiskers bristled.

Javelle looped her booty around her arm and left, climbing the back stairs to her favorite reading nook—a long-forgotten window seat set into an awkward twist in the tower.

She had barely settled down with her feet tucked under her when the cat vaulted up beside her.

"Go away, you don't eat tongue-sweets."

"Your father would say I needed to. You are a thorny girl! Most people would welcome a soft, pliant feline curled beside them."

"Yes, but you are neither of those. I've heard of your exploits in Rule and Edanvant."

"So the prejudices of the parents fall to the child." The cat took a mournful tone. "A sad world—or rather, worlds."

Javelle paused in stuffing the first ruby tongue-sweet into her mouth. "You've been in other worlds? What's it like?"

"Different." The cat hiked a hind leg over its shoulder and began thoughtfully tonguing the back of the leg. "I seem to harbor dim memories older than I . . . but they ebb and flow like fog, and likely are not half so interesting as I am at this moment."

A dislodged white hair or two fluttered into a shaft of window light while Javelle, speechless, confronted a cat's massive self-satisfaction in the flesh and fur. She was her father's daughter.

"The past is a valuable lesson we can learn from," she intoned dutifully.

"The past is overrated."

"Father says it's the best road to the future."

"What does he know?" the cat sniffed. "All cats are older than time, no matter how young, but Kendric the Skeptic is only forty years ahead of the most ignorant babe."

"Forty years!" That seemed an incredibly long time to Javelle.

"Though among mortal men," the cat conceded, washing its foot, "that is considered a good sum of survival. I wonder with all of his battles that he has lasted long enough to produce some silver hairs."

"Silver hairs?"

"Gray, if you must put it in common terms. I always fancy a touch of silver, however. Dark hair is . . . uninteresting."

The cat flicked a last hair into the air. Javelle watched it float from side to side toward the cushion.

"Silver hairs," she repeated. "Mother has not a one—"

" 'Mother' is a Torloc. She will live forever—or what will seem like that."

"But Father has magic—"

"Acquired, not inbred for generations."

Javelle had tired of the creature's self-satisfied tone. "Do *you* have magic inbred for generations?"

"All cats do."

"Hiding behind your breed isn't good enough. What do you specifically possess?"

The tail flicked airily. "An instinct. Good manners. Impeccable timing."

"That's not magic, that's conceit!" Javelle leaped up, dislodging the cat. "I'm tired of your implications and your silly, sly face. Go away!"

The cat, which had landed on its feet, stood its ground. "You go. I like this spot." It leaped into the cushion dent that had been warmed by her body and curled up into instant oblivion.

Javelle stood motionless, feeling anything but tranquil within. A round of ugly speculations was roiling her heart and mind until the pale metal snake, which had remained wound around her wrist for several days, sensed her turmoil.

Whip-quick it untangled itself, then migrated up her arm and into her hair, almost hiding at her neck rather than circling it. The metal had warmed to her body heat; for a moment Javelle, almost hopefully, took the ornament for a living thing.

"There," she said, patting it. "You mustn't be frightened. Surely there's more to this than meets the eye, especially the eye of a sleeping cat."

Felabba remained still, except that one green iris swelled open before slitting shut again.

The unusual act of addressing her birth-token had made Javelle play comforter to herself as well. She had never before confronted the idea of her father declining, had never noticed nor expected change in either of her parents in all the years she had known them.

She slowly descended the stairs, thinking as hard as Thane had. Irissa hadn't changed. She looked exactly like the self-portraits she had woven into the tapestries. In many ways, Irissa looked a great deal like Javelle.

Javelle took the more public turning of the stair, pausing when she saw her parents at the center of a knot of gilt-haired Rengarthians in the hall below, their dark heads making the pupil in a pale saffron eye.

Kendric, of course, loomed above the rest. Light lanced from the narrow windows at the hall's highest, striking silver highlights from the crown of his head just as Irissa's hair radiated blue.

Silver. Javelle leaned against the stone wall, upheld by its cold shoulder . . . not crimson, as in the tapestries, but silver. She noticed no silver among the flaxen heads of aging Rengarthians, and ludborgs had no hair to show.

She'd never confronted the signs of aging in her kind— or any other. Somehow she thought it would all be as eternal as Rengarth's unending summer. Her mother had looked the same from the days when Javelle's infant eyes could barely focus on her until now.

But Kendric did not.

And what was worse, for some reason, Thane, who was blithely indifferent to such matters, had known it before Javelle had.

Irissa paused before entering her room, a hand at her Iridesium circlet, as though she had a headache. Then she looked up, her silver eyes shrinking as her dark pupils swelled to meet the dimness.

"Thane! We wondered where you were. Why—?"

He nodded toward the hangings with a new terseness. "If you've been to the Spectral City and found no gate, then this world is indeed sealed. I shall have to look in other worlds."

"But how shall you get there without a gate?"

"Perhaps I can make one."

"From these?" Irissa moved toward her own creations.

"You made them from the magic of your memory. Perhaps I can use that as the key to my magic."

"Use a hanging as a gate?" Irissa smiled wearily. "An innovative notion, but surely such potential would have called to me." Her hand smoothed the tapestries' shimmering folds as if greeting old friends by strokes along their sleeves. "These hangings are as spectral as the city in their way. I have never mistaken them for portals to anything but pleasant memories—and some not so pleasant."

"Perhaps you cannot double back on your own past. Perhaps I can because I never lived it."

Irissa went to Thane, intrigued by his new resolve, his almost merciless sense of mission.

"I had not thought life in Rengarth was so pallid, that it offered so little challenge. Kendric said—" Thane waited. "He said you didn't find obstacles enough to interest you here. I see now that he was right."

"Have you ever thought, Mother," Thane said, "that Father might not welcome an extended life span in so static a place? That it is no service you do him if I return the sword?"

"No. No!" An idea illuminated Irissa's face. "Besides, if you do find . . . make . . . a gate, we can *all* use it to come and go by. We will be trapped here no longer."

"You've never said that before, that we were trapped."

"I suppose I never thought it. What was, was. And my life was changing so much within—I bore Javelle, then you shortly after—I never looked without myself."

"What's . . . the real Without like?"

Irissa leaned against the table edge. "The Without beyond the worlds, you mean? It much resembles the vast, unexplored territory within each of us, I believe. Yet it is a realm composed of all things unwelcome in our own worlds."

"Evil?"

"Perhaps. Or perhaps these things could be . . . better . . . than the things of our world. It isn't worth the risk of invoking Those Without simply to discover if they will devour or delight us."

"Are . . . Those Without people? Rulers? Monsters?"

"No one knows. No one goes Without until forced to. Why ask such . . . morbid questions? Have you felt the empty touch of Without?"

Thane shook his head. "Since I began staring at these tapestries, I find questions writhing in my mind like blue-worms. I . . . sense a pattern beneath the design of your weaving that even you have never sensed. I feel the tug of a new thread being braided onto the warp and woof of an old loom."

"Now you talk like a Torloc." Irissa rested a hand on his shoulder, surprised by how it had broadened recently. The sudden growth spurts of youth made Thane seem like some forced flower in the palace gardens—delightful but a bit nonplussing. "Can you do it? Find a gate?"

"I will do it," he answered with that peculiar intensity only she had ever seen, for it only manifested itself when he talked about magic. "What will you tell Father when I am gone?"

"The truth," she answered without hesitation. Then she laughed at her own temerity. "The truth. He will be—"

"Angry?"

Irissa nodded bleakly. "That. And wild to follow you, and worried and . . . wounded."

In the silence Thane cleared his throat.

"I am not afraid, Mother, but I wonder that you are not."

"Sometimes we must do things that others will not understand."

"For their own good?"

"For their own—and our—good."

"I wonder which will be harder," Thane mused.

"Which what?"

"My finding a gate from Rengarth—or your telling Father that I have done so."

CHAPTER
10

"SCYVILLA!"

The ludborg stopped, then cocked his hood at Javelle.

"Yes, little Lady Longitude?"

Javelle's nose wrinkled at the nickname. Scyvilla had begun slyly using it in the past two years, ever since Javelle's height had begun to rival her mother's. If she disliked comparisons in height, she didn't blanch at borrowing her mother's most no-nonsense tone.

"Where is my father?"

Scyvilla shrugged, then clapped his sleeves together. A limpid glass ball appeared between the prayerfully folded ends. "Does little Lady Longitude require a casting?"

"No, not the crystals," Javelle said. "A simple question requires only a plain answer. Where is Father? I saw him with some townspeople below, but by the time I arrived, he had vanished. Do you know where he went?"

During the ensuing pause the ludborg's hood leaned nearer to inspect her face. Javelle couldn't help fidgeting at this unnerving inspection, thus ruining her hard-won air of authority.

"Well," Scyvilla said at last, "you must have dawdled a good long while to miss the exit of that crowd. No doubt you had weighty matters on your mind."

"Yes, I did."

"Then a crystal casting is just the thing—" The wings of coarse fabric buoying the globe moved eagerly.

"No!" Javelle implored. A long silence and the tilted hood, dark as death within its oval, forced her to elaborate. "The . . . crystals never work for me, anyway."

"The crystals always work—whether as we would wish them to or not is another matter."

"The crystals lie!" she burst out, wishing Scyvilla had not forced her to such heartfelt heresy. Which was worse—the heresy or her high feeling, she couldn't say.

"How so?" Scyvilla's voice was soft, grave, and too calm.

Having committed to truth, Javelle outdid herself with frankness.

"Father is right; your crystals are a fraud! At my birth your casting predicted that I would bear a magic greater than any in Rengarth had known. People were fond of repeating this, this . . . tale . . . to me, until it became obvious that I bore no magic at all."

Scyvilla rocked back and forth on whatever he used for locomotion under the skirts of his gathered robe. Javelle, already regretting her confession, tried to maintain dignity by remaining absolutely silent.

Scyvilla's sleeve unexpectedly brushed her arm, an oddly comforting touch. She flinched.

"You have been thinking hard thoughts, young woman, and thus say hard words. Did my crystal casting at your birth say you would bear magic *from* your birth?"

"Not specifically, but when else—?"

The hood tilted. "Are you dead, then?"

"No—! But . . ."

"Why, then, if you are yet living, you may yet see the crystals prove their truth."

"So I am to live my whole life on a 'maybe'?"

"It is better than many have. Besides, be grateful for being spared the burden of magic, since my crystals . . . lied."

"That's what Father advises," Javelle conceded.

"Then heed your father and not the crystals. He is a doughty fellow who has seen magic work much pestilence. And I'm sure *he* never lies."

"Never! But . . . perhaps your crystals didn't predict an impossible future for me. Perhaps they took me for Thane. He should have been firstborn. . . ."

Something caught Javelle and shook her—a wind, a phantom, a disembodied outreach of the ludborg's will. Scyvilla's voice came high-pitched and yet stern from the fog of surprise enveloping her.

"No. Say what you wish of the crystals, but never deny yourself."

The moment had passed. The two stood conversing on a flight of shallow stairs midway between bottom and top. Javelle had the odd notion that for an instant they had stepped outside of time.

"I . . . won't," she promised. "And perhaps your crystals were right. I may be the wrong one. But—" she added quickly, "that doesn't mean I won't be right again."

"Good girl," Scyvilla approved.

For a moment Javelle feared he would attempt to pat her on the head, but she had grown too top-lofty for that. He scurried away, the unbroken globe glistening between the pincers of his sleeves. No doubt he sought another victim to impress his scrying skills upon.

Javelle sighed and continued down the stairs. At the next turning she met a linen-layer with her chin atop an armful of sheeting and a head full of just the information Javelle craved.

"The dungeons," this woman answered smartly when Javelle posed her prime question. "Some townsfolk came

—most agitated—and your father led 'em all below. Dark and dusty it is down there. I like my upper stories better, despite the stairs." And up she tripped the endless flights, as merry as Scyvilla about his errands.

Dungeons. Javelle, puzzled, began clattering down the stairs. Once the palace dungeons had been a magical maze that had held her father briefly captive. Now they served as a storage area divided into cellars—root cellars and wine cellars, spice cellars and flower-drying cellars, old-furniture cellars and empty, good-for-nothing cellars.

She and Thane had played hide-and-seek among the cobwebs and casks. Sometimes, they had frightened each other with ghoulish stories—she telling more terrible fancies than he, because she was older. Thane had retaliated with magical tricks, sending shadows marching against her and dropping phantom spiders as large as casting crystals onto her shoulders. . . .

Javelle's nose scented the half-remembered odors of the rooms below as she hurried down the kitchen stairs—they also exhaled a fetid reek that spoke of a new, rank dampness in long-dry places.

She rushed down the dark steps, guided by flickering torches ahead and the echoing murmur of voices. Something was happening. Something . . . exciting.

Thane, she thought a bit maliciously, would be angry that he'd been in Irissa's chamber mooning over tapestries and that *she* alone had witnessed the uproar. . . . He'd be sorry that he suddenly had "more important" things to do.

The first voice she heard clearly was not her father's.

"Poison," it was declaring in demanding tones, "is the province of Rulers and ruling clans."

Javelle burst around a corner to find a wall of backs blocking her way. The townspeople. Facing them all was her father. He acknowledged her arrival with a raised eyebrow, but he didn't question it, being more concerned with the townspeople's complaint.

"Why are you so certain that this 'poison' that taints your water supply begins here?" he asked reasonably.

For answer, a burgher hefted a glass vase filled with liquid. In the torchlight, filmy snakes of black writhed on the water's oily surface.

"This is the water we draw from our wells and rinse down our streets," she said heavily. "It springs from here because the palace was built over a natural spring to guard it from taint."

"And now you believe the source has been poisoned."

"Perhaps not intentionally," another citizen admitted. "Perhaps the poison was meant only for the ruling family and inadvertently leaked into the city's supply. We have not had a royal poisoning in many years," he added almost wistfully.

"And will not," Kendric said definitely. "Why couldn't the cause be natural?"

"Because—" The burgher was astounded. "Because poison is the way of Rengarth."

"Not since I have been Ruler."

"But when you are gone?"

Over their heads, Kendric saw Javelle's face whiten in the pallid light. "I don't intend to be gone for some time. Besides, I can't leave. None of my family can. Nor can you. We had better solve this problem for all our sakes. Let me see the vase of untainted water again."

The shopkeeper—who kept a stand fragrant with fresh tongue-sweets, Javelle remembered—lifted another narrow vase. Rengarthian water swirled against its clear sides, reflecting a faint glimmer of rainbow colors—red, blue, violet, gold, and green.

Water was not only life in Rengarth, it was beauty. For a moment poison was forgotten. They all smiled to see the fresh liquid swirling in its endless dance.

By way of contrast, Kendric lifted the burgher's darkened vase even higher, shaking the water into a clot of twisting black tendrils laced with poisonous green, crimson, and purple. All these virulent shades were intensified versions of the clean water's opalescent purity.

"This other," he said, "came from the town. Let's compare it with the palace source-water."

He bent below Javelle's line of sight. She pushed herself past the gathered people to see. Kendric was kneeling at the stone lip of the underground pool she and Thane used to pretend was the Outer Abyssal Sea. He dipped an empty vase in the night-black water and lifted it into the torchlight.

"Bubbles clouded the liquid, then burst. The water settled, clearing. Brows all around knit in puzzlement. Then the clearing water stirred and darkened. Rainbow-dark threads floated within the glass.

"The source!" the burgher crowed. "Tainted."

Kendric nodded, then shook his head. "Yes, but poison is administered by the pinch," he said, "not the pool. It is a specific, sneak-thief sort of weapon, a coward's choice—"

"We care not the nature of the beast, Ruler, only that it be vanquished," someone complained.

"You cannot vanquish a . . . beast, as you say, until you know its nature." Kendric put the vase on the ground and peered into the black water beyond it.

Javelle stared, too. The pool looked no different than it did of old. It had always seemed dark, because the under-cellars were ill-lit. Now, apparently, a new blackness was seething in its placidly lapping waters.

Javelle shivered at the thought of ill festering beneath the palace's very foundations. She shuddered so hard she dislodged the snake choker from her throat. It slipped down her torso, almost falling, before it looped her waist. She ignored its movement, wondering intently what her father would do. He was about to tell them all.

"I've heard it said that all the water on Rengarth—every river, brook, lakelet, fishpond, puddle, lagoon, well, and dimple—meets itself coming and going deep underground."

"Yes!" the sweetshop keeper shouted. "Thus our concern. Soon this one tainted spring could make all Rengarth an evil-smelling cauldron!"

"Or," said Kendric, rising, "some taint from elsewhere could have migrated here."

They had not considered that, or the enormity of that notion. In the silence, Kendric undid his belt with the ceremonial dagger and began wrestling himself out of his braid-gilded tunic.

"What are you doing?" the burgher demanded.

He sat down without answering and tugged off his boots.

Javelle noticed the worn soles, the scuffed orange hide. Shabby boots didn't become a Ruler, she thought, resolving only to wear the richest footwear when she came to the High Seat. Then she realized whom she would be succeeding, and horror overcame her unthinking vanity.

Kendric finally stood, barefoot and bare-chested among his subjects, unchagrined because he had never thought of them as subjects, any more than he had thought of himself as Ruler.

"You are going to . . . go in? Swim?" Javelle had finally spoken, because she could no longer bear to remain silent.

"Watch my boots," he answered cryptically.

She flushed, knowing he had noticed her disdain for his worn footwear, realizing that he treasured that very wear as a remnant of Rule.

"And you—hand me that torch." He reached out a hand.

"You're taking a torch into the *water?*" someone demanded incredulously.

Javelle was silent, not having refound her voice yet.

Kendric chuckled. He liked to confound those who would extend him some ritual obeisance, yet knew no more of him than they did of the central sun that daily drew its train of bright twins across the sky. And he welcomed a problem that required solving.

"I need to see where the underwater caverns and rivers lie."

"See?"

"See." Kendric passed his ring before the torch flame, each of the five shades within the central cabochon brightening in turn. The watery silver color flared brightest and bluer. Then the flame acquired the same silvery aquamarine hue. It fanned with a cool, ethereal light, seeming more a thing of liquid than of fire now.

Lunestone, Javelle reminded herself. Her father's ring numbered the cool blue silver light of Lunestone among its component colors.

Kendric stepped past the pool lip, his bare foot questing into the water and finding no support. With a shrug of massive shoulders, he passed the torch to Javelle, crouched, then braced his hands on the edge and lowered himself into the dark, chuckling wavelets.

She bent to return the torch, feeling its chill bright light beat across her cheek. He took it and smiled at her, for her. Then the black pool swallowed him as he submerged. Only the torch was still visible beneath the water, an exotic long-finned fish of azure flame skimming below the surface.

"At least he is brave," a townsman commented under his breath.

Javelle whirled on the speaker, fresh fire in her eyes.

"As well as wise," the burgher added quickly. "Though I fear in this instance . . ."

They turned back to the water, fear multiplying in all their minds in different manners. Javelle had always excelled at frightening herself, especially in dark, unknown, forbidden places. And she had learned of late—for the first time—to fear *for* her father. It was an unsettling notion and it took full form in her imagination.

He could drown. Or he could . . . breathe . . . the water and consume poison beyond saving. He could find an underwater river and be swept away forever, so far that they'd never find his bones. He could hit his head on a rock and drown. Or he could lose direction in the bottomless dark and drown—

The possibilities were endless, she discovered, watching with the sort of parental horror she had witnessed many times directed toward herself. She began to understand. Aging was just the half of it. Try to hold back the night and you soon grew too busy to deal with the dangers of the day. . . .

"What do you think he does?" someone asked her, deferring.

She shook her head, watching the water.

Kendric remained submerged for many anxious seconds that added like grains of sand into a pile of minutes.

"He's drowned," the sweetshop keeper wailed finally.

"Swept away to the Bubblemeres to be a wellwraith," predicted another. "Left us to the taint."

"No," Javelle said, but no one heard her.

Then the pool's center erupted into a fountain of spray, a blue flame burning at its center. Kendric's head surfaced next, sputtering into speech.

"My dagger—throw it to me, quickly!"

Javelle swiftly pulled it free of the belt. She hurled it haft-first across the black water, hoping her arm had sent it far and true enough.

Kendric's paddling left hand broke water, the ringstone shining azure in the torchlight. The dagger haft spun into his palm just as he was about to sink again.

"Are there underground rivers?" the burgher asked, hands braced on bent knees.

"Yes," Kendric answered, "and things that come through them."

While his words sank into their comprehension, he

suddenly doused the torch flame into the water—though it was not made to fade in water now that his ringstone had spelled it.

Yet he released it, let it drift down until its burning light hit bottom and cast an aquamarine glow throughout the obsidian water.

Their faces lit by reflected azure, townspeople gathered around. Kendric's dark form dove for the sky-glow of the bottom, as if to retrieve the torch he had so blithely tossed away but moments before.

Then another dark form glided into the blue-lit grotto—man-long and swift-swimming, a shadow that spread wings wide as a cloak.

"What is it?" Javelle cried. "No one has ever reported such a creature in Rengarth!"

"A wellwraith from the Bubblemeres," a townsman guessed.

"One of the devouring manfish your mother bound in a fiery circle to Swanfish Lake," the burgher said.

"Your father was ever interested in undocumented beasts of Rengarth," the sweetshop keeper put in dryly. "I believe he has found one he will regret discovering."

"It can't be a beast," Javelle insisted desperately, "it's a fish. Quick, someone send for Mother—"

Receding footsteps told Javelle her first royal command had been obeyed. She couldn't tear her eyes from the water. Her fingernails crimped her palms. She watched the two slow shadows converge at the heart of the blue light, and there was nothing that she could do but watch.

"Why?" she berailed herself. "Why am I here and Thane there? He at least could *do* something."

No one heeded her self-searching. Perhaps she had merely whispered when she thought she shouted. She finally clapped a hand to her mouth, as if to contain a scream that was only waiting for a reason to release itself.

Again time had passed in tiny accumulating grains of

agony. Again it was impossible that a man could stay underwater so long and still breathe.

The two shadows met, then collided, the force driving them both upright, pushing them upward like dark, folded hands.

Together, they broke water in a spray of cerulean drops that wept back to the pond surface like rain. Kendric charged out of the water to his hips, his dagger blade flashing in and out of the mated shadow as if sewing.

The two entwined figures seemed to be dancing atop the water. For a moment Kendric was lost within the flailing black wings that beat the pond into an azure froth of splashing liquid.

"'Tis feathered!" an onlooker marveled.

"No, 'tis finned," argued another.

"Both," suggested a third.

Kendric moved as if winged himself, the dagger plunging into the dark that had seized him. Javelle was reminded of the tapestry of her father among the mob of Ivrium's armed Heirlings, save that a static tapestry scene could hardly convey the motion and gracefully awkward force of true combat.

For that is what she witnessed, Javelle knew, although she had never seen its like before—a duel to the death with an alien creature found cruising within the heartspring of the very palace itself.

Both contending figures crashed into the water again, shrinking as their forms struggled down to the bright blue eye of light radiating from the magically waterproof torch.

Light was Kendric's ally; clearly, the creature he fought was an aquatic beast of darkness and depths unthought of. Javelle had never suspected Rengarth hoarded such monsters. She wondered how her father had known—guessed.

She continued watching, a bit less agitated. Kendric had expected and controlled this confrontation from the moment he had dashed the torch into the water and let it sink.

Every move the contending forms made played against the lurid azure light emanating from the spring bottom.

Limpid blue bubbles drifted up and burst on the surface —traces of both agitation and lost air below. Veils of taint roiled around the intruder's black body, interlacing with thin vaporous streams of red blood wafting upward.

Whose blood? Javelle wondered, wondering, too, what weapons the fiend-fish employed.

A moment after, the two forms clashed again on the bottom. She saw Kendric's bare feet braced on the gritty bottom rocks, saw the demon-fish's supple length writhe like a tapestry caught in a windstorm from Without.

For a moment her father's figure appeared to waver, to grow as slack as what he fought.

Then Kendric pushed close to the creature. Once again they shot upward together until they were propelled far out of the water. The fiend-fish's flailing wings beat ponderously now, towing itself around the pool, dragging Kendric with it.

Rushing footsteps down the stairs ended in Irissa's arrival, Iridesium circlet almost coal-black with anxiety. Then she was standing by the pool edge, the circlet and her ring flashing ropes of coiling color that lashed out at the water. Even as they fell they wove into an iridescent net.

Kendric, glancing up to see the flaccid rainbow arching toward him, made one last, long dagger stroke into the heart of the unnamed beast and suddenly broke free of it.

The creature paused a moment, great wings thrashing water into an arch of spray that moved through the descending rainbow net. Then the water dissipated and the net fell atop its target—a sluggish, rolling mass of darkness that floated now, rather than fought.

Kendric's sleek head resurfaced several yards away, a clean silver dagger blade between his teeth.

"I'll reel this unnatural fish in," Irissa said, the strands of her power even now drawing the beast to the stony pool rim.

It lay bound at her feet in a net of many pulsing colors when Kendric churned alongside.

"I'd already given it a death blow," he said.

"Better that it should not blow back," Irissa answered, unperturbed.

She watched as he lumbered out of the water, grunting. Droplets puddled around his bare feet. His breath came ragged and his words exploded singly, like beads he was spitting out.

"This . . . thing. There's the . . . taint. Found its way . . . here . . . from somewhere . . . deep and dark."

"Rest awhile," Irissa advised softly.

Kendric shook his head, spraying her and several bystanders with water. "Later. I want to see—"

He bent to examine the catch, extending a hand for a torch some townsperson immediately and reverentially provided. His beringed left hand brushed away Irissa's iron-woven net as if dislodging cobwebs.

He lifted one of the massive wings.

"Feathers!" chortled an onlooker.

"Fins!" a neighbor retorted just as gleefully.

"Both," Kendric mediated. He rose slowly, and everyone remained silent until he spoke again. "Scaled and feathered, finned and winged. It's a swanfish."

"No!" someone protested. "We've seen such fish, eaten them—they're white as the Frostrim and beautiful in their way. This thing is ugliness incarnate."

"A swanfish tainted," Kendric insisted. "A demon swanfish gone black and bad. True swanfish are docile, else why would we prey on them so successfully? This is their darker brother, who found its way here from who knows what black underworld stream."

"From beyond Rengarth?" Irissa asked quickly.

Kendric turned to stare at her oddly. "From beyond? No. I only meant that water underlies all this land, and surely there must be dark pools somewhere. Why are you so eager to look beyond Rengarth?"

"No . . . particular reason, except—"

He shook his head, this time dousing Javelle, who watched without blinking.

"This is natural evil . . . the decay that all things good and true come to in their time. Remote as it is, even Rengarth cannot escape such processes. That is all it is, simple degeneration."

Irissa and Javelle stood still, hearing these words with no answer. Their glances crossed. For the first time, mother and daughter regarded each other with an awful, shared, secret understanding.

"Come," Kendric carelessly told the townsfolk. "Bundle up your demon-fish and bury it in some deep remote place. Perhaps good grass will come of it. Well—you were so eager to seek the source of the taint, take it! The blue flame will purify the water and, that done, fade as flame always does. Home with you—and your prize."

They obeyed, gathering around to lift the sodden black carcass and carry it up the dark stairs into the streets.

"A good day's work." Kendric amiably draped each damp forearm over Irissa's and Javelle's shoulders. "Nothing like a bit of successful . . . plumbing to make a man or a Ruler feel useful. Javelle, fetch my boots. And if you, Irissa, will bear my belt, I think I may actually manage to climb all these stairs to the rest I so well deserve."

Leaning on them both, he made good his word.

CHAPTER

11

WET AND SHAKEN, JAVELLE LEFT HER PARENTS ON THE way to their bedchamber. She hurried through the dim hallways to Irissa's room of tapestried retreat.

She met no one—not even a stray ludborg or a serving person.

Thankful that she would see Thane alone, Javelle let her mind string and restring the words she would say to him—words that would adequately convey her shock, her fear, her sudden sense that the center of their lives was slipping away. She could confide in no one else what she had just seen.

For Kendric, despite vanquishing the beast in suitably doughty fashion, had been winded and racked. His limp at the dungeon stairs' bottom had become a hobble by the top.

He had never quite caught his breath, even on attaining the hall. And though he made light of his weakness, Irissa had not teased him in return, but simply drew more deeply into silence. Not long before, Javelle had claimed such

135

moody withdrawals for her own emotional territory. It shocked her now to see her powerful mother resorting to her own feeble defenses against confusion.

Amazed, Javelle felt herself the pivot of a spinning, multifaceted world that reflected her parents in odder and more fragmented guises. At least Thane would understand, she thought, racing toward the room. He had warned her of this very thing. Of their father . . . fading.

Javelle burst across the threshold to Irissa's chamber. By night the room was womb-dark. The shutters still hung ajar, but the impervious cloak of evening that lay beyond obscured the view more firmly than any human hand could.

"Thane?" she demanded of the dark.

No answer came.

Had he left? Impossible! He hadn't even heard about the battle below. Thane would never miss such a stir had he known, Javelle thought. He must still occupy the room . . . dreaming in the darkness.

Light. Where? Javelle wished at such times that she could clap some tongue of flame into existence as her family could. Snap her fingers—candelabras by the bank. Toss her head—a magical metal circlet spews out fireflies of candescent quickness. Draw the sword and the hilt's glow warms eyes and hands and everyone around. . . .

No, she needed to find a servant, Javelle concluded unhappily—just when she didn't want witnesses— someone to light the fire with tinder, or bear one lit candle to all the unlit ones and pollinate the dark with brightness as bees bow to flowers one by one.

Something brushed against her legs and she shrieked.

"Hush! Great baby of a girl. . . . Have you never felt a cat rub before?" a voice grumbled at her feet.

"Felabba! What are *you* doing here?"

"The same as you. Looking for a beam of light."

"I thought cats could see in the dark."

"Perhaps I search for a beam of light you can't see."

"I don't like riddles. They're . . . underhanded."

"But you like light. I could get you some if you're nice."

"I can get some, too."

"Not so speedily, nor so . . . privately."

Javelle stared into the darkness at her ankles, not really surprised when the alien embers of two green eyes glowed into view. "You call that light?" she jeered. "Not enough to see by."

"Odd . . . I can. Now."

Javelle heard a soft bound, then the cat's voice came from table height.

"What would you have? Gilothian fireworms linked into garlands and draping the chamber? A subdued circle of luminescent waxweed? Schools of glimmerfish in a casting crystal? A simple . . . torch or two, on stands of curdled amber?"

"Just ordinary, decent light, please!"

"Have you ever considered, child, that imagination is the tinder of magic? Oh, very well . . . ordinary . . . light it shall be."

A white tail flicked in the darkness. Actually, a white tail waved in the now gently ebbing blackness. All the room's wall torches and standing candles flickered into simultaneous life. The cat's eyes faded to bright, everyday green.

"That's better." Javelle wasn't sure whether she meant the light or the restored normalcy of the cat's eyes.

Then she examined the chamber in the light Felabba had evoked, and suffered her second shock of the day.

Thane was not there.

"Oh, no—" She turned in the empty room as if to surprise him hiding in a corner.

"What's the matter?" Pertly, from the cat.

"Thane . . . I wanted to speak to him."

"Perhaps I can suffice."

Javelle inspected Felabba skeptically. "You never did

before, to hear the tales my parents and these tapestries tell. Why start now?"

"Ah, you've been listening to Kendric again. I seem to recall him always rubbing me the wrong way—or perhaps it was vice versa. Let *me* set the stories straight."

"No!" Javelle didn't want any more illusions toppled this day. Annoyed, she spun again, as though to trick Thane into revealing himself. "Where *is* he? If he's not here, he never would have missed the crisis in the dungeons."

"I did," the cat pointed out, yawning.

"Small use *you* would have been. Mother and Father say you are not the real Felabba, anyway, but only an ignorant shadow."

"That sounds like the description of a child as compared to its parent. If I *am* an offspring of the creature you call Felabba, at least I bear some of my progenitor's magic. I made light. What have you made, child, besides mistakes?"

Javelle gasped. "You are . . . rude."

"Satisfied as to my true pedigree, then?" the cat asked with an oblique look as it shifted position. "If you want to find your brother, you had better speak more gently to me."

"Why should I soft-speak a fraud?"

"Because I know where what you seek is."

"Thane?" Again Javelle questioned the room's flickering shadows. He must be here, she told herself, unless. . . . She turned to the cat, her tone softer. "Felabba, has Thane found a gate and opened it? Has he left Rengarth?"

"Not hardly!" If a cat could be said to hoot, this one had. "On the other hand . . . he is, so to speak, somewhat out of this world—"

"Sense!" Javelle's fist pounded the table, making the cat's ears flatten in surprise. "Make sense, you aggravating palavering creature, or—"

"I recognize the tone, if not the words. Such impatience.

It took your mother many hundreds of hours of exquisite patience to weave these hangings. It would behoove her daughter to learn a lesson by reexamining them for a few paltry moments."

"I have not *time* for such lessons!" Javelle insisted passionately. "Something is changing beyond all my ability to understand it, much less halt it. Something . . . I . . . oh, it is not the same! It will not ever be the same again!"

The cat watched Javelle put her fingertips to her temples to contain the thoughts violently overflowing her mind. It lifted an admonitory forefoot.

"Study the tapestries," it advised quietly, then began to wash its paw in long sweeps of its barbed tongue.

Calming in the face of such sublime indifference, Javelle picked up a green-gold candelabra and stomped ungraciously to the wall. She let the flickering light sweep the brittle threads, catching on every metallic snag.

When she had illuminated the first tapestry, she moved to the next—and flinched. Never again would she be able to view these pictorial hangings as a source of wonder, as an unreal parchment upon which her father's and mother's lives were scribed with intricate stitches instead of lettering.

The weaving itself showed no age—nor did Irissa—but Kendric did. With new, uneasy eyes, Javelle saw a natural inequity recorded, beyond the past events the tapestries were meant to commemorate. She suspected that she would come to know the tragedy well—the unequality in her parents' life spans. Perhaps, she thought, even her own.

Her shoulders slumped. As she lowered the candelabra, the light sank on an Edanvant scene like the sun setting on its woven landscape. The past did not glimmer so glamorous when the future was even less livable.

"There are more pages in the lesson," the cat prompted from the table.

Javelle turned, light casting her own shadow across its

form. It sat as if eaten by the dark, a pale hummock of fur floating atop the table's burnished woodgrain sea.

Its legs were tucked in for warmth, its front paws folded like a ludborg's sleeves flattened against its body proper. At the moment it appeared to have no limbs—just a vague body and an aloofly observant face, each whisker a rapier of trembling silver spidersilk in the dimly lit room.

Still, something undeniable inhabited the cat's still form. Something that would not be gainsaid. With a sigh reminiscent of her father when forced against his better judgment, Javelle turned back to the wall and continued her circuit of the tapestries.

One by one the storied scenes passed in review—the bridge Irissa and Kendric had made in Edanvant to reunite the severed Torloc sexes . . . the icy lair of Delevant, first Torloc man to seize magical power for himself—and to lose it utterly . . . Felabba herself entoiled by a moonweasel in Rule, and Kendric about to dissect the murderous furred snakelike form with the edge of his mighty sword.

Then came the series' sole unpopulated scene—the empty tower room of this very Rengarthian palace where Geronfrey had opened his windows to eight alien vistas— one leading even to the dread world Without. From here Geronfrey had fled and left Rengarth to its legitimate heir, Kendric.

No wonder the chamber was shown unoccupied. Emptiness spoke most eloquently of its dire power. And to think, Javelle marveled, that this forgotten room existed still somewhere atop one of the palace towers. . . .

"An intriguing array of views," the cat commented loudly.

Javelle started, then turned. Felabba had deserted her tabletop and sat on the floor just behind Javelle, tail coiled around her forefeet for warmth—or perhaps merely neatness.

"I've seen these empty landscapes before," Javelle answered, ready to move on.

"Have you?" The inflection was as pointed as one of the cat's translucent claws.

Javelle studied the tapestry again, narrowing her eyes at the eight tiny vistas framed by each window. Miniature creatures cavorted in the land and skyscapes represented there. In one—a thunderstorm land apparently on the brink of an eternal lightning flash—Javelle saw something else, something . . . some*one* . . . new!

"Thane? It's . . . Thane! He's balanced on the window-sill, about to fall into the world beyond the window—what world is that?"

"*Where* is it?" the cat asked in turn.

Her eyes frozen to the frozen scene, Javelle responded numbly. "There, can't you see? There, in the stitching—he's no longer than my . . . my thumb. Oh, what shall I do? He must have found a gate—but to where?"

"What lies outside the window?"

"Why repeat me?" Javelle was stricken frantic. "What lies outside the window is . . . whatever lies without. I wish to know the *name* of what I see!"

"You have named it," the cat said.

Stunned, Javelle tore her gaze from her brother's tiny woven form to the pale puddle of fur on the dark floor.

"Named it? Just now?" Then she understood what even Felabba would not be guilty of telling her. "What lies . . . without the window, outside it . . . *is* Without! Thane has not *found* a gate, he has *mistaken* a gate. He teeters on the brink of Without. I must help him!"

"How? You have no magic."

The cat's indifference didn't madden Javelle, as it should have. It steadied her. Hearing it was like listening to a cold, sere voice within herself, a voice that had always been there but she had never heeded until this moment. A voice she had never truly needed until this moment.

"I'll find the original site of this tapestry. This . . ." Her free hand traced the shape of the tower room as if she were blind and memorizing every thread. ". . . this lost tower room."

Javelle whirled so quickly that the tree of candle flames in her hand snuffed out into a smudge of smoke. A nervous flicker from the other candelabra still lit the room, the cat.

"I will find Geronfrey's tower room," she announced as much to herself as the cat.

"Mightn't it be hard?" Felabba called after her. "Mightn't it be magic-hid?"

"Coming?" Javelle threw the lone word behind her heels as she snatched up a single fresh candlestick and rushed from the quiet room of dormant tapestries. "You don't want to miss anything."

She never looked back to see if the cat followed. Instead, she bolted up long-forgotten stairs to long-forbidden places —places that seemed permanently shrouded beneath a child's elaborate pall of dread.

Whether soft padded footsteps trailed her was irrelevant. She heard only the creaks and scrapes and long hushed silences of childish fears, felt the warnings reechoing in her ears: "You mustn't go—" "Stay away from—" "Never take this stair, that turning; never darken that threshold. . . ."

She didn't know if Irissa or Kendric—or Scyvilla—had uttered these proscriptions . . . or whether some distorted twist of memory was her only refuser. Whatever the source, these palace high places—these dark turning stairs . . . these forgotten towers and dusty rooms . . . these hideous, empty poignant spaces—warned her away even as she plunged higher and somehow deeper into them.

She became confused. Everything above a certain level was in disuse . . . it had been for years—and for decades before that. She tried to recall seeing an octagonal tower from the city streets, but could remember none. But perhaps the octagon was on the interior only.

She began to wonder which tower she climbed, even whether she climbed or descended. Her echoing footsteps became the only token of her progress, just as the candle flame's harsh sweep across age-dusted stones was her only light . . . and the haunting pursuit of her own shadow her only companion.

At last she had climbed so high that only one last door remained closed before her. When her palsied hand pushed on the ancient wood, it resisted opening.

Panting, she laid her cheek to its rough timber. "Thane?"

The name came out a whisper that a living person couldn't hear through fist-thick wood—why should a boy made of twisted threads two inches high in a room far below heed it?

"Louder."

She looked down to find the cat, sides heaving and tongue hanging, beside her. That the inherently idle creature had bestirred itself impressed Javelle with the urgency of her quest.

"Thane!" she shouted in the close remoteness of the tower stair.

"Go away." The faint reply leaked through the very woodgrain under her fingertips. "You can't help. Go away."

Javelle lowered her shoulders in an explosive sigh, then set the candlestick by her boot. Her shadow loomed grotesquely on the door. Javelle pushed into it, into that dark part of herself, the hard, closed, wooden facade of the door. Her hands clawed for handles and hinges, for locks that would turn and weight that would give way. She pushed so hard she felt her torso swell against the serpent belt until even the metal seemed to strain.

There was nothing for her senses to hold on to, but

perhaps something—her weight, her will—tipped the balance. The door faded from her path without a sound, and she was walking into a moonlit room . . . in a world that had no moon, had never had one.

But this is what moonlight would look like, Javelle decided, studying the icy blue-white light that gleamed like daggers on the edges of all eight stone windowsills.

Beyond the eerily lit sills shone the dim landscapes outside. Strange sights churned beyond each opening, but one was blocked by a human form, as a fly's trapped buzzing body interrupts the intricate tracery of a spiderweb.

Javelle ignored seven vistas of wonder and ran straight for the source of her worry.

"Thane, it *is* you!" She breathed relief to find him life-size and wedged into the windowframe. Beyond him the dark unrolled in great, noxious plumes, and eyes glimmered like dew on dawn-bright grasses. "You've found a gate where there is none—why?"

"Go back!" he spat, as usual—or perhaps more passionately than was usual. "I don't need you turning tables on me, following me. Go back, Javelle! And fear not. The gate won't take me, anyway."

"Then come back *with* me."

"I . . . will. In a while. Just leave now—while you can!"

"While *I* can? Then you . . . can't."

"Of course I can." He twisted like a fish on a line.

Javelle leaned closer to the window, though the whiff of fresh sulfur repelled her. A thin transparent film lay between her brother and the night Without. In that slick, almost-invisible surface, she saw a faint shadow of Thane —and a sticky, viscous material that webbed his hands and face and body. . . . She even saw the palest, vaguest shadow of herself.

"You can't leave, or you would have by now," Javelle realized even as she spoke. "You're . . . trapped."

"Trapped. Yes!"

"I must get help, then. Father. . . ."

"Not Father—Mother. Father doesn't—"

"Doesn't what?"

"Know . . . why. And he mustn't, Javelle," Thane pled, out of character. "As you've always loved him best and he you, keep this secret."

Silent, she couldn't say which assertion shocked her more—Thane's insistence that their father had no right to know of this attempt to prolong his life, or Thane's naming Javelle her father's favorite.

"You think Father wouldn't risk his very life to save you? Thane, you don't know him at all—"

"He would, of course he would. He will. That's why he mustn't know of this. Javelle, this is a window to Without! Only this one would open to me, of the eight, and now it will neither open fully—nor close. Mother begged me to find a gate from Rengarth, and I have. Perhaps she can find a way to free me—or at least a way to find the sword herself."

"What sword?"

"Father's sword." Thane panted, worn by the struggle of hanging between two worlds—and one of them deadly. "Not the mind-made one here—the original sword he left on Rule.

"It will extend the length of his life-thread as surely as confronting the dangers Without will snap it. Now leave me to my task—I got this far, I won't be stopped. Just . . . keep . . . quiet about this. Tell Mother, if you must, but don't upset her more than she already is."

"Mother—upset?"

"Haven't you noticed? She's worried about Father, ever since she saw that mortal years were taking their toll of him. Only the true, Rengarth-forged sword from Rule will give him a Torloc's longevity. But she can't find or cross a gate to go fetch it, not even she."

Javelle drew back, shocked. *"You* are her only hope, Father's only hope."

Thane resisted the web, tried to push himself forward into the darkness beyond. When that failed, he struggled to wrench loose, bucking against the invisible threads, not even seeing his shadow in the translucent veil.

Javelle moved toward the door. "I suppose I could get Mother. . . ."

Thane, rapt in his struggles, didn't answer.

She stood with her back to the threshold and those ranks of twisting stairs massed with all her childish fears behind her. There was nothing she could do. Thane had said so. She knew so. Mother would want to know, to hear, to help. As would Father, only he mustn't . . . for his own good. Father must hoard his own good . . . or die. Only he wouldn't, if he knew. And if she told . . .

Javelle shook her head. Too many shocks this one day. Too much lost. Her fingers felt ice-cold. She touched the metal snake at her waist and found it warm by comparison, even on the topmost scales.

Nothing she could do would help anyone. She was doomed to be a messenger bearing ill tidings of magic gone awry—Kendric's magic, that wouldn't do him the courtesy of extending his mortality . . . Thane's untried magic, which had ensnared him for trying too hard . . . even Irissa's magic, failing at last to preserve the one thing that meant most to her.

"I can't," Javelle told the windows beyond Rengarth. "I can't." Can't run and tell, can't help, can't do anything, and certainly can't use a magic she didn't possess. Useless. She was—the word formed in her mind like a curse—useless.

Her self-loathing found an echo. *Ussselesssss.* The word hissed around her like a wind, audible but disembodied. *Uselessss.* It keened into her mind with an alien voice—another's voice.

"Useless."

Javelle tightened. The cat at her feet hadn't spoken. Yet she heard the word as if it emanated from somewhere very near.

At her waist, the silver serpent stirred its metal scales. Her fingertips felt the cool rasp as it slithered from her waist and up her arm. Around her neck it coiled, nooselike, and insinuated its sleek metal head over the fleshy coils of her ear.

"Useless," it mourned into the seat of her hearing.

She sensed a kindred agony, much older than her own.

"Sssuch endlesss hopes. So many weary yearsss. Such promissse."

She glanced to her brother, to the cat. Only she seemed to overhear this dirge.

No, she thought. Nothing is as useless as all that. No one is useless unless unused. She felt a rising determination. Thane had achieved his mission. He had found the impossible—a gate from Rengarth.

Never mind that his gate led to the one place of all worlds most to be avoided—the world Without. Never mind that his attempt had webbed him in the curtain to that world.

Beyond the window awaited Without. Beyond Without —if one . . . or two . . . survived it—awaited more gates and more worlds. One of them was Rule and held the sword on which their father's life hung.

"I *will* help," Javelle spit between her teeth.

Before she could act on her intentions, while her will was still gathering and tightening, the snake stirred again as if roused by her resolve.

It writhed into her hair, making goosebumps rise on her scalp. It tangled its coils among her curled locks and untangled again to circle her skull. At last it came to rest—its smooth small-scaled metal belly over her forehead and its head hanging a bit heavy over her right ear.

Javelle had heard the tales of her birth—how Kendric had tried by force to wrest the birth-snake from her body, how it had settled at her temples like a scaly crown. Later, when she was again inspected, it had retreated elsewhere on her person. Never did it aspire to her head again . . . until now.

Old words from a bitter prophesy echoed in her mind. "—she shall bear a greater magic than any in Rengarth . . ."

Not within! Without! Outside herself. Not *in*born, but *beside*-born! The Overstone egg had delivered its own offspring the same moment Javelle took independent breath in this world of Rengarth. *She* could open the gate her parents sorely needed, because she had always carried the key.

Javelle moved to the window, slowly, purposefully. Thane shouted at her to go back, but she hardly heard him. She heard instead a dry, satisfied hum in her ear, in her heart. Now she knew.

"Thisss," said the voice at her ear. "For this I was born."

The Overstone snake lifted its glittering head, its darting tongue sniffing the sulfurous air as Javelle approached the veil between Rengarth and Without. The web dissolved without warning. Aghast, Thane caught himself a moment before falling through.

"You! You opened it! Thank you, sister; now stand back and don't breathe a word of this, except to Mother. But I think she will know."

He braced himself with one last look back before leaning into the roiling darkness Without.

Javelle jumped to the windowsill beside him.

"No! Don't follow." His spring was already in motion— he was plummeting into a new, unknown tapestry of dark and danger and vast empty places, growing smaller every instant as if shrinking into some new, unilluminated tapestry.

Javelle leaped, too, for the first time in her life breaking custom. For once, she followed Thane—impulsively, determinedly—right through the window into Without.

No wind howled in the room. No storm broke loose beyond the windowframe. No new figures grew visible in the dark it bounded.

The cat sat for some moments regarding the dark window, as if watching a mouse hole in hopes of the imminent reappearance of prey. Then it sighed audibly, with a peculiar, catlike trill.

"I suppose," it mused aloud to the empty tower, "that there's nothing else for it."

One bound brought it atop the windowsill. Moonlight from a source other than a moon painted it a softer shade of white.

The cat lifted a paw that had landed on some sticky fallen web filaments, then gathered its limbs into a taut assemblage of furred muscle and sprang gracefully through the window into the dark.

CHAPTER

12

KENDRIC SAT UP, MOANING IN LOUD SURPRISE. THE FISH that flitted within the bedchamber walls boiled in their lucid waters until he subsided.

"You must rest," Irissa advised softly, leaning over him.

Kendric recognized a tone he had heard applied to sick children and brushed the suggestion aside.

"I must have gotten chilled in the water, that is all."

He stood—or tried to—then sank back onto the great circular bed. "A stiffness. I feel as if I'd been beaten with thistleweed cudgels."

Irissa was expertly plucking at the bedclothes, drawing them over him. He'd seen that maneuver before, too.

"I'm not . . . sick, only—" he repeated, then stopped. The proper word wouldn't come. He had never felt as he felt now. Not just tired, but exhausted. Not cold, but frozen to the marrow. Not worn, but worn . . . narrow.

"Rest," Irissa insisted in a pleasant lulling monotone.

Everything seemed to have drawn back from Kendric's body. Even the bedclothes had shrunk from his skin. He felt that he still floated in some dark, alien substance that was half-water, half-air, as Rengarth itself was half-liquid, half-land.

"What's this?" Irissa was asking, the soft pillow of her palm resting on his shoulder. An ache had settled there that her flesh warmed.

"A bruise, no doubt," he admitted lightly. "That devil swanfish didn't bite, but it thrashed more than a mite. It flailed like a convention of whips . . . head, fins, tail, everything."

Irissa nodded absently, hearing Kendric's voice soften into sleep. No wonder his shoulder hurt, she thought as she let the linen softly drape it. A bruise as large as her hand already marked the skin with lurid Iridesium shades of purple, saffron, and green.

Kendric's eyes had shut. His hair, still damp, looked blacker against the pale pillows. The cowl of wet gray strands around his face shone bright as polished silver.

Frowning, Irissa skimmed fish-silent from the chamber. Thane, she decided, must not fail in finding a gate. And quickly. The halls were unpeopled as she rustled through them. The entire palace exuded a subdued air. Perhaps the tale of Kendric's battle with the tainted fish in their very midst had sobered the inhabitants.

Javelle's white, worried face—as it had looked at the dungeon spring—lilted to the forefront of Irissa's memory like a wailwraith's visage rising from a pondtop to frighten an unwary passerby.

Irissa paused, her hand on a wall supporting her. Deep alarm thrummed through her frame—not a magical alert, but more vague and therefore more disturbing. Instinct, that most human and arbitrary of skills, was pulling steadfastly on the sleeve of Irissa's attention.

She hurried to her receiving room. She could deal with whatever had upset Javelle later. First, she must find Thane, and ensure that he would find a gate. Otherwise—

Irissa froze on her own familiar threshold. The candles

were lit, wavering merrily against the curtained walls. The room was empty—and Thane would never have left without finding a gate or reporting failure directly to her.

Irissa moved to the table at the room's center. Some impish wind delved among the weavings, making the one-dimensional towers swell, woven waves crest, and small thread-dressed figures shift in their flat, hanging worlds.

Irissa shivered, feeling the Iridesium circlet tighten on her brow, as it did when she felt anxious. Her own domain seemed cold and abandoned and somehow hostile.

"Ah." A voice behind her sounded the genteel triumph of having found her. She turned to see a ludborg in the doorway blissfully nodding its empty hood.

"Good evening, Reginatrix. Scyvilla has sent me to announce that he is, ahem . . . assembling . . . one of his dinners to celebrate our deliverance from the devil swanfish."

"Dinner." The word was too simply domestic to mix with Irissa's darker instincts at this moment. "Kendric is . . . fatigued. I think another day—"

"Ah." The hood nodded sagely—or perhaps Irissa only attributed some change of expression to that expressionless hollow of cloth. "I doubt not that the innovative Scyvilla can keep his conjurings fresh under a casting crystal for another day."

The ludborg turned to go, then directed a slice of its empty hood and a parting thought over its curving shoulder.

"Besides," it added, "the young ones were nowhere to be found, and a family celebration would be hardly that without them."

"Nowhere?" Irissa's sharply sounded question pinned the ludborg to the threshold like an arrow through the sleeve.

"You sound . . . alarmed, dear Reginatrix. I would exile myself to the Bubblemeres were I to cause you needless worry. Scyvilla himself assures me that such young people are prone to sudden disappearances—and as sudden reappearances."

"Nowhere?" Irissa repeated, a bit nervously. "In the palace, you mean—?"

"The palace, the stables, the marketplace. We have a thousand hidden eyes and ears, my kind and I, and a certain instant communication is possible through the blue-worms. They are nowhere about—in any place we might look. No doubt they will reveal themselves at their whimsey, as many times before."

"No doubt." Now Irissa's voice faded in its turn. An invisible web of worry was pushing her a step back from everything around her.

The ludborg's hood gave a departing jerk that was meant to convey confidence or farewell or simply an itch within its commodious robes. Then it was gone and Irissa was alone with greater foreboding than she had sensed before.

Almost immediately she noticed a snuffed candelabra on the floor, its wicks like tiny wrought-iron tines jousting the air. She bent to retrieve it and ran her fingertips over the burnt ends. Cold and ashy, they smudged her fingers.

She knew why it—and the other candelabra that still flickered—had been lit: to lighten the room as sunfall darkened it. Thane must have still been in residence then. Then why had these candles—and they alone—been snuffed? And when?

Deliberately, she moved to a wall-mounted sconce. One by one the blackened wicks growing from her hand bowed to take flame from the lit taper.

She could have used a more magical and therefore more spectacular method to relight the candles, but she didn't want her magic to overpower any traces that remained of what had recently transpired in the room. She sought a kind of common logic that had naught to do with magical shortcuts.

Returning to the central table, Irissa set the candelabra down. Its flickering light revealed several fresh, fine white scars curving into the glossy dark wood. Her wetted fingertip elevated one to the light. A white cat hair.

Irissa smiled. Better. Thane had not been alone. The cat that claimed to be Felabba had been with him.

The restless chamber wind whipped past, forcing the candle flames sideways until they pointed like long-nailed fingers—pointed to the walls.

Not magic again, but instinct, made Irissa regard her tapestries. She had purposely kept this room bare and self-contained. The hangings she had woven from her fingers and memories were the only furnishings beyond a few tables and chairs and the tapestry screen itself.

The only life in the room wavered among the gently stirring tapestries, in the woven images that trembled under the candles' nervous illumination.

Memories shifted there, coming to eerie life more than they ever had before . . . simply because some gate in Irissa was open wider—as she skeined through threads and thoughts for her son—than it ever had been before.

Perhaps her worry over Kendric, broadened now by her unease at the children's absence, Thane's absence from this room, had opened a chasm in her emotions into which thoughts, insights, magical impulses, and some awful overwhelming dread were pouring in a jumble of glancing images.

A Swallowing Cavern of the self spawned and spit out and blended the images interchangeably, so Irissa found herself lost in the past scenes she had woven, standing under the suns of other days and dreaming through the moons of other nights in rapid succession.

The heavy hangings drifted around her like veils. She saw through their muted shades, her vision pierced by the metallic twang of threads that rang particularly true—the sound of a moonweasel slither across the forest floor recalled exactly, the way Kendric's laughter echoed from everything around him no matter what the world . . . the sun glancing off of Ivrium's Iron Tents, the glint of Chaundre's seeing devices slipping down his long and crooked nose . . . the smell of the burning forest of Edanvant, of her mother Jalonia's salad-scented hands, of black-mouthed Javelle when she had ravished the ebonberry preserves when she was three. . . .

Above all, Irissa sensed the sight, sound, scent, feel of Thane's sympathetic magic woven into the air of Rengarth since he had been born. . . .

She stiffened, ignoring the tapestries' unreal swell, as if she drew their specters to herself, or they drew her own ghosts into themselves. Amid the many things sensed and seen and simply remembered, one vital, unique thread was gone, had snapped. The lead of her son's magic, so linked to hers by birth, by nature—was gone.

Thane was gone.

Irissa beat her way through the distance between the walls and herself, flailed through shifting membranes of memory and magic. A ghost among the ghosts she had woven from her past, she moved toward a Spectral City of her own creation.

Transparent as samite scarves, the tapestries billowed around her. Kendric brushed her arm in the Inlands. Felabba bounded against her knee in Rule. Finorian tapped her shoulder with a long, bony finger in Edanvant. Her father, Orvath, shrugged and shoved her toward an open window in Citydell. . . .

Yet none of it was true contact, not even with the tapestries themselves. Irissa flailed around the room, reaching blindly for some trace of Thane, some thread that she could pull and reel him back to her by.

All threads intertwined, all threads made a bramble-wall of sovereign pattern. Irissa pushed through filmy veils that never settled to reach yet another woven world. A forgotten face of Rengarth confronted her—wing-borne swan-spawn black against the three-sunned sky . . . a bearing-beast with a scimitar of horn in mid-forehead treading the clouds . . . behind it all a darkness, a telling absence, a Thing that even she had not dared to weave directly into the tapestry.

Thane, she thought, hearing the word echo within her head like a plea. She peeled away several more veils to seek the emptiest of her reconstructions, and thus the most dangerous.

She had paused in weaving the tapestry of the tower room, she remembered. She had wondered if she should include at least the sinister flat oblong of the birthing box. No . . . better forgotten. A vignette of that unnatural foursome—she and Kendric and Geronfrey in all his velvet-gloved power and that . . . Other? No . . . all better banished.

So she had left the tower room empty, caught somewhere between who and what had contended there—and what would happen there after . . . if ever.

Irissa numbered the woven windows, glimpsing all the worlds she and Kendric had visited—and shared with the sorcerer Geronfrey, sometimes unwittingly—including this one of Rengarth. At the last, the eighth window, her eyes stopped their anxious roving.

Something pulled her to it. Instinct again, pure and not so simple.

The window to Without was Iridesium-black and stormy. No wonders lurked beyond it, only darkness. Except . . . Irissa came close enough to warm the interlaced threads with her breath.

Two pale motes—a mere cluster of stitches finer than gnat legs—lay embedded against the darkness Without. They were delicately done, enough to show detail in wondrous miniature, beyond the skill of an ordinary needle, beyond Irissa's intention or ability.

Two infinitesimal, lost figures drowning in the dark sea of Without. Thane—falling. Javelle—falling. And one last pale stitch, hardly bigger than a period in a parchment, too small to even name.

Realization swathed Irissa, wrapping her in skeins of the past, skins of herself peeled from many moments in many worlds. She grew too tangled to move. Her mouth opened to scream but only a sigh came.

And then blackness came, only blackness yet not black enough . . . because it was not from the world Without, but the world Within. Irissa darkened to her own speculations, and hid from them inside herself.

Kendric wakened in the morning to the birds stirring above the ceiling-hung cradle of netting.

They moved in the air like fish in the water, darting past in flocks, weaving in and out the open windowslits as if dodging constructions of coral.

It was a particularly peaceful way to awaken, but even twenty years in Rengarth had never made Kendric feel quite, well . . . certain . . . that birds that roosted in the palace eaves would remember to exit before relieving themselves.

He stirred and made the usual motions to rise. This morning every gesture rubbed him the wrong way. Every muscle, every joint, every scrap of flesh seemed reluctant to do its part in the common task of rising.

He forced himself upright and began to dress, observing the lurid bruises blossoming on his limbs and torso. He rushed into his clothing, hoping that Irissa wouldn't notice these badges of a battle she would regard as rashly undertaken in the first place.

Then he glanced at the bed, at the bunched feather quilt he had taken for Irissa's sleeping form.

She wasn't there.

He pulled back the quilt, rifled the bedlinens, unwilling to believe his eyes. Irissa had always been there, every morning of their lives together in Rengarth. Always. Some things were as immutable as sunrise and sunfall. He always woke first, and Irissa was always there.

Today she was not.

He finished dressing, unmindful of the snaps and strains of hasty movement. Then he went, ice in his veins, to find Irissa.

"No, no, we haven't seen her," the cook and helpers chorused in the kitchens. "Not in the larder, either."

"Not in the garden," said the slightly shriveled ludborg who tended to such matters. "Scyvilla? I know not, Ruler."

Kendric finally found the ludborg in question crouched at the lip of the dungeon spring, holding a candle over the murky water.

"Irissa," Scyvilla said absently upon being questioned. "No, not here. I've been alone here all the night."

That distracted Kendric.

"Alone here, all night? Why?"

Scyvilla's long sleeve—the pointed ends were soaking wet, Kendric noticed—lifted lugubriously to point to the swanfish carcass.

"The townsfolk must have been too superstitious to cart it away. I'll have it removed at once," Kendric said. "I would have seen to it yesterday, but was . . ."

"Fatigued," the ludborg put in mournfully.

"Yes."

"Worn to bone."

"Tired, but that is only to be expected—"

"When one wrestles a demon."

"Yes." Kendric heard a defensive edge in his voice he

didn't like. "What are you doing here?"

"Testing the water to see if the taint prevails."

Kendric pointed at his vanquished foe. "The source is dead and gone."

"But it infected the water, you know. Of course you know. You must have swallowed some of it." Scyvilla's faceless hood twisted to angle directly toward Kendric's face, as if confronting him about something.

"Some." Kendric frowned to remember the bitter taste that had coated his mouth after the encounter . . . that still tainted his mouth and throat. "Your experiments can wait, Scyvilla. I must find Irissa before I worry about swanfish taint."

"I do not conduct experiments. I know the damage that has been done. I seek merely to discover if the city folk are in danger as well."

"Perhaps you do not understand me. Irissa is missing. Irissa is not to be found in any of the places she would be on arising."

"Have you looked in places where she would not be at such a time?"

Kendric studied Scyvilla's perpetually eclipsed face. In the ludborg's dark empty visage he read his own slow thoughts.

"Where she would *not* be! Of course. . . .Thank you, Scyvilla!"

Kendric forced his leaden legs up the dungeon stairs three at a time. He raced, through the pounding of his pain, up narrower and narrower sets of stairs until he reached Irissa's receiving room. It was only in midafternoon that she came here, but this was also the only place he had not looked for her.

And he found her.

"Irissa!" Relief lightened his steps as he crossed the threshold. "You are up and weaving as early as a spider."

She started guiltily, half-rising from behind her tapestry stand. He saw a length of rudely woven fabric, saw an emerald-green glitter among the pattern.

"You must have risen early," he restated.

"Yes," she agreed, sinking back onto her stool as if too weary to stand.

Kendric felt more than ordinarily winded himself. He leaned against the central stone-based wooden table and regarded her.

The room, with its windows still shuttered, was lit by guttering candles. In that ebb and flow of sickly light, Kendric saw that Irissa's hands and face were both a cold wax-white. Her silver eyes shone dully in a tarnished setting—the shadows hollowed out around them.

"Sudden inspiration," he suggested, nodding at the rumpled cloth before her. "One cannot argue that. But"— Kendric twisted his stiff neck to survey the tapestries on the chamber walls—"where will you put another hanging? There is no room. And I thought the series complete?"

"The past is never complete as long as there is a present. And I will find a place," Irissa answered tightly.

He turned back to the walls, trying to locate a space for an addition. Behind him, Irissa rustled over.

"You needn't scout a vacancy. That's my worry. And you know these scenes by heart, don't waste your time eyeing them when you should be below seeking breakfast."

The words reminded Kendric that something empty occupied his center. Ordinarily, the mere suggestion of breakfast would have sufficiently diverted him. He knew that, and Irissa knew that—too well.

He looked into her eyes, which immediately darted away. She smoothed the lay of his tunic.

"A sudden inspiration," Kendric said.

"Go to breakfast. I'll be down in a bit. You went to bed without dinner last night."

"And when did you dine—or breakfast?"

"Before," she said lightly, moving away.

"Irissa!" He thundered her name, standing, even though needles of discomfort pierced every inch of his body. "You have never not quite lied to me before."

She turned back. "You think I'm lying?"

"I know you're not lying. But you've never been so . . . careful . . . to *not* lie to me before. It doesn't make sense, but I sense it. Irissa, what is wrong?"

Her face shattered like one of Scyvilla's casting crystals at the moment when it destroyed itself to reflect a few narrow splinters of truth.

"Irissa—?" He wanted her to tell him that nothing was wrong.

"Everything," she admitted.

"Everything?" Kendric was bewildered. "That is so unlike you, to talk of trouble in such blanket terms. You are the one who can reach into a knapsack of sunshine at every dark crossroad, who can weave the world around you to the shape of your will. You are the one who accepts nothing as a barrier. How can you say everything is wrong?"

"Because it's all my fault."

Kendric sat again, against the table edge that was pressing a groove into his bruised buttocks. "Tell me," he said simply.

She returned to the tapestry stand, as if looking for words woven there that had escaped her. Her fingers treaded the ridges of interwoven thread. Kendric suddenly realized that this fresh swatch of tapestry was a prodigious amount of work for Irissa to have accomplished so quickly, even if she had sat up all night.

"You are right," she began, "the walls are full." Her eyes took bittersweet inventory of the hangings all around them.

Kendric couldn't take his eyes off Irissa, not even to refresh his memory of the hangings. He had never seen her so hopeless before, so . . . wearily ashamed.

"And yet, the walls are empty," she continued, her voice as vacant as her words. "I didn't want you to see it, what I was doing. But you might as well. I knew you would have to know eventually. I just hoped the worst would be over and the end would be so . . . joyous that you would overlook the means."

He had arrived beside her by the time this speech was done, worry gnawing harder on his stomach than hunger. Irissa was not one for slow speeches, either, Kendric knew. Then he glanced down and saw the awful, familiar figure shaping itself in her work.

"You've never—" he began.

"I know."

"Why now?"

"I . . . need it."

"Why?"

"To do that which you won't like."

"Which is—"

"To pass through a gate from Rengarth."

"To—where?"

"Rule, I thought."

"Rule? And aren't you certain?"

"Now? No. . . ."

"When *were* you certain?"

Her eyes finally met his with an expression that was desperate, sad, and yet defiantly rueful. "Yesterday," she said.

Kendric regarded the darkly glittering figure she had woven into the tapestry. The background was barely etched, but the figure was worked with startling detail.

"Life-size," he noted. "Even I was not so honored in your hangings."

"You would have overgrown the space," Irissa returned with a hint of her usual humor. Then her expression dulled again. "And it must be *exactly* life-size."

"Why? Why now, Irissa, why resurrect that which has

been dead for nearly two decades? That which never really lived? It can't serve you well. It can't serve *us* well—"

"It *will* serve," Irissa insisted. Her hands fisted into the tapestry, puckering the cloth and making the jewels sprinkled over the woven figure sparkle.

Kendric studied the gemstones, recognizing colors leeched from the Iridesium circlet at Irissa's temples. No wonder she looked so drained! None of her magic had been used to weave the tales the other tapestries told. This . . . new experiment was fashioned of *all* magic.

"Why?" he demanded again.

"I was not the only one missing this morning."

"Who else?"

"Kendric, I would give my eyes to not tell you—"

He caught her arms in an embracing grip. "Keep your eyes and just give me answers, Irissa. The worst, tell me."

Her face shattered again, though some iron semblance of control still presided over its disintegration. Kendric prepared himself to learn what he would probably give his ears not to hear.

"They're gone, Kendric! Gone."

"Who?"

For answer she led him to the wall, to one tapestry—the hanging that showed an empty tower with eight windows each overlooking a different vista.

"I'd given him a task," Irissa began, the words tumbling forth now that she'd unstopped them. "A nigh-impossible task—to find a gate from Rengarth."

"Thane?" Kendric was beginning to sense the height, depth, and width of the tragedy.

"Thane. He was so . . . talented, so instinctive. I *knew* he could do it—"

"*Was?* Irissa, you speak as if he were dead—!"

Her head shook mournfully, and there was a flash of madness in her eyes. "Not dead. Only . . . gone."

"Then get him back!"

"I . . . will, only you must let me."

"Thane, gone. . . ." Kendric absorbed the news without question. Irissa had never lied to him—or anyone else. But he still didn't understand her response to that . . . devastation.

"Why are you showing me this empty tapestry, this old room where we once banished Geronfrey and saw her— that thing you weave into life again on your loom? We saw her die once, and yet again. Why do you evoke her now? You saw Geronfrey strike her dead to steal the breath of death from her body—that unborn babe he coveted so much he'd take it dead as well as alive."

"I must raise up old memories! There is a way for me to follow, to find my own gate. But I must have help. Her help."

Kendric frowned. "If Thane found a gate and took it, why are you so afraid that he can't return? He'll come back, Irissa! Why you think you must have a gate from Rengarth, I don't know, but if Thane is mage enough to find one, he's mage enough to return."

Hope lit her eyes to quicksilver. "You may be right. I perhaps have too little faith in him." Then her expression darkened again. "But, Kendric—"

"What?"

"Javelle doesn't have the skill to return, and if she and Thane are separated, if they separated in the gate, as you and I did once—"

"Javelle?" The news stunned him. "Javelle is gone as well?"

Irissa only nodded.

"You did say . . . 'they.' Both gone?"

With the worst known, Irissa straightened a little. She looked into Kendric's eyes and found—not the anger she dreaded—but a bewildered despair she found even harder to confront.

For once words wouldn't cross the threshold of her

tongue. She lifted his hand—he was so shocked that it hung heavy in her grasp—and put it to the tapestry, to the two tiny white figures against the dark background of a window.

He jerked slightly as his flesh touched the fabric, then his forefinger found the familiar forms. Lightning bolts of metallic thread danced in the stormy woven sky as Kendric's tracing fingers shook the tapestry.

"I can . . . see them." His words were reluctant. "Woven in. So . . . small. Not even as babes were they this . . . perfectly tiny. Irissa, what magical curse is this that sews our children into the dead skin of our earlier lives?"

"Curse, I hope not. Magic it is, yes. Thane's, I think, mostly. And then some other . . . element."

"Geronfrey?"

Irissa couldn't bear the baffled fury in Kendric's face. "No, I think not. I hope not." Her finger rested on a pinpoint of pale thread, one single stitch that had not been there before. "See here? I believe Felabba went through, too. Perhaps she helped open the gate, perhaps *she* left this . . . message in the tapestry."

" 'I think . . . I believe . . . I hope,' " he repeated. "Why don't you *know,* seeress? Your connivance led Thane to manufacture a gate and drag Javelle through with him. Am I supposed to rest easy because you 'think' Felabba is along?

"Worse and worse. That . . . callow meddler who doesn't even claim to be Felabba's shadow could be less use than its carping predecessor! Irissa, what have you done? Why have you done it? Can you undo it?"

"Yes! Yes, that's why I was working on the new weaving. There *is* a partial gate from Rengarth—in the Spectral City. Our friends there told me as much, but one can only pass through it if one is part spirit, so—"

Kendric shook his head. It buzzed as if a thousand flies

were eating his brain from the inside out. Even though his eyes discerned the unmistakable forms of Thane and Javelle in the tapestry, his heart refused to believe they had been reduced to a few tiny stitches in a vast plain of threads.

Irissa blamed herself, and he suspected she was right to do so, but he didn't want to add to the chorus of accusation, not when his own emotions were so unsteady.

"Perhaps you are right," he told her carefully, listening to his voice rasp in his ears as if spoken through iron filings. "Perhaps I am better off not knowing the worst."

"We are all better off not knowing the worst," another voice put in.

They turned to see Scyvilla hovering on the threshold, a smoky casting crystal in his grasp.

"But it is our fate to know," the ludborg continued in a heavy tone. He crossed the threshold in a smooth rolling motion. "And my fate to tell. I am afraid, friends, I come bearing dire news."

Scyvilla paused and his empty hood twitched solemnly from one to the other until the silence grew unbearable.

Irissa began laughing. She laughed until hands came and caught her . . . and voices jousted around her . . . and the figures in the tapestry came to life and laughed with her until they cried . . . and coldstone tears of every color piled so high in the room she could no longer see anything beyond the gorgeous glitter of her tears.

CHAPTER

13

THE WORLD WITHOUT WAS EMPTIER THAN ANY PLACE Javelle had ever imagined could be.

She crouched on solid *something* as if having landed there from a small leap downward, her fingertips lightly fanned on a surface that was hard, dark, and cold.

Darkness extended in all directions. Empty darkness.

"Thane?" she called. There was no answer, not even an echo.

Javelle stood in slow stages, feeling oddly unbalanced. No landmarks of up and down guided her motions. She wondered briefly if she had gone blind.

Then she turned and saw the tiny circle of lights in the inpenetrable distance. She almost toppled, the sight so startled her after the solid darkness.

But the lights were small, like the thick-clustered stars of other worlds that her parents had spoken of. She blinked, then shut her eyes. The lights' pinpoint brilliance pricked the dark behind her closed lids. She could follow their spark-lit path through her own inner dark as easily as through the vast outer dark of the world Without.

She began walking, each step a nervous assumption that the black surface beneath her feet would not fall away into greater darkness. Her thoughts grew as dark as Without.

I never should have meddled with Thane, she lectured herself. Never should have taken his mission so seriously. Never should have followed. Where *is* he now? More to the point, where am *I*? What will Father say when he finds out? Will he find out?

Perhaps Mother will come after and fetch us. But do I *want* to be fetched? Oh, yes! No—! It's all right, Javelle, you silly, the dark doesn't bite. . . .

Something nipped the outer rim of her ear. Javelle gasped and froze. Then something spoke.

"Don't fret. That was a pinch, not a bite. If I bit you, you would die, for I still bear the borgia taint I drew from your mother before both our births and will until I can release it into something deserving of it."

"Die?" Javelle was beginning to think that darkness was as close as anyone could get to death and still live. Yet any voice, however lethal, was welcome in it.

"Think of me as your guardian," the dry voice continued. "I will only bite in your defense, or my own. Ah, it's so good to be . . . alive, however briefly."

Javelle felt the serpentine circlet tighten around her temples. The snake's blunt metal head lifted off the ledge of her ear as if straining to survey the blackness.

"Biting is no doubt useful at times," Javelle ventured. "But what is there to bite here in this lightless land? Have you any other useful habits?"

"I should think opening a gate to Without was enough."

"*You* did that?"

"I and no other, not even your brother."

"Where is Thane?"

"I am not a cat. I do not see in the dark—and sometimes not even in the light."

"So you are only good for getting us into the dark, but

not out of it. To be so arbitrary, you must be magical, as Father would say." Javelle didn't wish to admit it, but she found it comforting to converse with something while treading the featureless murk.

"On the other hand," the snake hissed back, "I hear very well, even when . . . dormant. I have heard your father's theories on magic. For one so long-bodied, he is most short-sensed."

"Ah, but you do not say it to his face, do you? Why do you carry a borgia taint—and why speak now after such long silence?"

"The taint was passed to me by the Rengarthian poison-leeches who squeezed it from your mother long ago. She still carried you within her, and then just barely. The bad borgia flooded into my very birthing vessel. I, being a poison-leech myself, was untouched by the toxin. It shall stay safe within my scales until I find occasion to bite someone—perhaps in your defense. Then, if something venomous bites you, I shall be free to sip your poison away and hoard it until I find opportunity to rid myself of it again."

"Most generous." Javelle was impressed. "But what if I am bitten before you find reason to transmit your present poison elsewhere?"

"That would be . . . unfortunate. I would be unable to aid you, except to bite that which bit you in return. It would die a terrible death."

"I'm sure I'd be terribly grateful," Javelle said dryly.

The serpent took her thanks at face value and answered modestly, "Your mother bore me at her breast through three lands and many perils; it behooves me to avenge her daughter."

"Let's hope I don't require avenging for a while. Do you think those lights are getting larger?"

"No."

"Closer, I meant."

"I doubt it, but distances are not my strength. Nor is talking. The power of the gate ebbs and so must my voice."

Javelle sighed. A speaking snake that swallowed and spit out poison and also arranged itself artistically on her person was an amusing companion, but apparently not too useful a one.

She trudged on. The serpent subsided, apparently having exhausted its supply of chitchat after so many years of silence.

"At least I had more to do with opening the gate than Thane did, for all his imbred magic," Javelle mused aloud, aware also that no one would know to credit her for the deed—or, rather, her familiar's deed. Still, if she could find Thane and crow over him, it might be worth the risk of this catapult into Without.

"Wait!" The snake roused itself to drone authoritatively in her ear.

Javelle waited, wistfully eyeing the far ellipse of lights. She became aware of something eddying around her knees —something like a breeze or a current.

What moved in the dark so silently?

A great piece of that darkness erupted into sudden form—a massive, shapeless form that pushed her down and then rolled her over and over. All she could see were the occasional winks of spinning stars far away and three mean bright lights twinkling amber-red above her.

Air—hot, heavy, sulfurous—belched over her fallen form. It panted all around her and seemed to suck the breath from her body. At her ear, the snake hissed furiously, retreating with icy speed down her shoulder to her wrist.

Light seeped into the darkness—the murky red-gray glow of drying embers. Javelle saw clouded forms roiling at a distance and one great prowling cloud that stalked her with calculated aggression.

The cloud gathered into a huge, hump-shouldered shape, its brutish head lowered and the three eyes spark-hot among the stormy clouds. A slash of lightning seared from its opening maw, turning a murky world to a forge-bright furnace of heat and light.

Javelle threw her arm before her eyes without thinking. On her wrist, the serpent's coiled form gleamed in many pale, poisonous colors against her eyelashes. Its tiny jaws unhinged to reveal the silhouetted scimitars of its matched fangs.

On such a small scale, Javelle found this savage defense pitiful. And how could the snake strike something as insubstantial as a cloud-creature? She braced for the amorphous monster's full attack.

"Wait!" someone shouted. Some*one*. A person with a voice much like Thane's.

Javelle uncoiled from her defensive curl even as the cloud-beast rolled into its stormcloud self, its fire and lightning dampening.

The ember-glow persisted, radiating from the visible flock of clouds bouncing along the obsidian floor. Javelle stood up amid them, looking for the newcomer. Looking for Thane.

A gilt-haired boy came through the huddled mists— taller than Thane, a bit older than Thane, almost old enough to begin to call a man.

"You're not Thane." She hadn't meant to sound accusing.

He wasn't offended. "Are you sure?"

"Aren't *you?"* Now she sounded incredulous.

He thought a moment, narrowing eyes of light, silvery aqua. "My . . . father called me Eeryon."

"*Ear*ion."

"*Air*-ion," he corrected.

"My father named me Javelle. And my mother had something to do with it, too."

"Mother?" Eeryon sounded politely disinterested in Javelle's words, if not herself. His hand reached for her long hair. The serpent raised a hiss that sent chills down Javelle's spine.

The young man's hand retreated, but not the question in his eyes. "You're a woman," he said abruptly.

Of course I'm not, she almost answered. I'm just Javelle, she was about to explain, my father and mother's daughter, Thane's sister, someday heir to Rengarth . . . perhaps, and someday woman. Woman sounded far more serious than Javelle considered herself, or wished to.

She suddenly realized that to a stranger, seen apart from her family, she might indeed be considered a woman. She nodded uneasily, wondering where this interrogation would take her.

Eeryon smiled. "That's good. I've heard of them, of course. You don't seem so much different."

To that there was no answer, and it was odd, for although she felt herself very different from Thane—noisy, rude, teasing, childish, impossible Thane—she suddenly didn't seem much different from Eeryon. Or rather, he didn't seem much different from her.

"You've never seen any women?" she marveled.

"Father and I live here alone—except for the cloud-spawn, of course."

The attacking beast had shrunk to hound-size and was rubbing airily against Eeryon's hip. He ran his fingers through its vaporous mane as if he could feel it.

"Javelle. That's the third name I've ever heard. It's nice."

She shrugged. Her own name had ceased to intrigue her since it had become common to the tongues all around her. "Javelle, come here . . . Javelle, go . . . Javelle, do . . . oh, Javelle, don't . . . Javelle—now!"

"Only three names," she mused, struck by an oddity in what Eeryon had said. "You must mean yours, and your father's and now mine."

"My father has no name," Eeryon said abruptly, "that I

could report. Names are common, Father says. That's why I haven't named this." He patted the cloud-creature again.

"Then you and I must be equally common," Javelle said wryly.

"And this Thane," Eeryon added.

"My brother."

"Brother. I would like to meet a brother as well as a woman."

"So would I. Can you help me find him? We came . . . through together."

"Through?"

"A gate."

"A gate? But that's what I'm looking for! Do you know of one?"

"I know only that I . . . we . . . came through a gate and are now lost in the endless darkness."

"Oh, it's not endless, and it needn't be dark."

Eeryon hummed something at the clouds. They clustered together, swelling and shrinking like a bellows, fanning their inner embers of light into a rampant blaze.

"You have magic," Javelle accused, not knowing why disappointment stabbed her bitterly.

"Don't you?"

"No." She wasn't about to claim the serpent's skills for her own. Besides, it was dormant now, a piece of lifeless decoration. She didn't want to make herself ridiculous by ascribing powers to an insensate thing.

"Where do you think the gate was?" Eeryon moved to her side.

The cloud-creature accompanied him, forcing Javelle to edge away. Without knowing how, she found herself strolling toward the distant lights with them both.

"I don't know," she said. "I only saw the lights and thought something might be there. Why do you seek a gate, Eeryon?"

"I have a mission."

"So do we! Thane and I. For our father."

"And I also! For mine." Eeryon's face expanded happily, as it did with every similarity found or suspicion confirmed. Yet the expression was not quite a smile.

This Eeryon was pathetically easy to please, Javelle concluded, and far more polite than Thane. She studied the young man as he paced her, his thoughtful face illuminated by a soft miasma of clouds. Suddenly, she had new hope for Thane's eventual humanity.

"Perhaps we can find my brother and the gate together, if that's all right," she suggested.

"Of course. Besides, I am eager to learn more of women."

That, again. Javelle tried a safe question.

"What do you know of women already?"

"Nothing," he answered blithely.

"But . . . surely you had a mother."

She expected him to retort that "mothers" weren't women. It was the sort of thing Thane would say without thinking.

Eeryon stopped walking. "A mother? No. What is that?"

"Why . . . the opposite half of a father. The woman who bore you." Javelle was astounded that she should have to define the elementary.

"Bore me what?"

"Bore your . . . body, delivered it from her own; reared you from childhood, taught you to walk and talk and to see the world around you—"

"Father did all that."

"Not the . . . bearing part!"

"Perhaps. I don't know, I don't remember."

"Well, he couldn't have."

"My father can do anything."

"Not that."

"Yes, he could."

"Believe me, Eeryon, I know something about . . .

women, and a mother is as necessary as a father to a child, at least at the beginning. Perhaps yours died, or was lost."

The notion caught his mind and sent it bouncing after possibilities. "Why would Father have said nothing of it, then?"

"Likely her loss troubled him. I don't know what my father would do without my mother."

"What does he do . . . with her?"

"Lots of things. Rules a kingdom, rears Thane and myself, talks, argues sometimes . . . and other things."

"Other things?"

"Private things that I don't like to think about. It seems . . . undignified. But I do know that not even magic can create a person without a mother. You had to have had one, Eeryon, though like my father's mother, she may have died at your birth. Women do that now and again."

"It must be hard to be one," he said respectfully. "What is it like, this dying?"

Again Javelle stopped, aghast. "Haven't you ever seen anything die? Like a bearing-beast or a butterfly? A flower?"

Eeryon's hands spread to embrace the dark. "Everything here is . . . eternal. And the only things living I have seen besides Father and myself are the cloud-spawn. They change, not die."

"Oh. Well, dying is like . . . the dark, utter dark. I was just thinking that myself before you and your light came along."

"Then it's not so bad." Eeryon sounded relieved. He reached a finger to the serpentine bangle at Javelle's wrist.

"Careful! It's . . . sharp at the edges."

"What is it?"

"A . . . piece of jewelry."

Eeryon seemed puzzled until Javelle gestured at his somber garments, which glittered with silver stitchwork.

"Decoration." She stared ahead as the lights bobbled in her view. "Perhaps that's all those glimmers are, too—decoration."

"No." Eeryon squinted in their direction until his eyes seemed colorless. "I've never seen them before. I've never seen any light here that wasn't produced by my father or the fires stoked in the cloud-bellies."

Hopeful, Javelle increased her pace. Eeryon kept her easy company as the lights swelled into bubbles, then became illuminated globes the size of casting crystals.

Javelle stumbled on the smooth dark at her feet. Someone else was approaching the balls of light from the opposite direction, like a vague mirror image that moved off-step.

"Thane!" Her word of recognition fell leadenly in almost-empty darkness.

It was her brother, she saw as the figure converged on the bright congeries just as she and Eeryon did. Thane edged around the glowing balls that hung at shoulder level, light and shadow shifting across his face as he neared, making it momentarily unfamiliar.

"You followed!" was his accusing greeting. "Javelle, you shouldn't have. And who is this?"

"Eeryon. He lives here."

"In Without?"

"Your 'Without' is my 'Within,'" Eeryon said calmly. "This is the lost brother you mentioned?" he asked Javelle.

Before she could answer, Thane did. "I wasn't lost. She was." He turned back to her. "If I find the gate back, you must return through it immediately."

"If," Javelle sniffed. "And how will you open it again without my aid?"

"As I would have had your aid not interfered with me before."

Eeryon had edged away during their debate. Now he circled the globes, staring into their inner curves.

"Who is he?" Thane asked suspiciously, under his breath.

"A native of this . . . nothing . . . world. He seeks a gate to another world, just as we do."

"You didn't tell him of my mission?"

"Only that we wanted gates."

"Don't trust this stranger."

"But if he can help us?"

"Better we help ourselves."

"Oh, is it 'we' again?"

"For now." Thane glowered, then stalked over to Eeryon, who was staring into the most subdued of the globes. "What do you see?"

"Nothing." Eeryon looked up curiously. "All the other globes teem with tiny scenes of worlds and of alien wonders. This one is blank, empty—alone of the eight balls."

"Eight?" Javelle came over. "There were eight windows in the tower."

"You think these . . . bubbles are all that remain of those magical windows?" Thane said. "That would be nonsense. We have not grown so large simply by thrusting ourselves through a gate."

"Perhaps the worlds we left have shrunken." Javelle leaned over a nearby globe. "Perhaps all worlds seem this puny against the great Dark that imbues Without."

She studied the flitting scenes that sparkled inside the crystal contours of light. "This looks like the Inlands, as Father described parts of it."

"And this is likely Edanvant, this emerald glitter of forest," Thane added, eyeing another floating globe. He moved to inspect yet another and took an audible breath. "Rule! Or what is left of it."

"But where is Rengarth?" Javelle was circling the clustered balls, looking into seven wondrous eyes of light and one milky cataract of obscured vision.

"Rengarth?" Eeryon sounded startled.

"Rengarth," Thane repeated. "Does the name mean something to you?"

"Not the name. I am given no names except my own. But Javelle sounded like she missed it when she spoke, that's all. I wondered what kind of a place one would . . . miss."

"Home," Javelle answered promptly. "Won't you miss . . . this when you find your gate and leave it?"

"I don't think so. But you don't want to go back already, do you?" His questing eyes moved from sister to brother.

"No!" Thane was definite.

"No. . . ." Javelle was less certain. "Not until we accomplish our task."

"Task." Eeryon's gaze left the vacant globe. Its opaque glassy stare seemed to have sucked his eyes empty of color, until they were all pupil, all dark. "It's true, we have a similar task—"

Thane turned on Javelle. "You *did* tell him—!"

"We all seek a gate from here to elsewhere," Eeryon intervened, unaware that he did so. "After we find it, our paths will follow their own lead."

"I hope so." Thane frowned at the circled globes, the only light in the ever-encroaching darkness. "If these are the eight tower windows seen from Outside in, how will we pass to another world unless we squeeze ourselves to the size of marsh-midges?"

"We must begin by going someplace other," Eeryon declared. "Perhaps we must make that place swell to accommodate us."

"How?" Thane challenged.

Eeryon snapped his fingers, an odd gesture, for the sound fell flat in the vast unpopulated emptiness.

A snarl of dark cloud came bounding out of the deeper darkness, its eyes glimmering in a triangle of points. Thane reached for the short dagger at his belt, uncertain whether he should draw it or not. But the form brushed past him unheeding.

Eeryon never commanded the cloud-creature aloud; it leaped as if on its own volition into the heart of the illuminated globes.

Then its mobile shape expanded and it swallowed one crystal whole—a limpid, buoyant world as brittle as a bubble. Cloud-mist swirled within the globe, stretching it. The shiny pictured surface pulled tauter than skin. Images grew and blurred. Color dissipated. Shadow scenes and spectral figures thinned like fog.

The globe belled out beyond the other globes, pushing past the three young people—encompassing everything, even the dark. Javelle felt the brushing of a veil—and sensed a sudden hush.

They stood within the cloud, all three, within the expanding globe. She reached for Thane and instead clutched the velvet-sleeved arm of Eeryon. Another hand grasped her serpent-bound wrist from the other direction.

Linked, swaddled in mist and filtered light, the three felt the darkness lift and scatter, flap away like a great dark bird. Beneath their feet the ground grew warts and bumps. Sounds bleated in the distance and overtook them.

And air—cold air slipped through their mutual fog, sharp as frozen knives. At their feet, the cloud that was Eeryon's pet congealed into a coarse-haired form that juggled a growl at the back of its throat.

Something else took shape in the new world—or appeared—as the clouds of Without vanished.

CHAPTER
14

KENDRIC LAY ABED, ENGULFED BY A FEVER THAT DID NOT flush him so much as tarnish him.

Irissa paced and wrung her hands white, the gesture putting into red relief the measles of needle pricks infecting her fingertips.

Even Scyvilla paced, in a queer rolling motion that seemed like the hushing of some deep sorrow.

Kendric's collapse had coincided with Scyvilla's arrival and Irissa's bleak hysteria in the room of many tapestries. Now only aimlessly fanning fish stirred on the surrounding bedchamber walls, where a party of ludborgs had smoothly borne Kendric's unconscious form.

Irissa paused, lifting one of Kendric's hands. Fingerprints mottled the skin—gloriously colorful bruises black as ebony and blue as night skies and green as foreign seas and yellow as a sunfall horizon. Poisonous, venemous bruises tricked out in the hues of many shades of toxicity. His body was tattooed with them.

"No one," Irissa swore, pacing, "can convince me that

180

this great thrashing ... feathered fish ... could inflict so many subtle hurts."

"The bruising is a symptom," Scyvilla put in wearily, "of what I saw reflected in my casting crystal. 'Tis a pity he sleeps. I wanted to do a personal reading. It might ... make matters clearer."

Irissa swirled to a stop before the ludborg's ambiguous figure. Its overall rotundity framed the smaller circle of a silver-blue casting crystal rife with other colors, just as swelling colors bruised the black Iridesium banding Irissa's forehead. Hair tendrils twisted around her face like serpents.

With one blow, her fist crashed into the crystal's fragile surface.

"Read now. For me."

"Scyvilla's hood opening cinched as if to squeeze out the sight of fragmenting glass and flying drops of blood.

"Not so harsh and so hasty, seeress," he moaned, bending to watch the settling shards. "Better the crystal break of its own inner tension than be broken. I can't say good will come of such a forced scrying."

Irissa paced and sucked her pierced fingertips with a heedless, childish intensity. "Read, anyway. There is no Eye of Edanvant here and I dare not delve into my own inner self, it is so torn in so many directions. Read, I beg you, Ludborg," she urged, forgetting that he had not borne that name in almost two decades.

She finally crouched alongside him, her silver eyes knife-sharp in their edged despair. Her voice cut, too, low and vibrant, painful as broken glass.

"What must I do?" she whispered. "Complete the blasphemy of my weaving and revive my shadow self from the tapestry to pass a well-gate to Without? Follow Thane and Javelle? Or cast myself in another direction to preserve Kendric from this alien taint? Or ... stay here and save him better? Whom do I serve best—and how, and where?"

Even the dark within a ludborg's hood seemed to shrink from Irissa's penetrating agony of indecision. Scyvilla lowered his hood to the shattered glass, then spoke.

"Pick one shard," he advised, "for each person you seek to save, including yourself."

Irissa's hand hesitated over the glittering array, the ring on her middle finger wheeling through its range of colors. Everything within and without her seemed in flux, as liquid as her will and as quicksilver as her eyes.

She finally seized a long, wedge-shaped splinter. "Read for Kendric first, as you intended to do when you found us."

The hood nodded noncommittally. "Blade-shaped, like a sword. A good choice. But *you* must read for all."

"I?" Irissa glanced over her shoulder to the bed as if haunted. "I am empty now of all but anxiety. That does not make for accurate future-telling, Scyvilla."

"I am a mere crystal-bearer. You know that, Lady Longitude. I carry the crystals and shepherd the shards to wholeness again when the violence of reading is done. I myself have never seen more in the glass than a remote twinkle."

"But this time you saw something! This time you brought the globe to us, bearing dire news with it."

"Bearing dire *fear*," Scyvilla corrected. "All I *saw* was the clear blue of the glass run riot with a rainbow of other colors. I saw the taint, that's all, not any specifics of that toxicity. Read, seeress, the scenes you see in this broken carnival of glass."

Irissa reluctantly bowed her head to the long triangular shard that lay across her bloody palm like an ice dagger. First, she saw that Scyvilla was right: the glass, once a translucent crystal blue, had gone gaudy. Ghostly bruises marred its silvery surface, as if it had been fumed by some poisonous plume of vapor.

Yet . . . even in this diminished state, Irissa could spy a small scene trembling within the limpid colors.

"A bier," she said. "This shard is bier-shaped and that is what I see, a bier with Kendric on it, Kendric wearing an Iridesium skin as if it were mail and as still as death."

"And . . . nothing more?"

"Is that not enough?" Irissa had not raised her head or her voice, but the words were sufficiently terrible to make Scyvilla's hood quiver.

There was no answer. She lay the shard softly down. Her fingers hesitated over the other splinters, as if the mere chance of her choice could influence the reading's outcome.

In a moment she had elevated another glass sliver, this one needle-fine.

"You narrow your field of view," Scyvilla commented.

"I have seen too much already," she replied. Then she gathered herself and lifted the thread of glass to the aquatic light glowing from the fish-filled walls.

"Javelle," she said, and sighed. She stared deep into that silvery stiletto of glass. It seemed like peering through the narrowest windowslit onto a countryside she was leery to see in more than such mere slivers of view.

Irissa nodded. "I see Javelle at a mirror—a thin dark mirror that holds her shadow. Or is it myself I see? I am the one who once was held in thrall to a Dark Mirror! *I* am the one with shadows—why should Javelle be thus plagued? Is there no end to the consequences set in motion so many worlds and years ago?"

"There is no end to consequence," Scyvilla whispered hoarsely, "and if you have assigned this shard to your daughter, be assured that what you see in it relates to her."

"Impetuous Javelle," Irissa said sadly, "always flying in the face of her own future to shape it to her wants instead of her needs. Why must *she* tread the dark paths of Without and meet herself in mirrors? Without magic she is a voice keening in the night."

"You see nothing but darkness in these shards?"

Irissa nodded. "There is a slim silver thread that shifts within the shard. Sometimes it shapes the shadow in the mirror, sometimes it wraps Javelle in lightning strokes of illumination." She lay the second shard beside the first. "I fear it is nothing more than a flaw within the glass."

Scyvilla nodded his lowered hood to the piled shards. "Again."

Irissa picked up another quickly, as if drawing lots. "Thane," she declared, a tremor in her voice. "Hope, perhaps."

The piece was many-angled, with five sides, none of them even. Irissa elevated it, looked through it, into it. She nodded. "Thane. I see him reaching for a sword set high on a wall! Then he will find Rule, find the first sword that Kendric carried—!"

Irissa's excitement ebbed. She looked into the deep well of Scyvilla's shadowed hood, wishing for once to see a spark of light or life there. What passed for his face remained blank and her eyes were drawn bitterly to the glass again.

"But . . . all is altered now. What good is the possession of a sword reputed to prolong life if that life has already met its end? Thane risks himself, Javelle endangers herself, on a pointless mission—one I prodded them to. In seeking to save one, I have lost all, perhaps forever."

Scyvilla's sleeve end nudged the glass pile, making the fragments chime together. "You have yourself still, seeress. Pick a shard and read your own fate. Perhaps that one you will see the clearest."

"Perhaps." Irissa glanced to the bed. "That is touchword of all magical hopes. Perhaps. Kendric was right; perhaps is a fragile pillar to build a life upon."

"Still, the shards are here, as you are. And he . . . as well, still. Perhaps you should not let your pessimism predict the future but allow your eyes to glimpse some vista you will like better than 'perhaps.' "

"Even Kendric could not slice a hair with a sword, yet the rituals of magic sliver hopes finer than any thread." Irissa sighed doubly deeply and lifted a last shard—an hourglass-shaped piece that glittered madly as she moved it.

"Time is the key to my riddle, that the glass knows," she admitted. "And within my time I see . . ." She stared into the fragment for moments that became minutes.

Scyvilla finally stirred and spoke, a note of pleading in his voice. "Seeress. Share your private view. You have never read the shards for yourself. There should be great revelation there."

"Revelation." Irissa laughed a bit angrily. "A reveling in revisitation, more like it. This narrow slice"—she shook the piece admonishingly—"unfolds a panoply of visions —Rule, Rengarth, Edanvant; Geronfrey, long-dead Wrathmen, as-yet-unborn forms that flutter at the edges of my eyes."

Irissa threw the shard to the glass floor, where it shattered on the sharp edges of its counterparts. Fish scattered silently from the violence done above them.

"Too many visions, tainted by too many colors," she complained, "too many times and places devouring one another until little clear remains. I have learned nothing, Ludborg, except that I know . . . nothing."

The ludborg's brown sleeves swept inward, herding shards into a shining heap. The crystal reassembled between the points of fabric, but its surface was glazed with a thousand minute fracture lines.

"My crystals have always come together seamlessly before," he remarked.

The rosy end of Irissa's needle-pricked forefinger touched the globe. "This one won't. Our four fates have been cast into the seams between many worlds—Kendric's and Thane's and Javelle's and mine—perhaps even into the crooked seam that unravels forever between life and death. And still, I don't know what to do."

Scyvilla left her there, sitting on the floor with her limbs and garb fanned around her like petals, her head bowed. The ludborg glanced last to Kendric lying in state upon the bed, as stiffly formal in his way as Irissa was limp and disarrayed.

His homely brown hood shook with distress. "Dire news, as I feared," he mumbled as he retreated, "and a direr casting."

CHAPTER

15

CANDLES SHORTENED AND FATTENED IN THEIR CANDELA-
bras, weeping slow, waxen tears.

Tapestries stirred against the stone walls they clothed,
setting their woven scenes in faint motion.

Shutters, cast open to the empty, moonless Rengarthian
night, made windows into empty-eyed, blind witnesses.

Irissa's shadow fell humped against the wall, only the
thin lines of her fingers moving.

Beneath her in the tapestry, shifting like reflection upon
water, a figure swelled in the weaving—herself, worked in
sheer silver.

The threads she wove appeared between her flashing
fingers as needed—an endless supply so long as she kept
her seeress's eyes stitched to her work, so long as she drew
on her own inner magical silver and pulled it thin and fine
enough to thread any eye of any needle.

So she spun her power into filaments of thread. Then her
fingers shaped it into a design atop a background of more
common manufacture.

What she wove lay there, not quite within the tapestry,

not quite independent of it. Herself she wove, as the surface of that self had been skimmed in Geronfrey's Dark Mirror. Herself as Irissa had confronted that shadow self in the person of Issiri, the consort whom Geronfrey had consigned to dissolution when he had stripped away the unborn son she bore.

Nothing remained of Issiri—here in Rengarth, in Geronfrey's schemes, in the world Without where he had fled, in any world. She had died in a phantom tower at the Paramount Athanor almost twenty years before—if anything so . . . ephemeral . . . could be said to have lived enough to have died.

Irissa's eyes and fingers and magic resurrected her in life-size form, in a gossamer of silver thread laced over a lapful of coarse tapestry fabric.

Only the eyes remained to be done.

The candle flames were deadening one by one in their sockets. An aurora of thin light was dawning at the open windows. Irissa stared for a moment at the two black eyeholes she had left vacant from the first, then straightened, rubbed her neck, and sighed.

The tapestries echoed her aspiration with their own gentle sloughing as they swayed to the constant interior draught that laced through the palace like a dry current. Something else stirred, a drape of fabric that was not quite walls, not quite door.

"Scyvilla," Irissa said without turning to look at the open doorway.

The sad globe of fabric shuffled forward without speaking.

"I have a task for you."

"Anything."

Irissa turned to the footstool she had shoved aside hours before. An old falgonskin pouch lay on it, limp and shapeless, the feather-sheen dulled to a faint gleam.

Irissa's numb fingers picked it up and painfully worked it open. Then they blundered for some moments within.

Scyvilla's capacious hood bowed lower. The ludborg knew that that pouch had borne the Overstone egg, emptying only at the moment of Javelle's birth when it had disgorged its own offspring—a silver Iridesium snake that had attached its mobile, metal self to the infant girl.

"It's empty, lady," Scyvilla finally croaked.

Irissa's fingers still fumbled in the pouch.

Finally she elevated something between them in silent answer.

Scyvilla neared a glide or two. "A . . . stone, seeress?"

"A stone. And not a stone. You remember when I first came to Rengarth, before I had found Kendric again? Remember when we met the Hunter, that one-horned bearing-beast who was Geronfrey's creature, that had nearly gored Kendric to death in Edanvant?"

The ludborg's hood nodded unenthusiastically. Clearly he remembered all that she mentioned, and clearly he thought that Irissa had finally and fully forgotten, herself. The room was ripe with despair, with madness, with unspoken rhyme, and no reason.

Scyvilla edged closer, seeming to shrivel.

A bit of sunrise, some ray from one of Rengarth's three suns, pierced the smooth stone between Irissa's elevated fingers. The light transfixed the small cabochon, drawing a flash of blood.

"The Hunter's horn was still dyed red with Kendric's lifeblood," Irissa went on in a soft monotone that sang of memory. "I . . . cleansed it of that almost-fatal coating. Then I . . . collected . . . this remnant leeched from Kendric's body into one drop."

"A . . . Bloodstone," Scyvilla breathed.

Irissa glanced to the center finger of her right hand. "But my ring already bears an Inlands Bloodstone among its five integrated stones. This one is . . . redundant." Scyvilla's hood shuddered at the last word.

"I had almost forgotten this stone," Irissa mused, "after all these years. It certainly had no use. Now—" She stood briskly, throwing off her fey mood as if shrugging away a cloak that weighed too heavy.

"Take it, Scyvilla."

"No!" He backed away, his round form shivering in a way far different from its usual comical manner. "Bloodstone, lifestone, I want no part of it. Would that I had never mentioned Rengarth to either of you, would that I had never seen it again, rather than that affairs should come to this tragic pass—your children lost Without the gate, Kendric mortally poisoned by the spoiled water, you . . . become, become—"

Irissa advanced on him, her shadow looming above her, the Bloodstone held before her like a weapon.

"Take it. It holds some portion of Kendric's lifeblood. I have decided that these matters can only be unraveled beyond Rengarth, and there I must go, whether I ever return or not."

A shadow of a smile clouded Irissa's grim features. "I can't help but hope that if the threads of Kendric's life begin to fray completely while I am gone, Ludborg the Fanciful will find a way to use this talisman to sustain him—somehow—until Thane returns with the sword, or I find some other method to save him."

The ludborg's long, shapeless sleeve extended inch by inch, until its end cupped into a cradle of brown serge.

"I . . . am used to bearing casting crystals, not life," Scyvilla said.

"Yet you make what was broken whole again. Take this talisman. It will do me no good in the worlds beyond Rengarth. And if you find Kendric failing beyond the slow, seeping death that has been visited upon him, find some way to use it. Use it!"

The sleeve squeezed shut on the small ruby stone and Scyvilla's faceless hood bowed again, whether in sorrow or farewell it mattered not.

"You . . . leave now, seeress?"

"Almost. I have one last . . . task. Leave me, then. I would not sweep you out of Rengarth in my train."

"It will not be Rengarth again until you are all restored to us," Scyvilla said intently.

But Irissa had turned back to the tapestry falling across the stand. Scyvilla backed from the room, a sleeve clutched to what would be his heart were he human and arranged like one, his hood drooping until not even his vacant faceless face was visible.

Irissa felt the room close around her again in solitude. Behind her back, tapestried figures shifted against the wall, watching her, friend and foe alike.

She sat again and picked up the silver thorn of her needle. Now she no longer wove from the coiled skeins of her eyes. This time she reached to a large bag at her feet. Inside shone the satin skeins of many-colored threads. She reached in and pulled a tiny snake of green thread free of the tangle. It threaded her needle, then the implement was cutting like a sword in and out through the thick fabric.

Green eyes grew in the empty black orbs that filled her shadow's eyeholes. It only took a few dozen stitches. Irissa hesitated before taking the last, then glanced around the room.

Her eyes fastened on a tapestry of the Spectral City with herself and Kendric—and farther off, Sin and Aven—absorbed into its phantom architecture. She had plied that shape from gossamer thread mingled with the slightest silver of her eyes to give the Spectral City its true translucent beauty.

Now the ghostly woven city shimmered as the wind moved it, brightening under the regard of her seeress's silver eyes. She had not thought of herself as Torloc for some time, isolated from all others of her kind as she had been here in Rengarth for twenty years.

Now Irissa was Torloc through and through again, seeress solely. She didn't even glance to the tapestry beneath her fingers as she took the final, irrevocable stitch.

For an instant, even the air held its breath. The tapestries froze. Irissa hovered, needle poised, over the semblance of herself that lay—a glistening silver mist—over her tapestry stand.

Like winter-conjured breath, the shape swirled in the atmosphere. It swelled, lifted, wafted free of the anchoring fabric.

A spectral Irissa wavered in the air before her, a whitewashed figure true-to-life in all its detail, down to every silver eyelash. Thin and fitful as the lightest veil, as the finest sheet of wind-sifted snow, it settled over, into Irissa, drifting over her eyes, her hair, her hands, her clothes like glitter-laden dust.

Irissa's terrible resolve, her unspoken grief, shattered momentarily under that gentle assumption of another entity's phantom substance. Her body slumped as if bowing under an unseen weight, then straightened a moment after. Her entire form seemed webbed in pale gossamer, then the effect sank into Irissa's everyday presence as snow melts into the less ephemeral earth.

Her eyes gleamed green—Torloc-green—then softened to silver again. On her ring finger, the plain Drawstone beamed its dull, dun-colored glint and subsided.

The tapestries beat against the walls. A wind shook them until the green-gold rings they hung from chimed out of tune. The figure of Kendric flailed his longsword. A moonweasel from Rule wriggled into sinuous mock life. The empty tower room quavered as if struck by lightning.

And the Spectral City danced in a shimmer of silver threads until it, too, rose from its background and scintillated in the very air itself. It, too, stretched and swelled, swallowing tapestry after tapestry in its glittering, vaporous image.

Irissa turned at the agitation and the chiming to meet the Spectral City as it came open-arched to consume her. Smiling, she spread her hands. It fell upon her like rain. She blinked under the semi-invisible onslaught of spectral streets and spectral walls.

Despite the city's icy aspect, Irissa felt warmed. Her magic was working. She had taken the specter of herself into herself and now the Spectral City was infusing the ghost of itself she had long ago woven into her tapestry.

These moments of conjunction were fleeting, she knew. She must find a well and walk through it into another world while her being still housed a spirit-self. She must find Thane and Javelle, Kendric's lost sword, the secret to his mortal preservation . . . and return before all those quests should ring hollow in the presence of his death here in Rengarth. She must—there was so much she must do . . . and one quick thing that she must accomplish first. . . .

Irissa ran toward the misty architecture of the Spectral City, through its ghostly portals and down its evanescent streets. She ran to her own walls and through her own tapestries as if they were spirits.

She was boring through the palace walls, floating up its stairs, rushing through its stone as through air. She felt the Spectral City thinning around her, pulling her into its amorphous wake.

Irissa burst bodilessly through a familiar door, rushed over an unfelt but familiar floor, saw small finned creatures schooling undisturbed at her feet.

By the bed she paused, Kendric lying lifelessly upon it.

He had not moved since being stricken, but his skin had taken on a deeper bruising, until he seemed a metal man hammered from Iridesium—immobile, hollow.

She reached a transparent hand to his face and felt

nothing. Tears pooled in her eyes and fell like feathers, wafting into nonexistence.

Scyvilla, looking shrunken, stood guard, his sleeve pinched shut on a mote of Bloodstone.

What would happen here, Irissa wondered wildly, while she was gone? What would Kendric think of her mad commitment to an indefensible course?

She might never find her lost children or his lost sword. She might never be able to separate herself from the reborn shadow she had conjured. She might never be able to return in any state. She might never see him again.

But now she saw him—for one last, wavering moment, and she let that image burn into her mind and her magic—Kendric poison-forged into mortal metal and only her will and wit and magic to reweave this tapestry into a brighter picture.

The Spectral City tugged on her half-human being, calling the spirit she had made herself into. The corporeal world thinned and faded, even Kendric.

The last glimmer she saw of it all was a sharp flash of red as Scyvilla unflexed his sleeve to contemplate the Bloodstone lying ripe with possibility and futility in the cradle of his rough robe.

CHAPTER

16

"WHAT MONSTROUS BEAST IS THIS?" EERYON DEMANDED, facing it.

His arm made a supple motion. In an instant Eeryon's velvet sleeve was stripped of its decorative gridwork of thread. Only a dark arm remained—and a braided silver whip that coiled from his hand. It hissed through the air toward the creature who guarded this unnamed world found within the swelling globe of light.

"Wait!" Javelle beseeched, lifting her hand into the path of the sinuous lash.

"What an idiot," Thane said with disgust, turning his back on the scene.

The whip recoiled harmlessly from Javelle's intervening arm, but Eeryon's cloud-creature was less polite. It bounded past all three to confront the world's native creature.

"'Tis *your* beast that's monstrous and unruly, Eeryon," Javelle complained. "Stop it before it hurts something."

"My beast?" Eeryon examined the slavering creature at

their forefront. "I don't know this creature except as a disembodied cloud."

"Oh, a fest upon you both," Thane intervened. He stepped beyond Eeryon's snarling pet and bent to lift the creature that confronted them by the scruff of its neck.

It dangled from his hand, a four-limbed, furred beast whose ferocious maw was lined with white teeth as well strung as matched pearls.

"Horrible!" Eeryon shuddered, glancing also to the changed form of his pet at their feet. "Awful," he repeated. "I never knew the worlds beyond Outside housed such freakish creatures. What is this alien thing called?"

"Felabba," Javelle answered wryly, scooping the cat from her brother's rough custody.

Eeryon watched her cradle it in her arms—jumping back when its long body twisted and sprang to Javelle's shoulder.

"You must have followed us through the tapestry, hm?" Javelle crooned while the white-furred face sniffed suspiciously at the metallic snakehead festooning her ear.

Eeryon looked to Thane for explanation, but received his answer elsewhere. From the so-called cat itself.

"It may suit your self-conceit, young lady, to consider it 'following,' but I remind you that *I* preceded you here."

Eeryon found his voice rasping in surprise. "And it . . . speaks?"

"Doesn't your beast?" Thane asked.

Eeryon considered the fearsome yet miserable creature hunched at his feet. It shivered slightly, as if terrified of the new world's strangeness—or perhaps of its own new form, as well it might be.

The creature's hairy coat was long and ungroomed, resembling an aurora of gray-brown spines. Eeryon recognized it for his faithful cloud-companion only because of three gimlet eyes buried in a snarl-haired face—one to each side of a long-toothed muzzle . . . and one eye inset directly over it.

"You've met Felabba. What do you call yours?" Thane asked.

"Nothing. Why should I name it?"

"So it will come when you call."

"Why? It always has come without my calling."

"So you can call it *off!*" Thane explained. "It seems a brutal beast. You had better tame it or it will cause us trouble in this world. This is not Without any longer."

Eeryon shrugged uneasily, the fearsome whip pouring to the ground like a silver waterfall from his hand.

"It is still your . . . friend, I suppose," Javelle suggested.

The whip of waterfall flowed backward, up Eeryon's sleeve, separating into liquid threads and embroidering as it went. The sleeve resumed its previous appearance— velvet encrusted with coiling silver threads. Eeryon's empty hand uncurled. He placed a palm tentatively atop the brute's wiry-haired head.

"It's not so soft as your creature." Eeryon eyed Felabba, who was now loftily overlooking the land from Javelle's shoulder. The young cat sniffed audibly.

"Still, it needs a name," Javelle said.

Eeryon shook his head, looking bewildered.

"Call it Briarwhip, then." Javelle couldn't help sounding impatient. "Though you should name it yourself."

"I have no fondness for naming." Eeryon stroked the disordered hair. "Briarwhip." Three dully gleaming eyes glanced ambiguously at him.

"Just see that it does what you say, or you can't continue in our company," Thane said briskly.

"Does yours?" Eeryon wondered.

"Does ours what?"

"Do as you say?"

"I should say not," Felabba answered for herself, leaping to the ground.

"That's different." Javelle edged over to Thane, well beyond the reach of Briarwhip's drooling maw. "Felabba's a mere housecat. She can't harm anyone—not seriously."

Eeryon eyed the cat dubiously but didn't object. Instead he looked around to the wider world. "Is this Rule, then?"

"Rule? Oh, Thane, wouldn't it be . . . magical . . . if we should happen on it through the first gate!" Javelle smiled tremulously at her brother.

"You want Rule, too?" Thane suspiciously asked Eeryon.

"Yes." Eeryon looked from brother to sister, some trouble tugging at his features, then he smiled—stiffly, as if unused to the expression, but ensnared by Javelle's optimism.

His aqua eyes looked less silver in this world, and Javelle, for one, breathed easier for it. Silver eyes were her mother's exclusive coinage, Javelle liked to think, though she knew that any other true Torloc seeress would wear them.

Still, so far, only her mother could claim that distinction. If Javelle herself didn't share it, she wanted to find no other who did.

"I doubt this is Rule," Felabba pronounced in a cross between an elongated mew and a yawn, ending their speculation.

"Not Rule?" Thane was indignant. "It could be. We haven't seen for ourselves yet."

"Then do, and be quick about it," the cat returned tartly. "For nothing of Rule that my muddled brain remembers looked like yonder stone outcropping. Now, there's a monster to make much of."

They inspected the direction in which the cat jerked its whiskers. A broken prominence of stones thrust through the mist, looking like the standing bones of a huge rock-ribbed creature.

"How have we missed noticing that landmark?" Eeryon wondered.

Briarwhip's hair stiffened along his ragged spine and a sound part growl, part gurgle bubbled in his throat.

"This world is assembling around us," Javelle declared, her brow wrinkled in concentration, "as if seen through mist."

"Perhaps *we* are mist here," Eeryon answered, "as Briarwhip was in Without."

"It's true," Thane said sharply, grudging Eeryon his insight and Javelle her sudden wisdom. For a moment she had reminded him of Irissa. "We've passed a gate, and an odd one at that. It must take time for the world and us to make ourselves plain to one other."

"Mother never mentioned such a gap between arrival and the awareness of a new land," Javelle said. "And Father arrived with bone-bruising speed in the Inlands."

"Mother and Father are not here now," noted the cat. It paused in cleaning after the journey to stare intently in a new direction, then resume its licking. Its advice continued between licks. "Best . . . find shelter . . . before you find that . . . this world . . . holds uglier surprises . . . than that mangy abomination . . . you call by the singularly . . . uninventive . . . name of Briarwhip."

The creature thus named jerked at the word. Eeryon's hand smoothed its bristled head until its growls lapsed into a muffled whine.

"At least that one appears to mind," Javelle commented, regarding the cat. "I suppose, being a creature of habit, you wish a ride?"

"Of course, but not with you."

Strong back legs catapulted the lithe body atop Thane's shoulder, where its plume of white tail switched past his nose and mouth.

"Mother's familiar prefers you," Javelle said. "You're welcome to its weight."

Thane's slight shrug did not unseat the cat. He pointed to the sullen stones in the distance. "Let's make for shelter.

Whoever's cat she is, Felabba knows the way of unknown lands."

Javelle let her brother take the lead. The magical moment when the birth-snake had come alive to open the gate to Without seemed a dream—and a futile one at that. Now it remained a dormant ornament, reminding Javelle of power glimpsed but never truly shared. Eeryon fell into step with her behind Thane, Briarwhip loping at his rear.

"So your mother had a . . . familiar." He nodded at the brush of tail jolting up and down in the twilight murk before them.

"Felabba is everyone's better and no one's familiar, to hear Father talk," Javelle answered. After a bit she added less bitterly, "She—or the original Felabba, at least—attached herself to our mother years before we were born."

"What is that like?"

"To have a pet or a familiar?"

"To have a mother."

Javelle's dark eyes tilted inquisitively at Eeryon, but he was serious. "You ask me to describe what everyone knows—each in his or her own way. For me to have a mother like mine . . ."

"Yes?"

". . . is to know failure early. She has great powers, my mother."

"I know." Eeryon nodded soberly. "I know what it is to answer to one with command over everything around you."

"Command? Oh, Mother's power is not in command."

"Then why is she mighty?"

"Because she is what she is. And knows it." Javelle's eyes narrowed. "Maybe that's my weakness. I know not what I am—or rather, I know all too well I am not magic-blessed like my mother."

"You don't have magic?" Eeryon sounded even more amazed at this revelation than the possession of a mother.

"No. Most people don't, you know. Father didn't, though it was inborn, until he met Mother."

"Maybe you'll meet someone."

"Torloc men do not have powers to pass on that way."

"What way?"

"You don't know anything, do you? You may have magic, but you are very ignorant. It's as if you'd never noticed anything around you."

"Perhaps there wasn't much around me to notice." Eeryon smiled, less stiffly this time, and paused to let Briarwhip bound past him.

The hound gamboled with a puppy's abandon, its misshapen muzzle snuffling the ground, its three beady eyes glinting at the mist-shrouded bushes rasping by the side of their path. Despite its homeliness and ungainly carriage, a touching curiosity imbued it. Briarwhip lumbered through this new world in a new form, learning the everyday magic of motion.

"I like it better this way," Eeryon commented, "though you say it is ugly." He examined the rocky fog-drenched landscape. "And this land at least is fair."

"It's cold—and wet—and dreary. My boots are soaked to the insteps, aren't yours?"

Eeryon glanced down to his feet. A ghostly tide of fog swirled around his ankles, making them all look footless. "I can't see to tell," he said cheerily. "It's nice to see clouds that assume no form."

"Dawdlers!" Thane charged with a shout. He mounted a brow of rock, his figure outlined by the eerie light, the cat's erect tail quirked into a question mark by his head. "Come and see."

Briarwhip thrust long forelegs between his scrambling back legs and scrabbled ahead as if called. Eeryon, laughing, followed. Javelle waited a moment, her numb toes reluctant to stir sensation by moving. Were they all mad, to find wonder in such a woebegone world? She tramped after them, beginning to sympathize with Thane's complaint of always being the follower.

"Look!" Even composed Eeryon sounded excited now, and the miserable cloud-hound was leaping up and down at his side.

They all faced over the brow of the dreary little rise, humans and beasts, and no one turned to watch Javelle approach.

So she saw it last, she who of all of them most knew what it was. She saw it past their shoulders and over the lip of the hill—the fallen circle of stone-hewn bones, the crumbled pillars worn through at their crimped waists, the odd dancing sparks of multicolored light weaving among the ancient skeleton of older earth.

The two young men were straining to reach it, each one's separate wonder and enthusiasm spurring the other to action. Even Felabba forgot herself, deserting Thane's shoulder to pussyfoot through the soggy marshes that Briarwhip's scurrying paws whipped into a lather.

Javelle hung back, possessed of a dread that made her feel vastly older than the others. Her prescience was not born of magic, but of knowledge. Her power was not prophecy, but recognition of the past.

She had heard of such a place as she saw now—many times, in the stories her father told only to her because she was the only one with inclination to listen.

In such stories Javelle had heard much of what she saw before her and knew three things neither Thane nor Eeryon with all their magic could know: they had indeed come to Rule—or what was left of it; they had come to the sunken island of nomadic Clymerind and something had made it rise.

If these two things were true, then the sword would not be so easy to find as Thane thought.

CHAPTER

17

KENDRIC DROWNED IN DARK SEAS.

Over his head, a silver sun shone weaker than a full moon through midnight clouds.

Every muscle and bone in his body had been hammered on some inner anvil until the pain of it rang in his ears like beaten brass. His sight grew darker than his surroundings, his vision was—for the first time in his life—veiled.

A mote moved in the anonymous murk. A . . . bubble poised against the vast uncaring dark.

Kendric's eyes strained at the veiled barrier to sight. For a moment light broke through. He glimpsed a room—familiar; a robed figure—more familiar. He saw an inverted pyramid of green shining lamp-bright.

The familiar figure he could not quite name hovered over the brilliant green shape. Some fine dust drifted from a sleeve cuff into the green. The figure turned with—a glass goblet, Kendric saw now—clutched to its front.

Kendric remembered an ancient Torloc seeress who had armed her breast with an emerald touchstone. She was

203

dead now, and the emerald was long since broken, long since scattered into dust and then air.

Why could he remember the dead and their talismans? Why could he recall Finorian, and not this figure, this glimpsed place, any of the things essential to him?

Advancing, the form blotted out all light, all questions, all memories. Something cool . . . and then something warm, sticky, and liquid touched Kendric's lips.

He jerked away from this intrusive sensation, but his mouth caught fire from the caustic brew, and he could not protest.

He was drowning again. In the bottomless dark he shared with Finorian and others—others also not likely to . . . remember . . . anything at all.

Swept into the Spectral City's departing train, the feather that was Irissa dragged over the rumpled and dark Rengarthian countryside.

She felt no more contact with the rough informal architecture of earth than she had the walls and stairs of the palace at Solanandor Tierze. Something had filed the edges off all her senses.

Such muted feelings lightened her, made her skim along unthinking, like the last and littlest fish caught in a silvery net.

Only the Spectral City moved or glowed in that night. Rengarth lacked moon and showed few stars. Night was welcomed indoors where tapers could be lit, though few in Rengarth ever walked outside to see what was not to be seen.

Irissa sought the shadow self within her, but it was as fleeting as the city itself. The only sign that anything had changed was her muffled senses. Odd, she thought, that *adding* another to oneself should feel so . . . stifling.

Then the Spectral City began coiling into a fist of light. Phantom walls and streets and towers collapsed like fingers into a densely glowing ball. Irissa swirled behind the phenomenon's core, too little and too late again to stop it, her mind hopelessly disoriented.

Tighter and tighter the city spun, until it blazed daybright. Irissa shut her eyes to that ghostly brilliance, but she saw through her closed lids, anyway.

Nothing remained of the Spectral City but its ethereal vapor and the shining silver stones of a well that widened into a maw even as she hurtled toward it.

Irissa plunged into that well as cleanly as wet silk threads a needle. Darkness swallowed her. She screamed, plummeting head-first, eyes closed but still seeing, down a depthless corridor of gleaming stones slick as scales.

She spun as she fell, screwing herself deeper and deeper into a seed of darkness swelling far below, her scream streaming behind her like a veil . . . like the wail of a wraith. Ghost-bound, she told herself. I have taken a spirit into myself and have become spirit-chained myself. Where will it end? she wondered.

Her purpose, forgotten, trailed her—a faint filament connected only by chance. Then the well's silver funnel jerked into her rear.

Irissa drifted in darkness both wet and dry—part of her waterlogged, another part lilting over the surface like a leaf.

The darkness had motion and purpose, if she had not. It eddied her onward, pulling and pushing. Finally it grew still, suspending her in liquid blackness that was equally dense above and below.

Something made her reach up for the dark, the way some people unthinkingly flail the walls of a locked room, looking for a door.

The door *was* the darkness. It gave before her—or she, once supine, pulled upright as she pushed forward. She brushed past a veil and walked into a light-filled room. The chamber was circled by windows, but they didn't admit any light.

The scenes the windows framed were mere tapestries, and their subjects resembled nothing in any world Irissa had visited thus far.

The confusion of the journey brushed away, like cobwebs sticking here and there. Irissa's emotions, if not her senses, sharpened abruptly.

"Another world," she breathed with a sense of accomplishment. "I've taken a gate from Rengarth. To—where?"

She turned to confront her entry point to this alien room, hoping to find a last signpost of the world she had left.

There was only another window.

No tapestry filled it.

Instead, a smooth wet black surface reflected Irissa in its ample length. It was only a mirror, and she had encountered it before—a mirror that sometimes played a birthing box and a bier . . . and sometimes mocked a door. In this case, it had pretended to be a gate.

The Dark Mirror of Geronfrey reflected Irissa as a silvery fog-swathed figure. She knew then she had not so much escaped Rengarth as had been lured into the dread Without.

The eyes that regarded her in the mirror knew that, too, and glowed gently green in token of the new self that she had welded to her own nature.

Irissa had thought only to escape Rengarth for Kendric's and her children's sake. She had not considered that her action had released Issiri as well.

CHAPTER

18

IRISSA MOVED QUICKLY PAST THE TOWER WINDOWS THAT were webbed in tapestries. These were not the familiar hangings of her own invention, but iron-stiff expanses emblazoned with all manner of monster and alien vista.

A circuit brought her back to where she had begun, to her own image in the only untapestried windowframe. She lifted a hand to the seductive surface—so smooth, dark, peaceful—and recoiled to see her fingers thin to bone as they neared their reflection.

Death, Irissa thought, that way lay death now—in the past, in Rengarth, where Kendric even now died in gaudy inches. . . .

Irissa whirled to study the iron tapestries, to eye the mockery of motionless folds beaten into their forms.

"Unlike you, I weave my imaginings into weapons," a voice intoned in a metallic echo. Irissa spun to face the surrounding windows in turn, knowing her undefended back was always to one of them.

A sheet of brocaded iron stirred—or rather, an image

rusted free of its surface. Massive bearing-beast's forelegs and hooves stepped over the windowsill into the chamber, bringing its rider's upper torso into view.

His garments were patched leather, thick and plain. Age had settled like snow over his features, softening flaxen hair and beard to white, carving crevasses into the once-youthful slopes of his face. At some point in entering the room, his steed melted away, even the reins dissolved from his leather-gloved hands.

Geronfrey stood alone in the tower chamber with Irissa —tattered, torn, worn to the bone that shaped his skin.

"What brings you to Without, seeress?" he asked, his once-melodious voice scraping painfully in her ears.

She lifted her hands, then let the gesture escape itself, as if freeing an invisible bird.

"There must be a reason," Geronfrey ground through lips so stiff they hardly moved. "A Torloc never travels without reason."

"Without." Irissa tried to keep her dread of such a fell place from her voice. She was amazed to hear her words carry clear and ring almost sweet in the metal-shuttered tower.

"Without," Geronfrey repeated, "has been my home for all these . . . years."

More than eighteen years, Irissa tolled to herself. Javelle's birthday always marked the year of Geronfrey's escape—banishment—to Without. "We thought . . . I thought—"

"You thought me dead? No, I do not die, more's the pity and more's the trouble for you and yours. Without takes its toll, though." Geronfrey lifted a stiff arm, the gauntlet upon it rusty as caked blood, the fanciful threads gleaming with dull Iridesium glory. "I am not a thing of Without, and pay my price for sanctuary." His gaze, once sky-blue and now a bitter ebonberry-black, appraised her. "As will you."

"I don't seek sanctuary—"

"You should," Geronfrey snapped, his voice fairly crackling, "for that is all you will find here in Without—cold, empty sanctuary."

"What of Those Without—?"

Geronfrey's laugh was as empty as the world he claimed. "Those Without! Tales told to idiots. I have delved the true, hideous secret of Without—nothing. There is nothing Without, except more nothing. All you see was . . . woven by me—painstakingly—from my magic. Only this . . . structure that I have imposed upon nothingness keeps your being whole, keeps me alive. All else is . . . nothing."

"But . . . my children have gone here—that's why I have come!" Irissa immediately regretted disclosing her quest—or at least one part of it. Yet her worry had been too great to stifle.

"If your children came here, then your children are gone," Geronfrey responded shortly. "If I with my eons of magical practice can manage only these few small shards of an existence—shabby raiment, an iron-bound tower—how could your children survive here for more than a moment?"

"I do."

"Only because you were fortunate enough—fated enough—to be drawn here through the doorway of my Dark Mirror. I take it your offspring share no such umbilical cord to my mirror—?"

"No! Nor to you, either. So perhaps the purity of their hearts and minds will be a talisman through Without."

Geronfrey turned away, giving her his stiff-clothed back, becoming one of his guardian tapestries.

"I have . . . offspring, too."

Irissa's soul wanted to shiver at Geronfrey's mention of the unborn infant he'd torn from Issiri's dying body, but something in her stiffened alertly. An inner ear cocked.

Survival instinct prompted her to ask quietly, "Then your offspring lives in Without with no harm?"

"Without is his mother. It delivered him and suckled him and sent him off to his particular lessons."

"His?"

"My son." Geronfrey's voice strengthened. "He who will complete my quest and deliver me back to the worlds beyond Without. He is among my better . . . creations."

"Poor boy," Irissa murmured.

Geronfrey's face grew thunderous, then crinkled in unexpected self-mockery.

"You do not seem to appreciate my achievements, seeress. Think of what I have done! How I . . . drew . . . a flesh-and-blood boy from the stuff of spirit, how I reared him here—in the vast wilds of Without . . . without any of the things deemed so necessary to the nurture of a human. How I made a man of him and sent him to reclaim my . . . property."

Irissa felt a strange, irrational stirring rather like pride and more like possession. Questions thronged at her lips, but she quelled them.

"You must indeed have conquered the vast Without, Geronfrey," she probed with a calculated bow to his vanity, "if you can send a half-human boy back to the worlds beyond."

"A trifle." Geronfrey's gloved hand waved in stiff imitation of its former suppleness. "He has . . . inherited some small talent from his mother—his first and former mother, who is no longer with us."

Tremors of aimless emotion shook Irissa to her fingertips. It was as if something other welled up inside her skin. A silvery veil shadowed her sight, straining Geronfrey's grim figure through a deceptive mist of glamour. She felt herself sink to the bottom of her soul as another's indignant heart embraced her within and without.

Through the silver shimmer, Irissa saw Geronfrey's iron face freeze, if that were possible.

"What new powers have you assumed in Rengarth?" he demanded more of himself than of her.

Irissa broke the spell of the veiling shadow. "How do you think I found a gate from Rengarth? I came through the Spectral City, whose inhabitants are culled from a millennium's worth of your victims. They aided me. And aid me still."

"Ah." Geronfrey nodded, his brow knit into a scowl. "Perhaps your hidden spectral allies will help prolong your physical self here for a while, then. Without the proper safeguards, nothing human can live here."

"What of your son, isn't he half-human?"

"He is of Without, I told you."

"But you have . . . sent . . . him forth from Without. How will he survive elsewhere?"

The thought had not occurred to Geronfrey. "Survive beyond Without? Of course he will. For this purpose he was spawned—to return to Rule and . . . But you are truly beneficent to worry about my son when your own offspring face such imminent danger, if they are not already dead."

Waves of conflicted feelings crested against Irissa's throat, confusing her. She fought an insane urge to pester Geronfrey for his son's name, to curse him for the danger or death of her own. But her own son was . . . safe. She would surely sense it if Thane had perished, so her son was safe. No, her son was horribly endangered! The wild reversal of her emotions seemed a phenomenon impressed on Irissa from outside herself. Or from so deeply within she could not see it.

"You mentioned . . . Rule," she managed to say, trying to hide her inner disarray.

Geronfrey looked disconcerted, as if he'd said too much. "Don't fret about other places. The one you inhabit now is hard enough to survive." His pitiless eyes narrowed. "How many years is it, seeress, since I was compelled to leave Rengarth at the hands of yourself and that overlengthy consort of yours?"

"Almost eighteen as humans count them. Didn't you mark them in the birthdays of your son?"

"You forget, he was not 'born' in the common way."

Irissa felt a great wrench, as if time had wrung itself inside out. She could hardly speak for the pain, and didn't. Geronfrey, frozen into himself deeper than ever by his lonely exile in Without, failed to notice her paralysis.

"You keep well," he conceded, raising a snow-white eyebrow to study her. "Better than I. But then you are Torloc and have benefitted from living in a benign world all these years. In *my* world. Rengarth"

"Reclaim it!" Irissa challenged suddenly.

Geronfrey shrugged. "And your Wrathman, how does he keep?"

Irissa's mind winced away from the question, from seeing even in her mind the twin dangers that hung over Kendric like paired scimitars—the quick death of poison and the slow demise inherent in a human life span. Some other, cooler part of herself answered for her.

"Kendric keeps as Wrathmen of Rule do, strong and vigilant."

"He is Ruler of Rengarth—for now—as I was before and shall be again."

"But he seems ever a thing of Rule, does he not?" Irissa encouraged him. "Is that why you sent your son there—for a thing of Rule?"

"How did you know that the sword—?"

"Sword?" Irissa felt herself hold double breaths.

Geronfrey laughed. "You could never dissemble. Anxious motherhood has made you clumsier than ever. You know what sword, if you don't know why, and you are yet seeress enough that I will keep you ignorant until my needs are fulfilled."

"You think to keep me here?"

"Don't sound so indignant. You've propelled yourself into a cul-de-sac of your own making. There is no exit from Without—or none that will serve your needs. My barriers keep much that is unpleasant *out*. Pass them if you must and if you can, but you will not like their opposite sides."

Involuntarily, Irissa glanced over her shoulder to the Dark Mirror. She saw her own pale face vanishing into it and taking one last look back at her.

"Back?" Geronfrey anticipated. "I think not. What serves as a door moving forward would become a doom moving backward. Remember it is a mirror, with two sides. One faces the future and is a birthing box; the other turns to the past and is a bier. Stay here awhile, seeress, and contemplate, for that is all you have the power to do now. Think upon your failings, past and present. I doubt that there will be any future ones to regret."

Geronfrey turned to brace a cracked leather boot upon one windowsill. The harsh tapestry bowed outward at his impending presence, as if shrinking from it. The scene scribed upon its riddled surface assumed dimension, because the welcoming cyclorama of an unwelcoming world of dark and cloud and distant thunder.

Geronfrey walked into his bitter, ugly world and vanished.

Alone, Irissa clasped her arms as if to hold herself within herself, as if stifling an invisible outflow of some unseen substance—blood, emotions, spirit.

Geronfrey's words echoed in his metal-curtained tower room. At least Irissa heard them. Children—lost. Another, less natural child sent on a peculiar errand. To Rule. For the sword. The *same* sword that would extend Kendric's life, perhaps spare it from the poison.

She began pacing the chamber's coiled limits, eyeing the stiff metallic scenes. If Geronfrey and his . . . shadow son had survived Without, so could her son—talented Thane. And Javelle? her inner voice asked.

Irissa shook her head, though there was none to record the denying gesture. She didn't know . . . about Javelle. But if Thane could escape Without, surely he'd take Javelle on his tunic tails—hadn't he dogged her steps enough in Rengarth, didn't he owe his sister that?

Yes. Her children would survive Without, Irissa decided. Geronfrey had not even known that they had come here— another reason to think they had successfully passed through on their way to Rule.

But . . . what of him, that . . . other boy? That unnamed, unbirthdayed boy spawned upon a shadow and reared by a renegade sorcerer in an empty abyss.

She was harsh in her judgment, her prejudice, some inner voice warned her. Geronfrey's son was just a boy, like any other.

Not like any other!

Only a boy, beloved of his mother . . .

Not any mother—a travesty, as Kendric once had called Issiri, that which should not have ever been allowed to be. As this sorcerer's son should not have been.

He is, as Geronfrey is. As his mother is . . .

—is *not!*

Irissa clutched her middle and hurled toward the Dark Mirror. It had brought her to this entrapping end. It would bring her out. She was no stranger to mirrors, not now when her mature powers had learned to face her own reflection.

Another reflection shadowed her in the mirror, not her own—a silver aura that exceeded the contours of her figure and shone like twin stars from the center of her eyes.

Her own enhanced image enchanted her. She studied the luminescent softness of the reflection, stared into the mirrored eyes until she detected the phantom play of green beneath the silver. Her whole figure shimmered and shifted as it rang through the rainbow changes of Iridesium— mellow saffron, wild azure, deep crimson, emerald-green.

Fascinated, frozen, Irissa watched herself assemble and disperse, break into a million fragments and compress into a shape she knew to be her own—and no longer only hers alone.

Only a stab of will through her very heart enabled Irissa to wrench away from the glistening surface as ensnaring as tar. At last her vanity came back to haunt her—that tiny impulse to look where she should not. Geronfrey had used that temptation more than twenty years ago to trap a slim ghost of Irissa in his Dark Mirror.

Irissa herself had shrugged off that incipient vanity. But Geronfrey had not. He had nourished it into a full-blown persona, shaped a glancing momentary weakness into a being that could grow beyond its own inception—and yet . . . yet it could not escape its self-fascination.

Irissa knew a wave of sick insight. She had passed through the spectral well into Without only because she had taken a semblance of her shadow self, Issiri, inside her.

Now, because she had swallowed her own self, Irissa could never take the tunnel of Dark Mirror back to Rengarth or any place other for only one reason.

By taking her mirror-haunted shadow self upon herself, Irissa was now forever exiled on the wrong side of the mirror, helpless to aid anyone—even herself.

CHAPTER
19

SIX TALL STONE FIGURES CIRCLED IN THE MIST.

They guarded a bowl of rock scooped from the surrounding terrain. Tissue-thin rain sifted over them, mingling with the ground fog that eddied at their knees. Unmoved by the elements, the circled stones maintained their grim guard-duty.

"'Tis a fey-looking place." Reluctance tinged Thane's normally buoyant voice.

"It reminds me of Without," Eeryon said noncommittally.

Javelle was silent. At her temple the circlet snake stirred and warm belly scales tickled her neck as it migrated. The serpent finally curled discreetly around her throat beneath her tunic, like some considerate muffler determined to preserve her against the chill air without betraying its presence.

Briarwhip whined. A shake of his coarse coat doused everyone with icy beads of moisture. By the monster hound's side, Felabba sat assiduously licking a muddy forefoot.

Then the land lurched beneath their feet, casting cat into cloud-creature, and human into human.

The humans, startled, clung together uneasily until their balance was restored, but the animals hissed their separate distaste and leaped apart. A fissure in the ground snaked between them—not wide enough to swallow a housecat, but deep enough to twist any foot that blundered into it.

"Without never shook so," Eeryon said.

"Nor Rengarth." Thane sounded more shaken than the landscape. "Perhaps . . . we should explore the space below. It's the only sign of . . . habitation we've seen. Javelle?"

Shocked into further silence, Javelle chewed her lip. She hated to hesitate on such a rare occasion—her brash younger brother deferring to her judgement. . . .

"Yes," she heard herself say in steady tones, "we should explore. But I don't think this site has ever been a 'habitation.'"

Thane grimaced. "You know what I meant. Eeryon, you lead. That beast of yours might have a nose for danger. Our cat is no match."

Felabba kept her rear leg hoisted over her shoulder and interrupted her bath to stare icily at Thane. "You may think so, but if that Briarbeast has not warned you yet, then it has no sense of peril at all."

"I suppose you mean we're already in trouble up to our necks."

"Nicely put," the cat answered Thane, resuming her grooming.

"Then stay here and keep safe while we look around."

"I will," she replied, settling down with tucked-in legs until she resembled a moonweasel muff. The faintest hint of a purr hung on the damp air.

"Coming, Javelle?" Thane threw the question over his shoulder. He was already nudging Eeryon. The two, trailed by the cowering Briarwhip, jolted down the rocky slope toward the somber stone figures.

"They don't know, do they?" Felabba mused softly, her breath etching a delicate cloud castle in the air.

Javelle crouched beside the cat and sighed. "You'd think Thane had invented this place, the way he runs roughshod over it. He used to follow me all the time, whether I would have him or not. Now he goes his own way, whether I will follow or not."

"He knows not where he goes—or how close to the strings of fate his rash dagger cuts. But you do, my girl, oh, yes. What will you do about it?"

Javelle stared at the cat, into the deep emerald eyes awash in alien, animal wisdom. Seed pearls of moisture trembled on Felabba's sweeping whiskers. An odd tiny black cross of imperfection impressed the curve of one lush iris.

"I thought, Felabba, that you were our guardian. Isn't that why you followed us through the gate?"

"Only if you give me something worthy to guard," the creature snapped. "Your brother is a fool and you are mired in your own uncertainty."

"What of Eeryon? What is wrong with him?"

Felabba's limpid eyes drowsed shut. "Now you ask a good question . . . for much is wrong there. Though what is right with him will be all your salvations."

Javelle stood impatiently. "Father was correct. In any form—old or young—you are a riddlesome, canting creature, full of sly hints and no real help."

The cat chuckled, an odd sound coming from the svelte feline face. "You are your father's daughter, as Thane is his mother's son. Answer me this: whose child is Eeryon?"

The marquis-cut emeralds of its eyes slanted shut. It dozed, entrenched on its folded limbs, frosty breath tendriling from its pink nostrils like dampened falgonfire.

Javelle's boot heel spurned a spray of rocks as she rose

and hurtled down the incline after her brother and Eeryon, as she moved farther into the fog and the marshy ruins below.

"It must have been a great stone palace once," Thane was saying as she approached. "And these . . . figures are half-fallen pillars. But the walls are crude—" His hand stuttered over the half-wall of tumbled rocks.

Another tremor agitated the ground. This time the land buckled until the tall pillars trembled and the rocks ground their stony jaws. The three stood silent, Javelle still many sword-lengths from the others. They all fought to maintain their separate balance on a dancing tray of earth held in some palsied giant's hands.

Eeryon alone seemed unconcerned: tremors hardly moved one who had been reared amid thunderheads. Before the shudders had shivered to a stop, Eeryon was moving purposefully toward the six pillars. He stood child-slight among their seven-foot-high presences and studied the crumbling, carved faces.

"These men are most solemn-visaged, like my father."

"My father is not so solemn, but he is as tall," Thane boasted, coming to inspect the stones now that Eeryon had confronted them.

"Mine is not so long, but powerful—" Eeryon began, his face growing troubled with the memory.

"They *are* tall—and powerful." Javelle burst from the sidelines. "Why shouldn't they be? Thane, don't you remember anything of the tales told in the tapestries, of father's last stand in Rule, of his bond brothers?"

"Wrathmen?" Awe cracked Thane's youthful voice. "These are likenesses of Wrathmen?"

Impatient breath made Javelle seem to spit. "Not likenesses, *the* Wrathmen themselves. The Six. Or five of them, rather."

Thane's eager hand reached toward the vertical stone slash running from each man's chest to a point between his carven feet. "Then . . . this . . . is one of the Six Swords—"

"Sword—?" Eeryon's hand raised, too. Overeager magic sent a silver finger of lightning from his palm toward another stone blade.

"No—!" Javelle knew naught of magic, but she remembered how the Wrathmen living and dead had gathered at the Oracle of Valna. "Half of these are time-frozen effigies, not true swords and swordsmen. Some fell spell may—"

As if to contradict her and prove their mobility, the massive stone pillars began to crack. Shale flaked from their surfaces, pattering to the puddles at their mired feet.

The great gray longswords ripped free of the rock that sheathed them, stone blades lifting in unison. Five adamant faces cracked stiff eyelids to reveal stone-blind eyes glittering like mica behind them. Hands mailed in rocky gauntlets flexed creaking fingers.

Shards of encompassing stone splintered into a rain of pebbles that dimpled the fog-drifted water at their feet. Only the vacant sixth pillar stood whole and still. The other five had become living rock-warriors now, grinding with grim memory into battle, answering the call of ignorant magic with their own even more ignorant mayhem.

A gray fog of stone-dust dimmed the sheen of their Iridesium mail, but every link held its ancient shape. The five figures moved in concert toward the three intruders while Briarwhip howled and paced at the moving circle's rim.

"We have no weapons," Javelle cried, not really expecting even weapons to stay the revived Wrathmen, not expecting to do anything but articulate her tardy despair.

Thane ignored her warning, his sturdy figure braced while he delved desperately inward searching the unseen well of his magic for the salvation of a trick. Despite his talents, he was not facile in facing danger. Eeryon stared raptly at the oncoming warriors who churned the shallow waters with dragging, leaden feet.

As they revived, as the rock that encased them ground away, hints of their former character and grandeur twinkled from their aspects. The lancepoint one carried seemed to sharpen with each step, an amethyst vein jeweling the tip.

Fiforn, Javelle breathed in her mind, bearer of the lance. She was watching whole tapestries of elemental earth take living form, seeing names from forgotten Rule take on reality.

Another Wrathman cocked a creaking arm to sling a bow from his back. Javelle knew and named him, too—dead Thrangar, the Torloc, picked to bones in Geronfrey's undermountain keep, then reassembled at Valna for a final, after-death battle twenty-some years ago. Dead Thrangar, still preserved in monumental rock and coming when called, coming without present purpose to battle innocent foes.

The gray of one Wrathman's form glowed with a carmine undercurrent—Prince Ruven-Qal of the Burning Powder still smoldered in this lost, reawakened place, Javelle marveled. And Glent of the Stones—gray and stiff even in life—it must be he stalking forward in rock-semblance, bearing a gilt-edged axen invitation to battle. . . .

Javelle mentally tolled the Wrathmen's names and weapons, too awed to quail before them. Some had been her father's friends, others his foes—unwillingly. All had been his fellows. She could not fear them, though she should, although buried, coiled magic had been unsprung and would lash out no matter who stood in its path.

At the moment, Eeryon kept closest company to the revivified Wrathmen. The sword blade of one still shone like fresh-forged steel—the one Eeryon's impulsive magic had probed. A power bond linked that sword, its bearer, and the boy from Without. Now that power choked upon itself, turned back on its source, rebounded from the stony purpose of the oncoming Wrathman.

"Eeryon!" Javelle warned, the word catching in her throat. The name meant nothing here—in Rule, or Valna . . . Better that she should use her father's—or her mother's.

Eeryon remained fixed, as if stone-spelled himself.

The Wrathman's brilliant blade reared like summer lightning to crash down upon him. Thane, intent on finding his own magic, never noticed Eeryon's rebound upon him. Javelle, unused to magic, could do no more than watch and wish she did not see the danger so clearly.

Eeryon remained unmoved in his peril, even when the advancing Wrathman's mighty stone boots neared the verge of his. The stone sword grew liquid-bright with longing and aimed straight for his heart.

Javelle screamed. Thane whirled to face her, a spinning disc edged like a whetstone blurring between his hands. The Wrathman's sword—still radiating the spark from Eeryon's magical fingertips—drove straight at the boy.

And Eeryon vanished.

Just vanished.

Completely.

That gave even the Wrathman pause. Briarwhip howled from the rim of the rocks until his yammers ground on their ears like stone on stone.

Thane's spinning whetstone spun, redundantly.

"Where—?" Javelle wondered. "Did the stone sword shatter him?"

"I'll shatter *them*," Thane threatened, lifting the disc's flat lethal edge that turned and floated between his hands. "Stone will bruise flesh but metal will slice stone."

"Eeryon!" Javelle called into the mist. Briarwhip's bays echoed her. Nothing else answered . . . nothing except the grinding resumption of motion as the balked Wrathman turned to the next closest target—to Javelle herself, un-armed, too near to flee and too ordinary to vanish.

Against her throat, the serpentine necklace tautened nervously. It hadn't spoken since opening the gate to Without—at least she hadn't heard it. Now it seemed likely to throttle her. Her head shook in annoyance as much as denial. She felt anger that she wouldn't even be permitted to speak a last word to her slayer, but would go down silent and undefended, even by herself.

Speak? Javelle thought. Why speak in the face of a seven-foot-tall man of stone who doesn't recognize what he does or whom he does it to? Yet she had recognized *him* from the stories told her as a child. But what could she say to the stone-eared revenant of a man her father had slain, however reluctantly?

"Valodec."

The Wrathman's name on Javelle's tongue surprised them all, perhaps Javelle most of all.

All the stone men paused. Thane, his round blade still whirling within his spread hands, looked sharply at her. In their mutual gaze, he remembered who Valodec was and that the Wrathman would have no cause to spare Kendric's offspring.

The voice came with the low, lazy rumble of earth before it erupts.

"Who speaks to stone?" the figure asked.

Javelle held her ground. "Are you not Valodec, he of the golden voice and the Gauntlet That Never Fails?" She nodded to his hands clenched upon the sword hilt, where faint veins of color gloved one fist and forearm.

"'Golden,'" the voice croaked with something like irony. At least, Javelle thought, I've distracted him from destroying all around him. "How do you know of my voice and my glove?"

"You make a marvelously solid specter, Valodec," Javelle continued, hearing her voice ring uncomely and uncertain. She spoke along the path she had started nevertheless. "In the land I come from, there is an entire city peopled with specters, but they are mist—like the ground fog here at risen Valna. You must be a mighty spirit to take such solid form."

"Vaaaalna. Valnaaaa."

The word breathed from five grinding stone mouths, between their calcified teeth.

"How does she know?" asked another, stepping alongside Valodec and thus confronting Javelle with double danger. She answered this new threat, the new question.

"I know, Glent of the Stones, because my father was forced to battle you as well as Valodec in the last days of Rule as he and you knew it. You he was able to spare—"

"Spare! He left me bruised and broken in the Rocklands."

"You would have left him lifeless."

Glent growled, all the rage his half-frozen face would allow to escape.

Javelle rushed on, answering for another's past in her own behalf. "My father only defended himself from both of you. Glent, you believed him a betrayer of your brotherhood, as Valodec did, but who was at the gate with you to beat back the monsters from Without here in Valna?"

A third stone man lumbered over to the first two. "I know that man's name as well as I know my own."

"Yes, Fiforn," Javelle said, noting the amethyst glint of the lancepoint atop the staff in his left hand.

Rock could not gasp, but it could grind, as if chewing ponderously upon her words. Fiforn had not expected to be called by name ever again.

Only two figures hung back. Javelle decided to be done with it.

"And you, Prince Ruven-Qal of Tolech-Nal, and Thrangar, who could have been my sire had Finorian's plans come to pass, you know my father's name and have no reason to dislike it."

They came as if called like dogs, the last two towering figures. Surrounded, Javelle had forgotten everything beyond the broken wall she had drawn to herself, the rim of the living and the dead made moving stone.

"You have no reason to defend Valna against me," she finished. Her hands lifted. "I am unarmed, even of magic."

"What do you know of Valna, daughter of He Whom We Have Not Named?" Fiforn asked.

"Only that a wise Oracle once was said to speak here, and once a gate to dread Without opened here. That six Wrathmen, living and dead, fought back the outer monstrosities that would have destroyed Rule. That only one Wrathman left this place. The others were rock-entombed as guardians against another cracking of that gate. That only two people left to tell of what had transpired here. I have heard the tale from them both in their different ways—my mother and my father."

In the silence Javelle heard the rasp of her own breathing. No sound came from the Wrathmen, who stood as stolid as mountains.

"You come from Without," one charged in a bass grumble. Javelle turned slowly to see which of the five had spoken.

"I have passed *through* Without, but I come from Rengarth."

"Nothing survives Without unless it is a thing of Without. And the things of Without that invade our world we are sworn to slay."

"Is Rule so feeble these days that it must fear two boys, an unmagicked girl, and a four-legged creature too dumb to speak?"

One stone sword elevated—Glent's. Its blunt point lifted to Javelle's midsection. "Torloc. I see the strain now. You are Torloc."

"Partly. You had no time for Torlocs in Rule, but didn't a Torloc seeress stand with you here at the Oracle of Valna?"

"You are not she." The accusation was articulated by the most melodious of the grinding voices, Valodec's.

"No. But, Valodec of Clymerind, this very nomad island that now upholds our feet, you have most reason to remember her. You met her in the forest on your death-day. As she was the last woman you saw, she was the first I saw—my mother."

"Torlocs lie," Glent growled. "Have we not stayed our swords long enough? Must we heed every garrulous chit who plants herself in our path? Finish them all, I say, and be sure of it."

Three swords lifted, shadowing Javelle like limbs from a graven tree. She realized the magnitude of what she had braved and, panic-stricken, took her eyes from the Wrathmen to search the mist for some sign of Thane. There was none. The three swords lowered, their shadows twining into one.

"Wait!" thundered another voice. Stone scraped stone as Thrangar's sword crossed the descending trio of his bond brothers' weapons. "I am Torloc; I died and was immured in Valna with you. If prejudice be your justification, that is not reason enough to slay her."

Stone abraded stone. The mutual weight of three swords pushed Thrangar's defensive blade to the ground. Valodec hung back, uncommitted, the puzzlement upon his rigid features slim hope for Javelle.

She hunted for a chink in their circle, a space she could slip through while they debated. They were too massive. Had she magic, she might have become liquid and flowed through them. Had the snake proven a more reliable familiar, it would have done more than knotted itself around her throat and remained silent. Had Thane been older or Eeryon stronger, perhaps they could have saved her.

Thane! The Wrathmen's disagreement over the swiftness of her fate permitted Javelle another look around. All she saw was the same murky, mist-choked marsh—the same, except that Thane and his wheeling disc were nowhere to be seen, nor was Briarwhip. Had they all vanished like Eeryon?

"I'd rather vanish," Javelle muttered through closed eyes, "than be sliced."

A sound severed the air—and then a rush of wind came, the first she'd felt here. She braced for the crushing contact of a blunt stone blade . . . and felt a few quick taps upon her shoulder, followed by the sudden presence of a weight.

"Nonsense!" a voice hissed in her ear—or rather, hissed *beside* her ear. It was not the snake's. "Great silly statues of stone, has the drip of Valna's underwater caves in your ears all these years made you deaf to reason? Enemies from Without threaten Rule, but they do not stand here before you."

Javelle, finding herself still unsundered, opened her eyes. If stone warriors could be said to blink, the five Wrathmen were batting stony lashes.

She glanced to her shoulder. Felabba, her hair whipped into ill-kempt peaks from her recent grooming, was spitting wrathfully at the assembled stone giants. The cat's green eyes flashed lurid fire.

"Can you not hear your own future speak?" it continued in great umbrage. "Your day is done and only Valna's slow rise to the surface has wakened you. Would you destroy the heirs to your guardianship? Sleep again, stone men, and let those of us young enough to deal with fresh dangers get about it. You creak in brain as well as body."

"Who speaks to us so?"

"I, Felabba, who am Guardian. Know you that the sword has been found."

They fell back as if struck.

"Yet there is a gate here—to Without," Glent said

stubbornly. For a moment he reminded Javelle of her father. She remembered that it was for her father's longer life span she had dared Without and faced the circle of his lost bond brothers. She wondered if Wrathmen donned stubbornness with their armor, and wished she could stay and talk and know them better, exchanging tales and comparing the details of old days she had never shared.

The cat had no patience for Wrathmen frozen past their time or a young woman with a thirst for times before hers.

"You have been roused from a long dream too soon, brothers," it announced. "You have done your duty and asked who goes there, and she has told you all you needed to know and more. So sleep again and stay out of our way—time is short and the stakes are dire."

Whether it was pure feline ire or some other commanding quality the cat contained, the Wrathmen drew back, dragging rock-bound feet.

Javelle was almost sorry to feel their heavy shadows ebb away. She was moved to follow them, save that cat claws curved into her shoulder, carving warning into her skin.

The Wrathmen resumed their previous places, great lumbering dancers in a pattern too huge for them to see more than a portion of it. They settled into their frozen selves, the upright swords dividing their tall figures. Their eyes shut, one by one.

"Kendric," said one, acknowledging that which had been nameless until now. "Kendric," the others repeated in a whisper of dry pebbles shifting, admitting him once again to their number, in absentia.

If the Wrathmen gave their sole surviving member a parting benediction, Felabba had no such sweet farewell for them.

"Relics!" the cat spat, loosening its admonishing grip on Javelle. "More in the way than out of it when they were alive, and more so now that they are entombed."

"They were an awesome sight," Javelle objected.

"So you would have thought until they ground your bones to powder. The fact is they are rather stupid, an attribute your quest and Rule cannot afford at the moment."

"I suppose I'm glad Thane fetched you."

"Thane?" The cat looked as surprised as a cat will ever permit itself. "No one 'fetched' me but my innate good sense."

"Then . . . where is he—and Eeryon?"

The cat narrowed its gorgeous eyes and hefted a mud-caked paw to the services of its tongue. "Indeed. A most interesting youth. It seems you had better do something about finding them."

"I? I am no . . . sorcerer. Together, they have more magic than I hold, even with you sitting on my shoulder."

The cat cocked its head. "Don't expect me to leap into that disgusting dampness that soaks the ground hereabouts. I've bathed enough for half of my ninety-nine lives already today."

"Ninety-nine—?" Flabbergasted at the notion of a cat outlasting ninety-nine lives, Javelle turned her attention on the surrounding area without further argument.

The Wrathmen had faded into their pillars again. They looked less like men and more like stalagmites with human features scratched across their surfaces. She saw clusters of broken boulders that shone with the same pale phosphorescence that encased the Wrathmen. These must be shattered stalactites, she realized. What cataclysm had shaken sunken Clymerind, destroying the Oracle of Valna and bringing the island afloat again, after all these years?

Javelle ranged farther, the cat clinging docilely to her shoulder. The snake unwound itself from her throat and slithered into a circlet at her temples again, taking its tail in its mouth and thus ensuring its own continuing silence. Javelle suddenly envisioned herself exiled here with only Felabba and the snake for company.

The thought was horrific enough to urge her to call out. "Eeryon—! Thane!" A new absence struck her. "Briarwhip?"

In the distance, a lone voice bayed hopelessly.

She paced the brackish ground, brushed past the motionless Wrathmen, wove in and out of their forms looking for any sign of the others. Her encounter with her father's past had so absorbed her mind and emotions that she had been numbed to the departure of her companions one by one. First Eeryon, then Thane and Eeryon's cloud-creature.

Javelle glanced up at the brim of rock above. Much misty land spread in the dark beyond this focal place. She would be searching terrain as empty and unpromising as Without itself. She shivered, a chill finally seeping into her boots and her fingers, spreading fear into her heart.

And then she rounded the empty pillar—the sixth pillar that would have housed her father's form had he not been spared for further adventures beyond Rule.

Thane was there, around the unseen, opposite side, holding his magic disc before him like a shield. He was silent, intent, and almost frozen Wrathman-solid, and the disc was still. It shone sun-bright, reflecting in a dark blot upon the stone pillar's surface, reflecting in a *hole*—a window to Without.

"Thane—?"

But he remained uninterested, unanswering. His face was stiff with effort—eyes and nostrils flared, lips and eyebrows taut. He seemed to have been that way forever.

And dancing against the shining gold surface of Thane's disc was a small buzz of darkness, a restless gnat of force incarnate that flitted here and there.

Thane foiled its every foray, the glow of his disc forcing it back as a shield turns a clever sword feint. He looked as if he had been so engaged forever—no wonder he had not challenged the Wrathmen, no wonder he had not come to Javelle's rescue.

A switching tail beat Javelle across the back. Felabba's face leaned close to her cheek. There was no comfort in the soft blink of fur across her skin, just utter concentration, like Thane's.

"What is it?" Javelle whispered.

"A gate," Felabba said. "Those long-slumbering Wrathmen were roused by something more potent from Without than our poor party—a gate great enough for a gnat and no more. These Wrathmen would have pounded themselves to dust on this soggy earth before their clumsy swords would have repelled *this* monster from Without."

"Who is it, then? Perhaps if I can name it, that will help Thane repel it. Felabba, you can't afford mystery now— tell me!"

"Thane knows the name as well as its bearer does. A good thing you dealt with the antiquities yourself, girl, for your not-so-foolish brother had better things to do than save your fur."

"Who or what is it? Tell me, or I'll throw you to the puddle!"

"Wait. You knew the names of men long dead and took some pleasure in telling them so. Surely, there are other names you know from your parents' past that you so treasure, names not even they like to remember."

Javelle leaned as far over her brother's shoulder as she dared. "Geronfrey," she breathed. "You are right, Felabba, I have not forgotten him, though I would like to."

"Nor has he forgotten you," the cat replied in sardonic tones pitched deep within Javelle's ear, "be assured. Nor has he."

CHAPTER
20

LIKE A CHILD CLINGING TO HIS MOTHER'S SKIRTS, Kendric curled his fist into a tapestry fold.

His balance gave, but not his grip. Green-gold rings ripped from the rod twelve feet above. Collapsing tapestry fabric sagged with Kendric.

He released his grasp to preserve the hanging and lurched toward the central table of Irissa's empty receiving room. Broken rings clattered against the wall as the tapestry slowly lapsed into stillness again.

Kendric blinked beads of sweat from his eyelashes. His arms buckled as if stuffed with fabric. Even the table's sturdy stone pedestal could hardly uphold him. Sinking, his arms flung around it, he swept a candelabra to the floor.

The crash echoed in his eyes—not his ears. He knew that he should hear more . . . see more . . . but he was learning to lean on his will alone, rather than his senses.

Those senses were drowning in a lush interior tide of poison.

Something tugged on his attention—barely. Some words

came to him—remotely, though he recognized their source as the ludborg who had appeared at his elbow.

"How did you come here?" it demanded.

"Lurched," Kendric answered after long consideration. He was haunted by a shadow, that raven of stoic self-mockery that always came to pick the bones of a dying warrior. Black humor in a habiliment of phantom feathers.

Kendric stared at the tapestries, watching the designs swim fishlike before his eyes. For a moment he wondered if he had dreamed leaving the bedchamber. Then the ludborg tugged him alert again.

"You are ill, Ruler, and wander. You must return to bed," it insisted.

"Not wander," Kendric forced the words out in weary response. "Wonder. I wonder." The thought, like most thoughts now, hooked his fevered mind on a sharp curl of speculation. He flailed at the thin end of an idea—a rational notion leading somewhere far beyond what he could see in his present state.

Impatient, Kendric roused his flagging energies to brush the ludborg aside and lurch toward the windows.

"It is dark without, Ruler; opening the shutter will shed no light."

"Dark without," Kendric intoned thickly. "Darker within."

It was not the windows he sought, although he crashed into a pair of braced shutters. Kendric rebounded from them before the ludborg could scurry to his aid. A stool bounced away before the thrust of his unsteady leg. He leaned his ungainly, weakened weight against the cool stone wall and stared at what he had come to see.

"There's nothing here for you, Ruler. She has gone."

"Gone," Kendric repeated, his deep, slurred voice tolling the word like a death knell.

The ludborg wailed—an unheard-of event—and vanished.

Kendric didn't notice. An unfinished tapestry lay crumpled over Irissa's work-frame. The threads writhed like worms before his uncertain vision. And in the center of the weaving a great hole spread like a blackened bloodstain from top to bottom and side to side.

Kendric reached a mottled hand—he looked like some sun-bruised lizard now and hardly noticed it—to touch the blot, the vacancy.

His perception betrayed him. His hand never quite reached the tapestry's midnight center—or it receded from his grasp. Perhaps he did not move at all, but dreamed and in dreaming, died.

Something jostled what Kendric had used to regard as his shoulder and now was a far-flung part of himself he had not the energy to reclaim.

"Drink," commanded a distant voice, somehow—despite it all—familiar.

The always-green-with-borgia glass goblet appeared before his face, its incarnate color darkened by a swirling streak of brown.

Kendric drank—because he still trusted the voice, because his will had been strong enough to get him here and little more, because he never could resist an offer of borgia . . . that raven mockery again—pick, pick, picking at his bones and sorely welcome to them, most sorely. . . .

His lips never felt the cool glass, the warm liquor. But even as he drained the goblet and the green seeped upward to refill it, he felt a certain vigor warm his blood and bones.

Kendric shook his head to clear it. "Ludborg?"

"Scyvilla, Ruler, as I am called here."

"Of course. S-Scyvilla." Kendric sighed and pushed away from the wall, surprised to find himself still standing.

"You should not have left your sickbed. There is nothing here but old memories. She will find what she seeks. You must preserve what is here until she can return with a remedy."

"You mean preserve myself."

Scyvilla's hood nodded soberly. "It is not an ignoble aim."

"No, but—" Kendric leaned forward, his hands braced on the tapestry frame. The hole—the human-shaped hole in the fabric—was blank, an utter absence. He could not see through it to the tapestry table beneath. If he brought his hand to it, some force kept his flesh from passing through, from even contacting that flat black area.

Kendric drew upright and walked—fairly steadily—to the wall where a tapestry swagged low on one end. He lifted the draping fabric, smiling sadly at how much effort even such a feeble gesture took.

"I'll have that rehung by tomorrow." Scyvilla was scurrying after him, like a palace flunky or any random ludborg.

That is how people served him these days, Kendric thought ruefully, they scurried after—waiting to catch him when he fell. It was not a warrior's end. But then, he had not been a warrior for some time.

He paused at another tapestry. He studied another black blot of Irissa's making—the midnight-dark rectangle outlined by a windowframe in the scene of a many-windowed tower. He blinked several times to make sure his eyes were not bewitching him.

"Gone," he repeated, less dolefully. "Gone," he said, even hopefully.

"Ruler?"

"Call me Kendric," he growled over his shoulder. "The least you can do for the dying is to call them by name."

Scyvilla was silent. People often were nowadays when Kendric spoke the truth. His truths used to be less blunt and loomed much smaller.

Kendric ignored Scyvilla and concentrated on the woven window. "Gone. All three. Even that cursed cat. They must be . . . somewhere else."

Kendric began striding back and forth along the room's four tapestry-hung walls. Every so often his steps faltered. He stopped, swayed, caught hold of a fistful of fabric. Tapestry and Kendric swayed drunkenly together against the wall.

Scyvilla's drooping hood almost covered his hidden face, like an eyelid shutting out a sight too painful to view. Kendric kept muttering to himself, single words, meaningless phrases.

"Where? First, Without. Then—? Not Inlands—or the Cincture? Delevant? No. . . ." His fingers traced the threads, passing over whole worlds in a few moments. Like one blind he pawed the tapestries until they shivered under his raw, searching touch.

In the center of the room, Scyvilla moaned helplessly.

"By Finorian's great horned toenail!" Kendric roared, stopping as if thunderstruck.

Scyvilla jumped, quivering under his robes until he seemed struck by palsy.

"Look!" Kendric's eyes turned to him. Their warm golden brown had darkened to a rusty black in recent days, but no alteration in Kendric's aspect could disguise the tremor of pure excitement that shivered through him now.

His palm hit the tapestry, drove it to the wall—several times, until a veil of dust shimmered forth.

"Here," Kendric insisted. "And not here before. Here— in Rule, of all places. Clymerind! Sunken Clymerind. Do you see it?"

Scyvilla edged morosely over. "An island, Ru— Kendric. Only an island."

"A *new* island. Or an old island become new. Clymerind. They change, don't you see? Change to reflect reality elsewhere. And here—these . . . dots. Javelle and Thane and that cursed cat. Don't you see?"

In his excitement, Kendric caught the scruff of Scyvilla's

robe and pulled the hood to face directly at the small cluster of threads that represented the island.

"Don't you see?" he demanded again.

Scyvilla shrugged politely and wriggled—fruitlessly—in Kendric's grasp. "I see that you are optimistic again. That is good. Now if you would rest and let the Bloodstone work to restore you—"

"Rest?" Kendric spit the word out like a curse. He stared at the island. For the first time since his illness, a smile touched his sharpened features. "Rule. Then they will find a gate back to Rengarth. But—Irissa? Why is she not with them? And what are those . . ." His forefinger prodded the island. ". . . those *dark* dots with the three light ones. Three dark dots . . . one for each gatetaker."

"Simply knots in the weave, old friend," Scyvilla said in anguished tones. "Now come back with me to your bedchamber and rest."

"No! Bring my bedchamber here, then, if you must have me there. Bring a bed, anyway. I will not leave this room."

"But—"

"I will not leave my one set of windows on the landscape without, where all I hold dear moves like motes through interwoven worlds."

Scyvilla's robe collapsed as if deflated. "As you wish, so long as you rest."

"Rest." Kendric tasted the word. "Who are the 'rest' with my children? The others. *One* might be Irissa, but—"

He hardly noticed the ludborg easing away on a liquid gait. His hand smoothed the tapestry and cupped the tiny island of Clymerind. "Moving," he murmured, chuckling a little. "On the move, small island, as of old." His expression darkened. "Irissa. Where?"

Already the benefits of the Bloodstone Scyvilla had crushed into the borgia were ebbing. Kendric sighed and stumbled painfully to Irissa's abandoned tapestry. He stared into its central void, his clearer eye shaping the outline.

Something in his heart or mind told him that Thane and Javelle and even the cursed cat were alive and moving in a world he once knew well. Nothing reassured him similarly about Irissa.

She seemed to have dropped into a well, into the hole of her own construction. Not since he had known her had Kendric sensed such utter absence, as if part of his magic had fallen away, leaving the rest of it shored up only by his will.

"The sickness," he told himself, repeating the word again, as though finding himself fatally ill were some reassurance. If fading faculties were the only reason for his unease, for the hollow core of loss within him, then he could die happy.

If it were not—if he believed, suspected, that Irissa and their children were caught in some dangerous worlds-wide web—why, then he refused to die at all!

It would be just like Irissa, he thought, to leave him alone in the dark in hopes that he would turn terminally stubborn and live.

She had never known such despair.

Iron, the windows were buckled shut with alien iron and would not bend to her magic.

The one window's black tunnel to Rengarth was haunted by the ghost of her own being. To plunge into it would be to embrace full spirithood.

Geronfrey had not appeared again. She suspected his absence had more reason than an intent to disturb her peace of mind. She suspected he was . . . busy . . . elsewhere.

Irissa moaned and slapped one fist into the other palm. So she had seen Kendric chafe at inaction—and had never understood it. She paced the round chamber, growing angrier, thinking in circles, too.

Thane and Javelle had found Without and then found a way from Without, that she knew.

And so had Geronfrey's shadow son.

What was he—this ill-conceived twin to Javelle's conception—this awful . . . twice-stolen being? First Geronfrey had skimmed Irissa's reflection from the surface of his Dark Mirror; then he had nurtured his shadow Irissa into a shadow wife and finally the mother of a shadow son.

Now that shadow son pursued Irissa's and Kendric's son, haunted his unshadowed twin, Javelle, who had no notion of her terrible kinship to a twisted thing, a purloined soul.

Irissa bit her knuckles and paused at the black mirror. The ghost she had assumed radiated around her image, soft as mist over the moon. She would almost risk the plunge, if it would do some good.

But something prevented her—some impulse not purely her own. Some shadow force moved on behalf of the shadow son—moved within her, subverted her will.

She sat suddenly on the floor. This iron room iced her joints, made her mind stiff as well. Her magic had congealed into an impotent fist inside her.

Something else resided within her, she admitted nervously—the resurrected Issiri she had woven from the silver of her eyes and donned like a cloak. Even Geronfrey had not perceived that subtle . . . addition. Why should he? Issiri had been only a tool to him, a vacant repository of his ambition, his vanity. He presumed her destroyed these many years.

But she was not dead. Irissa had assumed the ghost of a ghost and paradoxically felt it stir within her—faintly, as wind on water. Irissa turned her face toward the Dark Mirror.

Her own face met her—phosphorescent as waterweed.

She saw the sad features disperse in widening rings of motion that dissolved like shivered moonlight on the ripples.

Like a wailwraith glimpsed through many fathoms.

Release. A wailwraith always sought release from its wet environs—why else would it wail?

Irissa heard a thin keening now—watery, woeful. She recognized it for an echo of her own—a mother mourning a lost son. Who else would find a lost magical son if not the magical mother?

Or—the idea made Irissa sit up straighter and breathe harder—if *one* mother might not go, perhaps another could. If *one* son could not be followed into the abyss, perhaps the other could.

She stared into her reflected face lapping at the edges of the mirror frame. The dark tide that had borne Irissa here underlay all the worlds, so Kendric thought. If so, it could sweep a spirit away, all the way to . . . Rule.

And if that spirit sought its own, its lost son, it would find Irissa's lost also—son and daughter. For Irissa knew with every mote of magic in her mind that where Thane and Javelle would go to fetch Kendric's forsaken sword, so Geronfrey's shadow son would ultimately come.

And the shadow Irissa? To whose aid would she go with her minor magic and her spectral emotions? She would help the other, Irissa knew that, the shadow like herself. But she would not assist Geronfrey, not he who had torn the half-life and the shadow spawn from her with one twofold blow of possession and destruction.

Issiri—or what remained of her—would not help Geronfrey. And that was who Irissa really feared.

She lifted her hands to the Dark Mirror, watching ghostly palms return the gesture. Her self-control loosened. An airy tension lifted from Irissa's mind and body. She almost saw it emanate along her fingertips and wreathe the mirror, infusing the semblance of herself.

A moment's regret made Irissa cry out. "Wait!"

Wai-ai-ai-ai-t, the echo came within her veins.

The pale reflection was spreading into the darkness of a single open mouth, screaming. Issiri—the remnant of Issiri—streamed away on the dark current, so rapidly its parting wail became a memory before Irissa's ears could even discern it.

Irissa felt suddenly hollow, even of hope. Unfelt as Issiri had been, her absence left a core of Dark Mirror in her host. Irissa saw deeper and darker into herself than she ever had before. What had she released—and to where?

Issiri could have dissipated into the dark river that underlies all worlds. Issiri could have flown like a death raven to pick the bones of Thane and Javelle and screech exultation at the survival of her own shadowy son.

Or, Issiri could have gone—as Irissa would have had she been able—to spare her own son while destroying nothing other.

It was all could and no certainty, at a time ringed round with ugly realities—Kendric mortally ill, and mortal besides; the children lost on a mission of Irissa's devising; Irissa exiled to one of Without's most confining corners.

Enemies free . . . and allies all endangered.

Irissa lowered her head until the Iridesium circlet touched her knees. She shut her eyes until she could no longer see what she wished not to see.

She was prisoner to Geronfrey for now, yes. But most of all, she was prisoner to her own hope.

CHAPTER
21

THE BLACK BUZZING MOTE THAT WAS GERONFREY
dashed itself at the pillar's transparent wall. Again and
again it met the glowing disc of Thane's magic.

Thane pushed the circle closer on each attack, until the
core of darkness in the pillar's heart narrowed like a cat's
iris. As it sealed, Thane thrust the disc edgewise in the
seam—a gilded scar to mark the place forever.

"Is it shut now?" Javelle worried.

Thane leaned his back against the stone and let himself
collapse. "Sealed now—and for forever, I think."

"It was from that very pillar," Javelle recalled, "that
Geronfrey reached through time and space to destroy our
mother—and failed."

"Well, he's failed again." Thane clapped gold dust from
his palms and noticed the stock-still pillars. "What happened to the Wrathmen?"

"I handled them." Javelle couldn't resist looking smug.

"You? With what?"

"Words. Magic isn't the only weapon, you know."

"Words? What words?"

"No spell, if that's what you mean. I simply reminded them of the past, their past."

"Hmpf." Thane sounded dubious but couldn't deny that the danger had ended. He took a wider survey of the area. "Where is that wild boy from Without? And his unattractive pet? They both bolted as soon as things got difficult."

"They . . . vanished." Javelle frowned her puzzlement.

"That's like a coward, winking away from danger."

"I don't think it was that. Eeryon didn't seem afraid of the Wrathmen . . . only intrigued."

"Well, I'm just as satisfied with him gone. I don't need extra baggage dogging our quest. Don't look so sour, I didn't mean you."

Javelle didn't brighten at Thane's grumpy admission—which she didn't believe for a moment—but neither did she belabor the puzzling matter of Eeryon's disappearance.

"At least we know we're in Rule," she pointed out.

"But where in Rule are we? If this is Clymerind, the island could sail anywhere. And with this eternal mist, we'll never see far enough to find another land. We should make for the shore—maybe there's a boat."

"Clymerind has been sunk all these years. There aren't likely to be any boats left. And why has the island risen now?"

"We can't answer any questions unless we go look." Thane bounded up the path leading to the rim rocks. "Come on!"

Javelle hesitated to cast a troubled glance behind her. The stone Wrathmen stood stolid guard, their features frozen into death masks upon the pillars, so the circle looked like a ring of upright effigies.

The stone swords both cleaved and united their forms. The blades were blunt, incipient shapes now, as rough as rudimentary spines. Nothing fearsome remained to the figures but their awful stillness, their funereal sobriety.

Javelle thought of her father frozen into such premature

stillness—not now, but in twenty, or twice twenty, years. She would be older herself by then, but could expect her half-Torloc heritage to extend her life span, if not bestow a full measure of Torloc longevity. Father had no reason for such a hope. Association was not the same as blood relationship.

Thane was right, Javelle knew. They two must be about their vague but vital quest. What happened to Eeryon didn't matter to them. Yet it did, in a way she couldn't name, and she knew that Thane wouldn't understand.

"Come on, Javelle! Or I *will* call you baggage."

She turned to follow him up the rocky path. Where the mist thinned at the top, Javelle could see Felabba waiting, her vertical pupils slit to needle-width and her eyes dreaming shut horizontally, so they formed a crossroad of north and south, east and west.

One last look—the stone Wrathmen, the thin puddles spilled over the rocky basin, wind swirling the mist into smoke—then Javelle scrambled up the incline. Her boot heels sprayed loose pebbles into a hail that pelted the water below.

"You must have a massive mind; you took long enough to make it up." The cat lingered while Javelle caught up. "But then one who can singlehandedly subdue a circle of walking, talking, sword-bearing stones with a few well-chosen words would be mighty beyond magic."

"You could have told Thane yourself that you intervened."

"Why? He is puffed up enough as it is. Let him wonder if you have unsuspected talents. I simply point out that it is unwise for *you* to be so deluded."

"Neither of you is very encouraging," Javelle answered glumly. Ahead, Thane's back was fading into the sour gray mist. She half-ran to catch him up, her boots smacking free of the adhesive mud stride by stride.

The cat followed in a disconcertingly silent trot. Its last words carried to Javelle with a mocking note.

"Encouragement is for children," it said, then fell behind and abruptly silent.

Behind the fading party of three, in the shallow bowl of fallen Valna, wind roughened the water and stirred the soupy mist.

Only these natural things moved—not the Wrathmen, not the empty pillar with a seam of gold sewn down its center.

Then, so abruptly it seemed some natural phenomenon had cut loose from the cloudy sky, invisible fists pummeled the shallows and slapped water, spreading droplets.

It seemed the beginning of a storm of gargantuan raindrops—slow and rhythmic, then faster and harder. The hollows in the water moved in a straight, rapid path, striking deeper, until they smacked into solid stone beneath the liquid.

The cloud whence these sudden drops came curled into view over their oncoming path—a curly, gray stormcloud that rubbed airy shoulders with the mist and shrugged it off.

Three dim glows sparked like marshlights at the cloud's lowered head. Eeryon's ethereal hound was racing across the deserted hollow, lacing through the pillared Wrathmen's mist-mired feet. Its small bright eyes sought eagerly for something.

With a yelp, the creature found it. Briarwhip, restored to his new yet unpleasant form, bounded up the path and stopped with ungainly haste. He sank on his haunches and cocked his snarled head.

The animal waited, patiently, as it must have done many times before. Mist shifted before it, slid belly-down over the slimy stones. Then mist parted. A thin script of silver thread was writing an undecipherable message on the dusky air. Air darkened to solid black as the thread laced up Eeryon's velvet sleeve.

Fog was suddenly drifting over his newly visible boots. Darkness had become clothed flesh. Only the pale glow of Eeryon's hands and face moved as he leaned forward to pat Briarwhip awkwardly on the docile head.

Even now the center of Eeryon's eyes were dark— empty, endless. Slowly, as though mist were seeping into the chalice of his being and filling it, the color changed to silver-blue.

He shook his head, not quite fully seeing yet and thus aware that he most likely could not be fully seen. But then he noticed that there was no one to see him.

Eeryon studied the circled Wrathmen, disappointed to find them mute and motionless, muffled by the stone as before they had come to life. His luminous eyes pierced the wandering mist, finding no sign of his former companions.

"They are gone, Briarwhip," he mused, patting the coarse hair again. The gesture gave him no pleasure; as a cloud the creature possessed a phantom fleecy texture. Here, in the world beyond Without, its texture was crude and brutal, like the other aspects of this place.

Eeryon shivered at the cold and the damp. The air of Without had been so indifferently constituted that Eeryon had never felt it. Yet here, as well as in Without, he was still subject to the same arbitrary absences from his self.

He turned to squint up the path. He could have been gone for moments—or hours. So, too, could they.

"Alone again, Briar," he told the hound. "I miss the company." He stood to survey the inhospitable landscape. "It's not so different from Without, with the dimness and the mist. But we know this is Rule, because Javelle said so. Come, we must find the sword. Then, perhaps, there'll be time to find Javelle and Thane again."

He started off, his silver-embroidered sleeves flashing in the ponderous air. Briarwhip gamboled after, long claws scraping the scattered stones beneath them.

The fog trailed them to the pathtop, then sank back into the cold cup of the land, swirling round and round the rocky rim.

Wrathmen were reflected in the shallow black water that cloaked the ground, their sword blades seeming to shine silver when clothed reflectively in the water's liquid alchemy.

More silver roiled in the flat, shiny water, curling in puddles formed from dimples in the rocks. Silver thinned and coiled, then coalesced into a pattern.

A face appeared there—more suggestion than reality. Glittering eyes blinked wide. A form almost seemed to surge up from the water's thin skin—features breaking through—a nose that sniffed something familiar, eyes that searched for something lost, a mouth that opened and spread and wailed its unspeakable loss.

A gasp shook the ground—an indrawing of presence and sound and water and air. Fog thickened into a smoky finger and pointed into the water's surface, into the face shattering there.

Then the silver was gone . . . and the face—even, for a moment, the fog. Unclothed, Valna revealed its bones—a stark, collapsed cavern fallen into boulders with stagnant pools surrounding a shabby circle of standing stones.

At last mist exploded from the water in a cloud of exhalation and softened the scene, rising to the very rim of rocks like steam and concealing everything in a thick veil of cloud-white.

Free, she was free. Motion sped past her, or she outsped it. She was not so much caught in current as she *was* the current, water fading into waves behind her. She turned as she streaked through the liquid foam, black glass walls gliding soundlessly by.

She was water-borne, tunneling through the long dark, but not water-bound. She could breathe water, or air, or fire, or freedom.

Free! She spun as she shot ahead, long silver hair tangling round her skin like satin threads. She caught flashes of herself reflected in the black rock walls to either side—a quicksilver form speeding through its element.

Quickstone Mountain, it was set in my hand.... A whole mountain of Quickstone she would see—soon. And ... and other things that belonged to her. Yes, she had not seen anything for so long ... to see now—oh, pretty, pretty, shining, flashing, speeding freedom.

Yet something tugged at her spirit, hooking her euphoria and reining it, a thin invisible line fixed to her heel. She couldn't always feel it, only now and then. It was not silver and precious, like herself, but it was like herself in another way, one that made her sigh and breathe out a cluster of bubbles.

Her freedom was conditional in some unspoken way, in a way she knew more deeply within her. There would be a price, but when had she not paid some price? And why worry?

Now she was skimming the dark water that seeped everywhere to buoy up many worlds, swept in its warm liquid embrace to a place where she would find that which was lost.

She had lost many things, including her life—not once but twice. Now it was her turn to find things—bright, sparkling, special things that were hers.

One thing—that had been hers and had been taken. That was not right, always she had been given things: time and jewels and once a bright silver stone as she lay dying. . , .

Now she lived, spirit and speed and quick, glancing

hunger. Now she would find. Her reflection twinkled back at her in the sober twin walls on either side.

Pretty, pretty, pretty. Pretty freedom.

Kendric awoke from fevered dreams—misplaced.

The room, lit by low-burning tapers, shivered around him, its geography alien, elusive.

Then he remembered. He slept in a new, makeshift bed in Irissa's tapestry room. Even now the hangings swam before his eyes, then wavered into familiar shapes around him, stirred by the faint interior wind that never ceased.

But . . . a vague revenant of dream tickled his unease. He would have sworn he saw a wink, a quick silver wink along the wall!

Perhaps he dreamed of his former bedchamber, where immured fish glinted through an aquatic glow. Perhaps he should be there now instead of camping stubbornly in this empty room where Irissa had been long absent.

For nothing had changed in the tapestries in days, despite moving his sickbed here, despite his vigilance. He pushed himself up, trailing the robe that weighed damp with his sweat, and lumbered to the wall.

No. He stared at the tapestry that depicted the mosaic map of Rule inlaid in the Circle of Rule's floor. Except for the sudden reappearance of the tiny isle of Clymerind— and he had spotted that days ago—nothing else had altered.

The white dots of the children and Felabba had become motes too small to distinguish against a mottled background once they had left the black rectangle of Without.

Even the three dark cinders that dogged them had sunk into the variegated weave—light or dark, his kin or his enemy, each entity made a single stitch invisible in the overall pattern.

Still—his dream sighting had been so vivid, so real.

Kendric pushed his weary body along the walls, studying the tapestry designs in the low candlelight, hunting a glimmer of change.

A thread winked at him from the Inlands. He rushed there to find a silver worm wriggling through Ivrium's red sands. And there! Another tapestry, another trace of silver, no larger than a blue-worm and less bright.

Like a single white hair woven into a head of midnight tresses, the silver thread trailed through a tangle of tapestries and worlds. Kendric paced it now—seemed to see it streak ahead, stitching through water, burrowing under buildings.

He wondered if he seized it and pulled, would all the tapestries curdle and draw tight? He wondered if he could rip it from its roots. He was pursuing it around the room until he stumbled against the leg of Irissa's tapestry table and paused, panting.

He braced himself on the frame's side struts, staring down at the great human-shaped hole in the center of her work. From that she had raised the spirit of Issiri. The vacancy remained impenetrable to the point of solidity. If Irissa's needlework had conjured Issiri's soul, what lingered was the opposite of soul, yet necessary to it, as the dark at the back of a mirror makes its silvery face reflective.

He almost touched it, the tangible emptiness, though he dreaded to . . . but then he saw that the black portion was shrinking, that tapestry threads were growing inward, together, as flesh mends after a wound.

Fascinated, Kendric watched the healing tapestry close upon itself. He wished he could aid the task, that he possessed any power now beyond the ability to falter. Painfully, he reached for the boarskin purse on the cord of his robe—flat, unused, worn for old times' sake, as a medal is after a war. Still, he never loosed it, as he never gave up his sillac-hide boots no matter how scuffed they became.

Turning the pouch inside out, he waited for flint and steel to fall to the crumpled fabric, then remembered he'd given them to Irissa on her quest to the Spectral City. His swollen fingers prodded the flat purse. Once he had carried a Quickstone—one of Irissa's coldstone tears transmuted to silver in his custody.

He had spent that rare, that unique coinage of Irissa's eyes and his faith, too, he recalled—given it to a dying shadow, to Issiri because she liked bright things, being born of a Dark Mirror. A single silver pence for the eyes of the dead.

He wished he had kept it now. He wished he still held some talisman to light his way into the dark, slow death poison offered . . . some hope of change in a hopeless and unchanging situation . . . some mirror to show where his children were, and how they fared. Where Irissa kept, and what she did there.

The shadow in the tapestry was swelling shut, or shrinking like the pupil of an eye when it sees too much light. Only a platter-size gap remained. Kendric leaned forward to stop it.

In a way, he felt it shut him away from Irissa even more than he had been. When this dark anomaly had dotted out, no trace would remain of what she had done, and how. No trace of Irissa's magic would linger in this room.

His fingers hesitated at the reweaving edge. Then he saw the dark had light—a fleeting cluster of silvery highlights. The dark eddied between his hands, as if he had shaken a bowl of water. Dancing light flickered into the semblance of a face—silver eyes and streaming shining hair, nose, mouth—Irissa's face! Or Issiri's. . . .

The face surfaced in the center of the tapestry, pushed up as if breaking water for air. But the black skin of Without held. Kendric could see a nose, chin, forehead swelling out the darkness and sinking back.

The mouth flared in a soundless cry and then the silver

was sinking again, fading as the threads interwove, locked together, closed the gap.

All the silver pooled into one drop, a tear at the inner corner of a vanishing eye. Tapestry threads writhed shut beneath it, marooning it there.

Kendric studied the smooth silver cabochon that reflected back in miniature the nearing impress of his trembling forefinger. It was hot to his touch—then cold, like stone. Like Quickstone.

He caught it in his fist and warmed it again. The door to Irissa had been sealed shut, but perhaps some benign or careless spirit—Issiri?—had left him a key to another door.

CHAPTER

22

SILVER SEA AND GRAY SKY SPREAD IN ALL DIRECTIONS. On a shingle of sand littered with dead things, a dingy ruffle of waves tossed to and fro.

"Rule was . . . bright," Javelle complained. "Neither Father nor Mother ever mentioned a rainy day."

"There must have been some," Thane said.

"Perhaps, but Clymerind was fabled for its beauty. This floating bone of earth we have walked has been picked clean."

"Ask the cat. It claims to know everything."

"I *have* known everything. There is a difference." The animal shook fine sand from a forefoot, wrinkling its face until the whiskers waggled. "I admit, my girl, that I, too, had more hopeful notions of Clymerind. But who knows how many years have passed here since its heyday?"

"We do!" Javelle was exasperated enough to stamp an emphatic boot on the packed sand. "Our parents wandered for some two years between leaving Rule and finally finding Rengarth. I was born within a year of their arrival in

Rengarth and am seventeen. Therefore, Clymerind has only been forsaken for twenty years."

Felabba pensively watched the waves play cat and mouse with a crayfish claw. "A pity that full laughter has not been granted to me," it commented. "I should be rolling upon the sand in mirth. I could use a good backscratch."

"Just say what you mean," Thane said.

"Indeed." The cat's white wedge of face lifted to Javelle, its expression excessively sweet. "What makes you imagine, dear girl, that the years tolled upon this once-magical land to the same tune that they sang into your parents' lives? Or that all worlds trickle sand through the same-paced hourglass?"

"But—" Javelle was stunned, but her brother wasn't.

"Don't try to tell us that we have to overcome time as well as gates!" he stormed. "You walked these lands yourself—not more than twenty years ago. With our parents."

Felabba batted wearily at the crayfish, flexing pearly nails into dainty scimitars. "I am Felabba, true—but somewhat more nicely preserved than your parents—or your father, at least. Even though Irissa looks as if she's stood still these twenty years, I have surpassed her. I have grown younger. Does that not . . . intrigue you?"

"Father did say you were a scruffier brand of feline earlier," Javelle conceded. "'Sharp-boned and sharper-tongued,' he said once. He didn't go into further detail."

"His restraint was commendable." Felabba licked a salty paw and made a face. "Children, children, children! Did I not mention my ninety-nine lives? Why do you believe the world—or worlds—to stand still because you seem to? I am a later . . . version . . . of Felabba, albeit younger. Your parents' Felabba has been gone these . . . well, many years. Many," it added emphatically.

The cat rose and strolled down the beach while Thane and Javelle watched speechlessly.

"Not only are we saddled with a nettlesome Felabba," Thane finally commented sourly, "but we are burdened with a fraudulent Felabba at the same time."

"You sound like Father."

"I can see why he took the back of his tongue to the beast. What is she doing now?"

"Digging."

"I'm hungry, too, but not for such things as wash up dead."

"I don't think she's digging for food."

"What, then?" Thane looked truly annoyed. He looked exasperated. He looked like Kendric when he didn't understand something and didn't want to.

Javelle pointedly examined the landscape. "It is sand, after all."

Thane's arms clapped to his side. "And we *are* hungry. No matter how much sifting time lies loose around us on this beach, it must still hoard driftwood and something to cook over it."

The two began zig-zagging between the surf's edge and the dunes, hunting for dry wood and any wet gifts of the sea that were still living. Within half an hour, they had a pile of gnarled, bleached wood smooth as picked bones.

They were just in time. Although no sunshine breached the mist, the silver sea was dimming into pewter. Even the fog darkened until they could only see a few feet ahead. Felabba was gone.

"Probably dug so deep she fell in," Thane grumbled as he helped Javelle tent the driftwood into a fire-worthy shape.

"The tide could have swept her away."

"Don't worry. With as many lives as she claims, she'll return to bedevil our descendents."

"If we survive to have descendents," Javelle amended, shivering in the dawning darkness.

"Don't worry about food. We'll find some. First I'll conjure a fire."

"Have you ever done it before?"

"No . . . Mother was most testy about my experimenting with fire. But there can't be much to it," Thane added cheerfully. "Even Father found it one of his first skills."

"Hm." Javelle sat back on her heels. "Before fire goeth pride."

"It's simply a matter of seeing properly—all magic is." Thane bent his dark head to the heaped wood. His eyes and his mind concentrated on the wind-carved shape of the sticks, tracing flamelike spirals and flares.

Javelle could see a glow halo the dry wood with every sweep of his eyes. Not so much flame as the pure heat that fire gives off, a silver-white shadow trembled over the wood. Cold fell like shadow over the beach as the light left. Javelle hunched nearer to the unearthly phosphorescence, hoping for Thane's success.

The ghostly glow burst into white-hot flames. Javelle jumped back even as Thane did, his dark eyebrows singed white by the flames.

"Too hot!" he admitted.

They crouched safely back from the sun-bright glare, attracted and repelled. A ball of cloud suddenly smothered the brightness. When it had passed, the fire burned low and meek.

A scaled fish fell to the sand next to the fire.

"Food!" Javelle crowed with suddenly released hunger, not questioning its source.

The cloud returned, shaking salty waterdrops over the pair, the sputtering fire, the still-flapping fish, everything.

"Briarwhip," Javelle hailed it, fondness in her voice.

"Filthy beast." Thane slapped sand and water off his sleeves, but he also captured the fish before the hound could run off with it again. "Where's your come-and-go master, then?"

"Here." Eeryon stood on the seaside of the fire, silver glinting on his tunic sleeves, his eyes the color of sand.

"Some help you were."

"Thane! He brought us food."

"We had the fire to cook it."

"Eeryon could have made his own fire."

Thane shrugged. "I suppose I get to gut the fish."

"Give me your dagger; I will." Javelle held out her hand.

"You?" Thane hooted.

"I." Javelle felt all too well that the getting of fish and fire were magical deeds the two young men had accomplished. The only feat left was introducing fish to fire—cooking, if you will—and she was determined to make herself useful no matter how distasteful the task.

The fish had suffocated on sea air and lay quite still as she brought the daggerpoint to its sleek belly. Ordinarily, she would have quailed at butcher work and let Thane take his male prerogative and do it, but she *was* extraordinarily hungry, for the first time in her life. And she felt, like the snake, useless—also for the first time in her life—a feeling that made her customary lack of purpose pale by contrast.

"I'll help," Eeryon said, crouching beside her.

And he did, holding back the shining skin while she made the long, slow cuts. Saying nothing while she concentrated on forgetting what she did and thought only of the outcome.

"I suppose I should . . . hack the head off."

Thane didn't answer and Eeryon looked uncertain. Javelle sawed the tough skin and flesh, then tossed the head to Briarwhip in the shadows.

Thane silently handed her a pointed stick. She handed him back a skewered fish, still loosely clothed in its scales so it shouldn't flake into the fire as it cooked.

Then she rose and went into the dark, toward the water's edge where the sea whispered to the sand over and over again.

"Thanks for sharing the fish," Thane said to Eeryon.

The boy from Without was silent.

"You could have shared our danger, too. We weren't greedy."

"I—" Eeryon began. Slowly, the fish began to cook as Thane rotated the stick, juice sizzling on the burning wood. "I meant to help, but was . . . called away."

"Can you always disappear like that?"

"Not always. I don't much like it."

"Why not? If I could disappear I'd . . . I'd be able to do anything—fight any foe, achieve any end. No one could stop me."

"Everyone can stop you when you're not quite there. Yourself most of all."

Thane regarded Eeryon's placid profile. "You're an odd fellow, but Without is an odd place to grow up. Listen, if danger threatens again, try to stay around for the difficulty. I can't look after Javelle all the time."

"Maybe Javelle doesn't need anyone to look after her."

"She has no magic," Thane explained carefully. "She has no business being along on this journey. Mother sent me, not her." In the silence, the returning Felabba's white form skimmed fishlike through the nearby dimness. "Not that wag-a-tongue cat."

"Perhaps I should leave," Eeryon suggested, moving.

"No." Thane didn't sound completely happy. "No. Stay as long as you contribute. Javelle would blame me if you left."

"You seem to blame each other a lot for things that are blameless."

"That's what it is to have a family, but I guess you wouldn't know."

"No," Eeryon agreed. "But I like company."

"Then stay. I don't care. I already told you."

Eeryon smiled, recognizing a grudging acceptance in the other boy. Briarwhip bounded over to settle at his side and watch the fish cook. Moments later, Javelle, several large shell halves in her damp hands, appeared from the darkness. She sat between the two boys.

"It smells good." She sounded surprised.

"It *is* good." Thane had pulled the fish from the flames and wrested off some meat with his fingers. He offered it to Javelle. Startled, she took the morsel and tasted it.

"Good."

Thane was scooping fish meat into the empty shells and passing them down. Eeryon shook his blond head.

"Go ahead," Thane urged. "Just because you missed the battle doesn't mean you can't eat afterward. Eat."

Eeryon lifted his fingers to his mouth, delaying eating as long as he could. His senses were particularly distant following one of his vanishing episodes. The sea's moaning came faint, like wind. He could smell neither the salt air nor the strong scent of cooked fish. His lips hardly sensed the hot flesh. His mouth barely tasted it. He went through the motions, watching Javelle and Thane wolf down their portions despite the heat.

When Eeryon quietly set his half-full shell to the sand, neither noticed it. Nor did they notice the white form that materialized over it like a specter to gobble daintily at the residue. When through, Felabba licked her whiskers interminably and rubbed once against Eeryon's velvet sleeve before melting into the dark again.

The fire subsided in subtle stages, popping now and again as sticks collapsed into charcoal or fish fat sizzled.

The three slept by it, wrapped in their own arms and separate concerns. Thane dreamed of finding a sword as tall as a tree and toppling it. Javelle slept lightly, feeling an odd comfort—and an odd unease—in Eeryon's returned presence.

Eeryon slept not at all, nor did he dream. He was used to the dark, and he did not use it for dreaming.

* * *

Far out on the Outer Abyssal Sea, something surfaced.

It was small and faint as a reflected star—a mere impulse glimpsed. It had whole great rivers of time and space to traverse, and vast, gateless empires ruled by vagrant currents.

Now it neared its heart's desire—near enough on the scale of things to recognize a heart's desire, however formless.

Formless. Yet it had form, could take form, as it had taken flight from the foundation of itself. Free. The word remained its touchstone. Free for the first time in its existence to answer to no one but itself.

A great illuminated pearl floated high above, painting a ladder of light on the ridged wavetops. It yearned after that far, perfect gleam that tipped every crest in quicksilver. Foothills and faraway mountains of gem-spattered ocean lapped around it—glittering scales drifted on the surface, ghostly shells stirred in the deep and the dark. Even the creatures of the deepest depths shone with fevered hues of ruby and amethyst, sapphire and emerald.

Aquamarine . . . The word had been born full-scripted in its mind. Like Quickstone. Somewhere beyond the sea lay a treasure of . . . aquamarine. It would search until it found and was no longer lost.

It dove, making a small maelstrom in the moonlight— one small flurry vanishing in the vast, shifting sea of treasured darkness and light. It was close—so close—to finding itself at last.

CHAPTER
23

IRISSA STARTED AWAKE—THOUGH SHE HAD NOT realized that she had slept. She was still a prisoner to Geronfrey's iron tower chamber, yet an overwhelming feeling of freedom tugged at her spirit. Perhaps she had dreamed of her own escape.

In the Dark Mirror's sleek center—the place Irissa's anxious eye ever wandered in search of comfort—a navel of light expanded. She pushed herself up from the cold floor and moved nearer.

Flames smaller than those reflected on the iris of an eye pulsed in the darkness. Their light spread, revealing three figures sleeping beside the blaze.

Tension cloaked Irissa's shoulders as she named and numbered the trio—Thane, his fist pillowed against his cheek, as he used to sleep in his cradle . . . Javelle, head turned one way, torso another in her customary restless disarray . . . and . . . one other, a boy who sat, not slept, his knees drawn up, his silver-threaded sleeves locked around them. The firelight painted the strange boy's hair the color of platinum.

Irissa warmed herself at the sharp though distant image, lost in memories. Another, harsher memory intruded, and she stiffened. She felt eyes watching her as she watched the scene in the mirror.

A hoarse chuckle echoed from the seven barred windows, though the room was empty.

"You have found my looking-glass," Geronfrey's degraded voice announced. "Apparently I, too, have mislaid a child. But now he is found, along with your lost ones. You study him now, seeress. How ironic our offspring travel together. A pity it cannot last."

Irissa's relief at the sight of her children alive and unharmed tightened into dread. She regarded the unknown boy again, knowing him now for Geronfrey's shadow child. Yet she recognized a favorite posture of her own in his, and she sensed an aloofness beyond understanding. But not evil. She saw no evil in him.

"A handsome youth, as befits his parents." Geronfrey sounded seriously vain, not mocking.

Irissa wondered how the sorcerer truly felt toward this son, this heir, this body-bought and magic-made offspring. Was he another tool, as his shadow mother, Issiri, had been?

Or had Geronfrey, having imitated life at last through his magic, learned also to imitate love? Certainly he had held no love for Issiri, his broken vessel, or Irissa, whose rejection had only spurred Geronfrey on to greater degradations of magic and power and parenthood.

"Both handsome boys," she conceded carefully. "How do you call yours?"

"I say 'Come,' and he does. Are yours so obedient?"

"No." Irissa smiled. "But they are more . . . honest. Besides, I meant . . . what did you name him?"

Geronfrey's laughter seemed shrill enough to crack the Dark Mirror's thick glass. "Names convey power. Do you think I would tell you?"

"I and mine are in your power. What do you fear?"

"What are *your* children's names?"

"Javelle. And Thane." Irissa studied the small images in the mirror. "Names only command those who can be commanded. You cannot take anything from my children, Geronfrey, just as you could take nothing from me."

"But I did! I took your essence. I made a woman of it, a mother."

"You made a mockery of it, poor hollow thing. You skimmed my surface, Geronfrey, and mistook it for self. Perhaps your son is all surface, too. All shadow."

"Does a shadow sit beside your own spawn? No. Eeryon is all I wanted him to be."

Silence held while Geronfrey contemplated his mistake in naming the boy he had so recently declined to name.

"I have never used anything's name to hurt it, Geronfrey," Irissa said softly at last.

"How do you remain so strong?" The sorcerer's voice was softer, too, carrying a bit of regret, a bit of envy.

"Because I am not afraid to be weak."

"Evasion! Wordplay. Glib, tongue-twisting half-truths."

"Half-truths have their place, as shadows do. No, I don't fear your son for your sake, or his own. I know nothing of him."

"Perhaps you feel a maternal bond."

"No! I have children enough, in danger enough. Don't give me custody of your guilt. I will not harm him, but I need not help him. He is yours, as you always wanted something to be. As I—even as that empty Issiri—could never be."

"Where is your Wrathman?" Geronfrey asked after another stormy silence in which Irissa could sense his gathering venom. The sorcerer had finally grown old enough to show it—and bitter enough to know it. "Why is he not thundering at the gate, at the brink of the Dark Mirror in search of his lost ones?"

"He keeps his place in Rengarth," Irissa answered with all the serenity she could muster. Within, her heart was pounding sudden alarm. If Geronfrey suspected her real weakness—and Kendric's—he would direct his baleful attention to Rengarth instead of Rule.

And Kendric, mortally poisoned, had no one to protect him there, except ludborgs. Geronfrey must be kept from inquiring after Kendric.

"A Ruler has an obligation to rule, you know," Irissa added blandly.

"I know." Geronfrey's tone was sardonic.

Irissa knew why: he considered himself the sole and future Ruler of Rengarth—that was the empty triumph that drove all his schemes.

"Will you ever end?" she asked curiously. "Does your lifeline dwindle or stop? Will . . . Eeryon become your heir? Or is he a stopgap? A . . . tool in your lust for immortality. Will you again sacrifice your own creation to your desire to create?"

"Questions! Torlocs and talking cats were ever fond of posing them. Answer your own speculations, seeress. You shall have time enough to do it in the bottomless hourglass of Without. And as you think, you shall diminish, in every respect, as I have."

"Age? I age in Without?" The note of not unwelcome hope in Irissa's voice silenced the sorcerer.

Moments after, the vision in the Dark Mirror winked out. Irissa felt a fabric tear in her mind, felt a distant tapestry amend itself.

"You have truly bequeathed all vanity to your dead shadow," Geronfrey's parting voice whispered against the stones. "It is something I shall never be guilty of."

He was gone. Irissa wryly found herself missing the company. She passed her hand over the mirror, hoping to raise a vision of her own . . . yet knowing it answered only to Geronfrey.

Finally, for boredom's sake, she searched her waistband purse. Inside were the forgotten flint and steel Kendric had given her for the journey to the Spectral City.

Like dull gemstones the two pieces clicked together in her palm. She smiled to remember Kendric carrying them through Rule and beyond, to recall the fires they had started and how comforting a fire always was to the children we all become in the dark.

She had seen her children by firelight. They carried no flint and steel—at least visibly—but still had learned to coax fire into their lives when needed. Her sharp eyes had spied the curled fish skin at the fire's verge: maternal anxiety eased remarkably when she knew that they had eaten properly.

So the scene Geronfrey had hoped would taunt had reassured her instead. Perhaps that is what she meant by a strength that he would never understand. Nor had his threat of Without's aging properties frightened her. Irissa smiled again to think how little she feared aging for herself if it meant keeping pace with Kendric.

Yet two disconcerting facts remained to trouble her. One was the odd lack of feeling she felt toward the shadow son—neither love nor hate. The other was an absence that Kendric, were he here, would consider the height of good news. Irissa did not. Felabba had been nowhere to be seen in the Dark Mirror.

Irissa would have felt better had she seen the cat.

When one's children venture into a hostile world ignorant and kind, when they sleep innocent as babes beside an unsuspected half-brother spawned from a shadow mother, it would be reassuring to know that something as wise, cranky, and chronically suspicious as Felabba was keeping watch.

CHAPTER
24

DAWN STRUCK THE SILVER SEA LIKE A SWORD ON A shield—the clash of sudden light brought Javelle and Thane instantly awake.

Eeryon had already been stirring; half-shells abrim with fresh water lay in a row by the fire shards.

"You rise early," Thane noted with a trace of suspicion.

"Water! Thank you." Javelle gulped down one shell's contents. "Where did you find it?"

Eeryon's head jerked over his shoulder. "Inland, beyond the dunes."

Felabba was crouched over a smaller shell, lapping intently. Briarwhip had already overturned his gigantic shell and was loping along the waterline.

"At least today we have sun to see by." Thane stretched and stood.

"To see what?" Javelle rose, too, brushing sand from her clothes. She glanced curiously at Eeryon's black velvet garb—still imperviously black despite the damp and sand dunes. It was as if nothing quite touched him. "It's island all around us, and sea all around the island."

"That's usually the way of it," Thane remarked. "Well, we shall have to find a way off the island. Perhaps a wrecked ship with wood enough to resurrect a boat from its bones will serve us."

"I'm not traipsing all over this island," Javelle objected, "in hopes of finding a shipwreck. Can't you two use magic, or something, to make us a boat?"

"Magic isn't that sort of servant, Javelle," Thane said. "You'd know if you had it. Besides, you're talking about make-magic, and that was never particularly Torloc."

"We won't get off the island," someone said.

Thane and Javelle turned to Eeryon with open mouths. Another voice had never intervened in their sibling debates before, unless it had been parental.

"I sent Briarwhip to cover the island last night," Eeryon went on. "The beast never sleeps. If it had found anything of interest—like broken ships—it would have told me."

"*It* speaks, too?" Thane was not about to believe that.

"No. But we have communicated without speech for so long that I know how to understand it—in any form."

"Then we have come to Rule only to find ourselves farther from it than ever," Javelle said. "Unless there is a gate here to another part of this world."

"There *was* a gate," Thane realized bitterly. "I sealed it to keep Geronfrey out."

In the silence, Thane condemned himself, Javelle mulled the situation, and Eeryon stood struck to stone. Yet of them all, he managed to speak again first.

"Geronfrey?" he asked uncertainly.

"An evil sorcerer who has haunted our parents." Thane waved an impatient hand. "It's our problem, and of no importance to you."

"Geronfrey. It's an . . . unusual name."

"I thought you didn't care about names," Javelle teased. "Eeryon, are you all right?"

His eyes were on the sea. When he turned to look at her,

she could almost see right through them. They were silver and green, like the sea . . . so aquamarine that for a dazed moment she thought she saw into saltwater.

"Tell me of Geronfrey, Javelle," Eeryon said quietly. "I should know the . . . danger you face."

"Tell him the old stories, if you like," Thane interrupted. "I'm going to explore the island for myself."

Eeryon had sunk to the sand, crossing his legs to sit.

"You *are* sick." Javelle leaned down to inspect him. "Was it the fish, do you think it was tainted?"

"No." Eeryon smiled palely. "Why should *you* think that?"

"My . . . father had a bout with a bad fish once, but he fought it, rather than ate it. And Rengarth, where we live, is rife with poison."

"I'm not ill." Eeryon nodded at the sand beside him until Javelle sat there. "Tell me about this . . . evil sorcerer."

"You say the word 'evil' as if you didn't believe in it."

"There is no evil. Except failure."

"Oh, I hope you're wrong." Javelle shook his arm, but Eeryon pulled away from her grasp. "If failure is evil, I am full up with it."

"What have you failed to do?"

"Find any magic within myself."

"Perhaps that is success, if magic makes for evil sorcerers. Tell me."

So Javelle did, glibly, with the ease of repeating a tale often told and retold. She told the boy who didn't know what a mother was that her own had once been a maiden coveted for the magical powers she would convey on her first lover.

"Geronfrey?" Eeryon guessed.

No, not *Geronfrey*. Javelle was indignant, rising to her knees in the sand to report how clever Irissa, her mother, realizing that she would have no value for Geronfrey if her maidenhood were given elsewhere, bestowed it on her traveling companion, Kendric.

"Then *he* was gifted with these Torloc powers?"

Well, not immediately, not evidently. And not willingly, Javelle went on. Kendric neither knew or approved of his new "gifts." Yet he learned to use them, and Irissa and Kendric traveled together until they found the lost Torlocs and came finally to Rengarth, where Kendric was heir to the High Seat, as it turned out.

And then everybody got rid of Geronfrey, who—it came out—had usurped the power in Rengarth for generations. And then Irissa and Kendric had Javelle and Thane, and it all ended relatively well, after all.

"But Geronfrey," Eeryon urged.

"Oh, I've heard about him since I had ears." Javelle strained fine, dry sand through her fingers. "I think he's a myth parents make up to cow their children, actually. He's always been out there somewhere, waiting. He still wants my mother, and she is beautiful, I suppose, but I wouldn't want to go against her will. They seem to dread his reappearance, my parents. And yet, I've seen no sign of Geronfrey in all my life."

"What is your mission here in Rule?"

Javelle hesitated. Thane had told her not to share their quest with this stranger from Without. Yet no one had ever sat and listened to Javelle for so long, as if what she had to say was important. As if *she* were important, whether she had magic or not.

Her dark eyes sobered. "He is only mortal," she whispered. "My father. Our father. He will . . . die . . . long before the rest of us—unless Thane and I can find his original sword that was left here on Rule years ago. You asked what having a mother was like, but you, too, have had a father, even if he was a bit distant. One does not want to lose that."

"No. That would be the ultimate . . . failure." Eeryon turned away from Javelle.

The cat was sitting on the sand, staring at him with its emerald eyes in full glory. He stared back, unable to look away.

"So that's the family tale," Javelle said, sighing. "I thought a quest to Rule would be more exciting than it is, but if—*when*—we find the sword, it will all be worth it. Oh, look, Thane's coming back. Thane—!"

Javelle jumped up and ran to greet her brother. Eeryon remained.

"You are quiet for a talking beast," he told the cat finally.

"Like you, I have much to mull."

"What do you know of what I must consider?"

"I, too, carry out another's mission—only in my case, it is a quest for another semblance of my self."

"You will . . . tell . . . them, then."

"Tell them what?"

"To say it is to arm you."

The cat stretched, flaring its claws into the sand. "I am already armed. It is you that are weaponless, shadow boy." Eeryon started. "I see you come and go. One day you will wink out forever."

"One day—soon?"

"I know things without knowing their pedigree," the cat mused. "Bits and pieces of previous lives shuffle like cards through my mind. I seem to know you for a thing of misbegotten shadow. I doubt you will endure long. But it does not take long to do evil."

"I will not do evil!"

"No one does evil until it is done. All act for good—their own or another's. All evil is done in the name of someone's good."

"Names again! I wish I had never heard anything's true name." Eeryon's fists pounded the sand. The cat batted at the motion, at one fist. Its velvet touch burned him like fire.

He jerked away, staring into the ambiguous feline eyes. "Tell me the truth. We seek the same sword for different reasons, different masters. What shall I do?"

The anguish in Eeryon's voice was enough to wring pity from a stone. From a cat it received a contemplative blink. "Learn more of parents, and less of masters. As a crystal caster of my acquaintance likes to say, the future chases its tail to the past."

Eeryon sighed in exasperation and pushed himself upright to meet the returning Thane.

"You were right," Thane admitted. "The island is mostly sand and rock. Its underwater sojourn must have drowned all the foliage. We're lucky it's been afloat again long enough for rainwater to collect in the rocks."

"So close," Javelle chaffed. "And yet too far."

"You know where we are?" Eeryon asked sharply.

"Clymerind was a nomad isle," Thane explained. "It sailed the Outer Abyssal Sea. When it sank, it lay southeast of the Six Realms, off Tolech-Nal."

"The sword was lost in Rindell Pond on the verge of the Shrinking Forest," Javelle took up the tale. "But much of the Realms altered in the gate's great collapse. Our parents saw Rindell Pond become a lake. It might be all dry ground by now."

"Besides," Thane put in, cheerfully toting obstacles, "we don't know how long Clymerind has been asail. It could have floated south to the Furzenlands, or north off the City of Rule—if there still *is* a City of Rule. Father was pretty clear about the upheaval as he and Mother left."

"Then we search for a raindrop within a deluge!" Eeryon's frustration came so sharp and sudden it surprised them all.

"You join us in our quest?" Javelle asked, her eyes shining spontaneously with a joy she could not explain.

Its innocence struck Eeryon silent.

"He has his own business here," Thane reminded her.

"Our business is the same now—to leave the island for realmland," Javelle said. "And, I've told him of our need."

"You didn't!"

"You were the one who mentioned Geronfrey. I think Eeryon wants to join us in our quest to save our father." Javelle turned to him. "Don't you?"

Eeryon looked from their waiting dark eyes to the cat's ever-observant emerald gaze. The creature said nothing.

"Yes," Eeryon answered slowly—so slowly he seemed to be answering another question entirely. "I want to join you."

"You see?" Javelle crowed to her brother.

"You must be an eloquent storyteller," Thane conceded grudgingly.

"There has to be something I'm good at," she said lightly. "Besides, with Eeryon along, we double our magic."

"Triple," the cat put in from the sand.

"Triple," Javelle repeated. She looked from one boy to the other, beaming hope and begging peace. Neither could resist her enthusiasm.

"Triple," they agreed, speaking together and then laughing.

"You had better begin your new alliance," Felabba put in tartly, "by concocting a way off this island. I've no desire to spend another night getting sand between my toes."

This time Javelle joined them when they laughed. The cat did not laugh. Nor did Briarwhip, who came padding over the sand to crouch by Eeryon, tilt his disheveled head, and remain unusually still.

In the creature's three small fiery eyes, only unasked— and unanswered—questions gleamed.

By late afternoon, the threesome, accompanied by the two animals, had located the island's narrowest end—a long spit of snoutlike land with waves sneezing on either side.

"We have found the head," Thane analyzed. "Now we must bridle it."

"How?" Javelle wondered. "With what?"

"Magic," Thane grinned. He was in his element. "Mother says that no matter how native magic is, you must find its specific paths within yourself. Sometimes it takes a lifetime."

"Father hasn't got that long," Javelle put in tightly. "Besides, I'm not interested in hearing how mystical magic is. I want to see results."

"A hard critic, Eeryon." Thane winked broadly. "But mark my reasoning. Rengarth is a world brewed of water and air and land, of birds and fish. I have an affinity for water, so it is to the things of water I will look for aid."

"Stop bragging and start doing."

"Peace, Javelle. I have, in case you haven't guessed yet, an idea."

"Say it!"

"Don't screech. It's so unbecoming a lady."

"I'm not a lady. I'm your sister and your elder and heir of Rengarth and I'll have you cast into a Bubblemere if you don't produce more than overheated air."

Thane bowed and pointed to the waves. "I will call on the powers of the deep, the great creatures of the Outer Abyssal Sea, of some of whom not even our parents may have been aware. Eeryon, being adept with the frippery on his sleeves, is a natural fisherman. He will cast the lines and nets to snare them, bridle them, harness them. Together, we will drive this nomad island like a chariot to wherever we wish."

The simplicity and sense of this plan struck them all dumb with admiration—at least no one spoke for several moments.

Javelle was the first to find a flaw in it. "You have no role for Felabba."

"She will . . . instruct . . . these creatures to follow our commands."

"What makes you think, young dreamer, that the creatures of the sea are mine to command?" Felabba asked tartly.

"You're a beast, like them." Silence greeted this two-edged answer. "You're . . . commanding by nature." Silence. "You'll probably be able to strand a tasty dinner on our shores as reward for your efforts."

"Now I see the logic," the cat said. "Magic always goes better with the promise of a full stomach."

"And I?" Javelle said. "What role have I in this joint enterprise?"

"You can fix the stranded fish once we get where we are going."

"Oh," she said, speechless for once.

Eeryon touched her arm. "You can watch us and guide us. Magic is highly self-absorbing. Don't let us spell awry. Don't let"—his voice lowered—"me slip away."

"No." Javelle didn't understand the task she had undertaken, but she knew from looking into Eeryon's oddly translucent eyes that it was a grave one. "All right." Their paths were set; matters had become serious. "You'd best begin before sunfall. If I'm to watch, I must see."

Both young men nodded. Felabba bestirred herself, moving to stand beside them. Javelle pulled back, drawing Briarwhip with her. The moment was serious enough that she felt a certain comfort in having the rough-coated creature at her side, a fellow witness.

Sunlight was already slanting through the clouds. Seabirds skirled along the headland, their wings beating heartbeat-slow in the salt-soaked, wind-laden air.

To Javelle, watching, it all evolved with the odd slowed motion of the birds. Nothing visibly changed. The trio stood looking to the sea, each silent, each lost in its own self, be it from Rengarth, or Without, or who-knows-where.

For the longest time, nothing happened. Javelle grew impatient, then remembered her father's words: magic is a great long Nothing with a Spectacular Period to it. She also remembered why she was here—and Thane—on this windswept spit of sand watching waves crash and hoping for something she didn't really believe in, because it had never believed in her.

Magic. Yes, Javelle thought. For Kendric, apostate of magic, let magic come. For Javelle, outcast of magic, let magic come. For Irissa, mistress of magic, let magic come. For Thane, born of magic, let magic come. For Felabba, reborn of magic, let magic come. For Eeryon, fading from magic, let magic come. For . . . Briarwhip, mismade of magic, let magic come. For . . . Geronfrey, misuser of magic, let magic come. Now!

"If Javelle had really believed in the magic of her mind, she might have thought her inner litany had taken outer shape.

For waves crested on the sand in faster rhythm. Clouds seemed to sally overhead at greater speed, as if racing the sun to its dying fall in the water. Wind hushed by with rapid caressing fingers. Sand rose in circling pillars and danced down the beach.

The salt-tang on the air grew heavy, like incense. A mist of whipped water and sand and air and cloud foamed at the sea's mouth, and ate at the island.

The land itself heaved, as if giving a great sigh, like a winded mount being asked for greater speed and longer service.

Something sang in the surf—many things. Shells reverberated to the notes of wind and water. Forms washed up, rising from the curling waves—finned, furled, tentacled, winged forms.

Among them the lancing silver whips of Eeryon's lines—spun from the endless reels of his sleeves—lashed like sprays of water. Captured leviathans reared above the water beyond the surf—great shining bodies sleek with scales. Human heads surfaced on fish-supple bodies, and fishheads with staring eyes and sucking mouths topped human forms—as if the dead of both kinds had found new commingled life in the water.

Life teamed upward at the island's fringes, every variety of water-breathing life summoned from the sea's soft sand underbelly. Silver lines secured it all in a gentle custody.

Then Felabba licked her chops.

The creatures ebbed from the sand and the surf, pulled out for the deeper water where the sinking sun blazed a bloody trail. Silver lines tautened, a thousand or more tied to as many submerged sea-steeds.

Clymerind the Wonderful shuddered from sand dune to shoreline. Its great, sunken body lurched forward. Waves sprayed at its rear as the island sliced shiplike through the sea.

On its quarterdeck—the sandy rise the three had commandeered—wind whipped their hair into their eyes. Sand, flying in multitudinous grains, sealed Felabba's green gaze shut. But it was too late. The island was moving. The island was under way, at sail. The sun moved into their lee, burning crimson.

Javelle looked to Felabba, an intent figure of wind-whipped fur, staring blindly into the future. Thane was braced, jaw set, looking more like Kendric than he ever had, making Javelle feel twice bereft for some reason, and twice blessed.

Eeryon was the last she looked at, and him twice. He seemed tauter than one of his silver lines. When she searched his eyes, she found their color had leeched into the flat silver sea. All that was left to Eeryon was the expanded pitch-black centers, holes in the mask of his face.

She stepped nearer, touched his plain black velvet sleeve. Her hand sank into the fabric as into night, vanishing. Her breath caught. She felt she was sinking interminably, drowning on dry land. Then she touched bottom. Herself. Her sense. That will that Kendric had tried to tell her was a better base than magic.

She struggled up, as if—breathless—she were racing through an alien element for a distant piece of herself. Javelle broke the sea's surface like a creature summoned, breathed wind instead of water. With her came another.

Her eyes crossed Eeryon's. Their dark focus had faded. The sea shone through him and found a salty echo in her pounding blood.

She smiled, nodded, and said nothing.

Clymerind sailed on into the twilight, drawn by silver reins fastened to a flotilla of sea-born coursers.

As land ahead—as lost realms—grew from a hairline . . . into a sandy scar . . . into a thickness on the horizon, the sun plunged its ruddy torch into the silent sea and the tangled wind hissed like snakes.

CHAPTER
25

MOONLIGHT STRUMMED THE TAUT LINES OF EERYON'S magic and dusted the sand with quicksilver. Clymerind glided toward the huge land mass the night obscured. Its ocean-called steeds remained invisible and unfelt, except for a deep tremor in the island's heart now and then.

Sunfall had come soon after they had sighted the mainland, so Javelle and Thane slept on the pillowing sand dunes. All had agreed to fast in deference to their sea-born coursers. It would seem . . . rude to fish among the shallows for small fry while greater fish still ferried them through the deep.

So, fireless and unfed, the trio began what they hoped would be their final night on the island. Only Eeryon kept watch on the silvered wires of his magic. Thane thought that unnecessary.

Magic was an unboiling pot, Thane had declared. No need to hover; once properly set in motion, magic would not fade at the maker's inattention. They could all sleep.

Eeryon had agreed pleasantly enough, but insisted on sitting up, anyway. He knew he could not sleep whether magic twanged the air or not. Even if sleeplessness were not a natural condition for him, he would have found it impossible after the day's numbing revelations.

Eeryon watched waves roll over the beach like lacy white clouds. Night in these worlds beyond Without was much like anytime in Without, he mused. Briarwhip sat attentively at his side.

"It is the same sword," he told the creature softly.

He took its silence, as always, for agreement.

"What my father demands of me will slay *their* father— or at least allow him to die in his natural span of years."

Again the beast kept silence, not even moving.

Eeryon sighed. "Their father sounds a man worth preserving, if their feeling for him means anything. And their mother sent them on this errand, so she, too, would be stricken if I obtain the sword instead of them." He revised his thought. *"When* I obtain the sword instead of them."

Briarwhip whimpered and nudged closer. The beach was cold in the dark, as the tepid air of Without had never been. Eeryon appreciated the beast's rough, more tangible presence now. He would miss the form—and the name—when they returned to Without. With the sword.

Of course he had to do it, Eeryon admonished himself. It was the ultimate obedience his father had demanded of him.

Geronfrey. The name had been branded into the dark behind the dark of his eyes when he had first heard it from the mage's own lips so recently. Its meaning had lain in the very novelty of it. Now the name was seared into his equivocal soul. He had never thought to hear it invoked as an enemy's name by those he considered his first—and only—friends.

Yet he had not been made to deny his heritage, his

purpose. Whyever Geronfrey wanted the sword, the reason
must be paramount. Nothing else could override it. Nothing.

Eeryon shut his eyes to the moonlit sand and sea. No
moon beamed on Without, and there was no sand, no sea,
hardly any sound except distant crackling lightning and
snapping thunder.

Eeryon wished he could be back in that undemanding
dark, answering to only one force—Geronfrey—instead of
to other eyes and ears, instead of to himself.

"I must!" he whispered fiercely. "Must, must . . . must
and . . . must."

His word seemed like the sea's suspiration hissing softly
over the sand. It was almost low and rhythmic enough to
lull him into the alien state of sleep, of temporary forgetful-
ness. Almost.

Briarwhip's abrasive coat rubbed Eeryon the wrong way
as the massive beast stirred.

The boy's eyes rolled open. The animal was fidgeting
beside him. He saw why. Before him the sea was sweeping
higher. Closer. Even as Eeryon watched, one high wave was
washing up the dunes toward his feet!

He leaped up to retreat. The wave had already flushed far
past the wetline. No backward pull diminished its size and
speed.

Instead of ebbing, it grew larger and higher . . . and
narrower—into a curl of liquid shape composed of moonlight and the sea's eternal silver spittle. Feet like shells
peeped from the ruffle of its watery hem. Arms moved in
the liquefaction of its flowing sleeves. A face crested to its
peak and stayed there.

The walking wave walked on, becoming more humanlike
with every step, until . . . a woman worked from silver
foam and seaweed neared Eeryon, the sea's deepest daylight glimmer greening her eyes.

Briarwhip growled and bared formidable fangs. Thick hairs along its spine stiffened to battle quills.

"Hush," Eeryon commanded quietly, glancing over his shoulder to Javelle and Thane. They remained sleeping, unmoved. Even the puddle of white that was the cat Felabba stayed curled into its inhuman dreams.

The apparition drew toward Eeryon as if seeking him. He saw now that the night, the alien moonlight, had deceived him at first. This woman was as real and human as, as . . . Javelle, though taller, though somehow both older—and younger.

Her damp fingers flicked to the taut threads leading from his sleeves as if using them as guidelines. The silver filaments thrummed at her touch like lute strings, emitting a sound sometimes high and sweet . . . sometimes as low and throaty as a warning cry.

Briarwhip's tail lashed the sand, thumping a drumbeat of alarm until Eeryon's quick hand on the animal's shoulder stilled it.

The woman paused opposite Eeryon, so close he could see grains of sand glittering on her bare feet like coldstones. A network of gems glistened over her diaphanous gown, glimpsed as fleetingly as living silver scales from the sea itself.

"Are you fish?" Eeryon wondered aloud, although in a hushed tone.

The woman's laughter fell more lightly than his softest syllable.

"I come by water, boy. I am not *of* water. I come by the dark water under all the worlds . . . and the silver lines of your magic calling to the voice of my freedom. You called for help, didn't you?"

She apparently found Eeryon as strange as he did her. She moved toward him, hesitated, then smiled her pale phantom's smile, studying him in mutual intensity.

"Who are you?" he asked.

The certainty in her silver-green eyes flickered. "I fear I have . . . lost my name. For some reason, also lost." Her face softened as she dismissed the notion of a name. "It doesn't matter. There are names that are greater than names, such as 'Mother.' 'Son.' "

Eeryon stumbled backward a step, nearly overturning Briarwhip in the process. He was not used to his cloud-companion making so solid an obstacle. He was not used to confronting strangers on the even stranger shores of another world. He was not used to having all his assumptions shaken in a single day.

"You're a dream," he accused. "I never dream. I *cannot* dream."

"How sad." Her wistful voice was as elusively seductive as the surf's. "I have had naught but dreams in my life, and most of them bad." Her hand reached to his arm as if to prove her existence.

"Who are you?" he gasped, forgetting discretion.

"I don't know," she answered honestly enough, a vagueness in her eyes that echoed her aspect. "But I know that you are mine. How your sleeves . . . shine—and your hair. I had a Quickstone once—liquid running silver in my hand. And then—" Sorrow took her eyes, drew her attention inward.

In the moment she looked elsewhere, Eeryon felt her compelling spell snap.

"Mother?" he intoned the alien word, even more out of step in this place and with this person.

"Mine," she said in a possessive way that soon became a sing-song chorus. "Mine. I have lost much that was mine, but something still remains . . . mine."

"Javelle said my . . . mother must have died at my birth!" Eeryon burst out. Let her be a ghost, a spirit, he told himself, an apparition from the swelling sea.

"Birth?" Memory stirred her vacant eyes. Her body moved uneasily, as if feeling unseen bonds tightening. "I remember no birth . . . only death. Slow, fading death. A man gave me a Quickstone once," she recalled, brightening. "So bright." Her eyes turned back to his. "Perhaps a Quickstone hastened *your* birth. *My* Quickstone. You are mine—"

She reached for him with her white, wet hands as vaporous as clouds and as grasping as bone. Her face blazed like the moon. Eeryon felt seared by light and mystery, as if Thane's overheated fire had sprung up into living form to consume him.

His horror raged high, along with another emotion new to him—denial. He felt the lines of his sleeve-sent magic slacken, felt everything around him loosen—sight, sound, feeling, scent.

Blessed darkness came to reclaim him. The scene around him faded, Briarwhip dissolved, too, into cloud form. The woman was the last object he saw, a bright mist dissipating on the beach as if drifting away in search of something it had lost.

"Where's Eeryon?" Javelle asked, waking in the night.

"Who knows?" Thane's voice was sleep-thick and grumpy. "Wandering around, as he always does."

"I thought I felt something—a fleeting fog—at my throat. It stings."

"Sea mist. Go back to sleep."

"My sentiments exactly," a new voice put in. Felabba stood, stretched luxuriously in the moonlight, then turned and settled facing in an opposite direction.

"Felabba, didn't *you* sense anything?" Javelle persisted.

"I only sense that night is for sleeping and daylight for asking silly questions."

"But I did feel something," Javelle insisted.

From the nearby dunes, Thane snored, asleep again.

The cat said, "Really," and flattened its ears as if to stopper them.

"Something . . . eerie," Javelle repeated to no one.

The silver serpent stirred against her skin, as if dreaming, but remained silent.

Morning showed the islanders an endless vista of immobile mainland—beach and birds and a fence of dark green forest beyond.

Eeryon had wakened the others without comment and now stood contemplating the land across the water as if too numb to see it.

"It looks like the Shrinking Forest!" Javelle exclaimed as she spied tall pinetops farther inland. "I can't believe that we've come so close to our goal on the first try."

"It *is* the Shrinking Forest," Thane asserted.

"For a forest that shrinks, it grows rather thick and tall," Eeryon noted.

He had been unduly quiet that morning and now avoided the others' eyes. Javelle tried to share a mutual glance, but found him quicker than she at evading it. All she glimpsed were the dilated black holes of his expression, his pupils.

Sometimes in bright light, his darkness-honed eyes became pure silver-blue. But now, in this daylight, on the brink of achieving their quest, Eeryon looked harder and more closed, as if he had let blinders shut his eyes. Or perhaps the remembered dark had done the shutting for him.

"How will we cross?" Eeryon was eyeing the river-wide band of water between island and mainland.

"Swim," Thane suggested exuberantly.

Eeryon's silence grew into unspoken disagreement.

"Are you afraid to ruin your black velvet finery?" Thane prodded. "Or the silver on your sleeves?"

Eeryon grew stiffer and seemed less likely to answer.

Javelle jumped into the chasm of silence. "I doubt Felabba could swim, or Briarwhip. And I certainly don't want to start the day wet, as well as chill and hungry."

"Then *you* think of a way for us to cross, Javelle," Thane promptly challenged.

"I will," she said, walking to the water's edge to consider it.

"It had better be fast," Felabba piped up in her sourest tone.

"Why?" they asked in unison, Thane and Javelle. Eeryon paid little attention to the morning's debates; he seemed marooned upon some inner island of his own.

The cat was delighted to explain at its considerable leisure.

"While you three were congratulating yourselves on the likeliness of the land before you, and while you argued methods of our party's conveyence over this last neck of sea, while you—"

"Tell us quickly, or it will be too dark to do anything but sleep again," Thane advised.

The cat blinked at such unseemly haste, then began stroking its whiskers with an efficient paw. "While you were doing all that I was merely attempting to remind you of, you neglected to regard the land at your *back*—always a bad idea on a journey, and a fatal oversight on a journey by island."

"Oh." Javelle had been the first to turn and see for herself.

Water was rising behind them—or Clymerind was sinking again! A thin rivulet of sea had seeped between them and the rest of the island, isolating them on the small headland.

"Why?" Thane wondered with more amazement than energy to confront the new threat.

"Our harnessed sea-steeds," Eeryon said abruptly. "All

the pull came from before us. The strain quite effectively broke the island's neck. We stand on the head while the body sinks behind us."

"And Valna," Javelle realized, "gone again. No one will ever see it again as we have—Wrathmen and all!"

"Thank Those Without," the cat put in dryly while wetting its whiskers further.

"Those Without." Thane spoke as if reminded of something. "You've never told us about Those Without, Eeryon. Surely, you must know something of them."

"Never mind Without or anything in it." Javelle pointed to the widening neck of water behind them. "We shall soon join the main part of the island in sinking—or at the least drift free into the wild Outer Abyssal Sea. We must find the longest pieces of driftwood possible and pole ourselves to shore."

"Pole ourselves?" Thane was torn between indignation and laughter. "The water must still be too deep for such a puny effort. Better that Eeryon cast his sleeve threads into cable, ensnare the shoreline trees, and we pull ourselves landward along the lines."

"Then let's do both," Javelle suggested, running past Thane to the prow of the headland.

Eeryon remained watching the main body of Clymerind soften into the waves foot by foot. No shocks greeted the island as it slowly returned to the depths. It simply ebbed, like a particularly tangible wave lost in a sea of more liquid composition.

At the opposite edge of their own tiny island, Javelle, her boot toes churning into the sand, was prying loose a half-buried log. Long as a bearing-beast—and almost as resistant—the log was not especially thick, but gnarled and stubborn as an old man's cane.

It would have been comical to watch Javelle battle this behemoth, save that the headland suddenly trembled under their feet. Both young men ran to help her, but Javelle's last mighty push heaved the log free as they arrived.

"Now that's magic," Thane approved.

"No, that's muscle," Javelle answered shortly.

"You? Muscle?"

"Will can make a mountain out of a mole," she answered stoutly.

Still, when she stood back and saw that it took both young men to twist the log around and drag it to the waterline, she began to realize the size of the task she had achieved without questioning.

"Is that all it is?" she mused, content to trot their wakes now that they were taking a hand in her plan. "Will? Father always said it could be so."

Felabba paced her with an urgent, paw-crossing lope.

"All? You are touching the unmagical secret within magic, my girl. I can't quite swallow that your father has led you in this sublime direction of self-sufficiency. Stubbornness, yes, now there was an art Kendric was master of."

"He mastered more than anyone knew," Javelle answered hotly, her voice breaking as she remembered the reason for their quest. "Watch whom your acid tongue scours, catling, or I shall teach you a lesson in respect for your elders."

"Ah, now they sing the same old doughty tune, father and daughter. You will need to age far more, Wrathman's child, before you can scold a cat in good conscience."

By the time Javelle and the cat arrived, Eeryon stood on the last dune that curled like a wave over the water. He faced the mainland, his arms stretched before him, the palms touching prayerfully. Once again the silvery threads embroidering his sleeves untangled, twisting into a thick rope. Like a flying snake the rope arched the water and disappeared among the trees.

"Come on, push," Thane urged Javelle.

She ran to help him raise the log upright and then, together, they speared it down into the waves.

"Don't drop it," her brother warned.

Javelle's arms ached as they probed for bottom. She feared it would be so far below that their pole would slip between their arms and back into the sea that had beached it.

But only half-immersed, the driftwood balked and bit into sand.

"It *is* shallow!" Javelle confirmed.

The sandy land beneath their feet slipped sideways, as if pushed. Thane and Javelle stabbed the log into the water again and again—always finding purchase, always pushing the submerged land behind them.

Before them, waves ate away the shoreline sand. The party found themselves moving backward; even anchoring Eeryon, who seemed as planted as some dark-barked tree on his spot of beach, was forced to backstep as their small island shrunk.

A seabird flashed white in the sun, then landed on one silver rope, balancing on the handy perch and cocking its big-beaked head.

"Away!" Eeryon commanded fruitlessly.

Briarwhip bounded into the surf and ran back and forth, chewing spray and howling at the bird's tempting yet secure proximity.

Spray stung the threesome's eyes shut. They fought their own tired muscles—even Eeryon feeling the strain of keeping his arms uplifted. They fought the unblinking gaze of the sun and the uneven footing of the beach. Felabba joined Briarwhip in hopefully eyeing the bird, then retired to groom herself away from the waterline.

Still, the opposite shore drew nearer, the forest's dark slash separating into ranks of trees and bushes. A few reeds bowed to the wind on the pale strip of beach, but nothing scuttered across the dazzling sand—no birds, no crabs. It looked utterly deserted.

"Almost there," Thane gritted between his teeth, shutting his eyes to drive the pole deep into the sandbar beneath them. Javelle pushed all her weight onto the lever, too, ignoring the water that soaked her garments hip-high and embroidered an uneven saltline on her tunic.

Eeryon shut his eyes to the sun, his arms trembling from the last effort of his sleeve-borne magic, almost transported by the task.

None of them even paused when a massive splash sounded behind them. They knew Clymerind had vanished as unwitnessed as when it had risen again.

A distant roar surged through the water toward the mainland surf, growing louder faster. That turned their heads over their shoulders—the sound of a million wings beating or five thousand horses' hooves pounding or hundreds of huge thunderheads colliding at the apex of the sky . . .

It charged up behind them, a boiling tidal wave that was the lost island's last gesture—the water it had displaced thrown up into a wall of unwanted force with nowhere to go.

The massive wave bore down on the tiny blot of land that remained the travelers' sandy raft—land had shrunk to nearly nothing beneath them and they had not noticed.

"Jump!" someone called, and they all did, forward without looking—toward deserted Rule.

Their feet sank knee-deep in shifting sand. Water churned around their knees, hips, shoulders. They paddled or swam or simply milled their arms. A rough dark head bobbled in the shoreline waves beside them, Felabba clinging atop it, her eyes showing panic-stricken whites.

The dislodged bird screamed its disapproval as it flew off. A thick silver rope coiled down into the water among the flailing swimmers.

Eeryon, his arms weighed down by his magic become reality, sputtered and sank. Thane and Javelle buoyed him on either side, Thane shutting his eyes and concentrating fiercely.

A weight gave, or a tautness, like a thread, snapped.

The three were stumbling onto the wet sand, through shallow water, feeling the waves sucking at their feet.

Behind them, the roar had become a wind propelled by a thousand throats. They turned to face their doom. An immense frozen wave was poised above them, looming over the last of the island, ready to roll forward to bury everything before it.

In that crystal-clear moment, they saw every glassy highlight in the watery wall, every silver thread of reflection that wove through it. For an instant it resolved into an image, as if capturing them all in a liquid mirror.

A figure floated there, limpid and distant, then the water collapsed. It fell upon the floating land that had been their barge and swallowed it in a solid blue-green maw.

Yet instead of crashing forward to consume its next morsels frozen upon the beach, the water withdrew— massed into a wave again and flowed *backward* toward open sea, where Clymerind had sunk again, dragging the headland's last, disintegrating sands with it.

Dazed, the three stared at the lapping water that had denied its own nature to spare them. Eeryon thought he had recognized the silver figure that had peeked through the window of that poised, watery wall. Javelle and Thane harbored sudden, unexplained thoughts of their mother that each kept to themselves.

None of them thought to turn and look behind them again—to the mainland from which the wave had fled as if impelled.

"As usual," the cat Felabba commented in a salt-rinsed tone, "you fail to find the obvious at your rear."

They turned as one—wet, weary, and still amazed. Both

animals sat on the drier sand beyond them. Briarwhip had flattened onto its rude belly, a ghastly blend of growls and whimpers coming from its soggy throat. Its three eyes stared toward the dark woodline.

Felabba was grooming again, bored again, contemptuous again. No help again.

She did not seem likely to be a help, not even when the man clothed in darkness walked out of the woods, a gloved hand raised to reveal one embroidered palm glowing fiery red in the sunshine.

Javelle's and Thane's heads lifted in unison, in mutual puzzlement and defense.

But Eeryon hardly looked up, only mumbling shamefacedly—as if he gagged on the words more than he could on any seawater.

"Greetings, Father," he said.

CHAPTER
26

KENDRIC WAS DROWNING IN A SEA OF POTENT POISON.

A rainbow arched the water, stewing in the light of a bilious sun. He reached for the sky-borne bands of color, hoping those airy ropes could pull him from the seething ocean of his own tainted blood.

Javelle and Thane floated by in an oarless boat— skimming the surface of his misery, their faces white and lost, their hands hidden.

Kendric thrashed long arms and legs. The water was warm, thick. It swirled with the colors of borgia and Bloodstone, with other shades too various to name.

He glimpsed Irissa in the form of a flying fish. Silver scales broke the lethal water, then flashed down into it again like a dagger buried at sea.

He had thrown a flaming dagger once and had never seen it land. He would have such a dagger back. Perhaps it could burn the poison from him.

Tossed and turned, Kendric could see nothing but the bottomless dark, could smell nothing other than the stink of his own mortality. Everything moved around him.

Everything shifted with the waves, the wind. There was no stillness here, no peace.

Scenes of earlier days were mirrored in the walls of waves crashing over him. He tried to focus on them, to grasp and cling to these straws of the past as a wrecked sailor would cleave to a piece of sturdier flotsam. But the insubstantial worlds within the waves' glassy walls foamed away, taunting Kendric with a glimpse of Rule here, a slice of Edanvant there. . . .

Walls. Not water, but *walls*. The walls were moving, shifting in waves. Tapestries. He knew himself—briefly— knew that he lay in Irissa's receiving chamber in Rengarth.

A ludborg hovered near—too vague to be named. Danger hovered, too, not near. Not here. Kendric battled upward from the ensnaring sickness, retching phantom seawater.

The ludborg thundered closer. Ludborgs were silent, but any motion agitated his senses now. Irissa's tapestries whipped against the walls, slapping the stones.

"Borgia," Kendric croaked.

Instantly, a green glass goblet hovered before him. Did *nothing* keep decently still anymore?

"Bloodstone," he ordered.

Dust the color of dried blood flaked into the libation.

"All!" Kendric said.

Motion stopped. A ludborg sleeve hung slack, the remaining Bloodstone still unshed within it.

"All!" Kendric thundered.

Someone murmured of husbanding the medicine, of waiting until someone should return. Kendric could no longer wait for someone other than himself to return.

"All." His voice had weakened to the squawl of a seabird, but he meant the command.

Murmurs of sure and terrible death, of nothing more to be done.

Kendric reached for the tossing flotsam of his death-world—for goblet and withholding sleeve and precious grains of life-preserving Bloodstone. . . .

The last red motes trickled from the lurid sky, fanning like a flock of birds that drowned in an emerald sea.

Kendric drank it, drank the bottomless goblet down thrice. Blood pounded redly in the poisonous green stream of his veins. Sound retreated, motion smoothed.

He was half-sitting on a cot in a room he knew, and it was indeed Scyvilla's sleeve that soothed his brow. He brushed away the fabric and almost overturned the bottomless cup of borgia as he rose with new—and bitterly bought—strength.

"Get out," he said.

Scyvilla stiffened.

He had not the strength to soften the words.

"Out," he repeated.

For a moment all hesitated. Kendric's strength abided wholly in his will now—his body and magic were drained to the bone, to the marrow. He could not make his small finger obey.

Scyvilla retrieved the fallen goblet—full again, green again—and scuttled away. A wave of gratitude almost knocked Kendric back on the bed, but he struggled upright, alone in the room.

Something was wrong beyond his own slow dissolution, he knew. Something had gone awry with Irissa and the children. He stumbled toward the walls, his weaving steps mocking the weavings themselves.

If Thane could unravel a gate in a tapestry and Irissa could weave herself into Without, then he could find . . . some . . . way of finding them, Kendric thought.

Through the tapestries. He lurched back and forth along the walls, trying to read sense into woven images, struggling to spy an exit among three blank walls hung with figured scenes.

He paused at a glittering depiction of the Empress

Falgon he and Irissa had ridden in Rule. Would a myth fly him free of Rengarth now? No. . . . He stood, swaying before the woven forms of Mauvedona and Verthane. Could dead sorcerers resurrect his powers now?

He leaned forward to study the scene of Finorian, his old adversary, reaching into the clouded sky of Edanvant, the emerald touchstone shattering on her breast as she prepared to throw herself to the winds and repel Geronfrey's evil from Without.

Even Finorian he would ask for aid, for mercy, but she was gone now—unhappy Eldress—and was able to offer neither aid nor opposition.

Who? What? Someone, something must help him! How?

The floor reeled. Kendric clutched a drapery to remain standing, then looked what his hand had fallen upon. It almost made him laugh . . . or cry.

His trembling fist had Felabba by the throat—mangy old Bitterbones, gone these twenty years and now back again in younger form. Where was she when needed? If her younger self were of any use to the children he wouldn't feel this cutting edge of danger honing all his warrior's instincts. . . .

Kendric's fist tightened on the tapestry and twisted. His arm swung back to wrench it from the wall, the past—so he would not have to see the awful future.

Something squealed.

Kendric called upon his ears to hear that sound again.

It repeated, faint and protesting—a call like a seabird's distant scream, an infant's cry. A cat's yowl.

Kendric's fingers uncurled, one by one. The crushed tapestry slowly unsprung. Felabba's screwed-up visage smoothed into its normal, sour expression.

Kendric stepped back. If everyone else could walk through weavings, why couldn't he? Other than being weakened unto death he couldn't think of a good reason. But he knew he needed . . . help.

"All right." He knew he was talking to himself, but approaching death conferred some privileges. "You may be deader than I, or distant in a more youthful form, but you sit here in this cursed piece of cloth looking as smug as ever you did in life. You will . . . *come back,* old cat. Felabba."

He couldn't believe that he was saying these words, that he was *beseeching* the worthless beast to come to a semblance of life, to help him.

Where would he find the magic—the will, the thoughts, the words—to make such wishful thinking true? Who knew how long the Bloodstone's restorative power would last? In his last conscious moments, was he to beg aid from a tapestry cat?

Kendric passed his hand before his eyes. The ring was cycling through its five colors, as lurid as his skin was painted from the poison. Among those five empowered stones was the Gladestone—a bit of forest green bright as a cat's eye . . . as Felabba's eye and Torloc magic.

He called on both—on talisman and the instinctual Torloc magic he had garnered from Irissa. He called on memory and fortune and his belief in something as sturdy as will, pure and simple.

He called on all that he remembered, and anything he might not remember. He called—for help, for the aid of anything that might assist him. He called specifically for old Felabba, because he knew her well, as he knew the sluggish thrum of danger in his slack veins . . . because her image was the only straw before him at this sinking moment . . . because the tapestry had mewed.

It was shaking now, the fabric, or his hand was. Lumpish stuff, tapestry—it thickened in his fist . . . or his sensation had thinned. Threads broke, parting like broken wheat before a long silver scythe. . . . Green flared around him, like Torloc torches spitting long tongues at the darkness.

A cat's head pushed through a hole in the tapestry—the

forehead fur carved in horizontal ridges, flattened ears, slitted eyes. Paws clawed free, forefeet claws—fanned and equipped with thread-ripping scimitars of nail.

Kendric reached for the illusion, grasped flailing fur. He midwived the rest of the animal free—long rangy body, the ribs like curled fingers beneath his palms; narrow hind-quarters, trailing tail.

He held a bit of warm bone and fur in his trembling hands and was amazed at feeling so proud of himself for so little reward.

The cat unhinged stiff jaws and yawned—or snarled—mightily. It looked irritated and fragile and impervious.

"At last," it commented tartly, as if just awakened from a catnap, "you have come to your senses, Wrathman, and to me."

Time did not touch Geronfrey's iron-bound tower in Without.

Yet Irissa sensed some absence. The sorcerer had not come to taunt her in some time. How much time? She couldn't say.

Perhaps she shouldn't complain. Time no longer held much meaning for her. Apparently some suspended state pertained here. She didn't hunger, nor need to relieve herself or sleep or eat. Her physical state had become less pressing, even as her mind and emotions sharpened.

Her magic remained distressingly mute, as if its ordinary means of expression had been bound and gagged. Worst of all, Irissa's instincts—magical and maternal and just plain mortal—had been lulled to sleep. She was almost content to remain here, quietly diminishing.

Almost.

She roused herself, pressing Kendric's flint and steel into her closed palm as if they were particularly sharp nails filed to prick her drowsing senses.

The distraction worked. Her vision cleared for a moment. She studied the Dark Mirror where the silver fog of Issiri had left with her spirit-self.

The mirror was empty now, peerlessly black. It showed Irissa herself in widow's weeds. . . . That image, that notion, was enough to bring her to her feet. No.

The room seemed to have shrunken. Her standing self pushed at the borders of it—ceiling, walls, windows. Cramped, confused, Irissa began to realize that she could no longer afford to remain a prisoner—not only for the sake of those she cared for, but for her own survival.

Yet how was she to breach this wall that separated herself from her magical foundation? Torloc magic was human magic, however unhuman Torlocs might seem at times.

Here in Without lay nothing that touched the humanness in her, nothing that reinforced it. No wonder Geronfrey had found Without hospitable; Irissa felt its empty avarice wringing her dry of everything—mostly of will more than magic.

Irissa's fist tightened on the humble flint and steel again. Kendric prized these things as helpful tools, not talismans; he would not let a loss of magic daunt him, he who had braved the world without magic for so long.

Flint and steel. Her palm opened as she considered their dull, workaday forms. Perhaps they would be her last token of Kendric—and of her children: steel for Thane's inborn magical nature, flint for Javelle's stony rebellion at her own lack of magic.

Where were they now, her children? How did they fare? And Kendric—fading as the poison fastened on his brightening flesh. . . . No! Geronfrey or not, Without or not, malaise of magic or not, Irissa must try something, must win free.

Free. The word unleashed an echo in her mind, along routes that were not quite magical. Free, the word wailed.

Not free, came an unbidden answer. Not enough, came the self-accusation. I have not done enough. Come help me.

Irissa shuddered, as if very cold or very hot. She looked again to the mirror. A fleeting silver form agitated there—a sliver of herself writhing in its own uncertainty, its own insufficiency. Come help. . . .

I can't! Why else send a forbidden fragment of myself? Irissa felt her mind churning these unsaid words at the mirror image. Are you worth nothing, can you do nothing?

Not alone.

We are all of us alone!

Not alone. They are no longer alone.

Who?

They we seek.

They?

Yours and mine.

Ours, you mean.

Mine . . . and yours.

Ours, yours—does it matter?

Yes.

Irissa had no answer to that. She paced, moving back and forth before the misted mirror, wishing she could shake the fog into physical form and then deal with it.

Yet she was moving, she realized, feeling the soles of her feet strike sharply on stone, feeling the gentle wind of her own movement. She had become too used recently to not feeling, to not moving, to barely being. . . .

Come help, mouthed the mirror in her mind.

Wouldn't I if I could? Can't you do anything?

I am half-here, you half-there. We are half again less than we could be.

Aren't we *all* half of what we can be? You must . . . we must do something.

We are alone.

"We" cannot be "alone."

We are alone, as they are.

Irissa's hands cupped her mouth to catch a whimper of fear. They were cold as flint and steel and her breath didn't warm them. She was aging, fading, icing over, as Geronfrey had predicted. Without did not destroy by fire and lightning. Without froze—softly, slowly, leeching life from limbs and senses inch by inch. Without . . . emptied.

Ah.

The mirror had sighed, as Irissa had not breath enough —or presence—left to do. It occurred to her that Issiri, spirit, phantom, stolen self, had more life and freedom than herself at this moment.

Pace. And think. And fight. And crush flint and steel, steel and flint, into the unfeeling palms of her disintegrating hands and mind and magic.

Flint.

And steel.

Irissa fell to the floor, collapsed to the floor. The mist swirled in the mirror, still wailing in her mind. She ripped her tunic hem. Her hands felt frozen as they tore the silk, and the fingers barely functioned. When the rip of thread from thread screeched in her ears, it sounded as if it came from the wrong side of the windows.

Yet she was tearing off ragged strips, coiling them into a pile. She opened one fist. Empty. Panic beat like a heart within her. She opened the other. Bloody bits of stone and metal lay there, unfelt, almost unseen.

Irissa took one between each thumb and numb, folded fingers. She struck them together. Nothing. She struck again, until her knuckles grazed, as if she were laboring at some phantom washboard, scraping her skin off and scrubbing a spark from the dark she lived in.

Brightness broke the gesture in two, made Irissa freeze again to see success flare and then wink out before her. She struck yet again, harder, drawing adamant stone across ungiving steel. Another bit of brightness. A spark in the encompassing dark of Without.

This time the spark fell into the nest of fabric. Irissa struck again—faster, harder. Another ember plummeted to limp silk. And another. She struck so fast and hard, her bruised knuckles ringing like bonewood bracelets, that a shower of stars fell to fabric and then ate through fabric and met each other blazing and then united into a tiny flicker of flame and then took hold and then . . . burned.

Irissa held her unfeeling hands over the blaze. Flames danced on the mirror of her ringstone, warmed the red of Bloodstone and the gold of Shinestone into a new conjoined semblance of blood and heat.

Irissa lifted the burning tatters in her icy hands. She felt only light, not heat. Then, bearing her flaming brand, she walked into the black oily veil of the Dark Mirror.

Fire met water with the hiss of a thousand serpents. Gold met silver. Without probed the worlds beyond Without. Hot seared into cold. Flint and steel broke glass. Body penetrated emptiness. Absence violated presence.

Irissa—or her mind or her magic—spiraled into the dark seas underlying Without. Fire flamed through water like a gilt crimson feather adrift on an endless stream.

Irissa felt herself—some part of herself—borne along a channel carved through adamant iron and spit out into a wider world. She sizzled through space and time impossible to penetrate in physical form, sensing the warmth of her hallowed flame shedding in her wake like a skin.

When the heat had abated enough so she could open her eyes, she was sputtering in salty water. She was cold, and wet, and barely able to breathe the air that came to her in fragrant gulps. She was struggling onto drier land with burning, bleeding fists that would not unfold into hands.

And, she was still in the dark.

CHAPTER
27

"FATHER? THIS IS YOUR FATHER?"

Eeryon stood frozen in his own footsteps as the waves smoothed away all trace of his earlier path. Javelle and Thane had waded ashore a few feet away. They stood together, brother and sister, while he stood apart. Alone.

As if addressing his solitary stand, Briarwhip came over and cringed at his side.

"Yes," Eeryon said, not knowing what to say next.

Javelle relieved him of the uncertainty by speaking before he could offer anything more self-implicating.

"Then your father must have stopped and turned the wave that would have smashed us. He *is* a most powerful mage, as you said. We thank you, sir." She smiled into Geronfrey's impassive face.

"I could have done that," Thane murmured. "If I'd thought of it." No one paid him any attention.

Geronfrey folded his gloved palm shut and tucked both hands into his wide sleeves. He stood regarding them, as stunned by their presence as they had been by his sudden appearance. Here, in Rule, his eyes were a pale sky-blue and his hair and beard were gilt. Eeryon barely recognized him, and kept silent.

Geronfrey's eyes turned to him, anyway. "You left without telling me," he noted pleasantly.

"I—we . . . had an opportunity to take a gate to Rule. I thought you wouldn't want me to miss the chance."

"No."

"Why send Eeryon," Thane spoke up, "when you can obviously go yourself on whatever errand you need done?"

The blue eyes took a long time to move to Thane's suspicious features, and a longer time to sum the boy up. Geronfrey peered into his youthful face as if searching for the lineage of an old friend, or enemy.

"Some things are only obvious to the young," the sorcerer said at last. "My presence here is strictly limited. I can only traverse small amounts of space outside Without, and then only in a pseudo-form. In fact, only luck showed me a way to Rule."

"Lucky for us that you came," Javelle put in. "I don't know how we'd have survived that wave—or turned it. How did *you* do that?"

Geronfrey smiled. "Sometimes I don't know my own strength." His look grew piercing. "Your strength is not magic, is it, girl?"

"No." Javelle hated confessing her lacks to too-perceptive strangers. "Not magic. Not like them."

"Them." Geronfrey eyed Thane again until the boy shifted uncomfortably. His regard fell last—and finally fully—on Eeryon.

"You have no time to waste, my son. I can bide here long enough to show you the proper path. This wood is thick and fey, populated by latter-day dangers even I have never encountered. Come."

They hesitated, all of them, even Briarwhip. Then Felabba, her eyes still half-shut from salt and sand, stalked stiff-legged from under the shelter of Briarwhip's belly.

Geronfrey's fingers snapped up like a whip. A five-sided ball of fire scribed with symbols flashed over the sand. Felabba smelled rather than saw it spinning straight for her. She yowled and sprang sideways.

The fireball dodged with her. For a moment, all the onlookers could see was a rolling white and red blur bouncing down the beach. Only the tangled limbs of the driftwood log stopped the momentum. A terrible hiss sputtered in the curling surf. Felabba lay long and limp in the foam. The fireball faded, branding red-hot script into the sand.

"Felabba!" Javelle was the first to reach the young cat and threw herself on her knees in the surf. "You have killed her," she accused the sorcerer.

Geronfrey stood unmoved, his hands tucked in his sleeves again, catlike. "I had not seen such a creature before and took it for a danger." He did not sound either sincere or sorry.

Javelle cradled the unconscious cat, its legs dangling over the crook of her arm. "Poor Felabba." She staggered upright with the burden. "Can't you . . . revive her, then, with your magic?"

"Alas. Magic never undoes what it does. Another's magic might wake her. Perhaps *your* magic, boy." He stared at Thane until the young man dropped his glance.

Despite Felabba's straits, Thane felt an instinct to hoard his magic, hide it from Eeryon's father's view. He touched the cat's wet forehead, Javelle's shoulder, in awkward consolation. "Maybe our mother could . . . cure her. I'll try—"

"Not now," Geronfrey's voice commanded. "I told you that dangers abound. You'd best retreat into the forest and find shelter." He stepped back like a host indicating his great hall and swept a hand into the leafy dark beyond him. "Eeryon."

Eeryon went, speechlessly, Briarwhip skulking at his

heels. "You don't stay?" he asked as he came abreast of his father.

"I told you; I cannot. Not for long. This world has aged beyond me, but it is new to you. Don't worry. I have left provision for you." Geronfrey's mild blue eyes lifted to the two young people lingering on the sand. "And your friends."

His gloved hand descended to just above Eeryon's shoulder—as if he were not really there to touch him—and squeezed into a fist. "You near your goal. You cannot afford to share it. Remember that."

Geronfrey bowed back into the woods, vanishing on the dark unreflecting curtain of greenery. For a moment his sober garb mingled with the branches and leaves—then only brush was trembling there in the soft sea breeze.

Javelle and Thane approached the place in numb wonder. Eeryon would have smoothed Felabba's lolling head but Javelle shrugged him away, turning so he couldn't touch the cat.

"I'm sorry," he said. Eeryon couldn't bring himself to say that his father had "not known" his spell's strength. His father knew everything.

"She's not dead," Thane put in, bored with apologies for spilt milk. "Javelle always thinks the worst. The cat just knocked herself silly on the driftwood. That was a most convincing fireball your father loosed—how does he do it?"

Eeryon shrugged. "I told you he was powerful. Somehow he harnesses the light and heat from the storms Without."

"Yet he can't . . . appear . . . in Rule for more than a few moments?" Thane asked.

"It's not easy to leave Without. Or enter other worlds, even in the image only."

"At least we've kept our family's archenemy from coming here," Javelle put in.

Eeryon stiffened. "Kept someone out? How?"

"It was when you were . . . lost," Thane said. "At the Oracle of Valna. I spotted Geronfrey trying to use the untenanted pillar as a gate to Rule and sealed it with the cutting edge of my magic. He'll never break through there. And if even your father is barred from physically appearing here, it should be equally difficult for Geronfrey."

"Yes." Eeryon was silent a moment. "If we are indeed in Rule, we had better separate and be about our own business."

Thane, so eager to be rid of Eeryon at first, was the first to object. "Why? We still don't know the location of our . . . quest."

"It might be better to part," Eeryon answered, his expression torn between annoyance and anguish. "Just take your path and I'll take mine."

"He's ashamed of us, Thane." Javelle approached them, the cat still lying limp in her arms. "He doesn't want his father to see him in the company of someone unpowered like myself. Perhaps even *you* aren't up to the powers they share."

"Nonsense!" Thane dismissed the notion.

"No!" Eeryon denied almost as violently. His sea-colored eyes pled with Javelle. "It has nothing to do with you or your powers, or lack of them."

"At least let us explore the forest together," Thane put in. "Javelle will be tending the cat and of no use. Once we find the lay of it, I'll be happy to part company. Besides, you can help me heal Felabba."

Eeryon hesitated, half-minded to plunge into the thick underbrush and leave them—and his conflicting feelings —far behind. Briarwhip whimpered at his feet, as if begging his agreement to Thane's proposal.

"All right. But I can't delay long. If my . . . father has violated his residence in Without, the circumstances must be dire."

"He came to warn you, Eeryon," Javelle told him. "He

knew you were in danger and somehow broke through an unbreakable barrier. A father will do that sort of thing. Ours would."

Eeryon stared at her, at her unshaken assumption that his father was like theirs, or anyone else's. It made him suddenly angry. It made him want to run away and hide in the deepest crinkle of Without—forever. But there was no way to run unless you first pretended you didn't need to.

"Let's do as Thane said," Eeryon decided, "and seek a way into the wood, and shelter." This time Javelle let his hesitant fingers brush Felabba's fur. "The cat feels warm. She may revive without magical intervention. Come with me if you want to."

Eeryon plunged into the forest's underbelly. Briarwhip turned its three anxious eyes on the remaining two.

"I don't like it," Thane said.

"Eeryon's father is a strange, terse man," Javelle agreed. "He seemed to be . . . laughing at us."

"Eeryon wasn't laughing at him." Thane shuddered.

"What an awful life Eeryon must have had in Without." Javelle pensively rocked the cat. "Will we find the sword, Thane? Will we find a way back?"

"Of course. We haven't got this far for nothing. And we'd be better off without Eeryon. He's a strange one. After we rest for the night—and sleepyhead wakes and can walk on her own again—I'm for following our Torloc noses to old Rindell and leaving Eeryon to his own bleak business."

Javelle looked troubled, but fell into step behind her brother while he parted the brush for them both.

"Oh, Felabba," she whispered into the cat's dry under-fur, "I want to go home, but first I want to find the sword—perhaps I can at least do that, find it. It shouldn't take magic simply to find something old that's lost."

The forest was oddly still. Wind barely stirred the branches. Other than choking underbrush, little foliage grew at their level. They wove through mazes of moss-covered trunks, moving deeper into darkness.

"It's odd," Thane said suddenly, "that sea and sand keep such close quarters with moss and shadow."

"I feel as if everything's been pinched together," Javelle added.

"Perhaps that's why it's called the Shrinking Forest," Eeryon said. "I fear our only shelter will be the interlacing pine boughs above our heads."

They paused to search for a likely resting place. Nothing appealed, especially not the bitter brown beds of fallen needles that carpeted everything.

Ancient pinecones scented the air as old pomanders might perfume a chest, a smell both stale and heavy. The forest felt unused, abandoned.

"What's that?" Javelle gestured with the cat in her arms toward a tunnel of oddly parallel trunks. Silver flashed far down the dull line of trees.

"Let's see." Thane moved into the unlit avenue under the pines.

The three heard only the fallen branches snapping beneath their feet and their own labored breathing as they struggled forward on a slick, shifting carpet of needles. No sunlight filtered through the interwoven limbs above, but the silver-white glisten ahead drew them on.

Soon they saw its source—glittering stalactites descending like gigantic snow-season ice daggers. A forest of such chill daggers plunged into the needle-strewn earth.

"Well." Thane stopped at an icy column and petted the surface sheen. "It's cold, but not icy, more like stone that has never felt sunlight."

"What shall we do? The way is barricaded."

Javelle was right. The wood had ended in a planting of ice daggers thicker than pine trunks, forming a construction that was not so much a clearing as a space the ice shards had forced between the trees.

It hung there in all its intricacy—a huge unmelting snowflake jammed into the pines.

"It almost resembles a building," Thane added, slipping under an arch between two huge fangs of ice.

"Wait!" Javelle advised too late. She clutched Felabba closer and sidled through the same opening, her shoulder bumping the chill surface.

Eeryon came last, dazed, silent. He had never seen the like of this.

Once through the ice-pillared passage, the party reached an inner open space. All around them soared plinths of ice, some swagging sideways to bridge each other. The frozen pillars met high above, glimmering in the dark where all the ice's internal shimmer could not reflect more than phantom light.

"It feels even colder here than it looks," Javelle said.

"You know what this reminds me of?" Thane prodded. "Think of the tapestries."

"*You* tell *me* to cite the tapestries?"

"The flaming castle of Mauvedona," he returned promptly, "only its opposite."

Javelle turned slowly, cradling the slumbering cat. The edifice of ice offered a certain magical sweep of form and excess of aspiration. It leaped up, almost as flame might, sharp and turreted. But so might falling water freeze.

Thane pushed farther into the cold dark heart of the place, lured by a twinkle ever out of reach. Javelle followed. She didn't want Thane out of her sight; every step within the bristling ice-dagger wood seemed to drive new obstacles between the threesome.

"Here!" Thane's voice rang jubilantly. "There's a chamber within where some light flares—"

Javelle glanced over her shoulder. Eeryon was hesitating at the twisted entrance pillar. She couldn't see Thane ahead, so took another step on the slippery surface. In her arms, Felabba stirred and began struggling free.

Javelle's heels slid out from under her just as the cat half-leaped, half-fell from her grasp. Javelle was skidding through space, her arms thrashing. She found Thane when her flying legs knocked his feet from under him. Entwined, they slid down a tilted passage of ice toward the maze's center, where light magnified itself from plinth to plinth.

Breathless, too shocked to cry out, they plunged over a precipice. They slid down cascades of frozen water as if descending an icy flight of stairs carved large enough for a mountain to climb. The light increased the deeper they plummeted—a sere, white light that gave no heat and threw no shadows.

The way narrowed and grew circular. They were tumbling around and around toward a narrow point below as if spinning down the sides of a funnel. They finally jammed to a stop, a tangle of limbs, at the funnel neck.

Above them, a widening gyre of ice yawned for hundreds of feet. They were caught in the twisted heart of a frozen water spout that had screwed itself deep into the earth beneath the forest. The silence was breathtaking, and Felabba had not fallen with them. No face peered over the ice's edge far above. They were alone, unhurt, unable to help themselves.

Eeryon stood as frozen as the pillars around him. Javelle and Thane had vanished as if sucked into the Dark Mirror.

He was not surprised when one of the icy plinths spawned a brightening shaft of light and revealed his father's image at the heart of it.

"What happened to them?" Eeryon demanded.

Geronfrey's ice-blue eyes were unblinking in the frozen surface. He didn't answer directly. "You are free now to pursue your own mission. Make haste and bring me the sword."

"*You* have diverted them into this cold maze," Eeryon

complained. "I knew when you appeared at the margin of the wood that you wouldn't be content to let me act on my own."

"You were *not* acting, Eeryon, that is the trouble. You have been seduced by the wonders of the worlds beyond Without. Your concentration fails. You forget to whom you owe your eyes, your magic, your very existence."

"I do not forget," the boy said leadenly.

"Then cease lingering and find the sword."

"Why is it so valuable to you?"

"You never asked 'why' before."

"There are no 'whys' in Without, but here—"

" 'Here' is a world to ensnare you, a trap for the unwary. Take example from this web of ice and preserve yourself from a more silken subterfuge."

"I was following your wishes. . . ."

"At your own pace, while you studied the will and wishes of others. There is no profit but self-delusion in such dallying. Go—before I forget what you are . . . or before I lose my patience and *show* you what you are."

Geronfrey's image shifted in the blurred ice—it blackened and silvered by turns. Hooves, tails, and horns blended into legs and arms and head. No matter how the form changed, Eeryon could always see the two matched pits of eyes, he could look directly through them into the unshaped vastness of Without.

He fled, not waiting to see his father resume his familiar shape in the ice dagger, not wondering how Thane and Javelle had fared in the maze's hollow heart.

Silver-white pillars of ice fled past him, rushing to his rear like white-barked trees. He breathed more easily as the trunks around him darkened. At last he was surrounded by unreflective forest again. He turned back to regard the silver light that had softened into a white glow.

When he faced back to the woods, Briarwhip was there,

scratching its spine on a tree root. Eeryon watched the creature writhe in earthy delight, its ugly limbs splayed to the branches above, and smiled.

The smile faded as another familiar form moved into his awareness. The cat Felabba settled beside another tree, watching him.

"I couldn't help it," Eeryon said quickly.

"Did anyone ask?"

"You ask with your eyes."

"You mistake my eyes. They tell, not ask."

"And . . . what do they tell me?"

"That you have company on your quest."

"No! You cannot come. My father will not tolerate it."

"He is absent now."

"He is never absent. You will see."

"I *have* seen. In another embodiment, Geronfrey struck me mute for a time. In this one, he has merely struck me. I fancy that his power—or at least his pride—weakens with long lapses of time. But I landed on my feet, as do all my kind. I suggest if you are to find the sword that we begin our next journey."

"They may need you within the ice-maze."

The cat never spared a glance beyond Eeryon. "They need me more with you."

"You will keep me from completing my quest."

The cat paused before answering, its mouth lifting in a mock smile. "To the contrary. I will *aid* you in your quest."

Eeryon stared into the sage green eyes for some time. The cat's expression never changed, nor its waiting posture. Suddenly, Briarwhip bounded up and dashed past the cat as if to play. Then the cloud-hound ran down the aisle of pines and waited, tail wagging.

Such a down-to-earth invitation to get on with it overruled Eeryon's reservations. He set out behind the eager creature, Felabba stalking silently behind him. He did not offer to carry the cat, and it did not ask.

From that moment on, Eeryon's path became simpler. He felt he trod old ground, and when a large gray stone loomed in his way, he edged around it, unsurprised.

Stones begat stones. Soon Briarwhip was dashing in and out of tumbled stone piles. The trees had drawn back in places, leaving cleared ground.

And then he came upon it—the still reflection of a pond. Rindell Pond, he knew it. Even the air struck him with a kind of rightness. Eeryon gazed down into the forest-shaded water, watching first Briarwhip's—then Felabba's —animal faces appear upon the water.

His own did not. Here, he had no reflection.

Graceful, limp-limbed trees trailed the water at either end. Eeryon studied the surroundings to avoid the painful absence of his own image. The pondwater seemed endlessly deep. Its shape followed no natural sway of the land, but held to a rigid rectangle.

Eeryon saw nothing that promised a sword, or a way to a sword. He might as well be trapped amid icy teeth, as Thane and Javelle were. Then he banished the others from his mind. To think of their plight, of their father's, was to undermine his own resolution, his own father.

Eeryon sighed, but it became a shudder.

Even as he trembled on the brink of the watery solution to his quest, an image began rippling over the pond. Circles of silver reflection surfaced and shattered, spreading wider. Again and again he saw the features of a face assemble— and dissolve.

A mouth that seemed on the verge of speaking dissipated and blew rings of expanding silver bubbles. Eyes widened to horror, or fear, and burst—only to grow again from pinpricks of light, like flaring pupils.

Finally the tendrils of reflection pooled into a single bright spot at the pool's center. They lifted from the liquid surface like fog until the silver-drenched figure from the sea hovered across the water.

"Mine," this apparition spoke, unseen arms spreading misty sleeves wide. Whether she meant the water, or the sword, or himself, Eeryon couldn't say.

"Where?" he asked.

Her finger, as ghostly as a skeleton's, pointed downward.

"How?"

Her arms swept wide, indicating the pond's edges.

Eeryon studied the vacant forest, the fringe of underbrush between water and woods. He shook his head mutely.

Her foot tapped water, raising no spray. But ghostly ripples flared from her shimmering figure. Eeryon's eyes helplessly followed their rhythmic outward progress. At the pond's edge, beneath his unreflected figure, he saw something more—a doorway, a wall, an entire architectural facade.

He jerked around. Under the intent scrutiny of his eyes, forms were shaping against the wall of trees, like a tapestry being woven from unseen threads. Phantom facades erected themselves all around the pool, each image as different from the one that sat beside it as many doors opened from many walls into many places.

The cat was trotting self-importantly along the fragmented walls and gateways, naming what it recognized.

"Lost Ashasendra. Old Clymerind before it sank. Soon-to-be Zelamizzary."

Each archway echoed in the water, as did its neighboring gates. All doorways opened on a furtive glow of many colors.

"Mine," said the water apparition, sighing.

"But the sword is *in* the water. Can't you bring it to me?" Eeryon asked. "I almost had it in the palm of my hand once, when I was in Without. Some silver figure severed me from it. Was that you?"

The woman's tendriled head shook violently.

"I know you mean to help me—"

She nodded with equal animation.

Eeryon clapped empty hands to his sides and began walking along the dozens of doors, glimpsing agitation within, yet nothing more recognizable than that. He sensed his insubstantial guardian behind him, waiting and watching.

Every door beckoned with elusive color and light and life. Only one would lead to a sword and the end of his quest. Some doors were timbered, others soldered from stained glass. Some were wafting veils of light—or constant shimmers of sound like falling rain. Some were Iridesium-sheathed or wood-carved.

Only one was plain—a rectangle of some dull wood or unembellished metal. It promised nothing but the fulfillment of curiosity.

Remembering his father's caution against seduction, Eeryon lifted his palm to the unadorned surface. A glow reflected there—not from the door, but from his flesh.

The living lines of his hand emblazoned their simple patterns on the door's surface—the upright central fateline crossed by horizontal head- and heartlines. They reflected the shape of a sword on the door and then it opened on a dark, undifferentiated space beyond.

Eeryon pushed through, into the dark, his flaming palm held before him as a lamp.

Briarwhip and Felabba watched in silence while the misty figure at the pond's center silently sank into ripples of stagnant water.

CHAPTER
28

"NOW," SNARLED THE REBORN FELABBA, HER HEAD JERK-
ing up as if caught in a noose tightened worlds away. "We
must make our way through the fibers of a gate. Where is
your sword?"

"In Rule. In Rindell Pond." Kendric found himself
confused beyond surviving. The Bloodstone potion's power was waning, leaving only poison waxing in his veins. He
had hardly the strength to answer the cat.

"The other one! Your mind-made one. We must have it,"
the cat replied.

"Here, then. You carry it. I have not the strength."
Kendric scraped the sword from the table where it lay.

"Have the strength," the cat advised unsympathetically.
"We must reach the prism-gate if your family is to survive."

Kendric straightened, as if infected with some of the
sword's enduring steel. "How? I am not as gifted as my son
or his mother in fashioning fabric into gates of passage."

"Fortunately," Felabba said, flexing her claws, "I am a
master at unraveling fabric webs and a mistress of gates."

She paced along the floor, staring intently at the wavering tapestries. "Surely Irissa did not neglect to weave the crux event into a tapestry . . . !"

Kendric bent and lifted the cat by the scruff of its neck so it could see the scenes at human height. "Tell me what you seek and I shall show you it."

"Softly, softly, Wrathman. My noble neck ruff, scant as it is, is delicate stuff." But the old cat dangled from Kendric's one-handed grip—the sword dragged from his other hand —its tail curling kittenishly between its legs, and perused the tapestry designs.

"Here!" it announced at last.

"That? That is the oldest of the hangings—and the simplest. Just Irissa and myself standing on a rock in Rindell Pond while a rainbow gate formed to take us on the first of our journeys together."

"So it shall suffice for the last of them."

Kendric started, struck by the dire implications of the cat's words. "You go through alone, then, old Bitterbones full of brutal predictions. Leave me here to perish."

"Cannot," the cat replied smartly. "The sword is needed even if you are not. And I cannot carry it, though I can open a gate big enough even for a Wrathman's contrary bulk."

"Do what you must," Kendric conceded, hearing his voice unwind to a hoarse whisper. Waves of sickness spun round him like grassweaver coils tightening. "I will do what I can."

Then not only phantom coils were closing in on him, but loops of rainbow mist spun from the rainbow woven into the tapestry, running its colors together before his eyes. He felt cold and hot, wet and dry, awake and asleep. He felt as flat as any hanging and wavered in the weakness of his illness like a wind-buffeted tapestry.

They wavered together—he and the tapestry, he with two equally leaden weights in either hand . . . an old cat and a second-mind sword . . . drawing him down, drawing him forward into the past, into another world he once knew well.

"Rule," Kendric muttered as everything melted into color and nonsense and multiple images of ill-groomed white cats. "Rule."

Cloaked in a halo of fire rushing through the dark waters, Irissa sensed the sudden opening of an underwater gate. Like a flaming fish she knifed across currents and through swift shadows. Her power honed itself on the whetstone of her consciousness, shaping her into an arrowhead impelled in one direction only.

She arrived with blinding speed, already centered on the instinctive target, a shining intersection of ice. She hung there for a moment, reasserting her shape and presence, adjusting to the rapid procession of time and space that had slid by her. Finally Irissa stiffly shrugged out of her frozen setting, stepping down an icy stair, pulling the tendrils of her hair free from a tangle of crystalline spires.

For a moment she feared she had returned to ice-bound Delevant's Maw in the Inlands of Ten, where her children would never have gone in their wildest journeyings.

She moved through a forest of ice daggers, finding order among the bristling pillars, finding aisles and chambers and finally a glowing circular stair of ice that led to a cul-de-sac far below. Two dark dots clogged the funnel.

Irissa crouched at the top to see them better, cold embroidering her relieved breaths onto the air in supple threads of mist.

Even as she watched, one tiny figure edged up the icewall. It paused to draw the other up after it, then inched upward again. Irissa pulled back from the edge, blowing warm breath over her chilled fingers. The flint and steel still warmed her palms, glowing like dying embers.

She longed to peer below again, certain that she had

found her children and equally certain that her observation of their struggles would be unwelcome.

So she waited, wondering what inventive form Thane's hybrid magic had taken, hoping Javelle would accept her brother's aid graciously for once.

Irissa sighed. Barely had reunion become reality before old differences resurged to exert their divisive ways.

It took a long time for Thane's dark head to surmount the edge of the ice. Irissa leaned forward to help him haul Javelle over the rim.

Both were scarlet-faced and panting, almost too worn to show proper surprise at Irissa's presence.

"How," she asked Thane, "did you climb the ice?"

He reddened more and brushed his hands behind his back like a child concealing a forbidden tongue-sweet.

When Irissa's look questioned her, Javelle simply shook her head. "Don't ask me. I merely climbed up the ladder of his legs." She brushed an errant hair under the snake encircling her brow. "It was I who slipped," she confessed, "and tumbled both of us down the slide."

"We all slip sometime," Irissa answered, turning again to her son. "Thane, I want to know as one Torloc to another, as seeress to seer. What quirk of invention has saved your skins this time? Let me see your hands."

He presented them with the evasive speed of guilt hoping to be overlooked.

Irissa took them in her own—they were raw and cold, as one would expect after a slow climb up an icewall. And also . . . *clawed,* as one—as she—would never expect.

"Thane!"

He snatched his hands back, fisting them. "There wasn't time for finesse. We had to get out. I thought of old Felabba falling down the deep hole under Falgontooth Mountain. They . . . just . . . grew. I haven't figured how to ungrow them yet."

"I suggest you concentrate on just that purpose. Javelle

and I will draw away so you may . . . divest yourself of your implements in peace."

Javelle, open-mouthed at the notion of a clawed brother, refused to move. "What about his feet?"

"I didn't need hind claws; my boots were rough enough to stick, as yours did."

"Yes, but—"

"Javelle." Irissa pulled her daughter after her until they were well out of Thane's earshot.

"You can't approve," Javelle demanded. "It's . . . unnatural."

"It worked," Irissa responded with a sigh. "I had no notion Thane had shape-altering tendencies. But I cannot complain of the results and am too weary myself to spell you out of the ice-sided hole you had fallen into. Now, where is the sword?"

"We don't know yet. Eeryon's father appeared and directed us into this wood, except I think it was a trap. Now Eeryon's gone and—"

"Who is Eeryon?"

"A boy we met in Without."

"A . . . boy—from Without? How old?"

Javelle stared into her mother's anxious face. She had forgotten to say how wonderful it was to see Irissa here amid the cold and alien landscape, and now it was too late. Now the omission would sound like one.

"Older than Thane."

"Older than yourself?" Irissa prodded.

Javelle had never considered that until now. "No."

"And he left you two here?"

"Perhaps he never saw us fall," Javelle said carefully. "Eeryon would not hurt us."

"But his father would."

Javelle shivered. "You may be right. I did not like that man."

Irissa smiled sadly. "He was not a man, but a mage."

"Not Geronfrey! I thought he'd be an ogre!"

"True ogres know better than to look it. Listen, Javelle—" Irissa put her hands on her daughter's shoulders, surprised by how closely their heights matched. "I don't want to worry Thane yet. But there is more urgent reason to find the sword now than your father's life span."

"Something more important than that?" Javelle looked bewildered, but her eyes were level.

"Yes. His very life itself. He has been poisoned by the tainted spring beneath the palace. Unless a remedy is found soon, he will—"

"Die? No. . . ." Javelle began, suddenly growing too old to deny the truth even as Irissa watched. "When? How long have we?" Now daughter's hands clutched mother's shoulders.

"We must find an answer as soon as possible."

"The sword?"

Irissa nodded. "Perhaps. It's a beginning."

Javelle relaxed her terrible tension, her mind working rapidly behind the open mirrors of her eyes. "Then we are close, for Geronfrey only appeared to us when we came to this shore—and this forest answers all the descriptions of Rule."

"A forest is a forest, Javelle—"

"But Geronfrey doesn't send his son there." Her eyes widened and grew wilder at the same instant. "Does he want the sword himself? Did *he* send the taint to Rengarth? Would Eeryon cheat us of our father's sword after traveling with us all this time?"

"Hush. You ask good questions, but let's not trouble Thane with them. His magic must be kept unmuddied until needed."

The boy was approaching, his hands dangling self-consciously at his sleeve ends.

"Well?" Irissa asked.

"Gone. I think," Thane added impishly. "Well, Felabba

has them. And who knows what a ludborg wears under his drooping sleeves?"

"Where is the cat?" Irissa wondered as the three moved slowly along the ice-slick floor. "I saw in the tapestry that she had followed you two through the gate."

"*We* were in the tapestry?" Thane sounded absurdly pleased.

Irissa realized that in memorializing Kendric and her own past adventures, she had neglected to weave the present into her walls. Perhaps she had taken it for granted and now paid the price.

"And you both shall be in several new ones," she promised. "Without claws, however. That is one secret we keep between ourselves, we three."

"Agreed," Thane said with a grin. "Wouldn't Father have a cat if he knew?"

Neither Irissa nor Javelle let the thought of Kendric shadow their faces for long, but their glances crossed significantly.

"Thane," Irissa said with sudden seriousness, "we think —Javelle and I—that this Eeryon is an . . . agent of Geronfrey, directing you to the trap that awaited."

"I knew we shouldn't have trusted Eeryon!" Thane burst out with a look at Javelle.

For once she refrained from arguing with him, instead regarding him with eyes as sober and adult as their mother's. He straightened, recognizing in Javelle a sad maturity he had never glimpsed before.

"What's wrong?" he asked with undisguised dread.

"A good deal," Irissa answered. "We must find the sword and take it to your father without delay. We may have to battle your friend, Eeryon—and even Geronfrey himself —to do that."

"Eeryon's not my friend," Thane repeated. "And I'm not afraid of him—or his father. Or *is* his father

Geronfrey? If that was Geronfrey, he's not so frightening as you said, just another man with hunger for eyes."

"Such men are always frightening, and doubly so when they are empowered. But I am here to help you and I have held the sword we seek in the palm of my hand, as the man who sired you has held it. The sword knows our right and will come to us if we find it—not the shadow son of one who has never borne the sword."

"Why do you call Eeryon a shadow son?"

"It was an . . . expression, Javelle."

"Because that's how he strikes me, as a fleeting thing." Javelle looked worried. "His eyes change, from light to dark. From full to empty."

"Forget him!" Thane burst out. "We must find the sword first."

"Agreed," Irissa said. "Let us make a pact upon it. First we find the sword, bending all our thoughts and magic and will upon that end."

The children's dark heads lowered as their minds repeated the charge.

"We will hold the sword," Irissa went on, her voice generating a seeress's weight, "against all claimants, be they living or dead, solid or shadow, from within or Without."

Her words echoed soundlessly in her children's attentive souls.

"We will take the sword to Kendric so he will take strength from it and remain always with us, our caretaker and our care."

And so they all swore silently in their hearts, each carrying a secret fear and a hidden sorrow.

CHAPTER
29

ONCE THROUGH THE SPECTRAL DOOR, EERYON FOUND himself moving through a vast darkness shaped by stone walls. Rooms with unseeably high ceilings and doorways large enough to accommodate thunderheads went on interminably.

Their interiors were an odd blend of the emptiness of Without and the fussily accessorized worlds beyond Without—the kind of worlds rife with trees and beasts and other people like Javelle and Thane.

Not that people or creatures occupied this deserted darkness, as far as Eeryon could see. Yet *things* did—the residue of people and beasts.

Dim light fell from windows cut into the high ceilings. By this lackluster illumination Eeryon spied metal-studded leather bindings for beasts hung against the walls. Implements of all description, yet old and rusted, twisted into shapes so outré Eeryon wondered if they ever had been natural.

And metal weapons glimmered everywhere. Those he recognized instantly.

He had charged the first sword he saw, thinking it the object of his quest. It was a sword, all right—a length of edged steel impaled in a block of pale stone, polished to the color of lightning from hilt to buried tip.

But he couldn't so much as touch, much less grasp, the sword. It and the space around it were sheathed in a slick invisible substance cold as ice. Eeryon's hands had shaped the frozen block that housed and isolated it. They shivered at the forbidding substance's touch even though his eyes were unable to see it.

Not even the heat of his magic-threaded palms could melt the unseen shield behind which the sword hid so publicly. After several attempts, Eeryon had fallen back, trusting an inner instinct he could not explain. This was not the weapon he sought—it was too light, too bright, too recently forged, and not nearly long enough.

Now the true difficulty of his quest had lain its weight upon him. This dark castle was *filled* with swords. Swords gleamed dully from every wall and even hung suspended from the unseen ceiling. They displayed themselves, openly beyond reach, in more of the transparent yet impervious sheaths.

It almost seemed that Eeryon wasn't truly there. The stones beneath Eeryon's pacing feet met his every step with an absence of echo. He glimpsed no reflection as he passed mounted shields of polished metal.

He made no sound and cast no shadow. If this place housed the sword he sought, he needed more than magic to find it among so many of its fellows.

Irissa stared at the rippling pool as it quieted. She and her children had followed every twist of the wildwood until it led to this small body of abandoned water.

"Look there! The wake of the wailwraith." She pointed to a dissolving silver reflection atop the lapping water.

"Something has disturbed this sequestered spot."

"Are we in Rule as it exists today?" Thane wondered.

Irissa examined the timid forest drawn back from the water, the retangular confines of the once-wild pond.

"If this is a remnant of Rindell Pond and the Shrinking Forest, it is not as I knew it twenty years ago. Why has the water shaped itself so rigidly? Why does the forest shrink from it?"

"We thought you would answer our questions," Javelle said. "Instead you ask more."

Irissa smiled and would have responded, save that someone else answered for her.

"Sowed questions are the seed of their own answers," came a familiar voice.

Felabba minced from among the underbrush.

"I haven't seen Felabba since I dropped her," Javelle realized. "We *have* taken the right path. Eeryon must have come here also."

The cat was unimpressed. "You did not drop me. I saved myself before you fell."

"What is *that?*" Irissa pointed to the blur of dingy fur that trailed Felabba from the woods.

"Eeryon's familiar," Thane said, "a stupid beast of no particular use."

"So we could say of our cat," Javelle pointed out.

Felabba refused to acknowledge this odious comparison. Instead, she sat midway between woods and water.

Irissa would not be distracted by a debate on the merits of one animal over another. She glanced alertly around the formal clearing. "Then where is Eeryon now? Has he gone into the water?"

"Why should a shadow boy go into water that will not even do him the honor of reflecting him?" Felabba answered obliquely.

"Well, *something* is in the water." Irissa stepped nearer.

"Take care, seeress." The cat spoke so sharply that Irissa

drew back. "Water was not kind to your Wrathman recently."

"Yet a wailwraith inhabits this unhallowed pool," Irissa mused from a safer distance. "I wonder if the sword still rests here?"

With a defiant glance at the cat, she moved nearer again, then knelt on smooth grass verging the water.

"I lifted it once, from a murky swamp, for your father," she told the children—or herself. "That was the first occasion I glimpsed my own magic. It made the heavy sword light and my a as strong as Iridesium. Perhaps I can draw the lost sw d from the water again. . . ."

Thane and Javelle edged nearer, enmeshed by the spell of Irissa's memories, by the odd convergence of her past and their present here.

Irissa spread her fingers and swept her hand across the dark water. Five gemstone colors flitted over her ring's single cabochon, ringing the hues' Iridesium changes— crimson, saffron, azure, translucent, and one indeterminate shade that absorbed the rest. The circlet at her temples pulsed with colors of the same stripe.

Disembodied sparks of color and light seemed to dance firefly-bright above the water. Thane, though only watching, felt an answering tingle in his palms and longed to add his magical reach to Irissa's.

He curled his fingers into fists instead. His mother was evoking the magical pull of a time before he had existed; as much as he felt that draw, it was not directed at himself.

"Will she conjure the sword?" Javelle whispered anxiously into Thane's ear.

"She doesn't need to conjure it; it exists. She seeks to call it to herself."

"But can she?"

"Besides her natural affinity for it—she has touched it magically before now—she wears the Drawstone in her ring. That might be enough."

"Could you have gotten it?" Javelle glanced quickly to his fisted hands.

"I don't know," Thane answered evenly. "And if Mother gets it, I shan't ever wonder."

"Careful, seeress," the cat cautioned in a hiss only the youngsters heard. "If you see the wailwraith's wake, so it sees you. . . ."

Irissa was oblivious to watchers and advisors. She delved deep in the well of her own magic and memory. She had been transported to a day when Kendric had been only a fallen stranger ordering her to retrieve his muddied sword from the dank marshwater.

This latter-day water she had not touched yet—nor did she intend to. It glimmered with the lucid darkness of the great black sea that underlies all worlds and springs from the Well of Endless Water in Without.

Rindell was gone, Irissa knew, and the Shrinking Forest. This . . . phantom semblance was a revenant of past places and past magic. Perhaps even the sword was gone, beyond retrieval by any means. She would know soon.

Her fingers felt chill, as if the water radiated cold just as flames cast light and shadow. The circlet at her temples hummed its peculiar metallic tune in time with her own interior, magical melody.

She remembered almost drowning in a Spectral City well, and drawing out a shard that bore the second Felabba. She wanted another shard now, another pointed weapon from another world. . . .

The sword—as Kendric had carried it through all of their adventures in Rule.

The sword—as it had bridged them in the rainbow gate, blossoming a gemstoned sheath between their steel-separated fingers.

The sword—as he had dropped it, gleaming and precious into the limpid water.

The sword—as some spectral hand had reached from what remained of Rindell Pond to catch and draw it under.

The sword—without its recently begemmed sheath, naked and natural, as it had been made in Frostforge at the Paramount Athanor in Rengarth generations ago.

The sword—as she had held the hilt and dredged its heavy length from Rulian water years ago.

A needle of lambent light pierced the dark waters. It swirled in a curdled current, around and around, balancing on the pinprick of its fine point. It was only a vaguely glowing splinter so far below that Irissa thought she was seeing through veils many worlds thick.

Her hand trembled over the water, then the fingers curved as the possessive palm cupped taut for its possession.

She called it with her mind and magic and memory, thinking not of impending death, but dawning life. She called to every optimistic moment of its making, in the name of Rengarth and Rule and everyone who had ever borne it. She called in Kendric's name, as last sword bearer; in her own.

And slowly, teasingly, rising and falling as with some underwater wind, the sword spiraled nearer. It grew to a silver thorn and then a thick splinter . . . became a dagger of light and then a longer dagger—or a shortsword. Its size swelled closer to the waiting cradle of her palm. Details shone in the dark water—a hilt wrapped in rotting strips of leather, a nick halfway down the blade where it had bit into something indigestible.

Ever closer the hilt came, crowning in the dark water, pushing through the liquid barrier—it was within easy reach should she care to wet her wrist in water.

Careful, seeress. . . .

A moment more, and the hilt tip broke water.

Behind her, Thane and Javelle gasped—and possibly the

cat. Irissa did not turn to see. She kept her eyes on the sword, her fingers tenting to touch the chill wet metal. . . .

Water rippled silver around the bobbing hilt. Broken reflections lifted like mist from the pond—five supple threads joining into five ghostly fingers.

Irissa felt a bone-freezing chill to her wrist, felt frozen in place. The fog crept up her fingernails, painting them silver. The tendrils stole toward her first knuckles. Irissa felt a corresponding icing of her blood, a removal of herself from this moment, a lessening of her senses.

A foot kicked over the water and spurred Irissa's hand from the sword. Irissa fell back onto the bank, under the forms of two contending children.

"Thane! How could you? She almost had it! I saw the very hilt." Javelle pummeled the arms that he had crossed over his face, then graduated to his defenseless back. "Why?" she shouted. "Why would you doom Father? Are you possessed? Has Geronfrey overtaken you? Or Eeryon? Are *you* Eeryon?"

Irissa struggled upright, her body separating her children so that Javelle's fury was forced into words alone.

"He did it! Broke the spell. Deliberately! The sword plunged back into the water again. Why? Do you want Father to *die?*"

Thane was quiet, pale. "No. Do you want Mother to?"

"Of course not."

He brushed the hair from his face, his slumped shoulders showing that he felt the sword's loss as keenly as they. "The sword may prolong Father's life, but calling it *would* end Mother's instantly. Didn't you see the emanation reaching for her as she reached for it, Javelle?"

"I saw a . . . shadow on the water," Javelle said. "A mist."

"Mist doesn't rise from water without the air's warmth to call it, and shadow does not fall where sun does not shine," Thane answered. "What has possessed *you*, Javelle, to hold our mother in such lesser light that you would sacrifice her to an uncertainty? There must be other ways of prolonging Father's existence, and I will have many years to find them."

"Thane." Irissa looked from her unshaken daughter to her unshakable son. "I should have told you, as I told Javelle. Your father is dying *now*. We don't merely seek some means to prolong his life, but one to save it. He was poisoned by some imported taint just as you and Javelle left Rengarth. I came after in hopes of helping you and him both."

"But—" Thane had sobered to near-speechlessness. "Didn't you see the silver shadow, Mother? That . . . inhuman hunger . . . grasping for you? It would have devoured you! I had to interrupt its ravening. Was it a wailwraith?"

Irissa sighed and stared into the dark water. Even her circlet had snuffed out. No rainbow reflection lit the Iridesium.

"I saw something," she admitted. "I disregarded it, so eager was I to grasp the sword." She peered darkly into the black water. "It has sunk beyond seeing now, beyond recall."

"But that . . . upwelling . . . would have destroyed you," Thane insisted. "I saw that it would."

"Perhaps. Yet I doubt it was a wailwraith. No one has ever seen such a creature, why should we be so blessed—or cursed? Perhaps I knew what it was—a shadow of myself I loosened to precede me here, to act for me, I hoped, against such dangers as Geronfrey."

"What was it?" Javelle came forward to join them, glancing delicately at Thane.

"This boy you call Eeryon. It was . . . is . . . his mother, I suppose. It seeks him first, and his good. I thought it wouldn't harm you."

"It hasn't," Thane said tightly. "But perhaps now that

it's free it wants to draw you into its shadow, as it has always walked in yours. It hungers for something. Credit me with magic enough to know a starving spell when I see it."

"I know." Irissa put a consoling hand to Thane's shoulder. "I thank you now. Like Javelle, I didn't quite feel that way at first."

"Such is the strength of a hungry spelling," he reminded her sternly.

"And Javelle." Irissa turned to her daughter with a rueful expression. "Thane is right. There is always another way. If I could almost call your father's sword from where it rests through this dark and haunted water, we can discover where it truly lies and claim it in reality. Your father is not dead yet."

"How do you know?" Javelle demanded hotly.

Irissa paused to think, or perhaps—feel. "I would know, as would you."

"You forget. I have no magic to discern such things."

Irissa hugged Javelle until her circlet rang lightly on the snake circling Javelle's lowered forehead. "You have a better casting crystal than magic on that subject—a special bond with Kendric. Perhaps that will mean more than all of Thane's or my magic before this quest is through."

"Perhaps." Javelle softened slowly. "I told Father once that I would not build my life on a 'perhaps.'"

"You have to, Javelle," Thane said seriously. "If Father is as deadly ill as Mother says, we all do."

CHAPTER

30

"WHY DON'T YOU," THE YOUNG CAT ASKED, "USE THE water for a mirror?"

"It's too dark to see anything in it," Javelle answered promptly.

"It's too dangerous," said Thane. "Dark Mirrors have done us all much harm."

"It's too shallow and too deep," Irissa said more paradoxically. "I seek in it too much that means everything to me to use its mere surface."

"Not as a magical mirror," the cat explained. "As a mere mirror. Find reflection just beyond your petty selves yet not so deep as your dearest hopes."

"Easy for you to say," Thane jibed. "You risk not so much as a whisker in this dusky water."

"Very well." As if treading an invisible tightrope, the cat's white paws minced one before the other until she balanced on the pond's very edge.

"I have never required a looking-glass for my toilet," she sniffed. "Perhaps that is why I can see past foreground reflections to the edges of the mirror. Forget glimpsing your own worried faces or lost swords and dangerous water-spirits. Look beyond your feeble selves to the tapestry of things that hangs rippling in the waters."

They all leaned forward to see the wonder the cat had evoked—Irissa and Thane fiercely, their Torloc eyes focused; Javelle far less confidently.

"I see it!" Javelle was the first to announce despite the handicap of purely human vision. "There, behind us—a kind of gray . . . wavering. It's a city—or one city street lined with many shops."

"Shops." The cat seemed in danger of laughing again, although that was quite impossible. "Such a plain way of putting it—'shops.' Yes, you see, half-blind child, what better eyes than yours have overlooked. Shops, indeed."

"What shops?" Thane was indignant. "I see nothing but filaments of silver threading the water and a glow far below."

"The same glow as when Father took the flaming torch beneath the springwaters?" Javelle asked eagerly.

"Father did what?"

"I forgot. You were tangled in a tapestry-thread gate upstairs when Father fought the dungeon devil fish. He took an unquenchable torch into the springwater with him."

"Then perhaps Father is—" Thane leaned over the pond, searching for the dim aquatic light he'd seen before.

"No." Irissa's hand clamped his arm before his balance could overtip him. "Water is not your father's element. But now I see what Felabba refers to—Javelle's spectral shop fronts. Only . . . they are not shops, but—"

"Doors of all descriptions, you poor blunderers." Felabba's tail lashed the flattened grasses. "Gates of many colors. This pondtop scum but reflects them. The reality lies beyond the forest archways."

"And the sword?" Javelle asked quickly. "The sword itself?"

"The sword itself rests in the world Rule has become since you left it. We are caught in prism-gate, which sits outside any world, even Without."

"The sword is beyond one of the doors?" Thane confirmed.

"Beyond one of the doors," the cat echoed complacently.

"Then—" Thane was rushing to the half-seen walls that hung before the dark forestscape behind him, pacing the rectangle around. "But which one, which door?"

"Felabba knows." Irissa bent to catch the cat's eye.

The cat refused to look at her.

Thane stopped. "If it knows everything, why do we bother to try to *do* anything?"

"Felabba's knowledge is less than magical, in this case. She saw Eeryon take the right gate, didn't you?" Irissa inquired.

Found out, the cat chewed upon its whiskers. While it mulled the most mysterious thing to say, Briarwhip lumbered up behind Javelle. Suddenly, the creature's unappealing maw opened to take folds of her tunic hem into its fangs.

Javelle batted at the three ugly eyes and tried to pull free. Briarwhip only whimpered through clamped teeth and shook its massive head. Each shake pulled Javelle a step or two backward. Briarwhip shook again—and pulled. Retreated and pulled. Shook and retreated.

Javelle found herself being drawn away from the others toward the dark woods, toward the vaguely outlined doors shimmering on the sylvan backdrop.

"Stop it!" she ordered, still edging backward.

Briarwhip finally did, more deliberate than obedient, freeing Javelle's clothing with a quick release of its jaws.

"Briarwhip saw, too," Irissa realized, laughing at the cat, at Thane, before striding over to Javelle. Her daughter was brushing her tunic free of wrinkles, unaware of where she stood. "Here." Irissa's finger lifted to indicate a plain door, barely recognizable as such beside the ornate doors and gateways neighboring it.

The cat had trotted over behind Thane, hissing some unkind feline curse at Briarwhip en route.

"True," Felabba said when she arrived.

"Why not simply tell us?" Thane demanded.

"It would not be a cat if it simply told us." Irissa smiled at the animal. "Its nature is to *teach* us by teasing us with either side of the truth."

"Its nature is not much help," Thane grumbled.

"So your father said."

Mention of Kendric sobered the party instantly.

"We must hurry," Javelle pled. "The miserable cat has toyed with us and wasted time that could be precious to Father. We must take the gate and find the sword."

"I'll do it," Thane offered brusquely. "You found the sword too heavy to lift before."

"You are no stronger!" Javelle objected. "Not yet, anyway."

"Neither shall go," Irissa decided, "now that I am here. I am stronger than both and I have lifted the sword before."

The cat sighed and sat at their feet, limbs tucked in, leaving one forepaw bent, as if ready for hasty rising.

"What is wrong now?" Irissa asked.

"And you talk of *me* wasting time." The cat cocked an ear to the pond behind them. "Have you considered that? *That!* That . . . shadow self. You dare not leave it untended, seeress."

"Leave it? I loosened it, bade it leave *me.*"

"That was in Without, where other rules apply. Flexible rules. Here, the shadow might fatten on your absence, might *become* you by the time you returned . . . might usurp yourself. You have heard of Usurpers before now, seeress?"

Irissa was startled into deep thought. "'Tis true,

Geronfrey provided Issiri a good example in usurpation. But I am the greater being—"

"Says who—you?" Felabba jeered. "Perhaps the shadow self has a shadow heart and mind and life, even a shadow magic of a sort. It has a shadow son, certainly. Perhaps the shadow self would seize its time, and who could blame it?"

"Then who will go for the sword?" Irissa demanded. "You?"

"Those sent for the sword. Why change the rules now?"

"A long, roundabout way to say you wish me to keep you company," Irissa noted.

"We will go?" Javelle couldn't believe that her wish was granted.

"But keep together," Irissa charged them both. "And you *have* dealt with this Eeryon before. Remember that he is on a countererrand to ours. Remember that he must serve *his* father, not yours."

"Eeryon wouldn't—" Javelle began.

"Eeryon did," Thane reminded her brutally. "He left us fallen into the ice pit. He's beaten us here—perhaps it's already too late. Perhaps he's taken the sword and returned to Without."

"No!" Tears made Javelle's eyes sparkle with almost-magical light.

She reached for the snake circlet as if to wrench it from her temples. But she was no more able to loose it than her parents had been at her birth. Her eyes fell on the ugly creature who had pulled her to the right—or the wrong—door. Did it serve Eeryon, or them? Was it true—or false?

"We have naught to guide us but this beast's impulse," Irissa said, reading Javelle's thoughts. She looked over her shoulder, shudderingly, to guard against ghostly selves stealing from the water. "This place is a . . . crux between worlds. My magic doesn't reach its full stride here. Perhaps Thane's will not, either. You both must go and carry the heavy sword together, face your erstwhile friend as one enemy.

"The cat is right: the shadow self I released haunts and impedes me. I doubt it will permit one as strong as myself to pursue its shadow offspring. Even shadow ties are sometimes stronger than magic."

Javelle lifted her palm to the door. There was no latch or handle; she could only push it inward. In the dark rectangle, a lurid, fire-scribed palm mirrored hers for a moment. She gasped and jerked her hand back, then pushed it forward harder onto the impression of itself.

The door melted before them as she and Thane walked through. Watching, Irissa saw her children pale to shadows. They swiftly became mere glimmers fragmenting into motes against the darkling forest.

"That is the hardest part of having children," Felabba observed from her lowly position on the ground. "Watching them leave."

"How would you know?" Irissa wondered. "You've never had any."

"Have you kept me company every step of my long way around the worlds? Have you trod in my pawprints? Who is to say what I have or have not had in my travels? Not I, who in this current life remember only the birthwaters of a spectral well. But I may have mothered . . . millions in my times."

"I hope not," Irissa murmured. The half-sketched facade shook like a faded tapestry into sight and out of it. "Kendric would not survive such news even if the children should bring all Six Swords back from beyond the shadow door."

Irissa suddenly collapsed into a crouch, her fingers reaching to smooth the furrowed catbrow.

"Oh, Felabba, *what* or *when* you are, I do not care. You may incarnate yourself in multiples and number lives in the millions, but there is only one Kendric. Can you do nothing—say nothing—that will aid us in saving him?"

The cat stirred uneasily and looked away. "I am young in my old age. My memories shatter with my multiplicity. I have come before and have not been . . . unnecessary. Perhaps I will yet prove myself essential here."

Irissa rocked back on her heels. The wood was dark, the black water still. The hideous beast from Without had curled into a waiting ball and laid its noxious head upon its paws.

"Once," Irissa recalled, "when I was temporarily blinded, you—or some past or future you—told me things I would have rather not heard."

"So is the way of a cat, if it can speak."

"What do you tell me now, young Bitterbones?"

"Only to wait and watch, as I do, as we . . . beasts do. Our time passes, yours and mine, even as Kendric's candle melts to its wick-end." The cat closed its eyes slowly. "Let us rest and let the children do it."

"At least it's a fortress," Thane said as he inspected the dim halls beyond the door. "Swords are often kept in such places."

"So are people—for many years, even lifetimes," Javelle answered glumly.

"At least Rule still exists. It has not sunk into the sea with Clymerind. We have a chance."

Javelle nodded, not liking the way Thane's words echoed from the great stones mortared into the soaring walls.

Nothing magical clung to those walls or this place. Stones were stones—cut into table-sized blocks and smoothly piled until they upheld a ceiling too high and dark to see.

The floor was inset with smaller stones, more rounded to the foot. There were no windows within—only shafts of murky light lancing the infinite dark from high above. The two moved through another looming archway—and almost collided with an eight-foot figure that clanged its weapons.

"An ice-wraith!" Thane swore as his hand jerked back from a cold metal greave as if it were hot.

Javelle retreated enough to survey the guardian. It stood upon a pedestal of some alien wood and wasn't eight feet tall at all. "Father would dwarf it. Don't be afraid. It's . . . mounted, like a lorryk head in the Inlands. Remember poor Bounder?"

"Will this thing speak, too?" Thane wondered.

"No . . . it's merely the skin of the monster. It's empty. Dead."

Thane cautiously touched jointed metal fingers, then darted back again. "Then they who keep the place have set this here as a warning of what metal-made beasts prowl the halls."

"Or of what beasts *used* to prowl such halls," Javelle said more practically. "I've seen no one here but our own selves. Not even—"

"He could be unseeable," Thane put in, "your fine-threaded friend. He could be lurking behind every pillar, around every corner. He could kill us with our father's sword and only one of us would know and neither of us would live to tell."

"Don't . . . frighten me like that." Javelle shivered. "It's cold in here—and where are the fireplaces? A hall this size should have hearths with mouths as high as an Empress Falgon's eye."

"You don't believe in Empress Falgons? That was just a tale Father and Mother told to embroider their travels. Besides, they rode the last one, anyway."

"And Felabba vanished in Edanvant, never to be seen again."

Thane was silent. He followed Javelle through the forth-right, foursquare rooms, never noticing that he had sub-sided into his standard place behind her. It wasn't that she was braver than he. Yet ever since she had been forcibly reminded of their father's fatal illness, Javelle seemed to have forgotten about fear.

She paused on a fresh threshold, putting a hand back to stop Thane.

"What?" he whispered, the word hissing back into his ears like surf cast back from the hard stones.

"Swords. I see swords."

"Swords? How many?"

"Hundreds," Javelle whispered back.

Thane stepped around her to see for himself. His mouth dropped to realize she was right. Not dozens—not swords by the foot, not hilts by the tens and twenties—but *hundreds* of swords hung naked against the walls, reaching up as high as the eye could see. Perhaps these doughty blades flashed their edged smiles even higher, but the upper darkness hid them.

Thane edged into the chamber—more like a great hall it was. No furniture impeded him—only more swords, sus-pended in air by some spell, or impaled in solid blocks of stone.

The air twinkled with swords, as a sky does with stars. Dim light glanced off polished blue blades and shiny gilt ones. It softly caressed old rust-sheathed blades, finding some winking luster under the dust of ages past. Light-burnished hilts shaped like fishes and deer and dogs hung alongside simpler ones fashioned from plain pommels and upright grips and curved crossguards.

"'Tis an armory," Thane complained. "What an army this lord must command."

"Yet they sleep," Javelle put in. "It must be night here. Be glad we happened to come in darkness."

"In darkness we will fail. How will we find one sword among so many in such dusk?"

Javelle turned around slowly, counting the glimmers from suspended blades as she would summer stars. The serpentine circlet loosened on her temples, only then reminding her how taut it had coiled. It clung lazily just above her eyebrows, and she sensed bright snake eyes searching the interior haze for its long, stiff, metal cousins.

"We've seen the sword before," she answered, "that's how we'll find it. We have the advantage of Eeryon. And we know it's longer than most. Even in this array, Father's sword would outmeasure the longest by a foot or more."

Thane was silent as he circled the room in the reverse direction to Javelle. They met at an opposite archway.

"Anything?" she asked.

"Not that I could see, although I've seen so many styles of blade and hilt I can hardly remember what Father's looked like."

"Then through here."

Again, Javelle led. Again, Thane followed and stopped. He groaned, softly but eloquently.

"Nothing but more weapon-hung walls," he complained. "Have these folk never heard of tapestries?"

Javelle pointed silently. On an end wall hung a fabric scene perhaps six times the size of their mother's weavings. A party of well-dressed people gathered around a white-wood fence in which capered a one-horned bearing-beast.

"An Edanvant scene!" Thane greeted it.

"These folk don't look like Torlocs, and the beast is too dainty to be the Hunter that skewered Father. It's as if the weaver had *heard* of us and Edanvant and depicted us from memories so worn that they have become lies."

"Who cares with what deceptions they hang their walls, as long as they have our father's sword? Shall we make our round again?"

Javelle nodded and the two split to either side, pacing along the cold stones, sharpening their gazes on the cutting edges of an eternity of swords.

At the next threshold Thane took hold of Javelle's arm. "We could be at this forever. There must be a better approach."

"What?"

His eyes cast around for a hook to hang his magic on. He found one in a great round shield hung low enough to touch.

"Quick!" He urged Javelle over to the circle of polished steel. "You seem to know the ways of the boy from Without. Think of him and I'll cast his reflection into this metal mirror."

She didn't have to try too hard; Eeryon's presence—or his absence—had dogged her steps through these deserted halls like a phantom Briarwhip.

As the water-borne semblance of her father's sword reflected the real weapon, so she felt Eeryon's duty to his father's quest—no matter the sorcerer's nature—echoed her loyalty to her own father. She couldn't quite regard Eeryon as a deadly rival, as Thane did, but as a fellow sufferer.

"Are you thinking?" Thane demanded.

Javelle smiled at his impatience. "Yes, of course. If you want to skim my thoughts, you must allow me the time and quietude to have them."

"Something's not working," Thane admitted. "I conjure a vision of another room, but it is empty."

"May I see?" Javelle brought her face before the gently curved steel surface. Her own reflection distorted, pulled her features apart like a wailwraith's shattered on the water.

Through the rended veil of her reflected face, Javelle glimpsed another room, smaller than these others, with a more intimate collection of weaponry glinting from the gray stones.

It was empty.

"Your thoughts and my magic make a disappointing blend," Thane said. "I only see more of the same."

"Yes, but . . . but, Thane—look! A sword lifts off the wall. By itself!"

Her brother's face dropped like a stone into the mirror image—pushed Javelle's reflection aside. They looked like twins joined at the jaw, and both jaws agape. Yet their own distortion was easy to see right past as they watched a sword levitate from its upholding pegs and float down the wall.

It hung in midair and turned this way and that, as if offering itself for their inspection.

"It's not the right one," Thane noted immediately, "but it might be worth having, anyway—a sword that wields itself. We must find that room."

"Yes, we must."

Thane suspiciously studied his sister's face, leery of such heartfelt agreement. It was more serious than his, but then, it often was.

"Thane," she said, her brown eyes narrowing. "That sword doesn't wield itself. Eeryon holds it."

"But . . . I saw no one." Then he realized the truth Javelle saw. "He is *invisible* again? How will we ever stop him if he has the sword?"

"Well, he hasn't, or he wouldn't still be looking. How is he to tell it? He's never seen it. He must be relying on his magic. We have our eyes. But I think we should hurry."

So they did, racing through vast chamber after chamber. Their eyes rapidly inventoried all the swords they encountered—none were long enough to be one of the legendary Six, none were familiar enough to stop their headlong rush from room to room to room.

At last the chamber sizes diminished. As the rooms shrank, Javelle and Thane noticed a different progression in the weaponry. These chambers held more exotic pieces —great, curved swords with coiled handguards; short, thick double-edged swords that could sever an arm or a leg at the joint; thorn-headed spears. It seemed likely that their father's lengthy sword would be among these other unusual weapons.

Yet in all the space and for all the mounted swords, they had seen no sign of Eeryon.

"There!" Thane indicated a sword high up on a wall. "That is the one we saw dancing by itself. He must be ahead of us—"

They dashed together through a doorway into another room, then paused as one.

Eeryon stood, his black velvet back to them as if dark itself had turned away from them, near the door leaving the chamber they had just entered.

He was motionless, unheeding.

Javelle was the first to approach him. "Eeryon?"

He turned without surprise, smiling distractedly to see her. Then he turned back to the room before him.

"What's wrong?" she asked.

"Nothing." His voice was distant, as his manner was— not from coldness, but confusion. "I think the sword we seek rests in here—I've been through every other room. But—" He stepped back from the threshold.

Javelle and Thane crowded into his former place—eager and possessive, according to their natures. The chamber before them was circular, the very navel of the boxy maze of rooms they'd passed through. Its walls were also weapon-hung—Javelle spied a great long slash of rusty steel on the wall opposite and gasped.

Thane had seen it, too. But when Javelle leaned forward to cross the threshold, to hurl herself at the wall and the sword and haul it down somehow as she had done once before, Thane caught her arms hard with both hands and restrained her.

"Don't look at me," he urged, "look at the floor. Why do you think he waited?"

Javelle glanced down to her feet. Thin intersecting beams of blue light lanced across the opening, lacing it shut a third of the way up. Javelle's eyes followed the barrier upward.

She couldn't see anything immediately before her, but as her gaze lifted, she saw again the thin, deadly-looking blades of blue light that sealed the opening as effectively as Thane's golden disc had closed a pillar to Without.

CHAPTER

31

IRISSA EDGED AROUND THE CONTAINED POND, WARY OF
Wailwraiths. The cat padded after her while Briarwhip
kept faithful guard at the doorway through which his
master had disappeared.

"Dogs are loyal," Irissa commented obliquely.

"Are you sure yon monster is a dog?"

"No." Irissa stopped and turned to confront the cat with
a wry look. "But then, I'm not so certain you're a cat,
either."

Felabba ambled by Irissa, favoring her with a swagger
past her leg. "Dogs are foolish, anyway. They only guard
the obvious."

"What do you guard?" Irissa asked. "The children have
committed to a venture into the unknown. I merely do
what mothers have always done—wait and hope for the
best."

"You don't fool me. You are taking soundings of your
counterpart in the deep waters. Are you sorry you released
it?"

"Yes." Irissa crouched near the water as if to tempt the indweller surfaceward. "I never guessed then that I would free myself. I had hoped that this pirated part of myself would find within it the need to protect these other parts of myself—my children. I forgot that it had a child of its own to guard."

"You ascribe deep feeling to a shadow."

"I don't know if shadows feel. Certainly, it clings to us—me . . . or Eeryon."

"Loyal as a dog?" the cat suggested sardonically.

Irissa rose and resumed her stroll that was more a pacing. "Not like a dog. Like a . . . creature with a heart and soul."

"But it is shadow."

"We all are shadow."

"Were you always so melancholy?"

Irissa laughed shortly. "No. Once I was younger."

Her walk had taken her abreast of the long wall on which the doorway to Rule beckoned. She stopped and stared at its blank, half-hidden surface, tempted herself.

"Where do these other doorways lead, do you think?" the cat inquired.

"You seek to distract me," Irissa accused, turning her attention on the other portals, anyway.

"I am a cat. I seek only my own comfort, remember?"

"Or others' discomfort. Ah, let's see. This well-embellished door has a Torloc look to it. Do you suppose it leads to Edanvant? Shall I send you through to see?"

The cat darted away, ears down and tail up. "Send me nowhere. It's bad enough being birthed by a well. I shall not now begin walking through walls."

"These are doors, as you well know."

Irissa's hand lifted as if to knock at the one she had called Torloc, then she stepped quickly down the line. The next facade hung on the air with a faint rainbow shimmer. Its door was shaped like a swan.

"Gateways," Irissa recalled fondly. "If I had to design a gate to Rengarth, it would be this. But no such thing exists. Thane and Javelle and I will be hard pressed to find a way back if they—when they—return with the sword."

"Perhaps Rengarth will come to you," the cat suggested.

Irissa snapped her face around again. "Sly, teasing creature. Be wary. I stand in a crux between worlds here—my children venturing into danger in one direction . . . Kendric dying in another. Do not try my patience. *You* may be the sacrificial key to any gate. If circumstances reverse far enough, I will not hesitate to turn any ally to my needs, as I will destroy any foe—even a sliver of myself—if need be."

"Oh, there is iron in your Iridesium, seeress. I am most impressed." The cat kept its distance, but winked one eye slowly shut. "Look upon your Rengarthian gate, then." Its ears flicked forward. "I hear a shadow breathing and a long-rusted hinge squeaking. I hear long bones creaking. . . ."

Irissa turned back to the ghostly door, drawn by more than the cat's jibes. There *was* a creaking in the air, faint as distant bells.

Then the softly colored dust motes lengthened into glossy threads of light. A shining tapestry wove itself onto the air. The swan-shape swelled into a satin-soft expanse, became swangate in the palace in Solanandor Tierze—so real it puffed out ebony feathers. The long neck arched, part from pride, part from strain. The bird's likeness seemed on the brink of exploding into a snowstorm of feathery midnight down. . . .

Even the swan's face distorted, changing into a shorter, furrier visage . . . becoming a white cat's triangular face. Irissa caught her breath and stood eye to eye with the cat-faced swangate.

The rest of the swan was stretching now, giving birth to a form that struggled through its fabric being. A hand broke through, clutching a sword hilt—no, clutching *the* sword hilt!

Had Thane and Javelle returned by another route, another world? But what of the cat . . . ? Irissa glanced to Felabba sitting placidly on the grass. The cat face newly affixed atop the swan's neck was not so calm. Its eyes squeezed shut in struggle, its ears had flattened to its shallow skull. It looked as if it were being drawn through a keyhole.

As for the hand bearing the sword—Irissa gasped and stepped back as an arm boldly thrust forth. And a knee! Then shoulder, legs, body.

She froze where she stood, no longer afraid, merely amazed. And then a familiar face broke through. Kendric was ripping through tattered tapestry, a white cat held high in one hand, the sword pushing hilt-first into the scene in the other.

Irissa lifted her hands to the Iridesium circlet, her eyes absorbing the scene in all its meaning. Rainbow skeins of airborne tapestry spun into tidy lines and looped around her head. They finally fastened to the swirling colors that played across the circlet's black base metal—and vanished.

Kendric bowed to put the cat on the ground, then his big hand batted away the last enwebbing threads.

"Kendric! You're all right!" Irissa hurled herself toward him, then held back at the last moment, fearing her delight should overpower him.

He winced in recognition of her restraint. "That is a matter of opinion. I am here, yes. And alive. But 'all right'?" He shrugged painfully and grimaced. "Can anyone who pushes from one place to another through mere fabric be completely well in one way or another?"

"What of the . . . poison?"

"What do you think?" he answered in turn.

Lightly clasping his arm, Irissa surveyed Kendric. At first glimpse, she had been heartened to see him standing upright. Now she saw that his ruddy face and hale appearance was an illusion. Poison still tattooed his skin with a universe of bruises and his hearty manner was a result of effort, not inner strength.

"Why?" she asked him. "How?"

"For how, ask the cat." He pointed to the ground, to a sharp heap of bones insufficiently upholstered by white fur.

"Fe-Felabba?" Irissa crouched beside it, trying to catch the focus of its faded eyes.

"Of course . . . Felabba," it snapped so sharply that Irissa darted back to avoid being bitten. "Let me get my bearings. I have come through two tapestries in one turn of the hourglass. Interrogate your Wrathman; he has only made his way through one."

Irissa turned her attention on Kendric again. *"Two* Felabbas?"

He eyed the other white cat—twin to the one he had carried through the tapestry, except its fur was smooth and its eyes clear as a water-emerald.

"Perhaps I merely see double," Kendric admitted. "Yet you, too, see them both—?"

"Of course. There *are* two. Kendric, how do you fare?"

"Well enough, once I'd persuaded Scyvilla to give me all of the Bloodstone powder."

"All of it! But that powder was like sands in a glass, it trickled your time out to the finest grain. I don't know if I can keep you . . . well . . . once the effect has worn away."

"It is not always for you to keep me well, Irissa."

"But the strain of moving through worldgates will surely hasten your—your . . ."

"Collapse?"

She flinched and was silent, not wanting to name his malady or the fatal stages of it.

"My sword will uphold me awhile," he said, leaning on the upright blade.

"Javelle and Thane search for the original even now."

"Where?"

"Through there, an adjoining amorphous gate. And another has gone there before them."

"Who?"

"You mean 'what.' Geronfrey saved that unbreathing infant he tore from my shadow self's body."

"Geronfrey has an heir?"

"Geronfrey has a blasphemy. I've never seen him, but Thane and Javelle have. Even now they struggle to find the sword before he does, in his father's service."

Kendric allowed his weight to seat him on the ground. "Tell me slowly, all of it again. It is more than I can comprehend standing up."

Irissa sank groundward with him, like a consoling weepwater tree drooping to the water. They had much to relate to each other, and perhaps precious little time in which to do it. Still, it seemed an idyllic moment to share the privacy of their own company beside a still pond, to forget for a moment the wear of others and the worry of outside concerns.

Irissa bent her head to his. "I am so glad to see you. I was afraid—" She left the thought unspoken.

"Yes, so was I," he answered. "It was too much to have you all gone—worry drained my will to live. Stay now."

"I will," Irissa promised through the crystal veil of her tears. "And Thane and Javelle will have the sword soon. You two shall be reunited, blade to blade, mind-made sword to master sword, wielder to weapon. Such a powerful conjunction will counteract the venom. You will live, Kendric, and live as long as any Torloc, I swear it! I will see to it."

"Just let me live long enough to see my children again— and"—he chuckled weakly—"those two white feline demons meeting face to face." His eyelids sagged shut as his head hung forward to his chest. He appeared to sleep, but

Irissa knew that Kendric kept so still only because he was hoarding the last shreds of his strength, his vitality, his very life force.

She turned on the old white cat.

"Why bring him through in such condition?"

"Would you have preferred me to wait until he was dead?"

"No . . . but it is not that close a thing yet."

"It is always that close a thing."

"And how do you explain yourself, disgraceful old hidey-cat, when you are a living redundancy?"

"You mean . . . this." Felabba pushed herself up on her rickety legs and stalked stiffly over to her duplicate.

The two animals eyed each other askance, sniffing noses and interlocking whiskers. Old Felabba was the first to turn away.

"Insignificant," she pronounced, returning to Irissa. "I have been long absent. Tell me what has happened. And speak up. My ears are not as sharp as they were."

"There is more that you could tell me," Irissa objected.

"Later," Felabba said. "I am most concerned about the fate of the sword. Your children trifle with a balance not only between worlds and gates, but between the sift of Time itself, and between all the worlds we know—even Without itself."

Alarmed, Irissa once again found herself asking when she had intended to tell. "They will not be harmed—our children?"

"Assuredly, they will." Felabba sounded even more impatient than of old. "The only questions are when and how much and by whom? Life will harm them, seeress. All your magic cannot stop that. But as for their quest here, it depends."

"Riddles," Irissa spat out bitterly. "Like Javelle, I find myself unable to live on a 'perhaps.' "

The old cat settled into the four sharp points of her leg bones, hardly noticing when her younger self padded over and sniffed cautiously at her ragged tail.

"Get used to it. We can do nothing—for anyone or anything—until the children return from the hidden gate they've taken."

"Even the great Felabba can do no more than wait?"

The cat's old eyes flicked to Kendric's self-contained figure. He looked frozen in death already.

"I have always done that," Felabba answered. "There is much greatness in waiting."

Irissa rose up on her knees, hissing her impatience. But the odd formal clearing was still and silent, filled with the act of waiting. The hound from Without waited for his master; Kendric waited for his immortality to walk through a doorway and his mortality to hesitate on the brink of a threshold of its own. Old Felabba waited for the ripeness of its predictions. Young Felabba had ceased pacing and settled down, mimicking its elder self even to the position of its ears.

Irissa looked to the pond. Within it, she sensed, some severed part of herself was waiting, too. She sat on her heels beside Kendric, her hand on his wrist so she should instantly detect any sign that the poison had done with waiting and had decided to be lethal.

"Blue-worms!" Javelle said. Then she frowned and was silent.

"Blue-worms?" Eeryon inquired. These were the first words he had spoken since their parting of ways. His eyes did not quite meet theirs.

"Strange creatures who associate with the ludborgs of Rengarth," Thane explained. "They are long, thin, and glow blue, but I don't think these rods of light are alive like them."

"The light rods are *something*." Eeryon lifted his right

sleeve. Along a swath from wrist to elbow ran a dark bristle of silver threads that had seared to black. "I tried to cross. Luckily, I led with my arm, else I would have sizzled like a fish over fire."

A smile flickered over Javelle's features as Eeryon's words reminded her of their beach encampment. That benign time seemed a thousand years away.

She glanced to Thane. His expression had softened, too. All three, she realized, wished for a return to the time when they had not guessed each other's danger—and vulnerability.

"We can . . . unite our forces to pass the barrier," Javelle suggested.

"A sword doesn't divide in two." Thane sounded angry.

"We can settle that later." Javelle was conscious of distant grains of sand passing an hourglass neck; their dying father couldn't wait on arguing children.

"How can we settle it?" Thane was unappeased.

Javelle's eyes narrowed thoughtfully. "Let you and Eeryon duel with magic to decide who keeps the sword. But first, we must get it."

Fear—and reluctance—and then a fierce aura of possession radiated from both boys' faces. Javelle couldn't understand them. They were as alike as twins in some ways— and implacably different. Above all, she knew she had to reckon with their matching vanity, their pride.

"All right." Thane was curt when he finally agreed. He knew the need for speed as well as Javelle, though he less liked to show it.

"That seems fair." Eeryon spoke coolly, as if his mind were deep in the reaches of Without. "How do we defeat the blue lights?"

Thane ripped a piece of braid from the side seam of his trousers and offered the frayed end to the cunning needles of light. They sliced right through the material with the high-pitched buzz of angry insects.

Powder drifted through Thane's fingers to the stone floor.

"What of the cable snake your eyes uncoiled to topple the onlookers in Rengarth?" Javelle asked her brother.

Eeryon looked so amazed that Thane quickly justified the trick. "A game I played. I can do it again, but if even Eeryon's magical silver threads cannot withstand the knives of light—"

"Eeryon's threads are material made magic." Javelle spoke with an unexpected authority. "The rope conjured from your eyes is *im*material, like this light. Perhaps—"

Thane was already concentrating. Under the hoods of his eyes, threads from the pale silver and gold of each eye met in the middle and formed a single bronze cable.

As before, the emanation wove through the air. It breached a space between two crossed blades of blue light and paused. Nothing happened, save the hovering cable trembled a bit. Encouraged, Thane directed the rope up and over the topmost lance of light. Then it wove in and out among the light beams, always drawing them down toward the archway's bottom.

When the tension drew tight enough for the magical cable to touch the unfathomable light, all three watchers held their breaths. Thane hesitated, then boldly pulled the slack rope tight. A humming vibrated even the floor beneath their feet. For a moment the sides of the doorway seemed likely to crash together as the cable pulled the blue lights from their roots.

Instead, the blue rods *bent!* Long they grew, like uncoiled snakes, flexing within the knot of Thane's rope until they were all caught and tied taut in a bundle near the floor. The doorway was not totally clear, but an inverted V of space waited for someone agile to cross it.

"Your silver threads might anchor my rope," Thane suggested to Eeryon.

The boy from Without whipped forth his left arm,

freeing lashings of silver thread to secure the straining rope.

Javelle clapped her hands in glee. "Who goes first?"

"You're not going," Thane said, "it might be too dangerous."

"You may need me," Javelle retorted. "Who thought you through the door?"

"We're not through yet. I'll go first."

"I'm first in line." Eeryon's taller, broader body blocked the path.

"You duel *after* we find the sword, remember?" Javelle told Eeryon. In fairness, she turned on her brother next. "Let Eeryon go first."

Thane allowed Eeryon to straddle the bundle of blue lights and pass it. "You made a bad bargain," he whispered to Javelle. "Who knows what trick Eeryon may treat us to? He may even vanish with the sword before I have a chance to duel him."

"I wouldn't have made a bad bargain unless I had a better way out of it," she answered mysteriously. "And Eeryon won't disappear. He knows he'd never have crossed this threshold without our help."

"I thought you were eager to find the sword?" Eeryon asked from across the opening, waiting politely.

Thane was so impressed by Eeryon's restraint that he let Javelle precede him through. She hopped over the bent rods of light so adeptly both boys caught their breaths for fear such confidence must end in a fall.

But soon all three were through the archway and staring at the great longsword high on the opposite wall. Dozens of other swords decked the same wall, some of them polished mirror-bright.

None carried the great age—the broad, long blade, the massive hilt with its leather-wrapped grip—of one rust-dappled sword that they all had recognized instantly, even Eeryon who had never seen it.

"It sings of magic," he said, moving to the wall.

Thane hastened to scramble after him, but Javelle caught his sleeve so violently he stopped.

"What?" he whispered in brotherly annoyance. "You must leave me alone so I can defend our right to the weapon."

"What of that other weapon?" Javelle pointed to another wall.

Thane spun unbelievingly to face it.

Another sword hung there—long and plain and rusted and right.

"What?" Thane repeated dully.

At the wall before them, Eeryon was studying the lay of the first sword they'd seen.

"Or *that* one?" Javelle said precisely, pointing to a third wall.

"Another sword?"

"And that and that. And that." Rapidly, she indicated three more swords hung at various heights throughout the chamber, each of them identical to the others.

"But," Thane said, and was silent.

"But," Javelle thought, frowning until the serpent circlet shifted on her furrowed brow. "It is not enough to find the sword. We must choose the right one."

"How?"

"Father said his sword bore the signs of every blow it gave and took."

"All swords bear nicks. Only Father would know his own."

"We handled the mind-made sword ourselves not many days ago."

"Not long enough to memorize its oddities. Besides, they all hang high. We shall have to struggle mightily to inspect them, much less lug them all down. There must be an easier way."

"You mean a magical way," Javelle retorted, eyeing the sword above her hungrily.

"Magic is hard," Eeryon said behind them. He stared up, numbering the swords. "Six swords are the same. What does this mean?"

"There were always Six Swords, forged together in Rengarth when it was more accessible and sent to Rule. Our father carried one, but the Wrathman from each of the other five Realms carried his own ancestral sword."

Eeryon was not answered. "These Wrathmen were those cast in stone on the once-sunken island?"

"Yes," Javelle said.

"But their *swords* were with them, turned to stone."

"Perhaps the *spirit* of the swords remained with them," Thane interrupted. "Obviously, the actual swords were lost in various parts of the land and refound by living descendants of the Rule our parents knew. There's a placard beneath this one, who can read it?"

"I can, if you'll boost me up." Javelle leaned against the wall to wrench off her boots.

The young men exchanged glances, then both bent to push her high on their shoulders so quickly she squealed her sudden fear and clutched a mounted ax handle to keep her balance. Yet she was near enough to read the severe black letters printed so perfectly and small that they must have been inscribed with a mouse-tail.

" 'A long sword,' " it says.

"That we can see," came from the ground.

". . . 'exceptionally long, the blade alone nearing five feet. Believed carried by me-medieval mercenary knights of unusual height.' "

"That we knew," Thane complained. "Except for the land called Medevil. Come down, Javelle."

"Wait!"

"We can't."

"The writing says more. 'One of six similar weapons recovered from various portions of elder lands. Although all are of the same age, C.'" Javelle stopped reading. "It just says the letter 'C,' with a period."

"Whoever wrote that obviously knew nothing of the swords' true history. You might as well declaim a ludborg's blue-worm mating rituals and expect as much sense."

"'C. undetectable. This particular sword bears more rust because it alone was . . .'"

"Well?" Even Eeryon sounded impatient now.

"'. . . was found in water.'" Javelle lifted her hands to the naked steel slung in a cradle of three metal prongs. Beneath her stockinged feet, two shoulders stiffened in unison.

Under her fingers, the cold metal warmed as if welcoming her touch. She knew their quest had ended with the odd words of the strange placard. She also knew that now would begin the true fight for the sword.

"Come down," Thane ordered tersely.

She hesitated. To descend would bring chaos on their uncertain alliance. "Perhaps I can unfasten it. . . ."

"Too heavy." Thane's hand tightened around her ankle. "You'll overbalance us all. Come down." He tugged roughly on her leg, almost toppling her.

Javelle screamed and clutched the sword by the upper, dull, false edge. It still bit into her soft palms.

Then the shoulders beneath her were shifting like angry earth when it murmurs against the beings above it. Another voice was calling into the confusion—an angry, irritated voice. Javelle finally toppled as predicted, grabbing the long hilt for purchase and pulling the terrible weight free.

The sword fell with her, on her. Buckling bodies broke her fall. They lay in a mutually bruised pile on the floor—Thane and Eeryon, Javelle and the sword.

"Don't move!" the strange voice was shouting. Distant stones echoed with the uneven, hurrying steps of an unseen newcomer. A ball of gold light bright as any multiplicity of suns swam toward them in the dimness.

They helped each other up, Javelle maintaining custody of the sword because she would not release it.

"Don't move," the voice behind the bobbing light threatened. "You have no right to slip in here by night. No right to disrupt the exhibits, to damage the installation, to dismantle a sword from its hangers. Give it to me."

"It's heavy," Javelle said.

"A girl! What's a girl want with a sword? I can see why you boys would think it smart—a sword to mount at home and boast about . . . but a girl has no right to be sneaking around in the dark stealing swords."

"We can't steal what belongs to us."

"Belongs to you? Crazy. Now, look here, I'm armed. I warn you."

The voice let the ball of light spin until it illuminated his own form. He was only a little old man with a white pointed beard like a goat's at the end of his chin and watery eyes magnified by circular lenses of coldstone.

"Is it Chaundre of the Inlands, do you think?" Thane whispered to Javelle. "I remember our parents talking of his seeing contrivance."

"What would he be doing here in Rule? Stonekeepers never even traveled from keep to keep in their own world."

Eeryon glanced from brother to sister and to the old man, mystified by their puzzling words.

"Rule?" The old man gestured with both the thick rod that cast the bright light and some Iridesium-dark metal contrivance in his other hand. "The Golden Rule is to do unto others as you would have them do unto you, you've got that right enough. But you three thieves have no right to take what's not yours—and even less to lose in exchange . . . but your liberty—oh, yes, a lot of long months you'll spend cooped up for this trick."

"We have a right," Javelle said hotly, "and we are not thieves. This is our father's sword."

"Is it?" Eeryon asked suddenly. "Perhaps his day is long past. Time may not run the same in every world. Perhaps another has inherited it and you steal it."

"Our father lives—how can another have inherited his sword?" Thane argued.

"Your father left this land—"

"As yours did—" Javelle put in. "Geronfrey abandoned Rule also. He has no more right than our father. . . ."

"Fathers be damned," growled the old man. "And rights. I'm in charge here, I'm armed—and no one shall take any property anywhere for any reason. It belongs here. And you three will be the only ones leaving, for quick incarceration."

"I see," said Thane. "You are the guardian of the place."

The old man straightened. He was wearing dark trousers and tunic, with a medallion glinting from one shoulder.

"Guardian, yes."

"But we wouldn't have been allowed through the gate," Thane explained, "had we no right to be here."

"So you had an accomplice inside. Who?"

"An accomplice Without," Javelle said, smiling. "The secondborn cat, Felabba."

"Cats!" The old man shuddered, making his light dance and blind their eyes. "Can't stand them. Sneak thieves, every last pussyfooted one of them. No one takes what I guard. No one. Now march!"

He gestured with the light of one hand and the darkness in the other. They consulted each other's eyes and shrugged.

Javelle had held the sword during the interrogation; the young men bracketed either side of her, each ready to claim the weapon should her custody falter. She knew it as well as they, and was determined to hang on to it, no matter how heavy it weighed, to maintain the truce. She remembered her father's lesson that she could carry more than she thought.

Javelle took a step, dragging the sword with her. The tip struck stone, scraping tunelessly.

"Leave it," the old man ordered. "It's mine. It belongs here. You three have brought nothing here but trouble and that's all you'll take from here."

"No," said Javelle, stepping forward again.

The old man raised the darkness in his right hand. The light in his left shook unaccountably.

"I don't care what claims you have. I don't care if you're just youngsters. No one takes from me—"

Simultaneous loops of silver and gold lashed from either side of Javelle like a forked serpent's tongue. With the same motion they entwined both talismans of light and dark and wrenched them from the old man's grasp.

The light hit the floor with a clank and rolled away like a renegade sun still shining fiercely. The dark implement clattered floorward also, sliding along stones until its form was lost.

The old man wailed as Thane and Eeryon each grabbed an end of the sword—Eeryon's shining palms, little suns in themselves, caught hold of the cutting end with no difficulty—and ran.

Javelle, disinherited, followed them after stooping to retrieve her boots. Her foot stumbled over something hard on the floor. She tripped forward and ran, guided by the glow ahead—a mellow needle of light that was not the implement of a greedy old guardian wizard, but one she had seen before.

She followed the fleeing hilt-light of Kendric the Wrathman's magic-ridden and one true longsword.

CHAPTER
32

KENDRIC'S HEAD LIFTED. HE LISTENED.

"What is it?" Irissa's voice was husky with worry.

Kendric pushed himself upright, using his sword for a cane.

"Something tingled my palms," he said with a weary smile. "I took it for the old battle-itch, but my sword resonates so much that I can hardly hold it. Touch it."

Irissa's fingertips lightly pressed the naked steel near the hilt, feeling a deep vibration. "How can you hold on to it?"

"Not easily," Kendric admitted, lacing his fingers around the leather-bound grip.

He balanced the point on the ground, actually dug into it. Nearby grasses shivered as if possessed of an ague. Then the earth itself trembled. Sudden wavelets dashed against the pond sides. The translucent veils of the facades to many worlds shook as if caught in a wind-wrack. Briarwhip jolted up to four unsteady feet and the two Felabbas leaped as with one mind to the lower branches of a pine, where they swayed with the moaning tree limbs.

"We will not hold our feet," Irissa chattered between her

teeth, barely keeping them from clamping her tongue. "What's happening? What brute magic is about?"

Kendric shook his already shaking head. Coldstone sweat dewed his particolored skin. He stood as if forged from the metal he resembled, unmovable in a madly mobile world.

"The crux is shifting," Irissa thought aloud. "Soon we shall lose sight of the prism-gate. With that goes all chance of . . . of seeing our children again!"

"And the sword," put in young Felabba sourly from her unsteady perch.

At that very instant the sword hilt bucked from the clasp of Kendric's hands. Only his quick grab kept it upright and in his custody.

"You must not lose the sword," Irissa warned.

He only grunted his agreement, shaking like a man mounted on a wildly bucking bearing-beast, his muscles strung taut as bowstrings while he battled for control of the sword.

"Wait! What is that?" Irissa pointed to the elusive windblown image of walls and doors. A feeble glow was blossoming at the heart of the plainest door.

"I cannot hold it!" Kendric burst out, leaning with the sword at an angle toward the door.

Then two booted feet and one unbooted broke the spectral door's tenuous surface in unison. A bolt of bright light clashed through, then several arms and faces. Three young people stood in the clearing before Irissa and Kendric—their faces flushed, the sword borne horizontal in their arms, like a dead body being returned to its kin from a far-off war.

"Here! Bring it here!" Kendric urged.

The gilt-haired boy on one end hesitated, but the others were too strong for him, and too obedient to another. All three moved forward, lifted the weapon upright. As sword raised to parallel sword, the earth softened its shaking.

Grasses stood vertical again and waves flattened to mirror-smoothness. The restless trees hushed and only Kendric shook—in his arms alone, so weary were they from restraining the whole wild earth's will through the reins of his sword.

Kendric took several deep, ragged breaths. His face had paled so all could see the poison bruises running riot on the livid skin. Kendric looked nothing like himself, but he did resemble a man sick unto death.

Eeryon suddenly whirled away from him—saw Irissa, started—and spun away yet again. "You can have it," he said, so low hardly anyone heard it. Irissa did, and so did Briarwhip. The beast advanced on spindly legs to Eeryon, whimpering.

Kendric reached a palsied hand to the leather-bound hilt Javelle and Thane kept custody of. Ancient leather flaked from his fingers like the disintegrating cover of a book old beyond memory. More light poured from the rune-inscribed hilt beneath, fanning the flame within the duplicate hilt in Kendric's other hand.

"My blood was running cold," he admitted, his face hopeful in the double hilt-light. "How did you find it, obtain it?"

"Javelle got it," Thane said suddenly. "Javelle climbed up as she did before in Rengarth and got it down. Javelle found it. And then . . ." He looked over his shoulder to the dark silhouette that was Eeryon. "He helped."

"He did not hinder," Felabba the Younger said, mincing around the boy's dark-booted feet without touching him. "That much is certain."

"I thank you," Kendric croaked in a poison-roughened voice. "No children can gift their father better than employing their separate talents—together—to bring him hope."

Javelle and Thane stood rapt, silent, terrified to death. They had never seen their father stricken—even his limited mortality had only been a distant, unfelt threat to them. Now Kendric's altered aspect was dreadful enough to wring the hearts from them. Even Irissa's warnings of his mortality had not prepared them from the awful evidence of it.

"We must . . . join the two swords somehow," Irissa said briskly, stepping into the triad. She'd agonized at the delay even as she'd allowed father and children their moment of mutual reunion and reevaluation.

The time of utter understanding and harmony between them passed. Time-suspended emotions between father and children broke like a bubble, a casting cyrstal. Eyes fell, feet shuffled back. Irissa caught the original sword's hilt in her own hands as the children surrendered it, already braced for its great weight.

"Somehow," she repeated, narrowing her silver seeress's eyes at both weapons. Now came the moment when she could do more than wait and worry. Now she could act!

"A most touching reunion," came a cold coil of whisper in her ear.

Irissa's head jerked up to Kendric. "Who spoke?"

"Not I." He frowned beyond her to the forest. "I see a black bird perched in yon tree. Perhaps it talks."

"Felabba!" Irissa ordered, never turning to see the tree in question or its dark-feathered percher.

Like paired hunting hounds the two cats turned with a liquid bound and made for the tree. Sharp claws sprang them up the trunk, but the black bird swept to earth like a big dark leaf just as they crawled out along the limb.

The leaf wafted in an unseen updraught and rose higher —became a bat. It circled Irissa's head, flapping and croaking.

"Loose the sword, seeress, or it shall cut you," the bat croaked.

"I'll cut *you,*" Kendric responded, lifting his mind-made blade.

It . . . melted. Five feet of steel wavered, the hilt bent in his hands like a wand of butter.

"I'm weak—" he began, as if blaming himself and ashamed.

"Not you." Irissa struck at the flapping leafbat with one hand, but it tangled in her hair. She tossed her head in revulsion until her strands of dark hair snapped like whips. Iridesium sparks shot into the glade's murky air. The bat's fragile, leafy form cracked into brittle bits.

Irissa screamed her distaste of this sending shattering on her person. Javelle and Thane rushed over to help flail the remnants from her hair.

A flotilla of jet-black moths, their wings softer than moss-velvet, fluttered around everyone's heads, circled like veiling spots before their eyes.

Irissa almost lost the sword as she evaded the airborne attackers. Javelle helped uphold it while Thane sent a glittering array of gold and silver flutterbys against the dark moths.

Fluttering wings clashed like swords until only dark and bright powder remained to sift to the grass.

A snake with shining black scales the size of leafmeal scraped over the flattening grasses, the passage of its body strumming a sinister song.

Wind and water moved to the notes of that melody, stirred like motes in the sun-slashed air. There was no sun here, only a leaking light that filtered through the thick needles of the pine trees, that reflected from the secret bottom of the pond, that came from twin hilts, both gleaming desperately against the dark.

The black snake shed its skin as it crawled, each unveiled self growing larger and darker. It reached the boots of Eeryon—forgotten Eeryon, who seemed to have vanished although he was still clearly visible. The snake began weaving upright on its fattening coils, a thing of such black velvet subtlety that the onlookers hardly believed they saw it.

Dark spiraled around the unmoving boy and then it whispered in his ear.

"The sword is yours. Take it."

He edged away from the wall of swaying scales. "I . . . cannot stand against them all."

"You cannot stand against *me,*" the voice as dry as dead leaves said. "Take it. Claim it. Claim your reward from me."

"No!" Eeryon turned away from everyone and everything—serpent, sword, the people witnessing the scene.

The blackness—and the snake form was not so much a real presence now, as an *absence*—screwed tighter around the boy dressed in black until it seemed to garb him in something even darker.

"I have my means, my vengeance, and my rewards. Everything you are is honed to claim that sword. Do it!"

"No! I don't know why you want the sword, but I do know why they do. And their need is life and light. I've seen enough of the worlds outside Without to know the needs of such as you and I have no weight here."

"Spoiled!" The serpent roared like a wave of wind. "Spoiled son. For this did I nourish you? It is not yours to ask questions, only to answer my needs."

"Thane and Javelle answer their father's needs without his asking them, without defrauding another. Theirs is the deeper claim, the greater need. You have life eternal, Father, and magic and Without. What can these people have that you would need?"

"Loyalty!" the voice thundered. "Gratitude. You are bereft of such qualities."

"You never taught me that," Eeryon said quietly, although the anguish of his answer shook in his voice. "You taught me only what I needed to know to serve you; you never taught me how to serve you even if you didn't know what you needed. My loyalty and gratitude go to these others—"

"And your obedience?"

"To you, as always. I shall return to Without—"

"Without the sword?"

"I shall return to abide by your will. But here I am not myself, as you have shaped me. Here I am . . . something other. If you do not like it, let me return."

"If you do not bear the sword, there is no reason for you to return, shadow! You are mere scum from the top of an old well. Without fresh water beneath, you grow rancid in my sight. Go. Or stay. You shall fade in ignorant inches and never know why."

Eeryon began trembling—not in the way Kendric had moments before, or the earth had, but in the manner water quivers at the buffeting of raindrops, like a substance being torn apart by the bludgeoning of its very kind and nature.

He didn't speak now. The others could barely distinguish his dark form against the encompassing blackness. Only a few wispy tendrils of silver sparkled on his sleeves—and they were snapping, breaking into lint.

Irissa could stand it no longer. She moved toward the entwined dark, her silver eyes about to flare.

A smooth black snake's head, so velvety it was furred, lashed out of the air toward her. "Would you interfere in family business?" the serpent demanded. Its coils—and they seemed to be endless—looped toward her, hovered at the edge of the sword still in Irissa's hands.

Behind her, Kendric stirred, his mind-made blade lifting.

Before either of them could challenge the interloper, a bay sounded behind them. Briarwhip came rolling forward like a thunderhead, its form changing even as it charged.

With a draught of noxious sulfur it sped past Irissa and

swallowed the snake into its expanded form. The two elements boiled together—the invisible darkness of the serpent, the altered, elongated shape of the cloud-beast.

Eeryon watched numbly from beyond the combatants, knowing no more than the others why his faithful pet should now bite the unseen yet magical hand that had fed its very existence.

The serpent form was swelling now, too, bubbling into a great black thunderhead. Gray and black cloud contended in their vaporous way, and each mixing of the two resulted in a re-forming of the individuals.

Now there was no doubt that the serpent had been a sending of Geronfrey, for the sorcerer's shape was growing detailed before them, down to the dark gauntlets that covered his hands. And Briarwhip . . . the creature was growing human by the inch, its backbone spines elongating into flailing hair, its coarse coat billowing into flowing robes.

"You have your chance, Geronfrey," a new voice crackled from the gray cloud—a voice of echo and distance, yet strong for all that.

Kendric stepped forward, shocked. "I *know* that voice."

"Who?" Javelle and Thane asked in unison, watching the conflict with wide eyes and little understanding.

"The dark cloud is Geronfrey," Irissa put in, "or, rather, Geronfrey's emissary in this world."

"We guessed that," Javelle said. "But why does Eeryon's cloud-hound attack its true master?"

"Perhaps it has never been Geronfrey's subject." Kendric smiled grimly. "First his shadow son turns on him, now the shadow's clouded shadow. I almost pity the man."

"Don't," Irissa advised with a shudder. Sudden comprehension swept her face free of worry. "But can't you guess what—who—Briarwhip really is?" Her eyes studied the children's puzzled faces.

Javelle's cleared first. "Finorian! Can it be? Are you sure? She strode into the sky to fight the evil over Edanvant. Afterward, only dark and light clouds could be seen clashing in the forms of Finorian and another, but . . ."

"If something of Finorian survived that encounter, why would she embody it in a thing as lowly as Briarwhip?" Thane objected.

"If something of Finorian survived," Kendric ruminated grimly, "it would take *any* form to survive."

"Finorian may not have perished in her battle with Geronfrey. She must have been cast into Without afterward." Irissa smiled suddenly. "She was *waiting* there, all this time! Long before Geronfrey was forced to take the gate to Without to flee us in Rengarth, Finorian was already there, although perhaps not in physical form. She . . . attached herself to that shadow son. Finorian had always been hungry for a young one to rear. She watched him, shadowed him, saw to it that Geronfrey would never break his will—"

"You give a cloud great credit," Kendric sighed. He looked weary, too weary to stand and too weary to seek to sit.

Irissa was enchanted by the rightness of her theory. "So now, cloud battles cloud once again. Finorian fights to stop Geronfrey from impinging on a world forbidden to him, for Geronfrey remains barred from acting directly in the worlds outside Without."

"Then he stalks us from afar still," Thane said in sudden rage. "We will never be free."

"He *fails,* Thane," Irissa said. "He always fails."

"Does he?" A tone of adult challenge made Irissa look quickly to Javelle. An expression of bitter reality curdled her daughter's face. "Look to Father and say again that Geronfrey always fails."

Frozen for an instant, Irissa stared at her daughter,

stared at the silvery metal serpent banding her brow. The
tiny pale scales teemed with an aurora borealis of light and
color, bright as bruises.

She turned to Kendric despite the seething contention
between the clouded forces only a few feet away.

He was nearly unconscious on his feet. It was a moot
point whether man upheld sword or sword supported man.
Neither seemed likely to stand upright long. As both
swayed to the whim of the earth's magnetic call, Kendric's
eyes were falling shut. And the sword's hilt-light was
dimming.

"Quickly!" Irissa gestured the children over. "Support
your father. I must meld the swords—"

With an effort that looked beyond her strength, she
swung the ancient sword alongside the one that echoed it in
every line. Between her entwined fingers, only a faint
luminescence leaked from the hilt.

Clouds towered over the five figures, boiling as if formed
from corrosive steam, black and white blended into an
overhanging gray.

Irissa sensed the force hovering to distract her. She even
sensed a familiar if not well-loved voice advising, "Pay no
mind to so much disembodied vapor, seeress. I will blow it
away to the farthest reaches of Without. . . ."

Join the swords. Irissa repeated her own instructions to
herself. Easily thought, not easily done. She was aware of a
darker cloud hovering on her inner horizon . . . one that
could end Kendric's fading life force here and now—

Yet another cloud formed behind Kendric—a yearning
glimmering puff of silver mist dappled with a Quickstone
waterfall of gems.

Irissa caught her breath. Even as she opened her mind to
her magic to rejoin the swords, so she opened herself to
another natural rejoining—between herself and the spectral shadow self once called Issiri!

Then another shadow slipped between Irissa and her

faint self-image . . . had a new champion—as unlikely as Finorian—intervened? Or could the child betray *both* its parents?

Eeryon.

Irissa barely waited to consider the shadow son's motives in separating her from that side of herself that had been his phantom mother. Instead, Irissa cast motives and fear and anger aside, delving into the pure silver well of her magic, intent on dipping from it freely no matter who sought to steal the silent thunder of that inner storm.

Her hands tightened on the conjoined crossguards, feeling the metal warm to the rhythm of her pulsebeat. She saw the hilt-lights well up silver in the center of her eyes. Both weapons had been made—and unmade. Now they would have to be made one—reforged a fourth and last time into one indivisible, perhaps immortal object.

Such matters took all of Irissa's heart and mind and spirit. She had no time to mind anyone else, not even her children, not even Kendric.

"Let me pass." The creature from the sea glimmered moonlight-bright, and its loveliness made Eeryon ache. "Your silver sleeves have gone ragged, boy, since last we talked. And they were so pretty. . . ."

Eeryon wasn't sure how he found himself standing guard between his once-private apparition and the family behind him. That was odd. He'd never considered himself to have enough "self" to stand in anything's way. First he had defied the sending of his father's powers. Now he played barrier to a wave of fog that could easily flow over him—even through him, he suspected.

It didn't. The figure remained scintillating on the heavy air above the dark pond as if hung there to dry. A vaporous finger unfurled from its cloudy robes and almost touched him. He flinched but felt nothing.

"She glitters so," the figure wailed, "her silver eyes, her hands that hold sunshine in their fists. Let me pass. I am made for light. I must . . . absorb it, warm myself at it, taste it, suck it, swallow it. . . ."

Again the mist shifted as if to surge past him.

"No," Eeryon said, not knowing why the refusal hurt him. "You can stay where you are and talk to me."

"Talk to you? Mutter at a shadow? You are insubstantial, shadow boy! And dark and unbright. Nothing. Not solid, as I shall soon be . . . oh, just let me pass a few tendrils of my hair—" Smoky serpents drifted toward him, but he recoiled from their spectral touch.

"No."

"You are mine!" the creature suddenly cried. "My . . . belonging. My living gem. I know you. I *died* for you!"

"But you never lived for me." Eeryon felt calm, listening to the truth falling from his own lips after a long time of hearing and seeing and feeling only lies.

He had never felt more real. He had never felt *more*. Emotions collided like contending clouds within him— love and pain and hate and pride and sorrow and gratitude and regret and shades of them all blended together.

Most of all, he felt pity for this pulsating remnant of being straining before him for a raw piece of life, no matter how secondhand, how shadowy, no matter how stolen. His father, Geronfrey, for all his power, was equally pathetic in his way.

"Remnants, Mother," he soothed the apparition—and himself in a deeper way. "We are all remnants of other people's lives. The magic of it is that we think ourselves our own selves. That is when we become dangerous. Hold back and let be what will be."

"But I will not *be* if I do not hunger, do not hold—"

"No," Eeryon said simply. "No, you will not be."

This silenced the phantom, this stopped it as perhaps his ragged magic never could.

"How can shadow be so strong?" it asked him wistfully.

"By facing shadow," he answered. "By finding shadow within oneself."

"Will . . . shadow see shadow . . . again?"

"I don't know. I can barely see you anymore—or any of them."

"Yet you defend them, and their unshadowhood."

"I defend you, and him, and whatever bit of myself I call my own."

"Let me pass," it wailed again, as if to break him.

"You can pass," Eeryon said, spreading wide his shadow arms on which ghostly threads still scribed a broken pattern. "You have only to be willing to pay the price."

"You mean . . . to risk destroying myself?"

"To risk destroying me."

The apparition coiled into its melancholy fog, silent for a long time. Then it sank into the water, in stages, thoughtfully.

When Eeryon turned back, they had all forgotten him again.

The unleashing of her full Torloc powers had made Irissa resemble her shadow even more. An aura of silver light overlay her figure. The Iridesium circlet and her eyes shone with an icy sun's brightness.

This moonlit nimbus broke wavelike over the sword's metal shores. Quicksilver drops of it spattered from blade and hilt to rain upon the ground like steel tears.

Within the living halo of light the sword melted and hardened in turn, glowing copper, then red, then black, then white. All these shades were natural stages to heated metal, but then another series of changes added their colors to the transition—the blue of Irissa's Skystone dominated, then faded into gold Shinestone into red Bloodstone into beige Drawstone and finally into a clear color that bordered on translucence—the shade of Floodstone.

Within the single cabochon of her ring these selfsame hues flared.

From outside the magical corona of color cloaking Irissa and the sword, two hands intruded. The aura flickered as they broke the veil.

Then Kendric's hands—bruised to the gaudy brightness of Iridesium—joined Irissa's on the crossguard. It seemed for an instant as if this intervention had shaken the spell, had broken its caster.

Irissa quivered like a flame. The swords buckled, their straight blades wavering. Then the ring on Kendric's left hand ran through its colors—copper Sandstone, plain Shunstone, Torloc-green Gladestone, silver Lunestone, and, finally . . . black Nightstone.

The two swords—blade and hilt—shifted through every change, their forms overlapping as Drawstone made them water-clear and ran them together, and separating as the Shunstone's plain power rended them from each other.

Irissa struggled to keep them conjoined and added her ring's round of changes to Kendric's. Soon the shades melded in turn—silver and gold to bronze, blue and green to aquamarine, black and red to purple, and copper and clear to burnt gold. When the Drawstone's translucent plainness coincided with the Shunstone's solid dullness, all color exploded, evaporated from Irissa and Kendric and the swords.

In that battle between opposing forces, that which draws together won over that which pulls apart. The swords gleamed translucent like great ice daggers, then melted their solid forms together—into one ice-forged sword.

The escaping colors united into a rainbow and bowed into the air underneath the dark arch of pines, spanning the pond and stretching to both ends of the facades to other worlds.

Thane and Javelle looked up to the thin, colorful canopy over their heads. Irissa and Kendric remained fixed, as if impaled in the ground, like the swordpoint.

"What have you done?" he asked her.

Her fingers lifted from the crossbar and stretched one by one like an awakening cat's toes. "Mind has infused reality. Your original sword—and the evocation of it—are one again. Your lifeline no longer divides into two separating strands. You will live—"

"Forever?" he asked wryly.

"Not forever. Just . . . long enough for a Torloc."

Kendric frowned. "Is this why you risked our children in Without—to claim a talisman for my longer life?"

"Yes! You wouldn't . . . couldn't . . . see that you were destined to fade faster than we."

He sighed and tried to focus on the new-made blade. "I still see them double," he said. "And there are two edges to your quest. I may live to regret long life, or die of an unforeseen blow long before this magic sword would cut the twisted thread of my fate."

" 'May' even a Torloc must live with. Your early death was certain; I saw it in the clouds across your eyes."

Another cloud came to Kendric's eyes, but before he could answer, Thane's voice broke into his parents' troubling discussion.

"The . . . clouds are gone," Thane reported in wonder.

Irissa turned to the phantom wall of doors behind her. Against one lay the exhausted form of Briarwhip, its three eyes fading from a faint green color to their ordinary bloody brown shade. The two Felabbas had deserted their tree limb to flank it and rake their tongues over its disheveled hair.

The dark cloud was not to be seen.

"You've banished Geronfrey's presence!" Javelle congratulated her mother.

"And given birth to another rainbow." Kendric lifted his head slowly to the colored bands above. If he saw the sword in duplicate still, the rainbow multiplied until the clearing seemed netted over by strips of gaudy mist.

"And the sword is one again," Irissa congratulated herself. "All we need do now is find a gate back to Rengarth."

"Fool!" Felabba the Elder stalked over on stiff legs. "You *have* a gate an Empress Falgon could fly through, thanks to your sleight of sword."

"What's so wrong in that?" Irissa bent down to inquire politely, so fine a mood she was in. "We can go home now."

The cat ungraciously spat a few spirit-quenching words into her face. "What's wrong is only that you have averted one distant danger, not the nearby certain peril. Only that you have inadvertently opened a high road to one denied any road. Only that where *you* can now exit, another can enter fully."

Irissa looked up at the wavering ghosts of many gates. One was split open, as if something tore the dark asunder. A double form was spilling from the torn doorway—the gilded Hunter grown ebony, and a rider merged to his mount.

The Hunter's hooves thudded over crushed grasses as the facade of gates shook and shattered and gave birth to a misbegotten blend of man and beast. Geronfrey's gauntleted hands controlled reins of chain that clanged together, his legs sank into the contours of the beast's ribs. Years of slowly diminishing in Without had forged man and mount into a union of living death.

"I will take the sword," Geronfrey challenged. "And with it the soul of he who bears it. And none will stop me."

Geronfrey raised his own weapon—an obsidian sword as slickly black as the Nightstone—and pointed it at Briarwhip. "You, ancient whisper of a seeress, cannot long vacate your cringing form here outside Without. Either as cloud or hound, you are unfit to deal with me directly. I will address your perfidy later.

"You, persistent pest," his raw voice thundered as he leveled the sword at the two Felabbas, "are cut in twain and your powers thus are halved. I shall further mince you both when I'm done with bigger prey."

The Hunter's dark forelegs stamped toward Javelle and Thane.

"You, the young disinherited, will have to find a world other than Rengarth to frolic in; empty of all your ilk, it is mine once more. You will not slip through Without again unless you pay a bitter price."

The bridle chains tautened noisily as Geronfrey reined the Hunter before the slim stab of darkness that was his son. "Your craven betrayal I do not overlook. You will have to demonstrate a reason to exist to me."

At last he reined the beast onto its hind legs, turning simultaneously so it reared like a hoof-armed wall over Kendric and Irissa.

"As for you two, you no longer share a kingdom and soon will share no sword. My exile in Without hampered my powers, but they flower here and now. Give me the sword and I shall leave you and your children to find your sorry way to whatever place will take you."

"Without take *you*, Geronfrey!" Kendric challenged back. "I thank Irissa's rainbow gate that at last you are not hiding behind emissaries, but come in person to do your ill."

Kendric lifted the sword, feeling a surge of optimism that the reunion of the weapon's separate selves—and its reunion with himself as bearer of both its aspects—had returned his poison-leeched strength.

Geronfrey and the Hunter made a formidable adversary, but Kendric had dueled them before in mirrors and shadow form. He would take his stand in his adopted land,

Rule, eager to end the unwanted association where it had begun.

"I had hoped you would make a fight of it," Geronfrey croaked, his now-black eyes gleaming fitfully. "My sword is the twin to yours, forged in the Dark Mirror. We shall see which shatters first before the power of the other—my darkness . . . or your light."

CHAPTER
33

"WE CAN HELP HIM."

Thane had sidled up to Irissa as Kendric and Geronfrey warily circled each other in clear space.

"'Can' and 'should' are not interchangeable," she reminded her son.

"But it's unfair! Geronfrey is mounted—and on a beast beyond normal ken."

"Kendric is beyond normal height," she answered mildly.

"How can you stand idly by and watch?" Javelle demanded in tones as disturbed as Thane's as she flanked Irissa's other side. "How can you quest so far and hard for a sword to prolong his life, then see him risk it in a contention with a deceptive sorcerer?"

Irissa could feel their fear and impatience, palpable as fog. She watched while the two white cats drifted over on soundless feet, each bracketing the trio.

"We make quite an audience," Irissa mused. Thane practically huffed and puffed his impatience, until Irissa put an arm around each of her children. "This is your father's work," she said. "You have never seen him do it before. We were unnaturally protected in Rengarth. This is the world Kendric and I left—one full of many pitfalls and hidden pockets of power."

"We can do nothing?" Javelle worried, laying her head briefly on her mother's shoulder. The gesture was an old one, not practiced recently. Irissa brushed back Javelle's always disreputable locks, found her fingers sliding over the snake circlet's smooth cool scales.

"We can do everything—when it is necessary. Until then, it is your father's challenge and he must answer it. Besides, despite all Geronfrey's assumed advantages, Kendric has one or two you forget."

"What—us?"

Irissa smiled at Thane. "I was thinking of the newly reforged sword—surely it must be doubly powerful now that it has met itself coming and going. And he has us, in a sense. To protect."

"But we wanted to protect *him,*" Javelle complained.

"Sometimes giving someone a reason to survive is the best protection anyone can offer."

The two mulled the paradox Irissa had given them, as paired kittens worry a skein of yarn. She glanced across the field of challenge to the shadowy woods beyond it. Another shadow watched from there, alone and unnoticed save for herself.

For a moment Irissa felt a surge of sympathy for this dark twin to Javelle, a fact unknown to either of them. She almost motioned Eeryon to her side, then considered what price he would pay for such a public defection if Geronfrey —as usual—managed to survive this encounter. Instead, she sighed and watched the battle commence. She couldn't say she approved of it.

Geronfrey had spoken truly: it was to be a battle between light and dark. His blade gleamed like a midnight sky as it sawed the air above Kendric. The Hunter's neck bowed this way and that, precisely tuned to his rider's motions to avoid blocking a blow. The beast added a quill from its own quiver to the contest—the probing thrusts of its wicked spiral horn.

Kendric avoided the pair's preliminary posturing with broad sidesteps. Each move was plotted, quick but effective, to preserve his strength. Each time the Hunter pranced to turn and follow him, the chains girding its belly and hanging in a skirt over its muscular hindquarters rang out a flurry of metallic incantations.

Geronfrey's sword sliced the air, making a great black comet of itself, but hardly ever threatening Kendric.

Still, as much as the sorcerer enjoyed cutting such a formidable figure, the Hunter and the sword edge were swiping closer and closer to their prey. Kendric's evasions turned around the pivot of a tighter and tighter center.

No monsters were aborning and dying in the hole to Without behind Geronfrey—he was monster enough astride his four-hooved bearing-beast. It was the most direct confrontation between the two, between even Irissa and Geronfrey, as if the mage disdained to use his full range of magical resources, as if he despised his enemies too much to fear them.

Irissa and the children watched in silent stillness while the Hunter's mincing hooves thudded the ground, while Briarwhip cowered at the half-seen facade wall, while Kendric became the center of a turning circle of man and beast.

Suddenly, the sword lifted in Kendric's two-handed grasp. Even as it rose, the molten glow of the hilt-light flashed down the steel's entire length. A thin tongue of flame lashed the Hunter's bunched hindquarter muscles, severing chain links that fell to earth in a shower of chimes.

The Hunter stumbled, dipping momentarily to its knees. At that moment, the second sweep of Kendric's melded blade met Geronfrey's shadowy straight-edge of stone.

The clash shook the needles from the hovering pines, set the Hunter's war chains dancing on its muscular body. Its black hooves minced away, striking sparks from the fallen metal links.

Kendric straightened from his battle crouch, his hands tingling from delivering the blow. There was no denying the brunt of it, but he felt as if a helmetful of blood had just flushed from him. His knees grew watery and the echo of the chains pounded in his head.

Worse than that—where before man and beast had stood in one conjoined form, now *two* such monsters waited bearing two shadow swords.

Kendric blinked his eyes and shook his head, hearing something within rattle. It wasn't the Hunter's chains, but something loose within the skull of his senses. Black moths danced again before his eyes and buzzed in his ears in a high-pitched skirl of sound.

The ground seemed to heave beneath his feet—to a different tempo under each one. Many voices droned in his ears—the children's, Irissa's, Finorian's, the cats', the hound's, the Rynx's even. When he glanced to his defense, his blade, he saw the glowing steel had forked into a serpent's tongue of living light. He saw it wavered and did not cut straight anymore.

The rainbow above seemed to be sinking over him like a softly scented veil. Grasses grew up to meet it—tender green shoots pushing past Kendric's knees, his elbows, his eyes. . . .

Only the dark center of his vision seemed real—where an unfamiliar face hung over a huge horned head and watched him as if witnessing a drowning.

Kendric struck out—blindly—at the dark. The bright sword cleaved it, again and again, engaging and shattering a curved ebony horn, meeting a black blade and smashing it like a crystal.

Kendric fought forward, his feet churning through the

ensnaring marshgrass. The sword struck chain and melted it. It fell on Iridesium gauntlets and bounced off.

Kendric almost lowered his blade, confused. Did he fight Valodec again? Valodec of the golden voice and the falgonskin glove that failed him not? He would not want to slay his bond brother a second time. . . .

And then he saw Valodec himself striding into the dark pupils that had swollen to encompass his entire field of vision. Valodec moved as a specter does—in an unnaturally even gait. Valodec smiled and stretched out a gauntleted hand webbed in all the colors of the rainbow and asked for the sword.

Kendric leaned forward to surrender it. Only at the last moment did his nature revolt. He struck instead, straight for the heart of Valodec, straight for his inner darkness.

Kendric heard the distant tinkle of bells ringing or chains breaking or glass shattering.

And then he fell forward, into the dark.

CHAPTER
34

"NOW?" THANE ASKED.

Irissa nodded. Kendric's sword blows, wild and yet guided to their retreating target, had forced the Hunter's hindquarters to back into the black gash from Without.

Geronfrey clutched an obsidian hilt with both gloved hands, trying to conjure a blade to replace the one broken by Kendric's sword.

Kendric's sword still grew from his fist, but its bright gleam was faltering, separating into the vapid, misty colors of a rainbow seen through clouds. Kendric himself was falling slowly, to his knees, to his face.

The hole to Without puckered suddenly and sucked the Hunter and Geronfrey through. It sealed shut, presented a bland, flat black face to the clearing.

"What's wrong?" Javelle cried, reaching her father even before Thane. "He was winning—!"

They gathered around him and together managed to pry his fingers from the still-warm sword hilt and turn him on his back.

"He has the sword!" Javelle told herself, the world around her. "Why has he fallen? He has the rejoined sword—he should live forever."

Irissa had sunk on her knees beside him, shocked to silence.

Kendric lay as one dead. She had seen him thus before, when the poison had first taken him. She had seen him throw off this malady to come in search of them, braced by the Bloodstone powder Scyvilla had administered to him.

Now that preservative was gone—and so was the temporary strength lent by the sword. Even Geronfrey was gone. And Kendric, too, would soon be going. . . .

"What is it?" Thane shook Irissa's shoulder, shook her until her faculty of speech was jolted loose again.

"Oh . . . Javelle, the sword was for his *future* longevity. It cannot affect the present poison, other than to allay its consequences awhile. It gave him strength enough to repulse Geronfrey. . . . As for the poison—if only Neva and Ilvanis were here! They could leech the taint from his veins."

"Can't we?" Javelle asked.

Irissa shook her head. "If I could have banished the toxin, don't you think I would have done it before leaving Rengarth?"

"But we are so *close!*" Thane pled. "We have the sword, we have reunited the two swords and ourselves."

"I know," Irissa mourned. "I know." She reached to touch Kendric's face. It was steel-cold. "Felabba!" she called in a voice of utter command.

Both cats came instantly, meekly. The old one sniffed long at Kendric's pallid lips. The young one moved on tentative feet around his head.

"The venom springs from the black water underlying all the worlds," Felabba the Elder diagnosed. "It has worked long. Were he not so strong, he would be dead by now. Had we Finorian's touchstone—"

Irissa snapped her head to the pathetic creature collapsed against a pine tree trunk. Its central eye glowed green in response, then faded.

"You see a remnant of the touchstone's power," Felabba the Younger said mournfully. "That's why the beast had three eyes. But its contention with Geronfrey has robbed it of all but a shadow of strength."

"I am weary of shadows," Javelle raged, rocking a little and unaware of it. "Shadows bring nothing but death and destruction." Her palms pounded impotently on the serpent banding her forehead. "My Overstone circlet is merely a shadow of my mother's Iridesium band, as I am the mere shadow of my mother. Had it—had *I*—any independent powers, it, I, could save Father."

"How?" Irissa's hands caught Javelle's wrists, pulled her hands from her head.

Javelle's anguish was beyond easy answers. "It . . . bears your poison."

"My poison?" Irissa feared she was losing not only a helpmate's life but a daughter's sanity. "I bear no poison."

"Not *now,"* Javelle moaned. "But you did, years ago . . . in, in Edanvant. Remember when Neva and Ilvanis leeched the poisoned borgia from you? They . . . discharged it . . . into the Overstone. Hence the serpent inside it that was born with me and became my circlet has always borne it."

"How could that help Father?" Thane was scathing in his helplessness. "We should poison him again, is that it?"

"No," Javelle said, "but if the snake had spent its poison, it could leech the taint from Father. But it's not free—it's still tainted."

They sat and absorbed Javelle's jumbled guilt and sorrow. Even Eeryon came over, as if drawn by her heightened emotions.

"This is dying?" he asked softly, looking down on Kendric.

"Look at us," Irissa said, lifting stark silver eyes to him. *"This* is dying."

Eeryon crouched beside Kendric. As his profile bent to see him better, Irissa caught a fleeting likeness between two aquiline noses and shuddered. She would have reached to push the shadow boy away, but his face was troubled and a darkness was spreading in the pupils of his aquamarine eyes that she couldn't deny.

"It is only dim—death," Eeryon said. "I think I've seen it. It doesn't hurt—"

"Only the leaving and the left hurt," Irissa said. "He cannot see us now, feel us now."

"I think you're wrong." Eeryon's voice had intensified. "He feels it all. You simply don't notice him anymore."

Before Irissa and Thane could respond to Eeryon's callous disregard of their grief, he looked at Javelle. "You said it was like Without, like going home."

She stared uncomprehendingly.

"Like not . . . feeling anything." Eeryon's eyes turned inward, swelling into utter darkness, like his father's transformed gaze.

He nodded, his gilt hair dulling even as it moved. The velvet of his garb softened to shadowy gray, paled to the color of his skin. His skin melted, dissolved on the air.

Eeryon was no longer there.

Their silence rang as heavy as their speech had moments before. Irissa clasped Kendric's limp hand as if to preserve him from a similar vanishment.

"He's gone!" Javelle's heartsick madness turned to passing marvel.

"Just like him," Thane said after a pause. "Coward. Can't see a quest through to the bitter end. I'll try my magic, Mother. I may be able to, to—"

Irissa shook her head. She could feel the life seeping from the hand in hers. On the central finger the color-jeweled cabochon was turning a cold, dead gray.

"Too late," Irissa said, her voice as gray as the ringstone.

Javelle suddenly fell over on her heels.

"Oh!" she cried. "Something pushed my shoulders."

She tried to rise, but was knocked back again. Her face jerked sideways as though struck. Her screams were not so much from pain as from surprise and disbelief.

Irissa rose to her knees but kept custody of Kendric's hand. Thane stood, prepared to deal with the new threat, once he could see it.

Javelle scrambled away from them without rising, using her hands to escape a bewildering attack. Tears were streaming down her face, hoarded tears meant for her father, but shaken loose by the bizarre moment.

Suddenly, she stopped, lifting a hand to her brow. "The circlet . . . it's—"

The serpent came alive so fast no one saw it strike. One moment it was coiled docilely around Javelle's forehead; the next it was unclasped, its sleek head and upper body snapping once at empty air.

It sprang fully free and wiggled in midair like a whip being snapped by an invisible wielder. A bright green color welled over its livid body, scale by scale from foot to head—and faded in the reverse order.

Then it paled to pure silver and fell into the grass, coiled and still. The Felabbas came to inspect it.

Javelle put her hands to her now-naked brow. "I don't understand."

The grasses beside her crushed suddenly in a long, wide swath. Javelle, her emotions racked beyond enduring, screamed and crawled to her mother's side. Irissa absently put an arm around her, her eyes and attention never leaving Kendric. Everything seemed far away, unimportant, save her vigil. She would know the last moment even as it came. He would know she was there.

The grasses darkened. Something was lying upon them, a

fallen black branch like one of Geronfrey's failed sendings. Its outline hardened limb by limb.

It was a man, a boy, a shadow.

"Eeryon." Only Thane was still vocal enough to name the essence that lay on the grass. He watched the black eyes lighten to aquamarine, then green with a Torloc glow. Or the lurid green of a borgia glow, old borgia. Briarwhip crawled on its belly to station itself at his half-invisible head.

Javelle stole a look in that direction, then her eyes flared in astonishment. "Eeryon, why have you gone, and come again?"

"To come, and go, again." His voice was faint, as was the outline of his face. "You promised it would not hurt."

"I never meant . . . I never spoke seriously." She crawled over, appalled by a sense of responsibility for something she didn't even understand.

"But . . . why?" she asked.

His head shook. Through his features, she could see the grasses stir and flatten. "I usually feel nothing when I vanish. This time I felt everything. I felt . . . alive."

"You *are* alive." Javelle was not prepared to witness another death, to make another leavetaking in her heart. "You can come with . . . us." A sob choked her to silence. "Come . . . back to Rengarth," she finished. "And . . . Briarwhip, too."

The pools of darkness that were his eyes lifted to the figure of his faithful hound. "We belong in Without, as you do not. As . . . none of you do."

He faded, mote by mote of his being, until nothing remained but the broken grasses.

Javelle felt deserted beyond bearing. She hardly noticed another absence—the loss of her constant companion since birth. But it struck her suddenly and she turned to pat the grass, trying to see through the thick tears coating her eyes.

Something rattled in the grasses. Something rasped over the bent stalks like quicksilver wind. Javelle pursued it, almost mad to keep something that belonged to her still— anything!

Silver flashed like running water. Javelle pursued it on hands and knees, a small child chasing cloud-shadows it can never catch.

The silver snake slithered around the frozen form of Irissa. Javelle plunged on, seeking the glint of her lost birth-snake, feeling nothing now but the chase.

She found it where it had first appeared to the eye of human, coiled around a forehead. Like her father before her, she rejected this dependency. She reached for it to tear it free, hardly realizing it was her father the thing had claimed, not seeing the tiny silver teeth biting like needles into the flesh just above his ear.

Irissa had, and—waking like a dreamer of dark visions blinded by fresh light—caught her daughter's hands in an Iridesium grip.

Her mother's voice rang like bells in Javelle's deadened ears and eyes and heart.

"No! Leave it. It doesn't dispense venom, it *feeds* on it."

"It feeds on Father—!" She reached again for it, to pry off the sinuous coils so strong and inflexible.

"It feeds on poison, as you said, Javelle!" Her mother was shaking her with a combination of fear and aggravation Javelle had not seen since she was very young and had taken some dreadful risk. She barely heard her mother's voice as Irissa suddenly clutched her tightly.

"Javelle, hush, child. You've saved your father. Look, his unnatural color ebbs! See, the snake bloats and bruises with the burden of the taint. So Ilvanis and Neva saved me twenty years ago. So you have carried this strange metal serpent all your life. It's all right. We're all right."

Irissa rocked Javelle like a baby while she watched Kendric. His stiff figure softened, as if the blood were free to flow in it again. His taut lips parted for the rapid passage of reviving breaths. Beneath his closed eyelids, his eyes quivered like flutterbys; his nostrils flared.

At last he moaned and struggled to sit. A fat silver snake fell to the grass, immobile, forgotten as Eeryon had been forgotten.

Kendric clapped a hand to his temple as though smashing a marsh-midge. He blinked and toted up the members of his sober family—Thane serious and white-faced, Javelle smiling at him through reddened eyes, Irissa . . . Irissa shaken and yet shining in sheer silver joy. He eyed the two cats, who were chasing something quick in the grass. He saw the unfortunate hound hunched over a vacancy in the same grass.

He stretched out his arms and listened for the customary creaks. There were none. He sat up. His back didn't crack, nor did his knees. He saw plain and straight—one of everything, except for the cats. He felt . . . light, and tight and extremely pleased with himself.

Then he remembered beating Geronfrey back with the flat of his fresh-forged sword and looked around for signs of the sorcerer. He saw none. He never missed the sober, self-effacing shadow of Eeryon.

Yet he saw his family through clear, untainted eyes. He saw a pond and glade and the phantom shimmer of gates to every place in the worlds one might want to go.

He grinned and announced his general good will toward this world, this place, this moment.

"Nothing," said Kendric modestly, "like a little exercise to get the circulation going again."

He had no idea why they all collapsed upon him with cries of sorrow and joy and nearly bore him back to the earth he had just so arduously escaped.

CHAPTER
35

"MAUDLIN," SAID FELABBA THE YOUNGER, PREENING ITS
fluffy neck ruff.

"I quite agree," said Felabba the Elder, biting a knot of
fur on her slack belly pouch.

Irissa and Kendric, Javelle and Thane, all sat together on
the ground like play-worn children, beaming at each other
in vacuous self-congratulation.

Briarwhip kept a disconsolate vigil at the place Eeryon
had last occupied. The sword lay where it had fallen with
Kendric, forgotten. Javelle smiled in the circle of her
family, the circlet upon her brow missing. That, too, had
been forgotten.

"Danger always threatens most in the moments just after
one rests from danger," Felabba the Elder noted sagely.

"Quite true." Felabba the Younger looked up. "Shall we
tell them?"

"When have they listened?"

"On occasion."

Felabba the Elder's ears flattened and its gaze shifted

sharply to the backdrop of trees on which the outlines of gates still scintillated.

"My ancient eyes spy a disruption in the gate from Without. Geronfrey still craves the sword."

"Why?" The younger cat gave its bib a long, luxurious lick.

"He must have *something* to show for his trouble."

Felabba the Younger twisted an agile head over its shoulder. "Surely he is no longer able to enter this world? Yon Wrathman has battered him back with the newly reinforced sword."

"Being forbidden something has never stopped Geronfrey before."

"How true. I suppose we should alert them—look, the sword's hilt-glow dampens as the dark draw of Geronfrey's shadow falls upon it! And they do not even notice—they are too busy gawking at one another."

"I've warned them of that very thing again and again." Old Felabba yawned. Lengthily. "No, let them enjoy their false sense of security. At my age, one mellows."

"But—"

"Fear not, young one. Geronfrey cannot come forth here in full form any longer."

"Perhaps not. But I remember—or rather, I believe *you* remember—an occasion in Rule when he reached through a rock pillar in the Oracle of Valna to seize Irissa. His hands and arms actually penetrated forbidden space and time."

"And he paid for it, for did not his flesh shrivel to bones? Why do you think he went gloved to the elbows ever after?" Felabba the Elder scrubbed her back foot vigorously against her neck. "Must be one of Geronfrey's cursed moth-things—teeth like a bat's, I tell you. Watch your tender portions."

"Thank you so much, but I must confess I do see a presence pushing at the door from Without—and the sword's light has dampened utterly. Do you not see the weapon edging over the grass to the door as if drawn by some unseen line?"

Felabba the Elder squinted at the sword. "It is quite still now. Though my eyes may deceive me."

"We really should warn them. Why else have we been summoned—I from my shard in Rengarth and you from . . . how exactly did you rebirth yourself?"

"Through a tapestry depiction of my old self. The Wrathman thinks he had something to do with it, but of course, it was all my doing, as usual."

"A tapestry? That *is* a remarkable method. We are very clever."

"Yes, I think so." Old Felabba stopped grooming to stare pointedly into the distance. "I think you are right; the sword has moved almost to the door."

Felabba the Younger arched her back as she rose. "Really, I can't permit them to go unwarned. All our hard work, and then it should be undone so easily—"

"Be patient. I have seen much more than you. Geronfrey may have lured the sword within reach, but he cannot levitate it through the door. I know his limitations."

"Indeed. The weapon appears to lie still. Yet . . . I see hands—black-gloved hands—pushing through the flaccid skin of a Dark Mirror. He will reach through the gate in defiance of the elements to seize the sword—!"

"Calm yourself."

"You may be my older self, but my conscience is fresher born than yours. I cannot let these poor fools lose the object of all their conjoined quests simply because I forbore to mew bloody murder—!"

Felabba the Elder boxed her younger edition lightly on the ears. "Enough hysterics."

"But I *see* Geronfrey's thieving arms reaching through! In an instant he will have the sword—!"

"Watch a bit longer and you will see that in an instant

something else will have *him.*"

Enough command drenched Felabba the Elder's voice to freeze young Felabba in mid-spring.

Both cats hunkered down in the grasses, tails and ears flat, faces extended like striking snakes' heads, whiskers twitching. Young Felabba's hindquarters waggled its impatience; the animal seemed a spring about to unwind, no matter its senior self's advice.

Under the watching cat's intent eyes, a pair of dark gloves stole soundlessly toward the dormant sword. Young Felabba crouched lower, all the better to spring higher and farther and faster.

Then gloved fingers curled around the hilt. A silver flash came bounding from the long grasses, hurling at a small bit of sleeve just above the gauntlets.

There it fastened like a gleaming pin.

The dark arms tried to retreat back within the plane of the doorway, behind the mirrored curtain that hid the owner of the arms. For a few moments the arms flailed and the silver object clung despite being violently shaken.

Then the silver arrow fell away and the arms retreated.

"You see?" Felabba the Elder hoisted a rear leg over one shoulder and began wetting the pantaloon of hairs on her upper leg. "Nothing to worry about. Geronfrey has received a dose of his own medicine—and then some."

"The serpent circlet." Felabba the Younger sounded suitably admiring. "It was waiting to discharge the venom it leeched from Kendric."

"Exactly, my dear lesser half. Observe and learn from your elders."

The younger cat stared at the sword, lying untouched now, and the closed doorway to Without. "Did Your Excellency predict *that* as well?"

"What?" Felabba the Elder froze as a sound keened

through the clearing, the sound of a massive door being driven open.

Felabba the Younger looked very smug. "That."

"What was that?" Irissa's magical instincts jolted her from a state of delirious happiness.

Around her, Kendric and Thane stirred uneasily.

"Something's been nagging at my composure," Kendric admitted, "but I didn't want to cast a sour word into the sweetness of our reunion."

"I felt something, too," Thane agreed.

Javelle considered. Despite the ordeals they had passed through together, she still remained the odd unmagicked one out. "I felt a sudden headache," she contributed.

Irissa stared at Javelle's naked forehead as if just noticing it. "Of course you do—you miss the circlet. We must find it."

Kendric looked around skeptically. "Where? It's hardly bigger than a blade of grass."

"We'll find it," Irissa promised.

They fanned out in four directions, studying the trampled grasses. Thane walked politely around the grooming cats.

"How did my sword get all the way over here?" Kendric asked.

Irissa glanced up fondly. "What we seek is long and silver, but a bit smaller."

"I know what it is, but how in the name of all Without did a sword this heavy . . . walk . . . all the way to the tapestry of spectral doors?"

"Here it is!" Javelle unbent and waved a limp silver cord.

They gathered around it.

"Puny, isn't it, really?" Thane noted.

"It's lost the colors of Kendric's taint already," Irissa marveled.

"It seems weak, exhausted. That I can sympathize with," Kendric said.

"Don it again, Javelle," Irissa advised. "It may gather some strength from you."

Javelle hesitated. She had never been free of the serpent's migrating presence upon her person. To accept such an attachment again—freely—went against her grain.

"It opens gates to Without," Thane encouraged.

"No longer."

The last speaker was none of them. The voice had come from high above, and whistled like wind in the pinetops.

They instinctively looked up. The pine trunks had softened into the folds of many towering gowns. Dark limbs shook gently above like shaking fingers. The voice of the wind admonished them further.

"No gates to Without remain open. He who has taken has been given full measure of his treachery. Resume your circlet, child of Rengarth. As you have lost one birth-twin, so you owe sanctuary to another."

Javelle stared questioningly at her mother, then set the metal serpent on her forearm. It coiled there gratefully, as if weary, and stiffened into unliving form again.

"Good." The voice was not one, but many. It moaned high in the unseen pinetops, but it spoke as if it—they—could see the party on the ground perfectly.

"We have come to claim our own. One returned of free will and is welcome. One sought to overmaster us and is mastered. We call back a third who has served and is too weary to come on its own power."

With a sense of dread, the four eyed each other. This terrible voice did not seem to brook disobedience. Had they all come so far, through so much, to lose one of their number now? Hands joined hands even as tongues kept a dread-filled silence.

"We call the creature of clouds and undying guardianship. This world will not welcome its unfortunate semblance here—and honor awaits it Without."

Briarwhip staggered to its unwholesome paws, still whining.

"It will find friends and surcease from its struggles," the voices promised.

At that moment, the light of the three eyes died. A column of gray smoke drifted into the treetops. The voices intoned as one again.

"We call upon the guardians of many worlds, so tireless in their duties that they have splintered themselves to better fulfill them, to merge their separated selves and become beings more apt to their worlds again."

Felabba the Elder bristled. "I, merge? Lose my hard-gained wisdom, my great age, my . . . mystique? Never!"

The younger was equally adamant. "I—sacrifice my noble ruff, my liquid limbs? No—!"

A cloud swept down from above, bruising them together. Two white cats spun in a fierce fight, spitting, yowling, and hissing, turning over and over.

Irissa and Javelle ran to separate them, but found themselves helplessly witnessing the fray. When the cloud cleared, one disheveled cat stood blinking on four unsteady feet.

"Which one is dominant, I wonder?" Kendric inquired ominously.

"Time will tell, Wrathman," the surviving cat observed, "and no doubt you will be the first to know."

"One more anomaly from Without remains illicitly in this world," the voices resumed. "We would summon it, but it was false at its first inception and is doubly false in its second. We would let it waste away here, but it has a claim on one yet living."

The four exchanged mystified glances.

"Seeress," the voices howled, and the word was terrible

in their disembodied mouths. The pinetops shook; grasses rasped and trembled at everyone's feet.

"No," Kendric said hoarsely, lifting his sword against the depthless night of Without.

"Peace, Torloc," the voices addressed him so suprisingly that his anxiety vanished. "The seeress shares her worlds with a stolen self she herself recalled. We cannot accept so severed a being into Without. Yet, unharnessed, this unanchored spirit will ever seek to claim a foothold on she who spawned it. The spirit also yearns for another portion of itself Without has already claimed."

"Eeryon!" Irissa saw in an instant.

"This shadow cannot return to Without except through the great dark waters that underlie all worlds. You who remain—and the . . . cat—must accomplish this last task before you can call your lives and your worlds your own again."

"How?" Kendric asked pointedly.

"You have many long years to consider it now," the voices replied with almost-mocking echoes, "but we suggest you waste no time. Take your worlds and your magic and make of them what you will. Tresspass on Without no more. You shall not be as welcome as before."

"'Welcome,' they call it," Thane muttered under his breath.

The wind whooshed away, swirling loose pine needles and grass dust into the trees' dark arms.

Those remaining in the clearing examined each other with a gingerly sense of wonder. The cat Felabba minced over on familiar feet and spoke—in vastly familiar, though singular, fashion.

"I suppose I must pull all your fat out of the fire again. Where is this . . . stolen self?"

Irissa pointed wordlessly to the water.

Felabba paused in distaste. "Water. Not my favorite

element, but then, Rule was never my favorite world. Hmm."

Everyone gathered around while the cat inspected its own reflection in the dark pond with more than a trifle of vanity.

"My prepossessing appearance seems intact at least," Felabba announced. "Let us see if my powers and insight have held up as well."

Irissa moved beside the cat. "This shadow sprang from a moment of my thoughtless vanity, and I re-created it from the silver of my eyes. I even sent it thither. I should bear the risk of releasing it."

"If Those Without thought you suitable for the task," the cat replied, "they would not have sacrificed our sublime separate selves. As we could not remain cut in twain, neither can you. Besides, the impulse of the shadow to join with its caster now that Eeryon has left this world is too strong for you to banish. Stand back and let me get on with it."

Kendric pulled Irissa away from the water. "The cat is right for once. You have risked too much of late, as have we all."

Irissa tightly clasped her hands. "Yet I feel so responsible for its well-being. I resurrected it—"

"Hush!" the cat hissed over its shoulder. "I call a wailwraith."

"A wailwraith. . . ." Thane crept nearer the still pond. "I've never seen a wailwraith, though I've heard you and Father talk of such things."

"No one has ever seen a wailwraith," Irissa said. "We've heard its inconsolable call through many worlds, but perhaps they were only echoes of our own uncertainties."

"No one has seen a wailwraith because a wailwraith doesn't exist," Kendric put in more gruffly. "It's a tale to scare children from the dangerous rims of ponds and pools. If the cat manages to raise one, I'd ask its pedigree."

"How sweet these big blunt words fall on my little pointed ears," the cat commented. "A skeptic to the last. Now be still, all of you!"

The cat lifted one paw and tapped gently on the water's still surface.

A sound like the tinkling of distant bells pealed through the clearing. From the tiny dimple of the cat's touch, the water rippled outward in swelling silver rings. Concentric circles scribed the pond to the edges of its rectangular shape.

Then the water hardened into black ice; circles froze where they were. The cat patted the surface again. This time the water rang with a dull thud, like a door that is knocked upon.

Each of the thin silver circlets shattered. Cracks ran from ring to ring, drawing a disintegrating web over the pond. The web itself lifted and tented into a peak. Silver glinted among the blackened veins of some ancient cobweb. Other peaks lifted alongside the first. Baleful eyes of weary wariness beyond belief peered through the aged veiling. Long strands of waterweed tangled in its broken skeins.

"It is . . . huge," Thane whispered.

"Something dwells within," Javelle added, "and my serpent circlet tightens until it's likely to choke off circulation in my wrist."

Irissa put a hand to her own circlet. Her fingertips traced a pattern of tiny fissures fragmenting the impervious Iridesium. In moments the magical metal would shatter!

"Hurry, Felabba!" she urged.

"Now you see it," the cat muttered. "A great, damp, uncomely creature—and you haven't heard it sing close up yet. Aid me, seeress. Call your shadow."

Kendric's hand clasped Irissa's shoulder as she gathered her powers to summon this unwanted but essential part of herself. The task was easier than she had thought. She merely let Eeryon cross her mind, merely let regret rise until it left a sliver of an opening in her mind, heart, and magic.

A silver snowspout was spinning free of the water, sifting up through the web. Issiri took shape there, sparkling, dancing, eager to be a free spirit again.

"You call me," her joyous, childish voice wafted over the web-crusted water. "I will have self again—and bright son, and Quickstones from the man who gives them. . . ."

"You will have all that," the cat said, "but only in the world Without. Not here. Here is for humankind . . . and creaturekind . . . and a few of us that are neither. You are shadowkind and belong to Without. Accept the wailwraith. It will carry you swift and sure to the dark rivers below into the darker seas beneath all the worlds. Those Without will end your sorrows on their unreachable shores."

"Not Without! Here. And now. I weary of coming and going at all others' beck and call. I . . . know this world. I like it. I—"

"You will like the illusions of Without better, dream-eater. Embrace the wailwraith. It has known the same sorrows as yourself."

The shining figure upright on the water turned to regard the huge shrouded face beside it. "No!" it pled.

"No . . . !" Irissa echoed it, moving to water's edge to intervene.

"Now!" the cat commanded.

And the wailwraith, with its sightless eyes and toothless mouth and great skeletal limbs like tree roots, submerged, drawing up the skirts of its tangled net, trapping a twisting, sinuous silver fish in its watery toils.

Issiri vanished with a last, heart-stopping wail. The cry was joined—and then surmounted—by a hideous scream of loss wrung from the wailwraith's vanishing form.

Their cries lengthened and interwove into a single plaint, then grew thin and faint and faded away.

Irissa's hand dropped from the circlet, which felt whole again. She felt whole again, but she also sensed an emptiness despite the fullness in her heart. The salvation of all that was dear to her had come at the extinguishing of this last, unlawful segment.

"It had to be." Kendric kept his hands on her shoulders as though to lend her his strength. "Those Without recognized a duty to provide for such a half-life as hers. She will see Eeryon again." Irissa's quick glance to his eyes was both stricken and incredulous. "I know it, Irissa. Neither of them will suffer, because neither of them wronged their own natures, however ill-begotten by Geronfrey."

"I wouldn't want to be in Geronfrey's gauntlets now," Thane put in. "Those Without seem merciless to those who betray Without—and within."

"I hope Eeryon is happy in Without without Geronfrey," Javelle said to no one in particular. The cat came by and rubbed genially against her leg.

Its touch was fleeting. Felabba moved with stately grace once more to the party's head, where she sat and began to clean the wet paw that had begun the summoning by wetting it further.

"The shadow boy and his mother will have a happy reunion," the cat declared. "No doubt they will share their world with that unprepossessing hound—or its spirit."

"Finorian!" Irissa realized tardily. "Her spirit has been called to Without, too."

"Imagine . . . ," Kendric began.

Irissa smiled at him. His flesh had regained its healthy color, although his extended life span was apparently not retroactive—gray would streak his dark hair for decades and decades to come. He smiled like a callow youth, however, while he added the last unlikely image to their sketchy knowledge of Without.

"Imagine having Finorian for a . . . grandmother!" he concluded. " 'Poor Eeryon' indeed."

"Perhaps not. Finorian taught me a thing or two. We might see Eeryon again yet," Irissa suggested.

Kendric's arm clasped her shoulders and turned Irissa firmly to face the wavering world gates. "First we see more of ourselves in our natural places. How do we go back—and to where?"

"These gates lead to many worlds," Thane said. "And they've been left ajar. We can go anywhere we like—within reason, and more. . . . I think we can come here again and take different paths."

"Edanvant." Javelle idly burnished the serpent bracelet with her palm. "I'd like to see my . . . grandmother."

"And I my grandfather, Orvath." Thane was definite. "He cannot be such an ogre as you two have made out."

"We had no idea," Irissa said, "that you missed such contact." She smiled half-hopefully, half-anxiously. "And I have a . . . sister I have not seen."

"Really?" The children were amazed.

"About your age, Javelle," Kendric put in. He looked at Irissa. "Really," he mocked the children's disingenuous curiosity. "Really . . . do you want to return to Edanvant?"

Irissa sighed and examined all their faces in turn.

"Later. Now let's go home."

"To Rengarth?" he asked.

"To Rengarth."

"This doorway," said Thane, "I'm certain of it." He led them to the tattered satin sheen of swangate. "Someone large has already blundered through."

They paused on the brink of the gate, each needing a moment's contemplation before passing back into the past . . . and the present . . . and the future, before leaving the every-time of this place where all gates met.

Then Thane stepped into the gate—and vanished.

"I suppose I'd better follow the brat," Javelle quipped, and bowed to slip through.

"We go together." Kendric, still untrusting of any gate, took Irissa's hand.

At the last moment he turned back to regard the cat lagging in their wake. "And what of Felabba? Does she come, too?—not that I am deeply desirous of her company."

"Wait and see," the cat retorted, its white muzzle lifting into what either was a smile—or a smirk. "Just wait and see."